UNCLUTTER

A Survivor's Story

Winnie D Pagora

BOOK ONE OF THE INNER VOICE SERIES

First paperback edition April 2023

Book design by Laura Boyle

ISBN 978-1-7779003-0-4 (paperback)
ISBN 978-1-7779003-1-1 (eBook)
ISBN 978-1-7779003-2-8 (hardcover)

https://winnzwordz.com

This book is dedicated to my mother, Amma.

Dearest Amma,

There was once a mother who had a daughter
Who thought she could never be an author
Amma insisted; Amma encouraged her
Amma persisted; Amma motivated her
And the daughter finally overcame her fear

Thank you for always believing in me.

CONTENTS

CHAPTER 1

"Way to go, T," Rory Matthews congratulated me. "All your hard work is paying off. You deserve this success."

I turned to my best friend, who towered over me at six foot four, a whole foot taller than me. His smile reached his warm, coffee brown eyes. He helped me arrange the furniture for the press conference later that afternoon.

I watched in awe as he lifted two heavy chairs effortlessly with his athletic swimmer's arms and smiled at him. "Thanks, R. It means a lot to me that you could come."

"I wouldn't have missed it for the world," Rory said. "It's not every day that I get the opportunity to be around a star."

I blushed at Rory's compliment. "Stop it. All I did was lead the team that created the Strollfield Cultural Festival app."

Rory scoffed. "The youngest person ever, a high schooler in Duckville, to develop an app for such a prestigious event."

"Well, we are almost out of high school, and Duckville is a really small county, where everyone knows each other," I argued.

"Oh yeah? Then why did Strollfield, a metropolitan city, select you as the leader of the app development team?" Rory questioned, his irritation apparent. "If this wasn't huge, you wouldn't be presenting our 'star student' speech next week."

"Star student" was a special award presented to the student who not only had a great academic record but also excelled in sports, extracurricular activities, and community service. The awardee was selected by students and teachers every year. They would present a speech at the high school graduation ceremony, just before the valedictorian.

I laughed. "Thanks. I'll stop trying to be modest."

Rory laughed with me. "Good, because it's unnecessary."

"Have you heard from Laila or Harriet yet? Are they coming?" I asked.

Before he could respond, one of my teachers interrupted me. "Tina, you need to get ready. We'll be starting soon."

"I'm all set, Miss White. We just need to get the chairs together, that's all."

"Rory will help with that. Tina, you're coming with me to the green room," Miss White said.

Rory nodded obediently and continued the arrangements as I followed Miss White.

"It's almost June, Tina. Why are you wearing a high-necked shirt under your blazer? And where is your makeup? You have to look your best for the cameras. It's your big day."

She didn't wait for my response but gestured for the professional makeup artist to sit next to me. The woman pulled my arm gently to the side to get better access to my face.

I jumped up. "I'm sorry, but I'm allergic to cosmetics," I lied and ran out of the room before Miss White could protest.

I sped down the long corridor and stopped when I reached the abandoned stairs of our newly renovated high school building to catch my breath.

Still panting, I squeezed my eyes shut, trying to shake off the icky feeling in the pit of my stomach. I disliked it when people didn't respect my personal boundaries and *despised* it if anyone touched me.

She didn't mean any harm, Tina. She was just doing her job.

I knew the voice inside my mind was right, but I didn't want to accept that right now. I was also not ready to admit that it was rude of me to leave the place so abruptly. I sighed and shook my head.

After what happened to me back then…

My phone rang, and I startled out of my reverie. It was Miss White, and I let it go to voicemail. I fumbled in my pocket for my lip gloss, the only cosmetic I owned. For everything else, I would need a mirror—another thing I avoided.

Again because of—

I shook my head vigorously to get rid of that thought and almost lost my balance. I clutched the sturdy, classy, handcrafted wooden railing that had saved me from embarrassment. As I examined its carvings, I smiled, remembering the time Rory, Harriet, Laila, and I had petitioned to save our ancient school building from being demolished and rebuilt.

The thought of destroying our one-hundred-fifty-year-old school, which had faded only slightly from its original deep maroon shade over the years, pained my friends and me. We wanted to preserve the luscious green trees, where robins and blackbirds frolicked during summer, and the elegant flower garden for our beloved butterflies. Thanks to our tireless efforts, the school authorities had given in and settled for a less-extensive renovation and modernization of the building.

That seemed like just yesterday. I still couldn't believe that I would be graduating from this place soon.

As the "star student," no less.

I smiled with pride at that thought. I applied the lip gloss, feeling better about myself. I knew the color hadn't smeared, but I ran my fingertips around my mouth to make sure. I closed my eyes and imagined looking at myself in the mirror. Absently, I touched my face.

I smiled, thinking about the dusky brown complexion I got from my mother. I was proud of my half Bhutanese, half English ethnicity. I ran my hand over my shoulder-length, smooth, stick-straight, brown hair, tied up in a neat ponytail. Oh, how I wished my hair was curly or wavy. Absentmindedly, I fiddled with the bee-shaped pendant I had bought as a part of the "save the honeybees" project. It was the only jewelry I wore, other than the matching earrings.

"You're too covered up for summer, sweetheart," an unfamiliar male voice said. A handsome face with high cheekbones smirked at me. He scanned me from head to toe with creepy eyes. "Haven't you heard of short skirts or dresses?"

"And haven't you heard of manners?" I retorted at the rude stranger, who continued checking me out lewdly. I dug my nails into my palms to stop my body from trembling. It took every ounce of my willpower to put on a brave front. "A-And I did *not* ask you for your advice."

He stepped closer to me and winked. "But you need it, sweetheart. What's your name?"

I didn't utter a word, knowing well that my stutter would only encourage this stranger's lascivious behavior. I swore under my breath when I realized that I had climbed up the stairs absentmindedly and had reached the landing. I bent my head and tried to descend the steps calmly, but he blocked my path with outstretched hands.

"I'm Nick. Nice to meet you."

I tried to duck under his hands and escape, but he held me firmly by my shoulders and removed my scrunchie.

"I'm talking to you, sweetheart."

I abhorred the feeling of his slimy fingers; however, his grip on my arm was too strong to escape.

He bent forward and whispered in my ear, "I want you."

His breath against my ear made my skin crawl, but I spoke with clenched teeth. "This is harassment. I will report you."

Nick snickered as he pushed me against the wall forcefully, covering my mouth with one hand. "Try."

"Tina, where are you? The press conference is about to start in twenty minutes," I heard Miss White yelling from the bottom of the staircase.

As Miss White's footsteps indicated she was advancing closer, the creep released me and vanished within seconds. I trudged toward the steps, still dazed.

"What are you doing here?" Miss White questioned me. "We're getting late."

I opened my mouth to answer, but nothing came out.

Miss White sighed. "Never mind, let's get you ready before the reporters arrive."

I nodded and followed her back to the venue. Even though I tried to shake it off, the creepy stranger's lewd behavior cluttered my mind. Blood still pounding in my ears, I tightened the blazer around my body and silently thanked my teacher for saving me.

***

I gritted my teeth and bore the makeup artist's fingers on my face as my baseball player friends, Harriet and Laila, pinned me to the chair with their strong hands, on Miss White's request, lest I ran away again. I knew I was in no position to argue with my teacher anymore. Especially now that my friends had told Miss White I was not allergic to makeup, and my teacher gave me a disapproving look.

I hoped and prayed that my face didn't betray the nausea that was coursing through me persistently. Mutely, I tugged at my shirt, trying to cover myself up further, still feeling icky at the memory of that creep's touch a few minutes ago.

"Why don't you just wear an Arctic parka?" Harriet Shelby asked, rolling her ocean blue eyes at me.

I let go of my shirt and laughed humorlessly. "Ha ha."

Laila Yousuf, my other friend, put her arm around me and smoothed the foundation near my mouth. "At least your face looks presentable."

I gently removed Laila's arm from my neck, being careful not to let it tangle with her luscious, straight black hair or smudge her perfect makeup. Laila flashed me a hurt look with her light sandy brown eyes and pulled her hand away with a sudden jerk.

Harriet saw this from the corner of her eye while checking her own pretty face out in the mirror and muttered under her breath, "Miss Touch-Me-Not."

My heart sank at my friends' reactions. I didn't get why they didn't understand and accept my dislike of proximity. After all, I had made this clear to them ever since the first day of high school four years ago.

"Where's your scrunchie?" Laila asked me, running her fingers through my hair as Harriet brushed it.

Feeling guilty from earlier, I clenched my teeth, waiting for them to move away.

Miss White interrupted us. "Her hair looks fine as is. Let's go."

Why this fuss about my hair and makeup when I am not even going to present the app? My only job is to answer questions if there are any.

I sighed and was walking toward the audience seats when I felt someone tugging my hand. I scowled at the sudden contact and turned to see who it was.

"Tina, we have a seat reserved for you on the podium," Miss White said, and my frown turned into a wide smile.

I followed her and silently squealed at the prospect of being on the stage during a press conference. I looked for Rory, to share the exciting news, but he was nowhere to be found.

I strode toward the raised podium, grinning from ear to ear, when someone caught my eye.

"Good afternoon, everyone," the master of ceremonies announced into the mic. "Welcome and thank you for making time on a Saturday to join us for this press conference to unveil the Strollfield Cultural Festival app prototype. As you all know, SCF, held in April every year, is Strollfield's biggest annual event, and preparations start months in advance. This is required because thousands of people gather from across the world to enjoy a variety of foods, music, dance, art, and cultures of our country. This year, for the first time, high school students are designing the fest's mobile app. And this would not have been possible without the help of our main sponsor—Parker Industries. Today, representing Parker Industries, we have with us Nicholas Parker."

I watched in dumb disbelief as the perverted guy who had tried to molest me earlier got up and coolly stood on stage as the audience applauded and cheered. Instantly, I turned around and walked toward my friends. There was no way I would be in the same vicinity as that creep again.

"Nicholas is here on behalf of his father, who couldn't make it today," the announcer continued. "However, we will not miss Mr. Darren Parker's presence, because Nicholas is well-accomplished himself. Despite being only eighteen years old, he has won three nationwide youth business plan competitions in the past year, in addition to standing first in his school."

"That's impressive," Laila whispered to Harriet and me. "Those contests are tough."

What's the use? When he's such a douchebag. It was the voice inside my mind.

Harriet nodded, playing with her light brown curls that I envied so much. "I heard that he is also the captain of the Strollfield High basketball team. He's tall, though not as tall as Rory."

"He's not even six feet, so he's much shorter than Rory," Laila replied. "But he is definitely better looking. Look at those perfect facial features and that chiseled body. And that soft, black hair…"

"Yes, and did you know that he hardly ever repeats his shoes or clothes? They are always custom-made, designed by the best designers in the world."

I tuned my friends out and focused on the presenter.

"Despite his hectic schedule, Nicholas volunteers at the fest every year and mentors each SCF performer during rehearsals in person—"

If he's such a good person, who was that demon from just moments ago? And why did he pick me? Did I make him that way? Was it my fault? I heard another contradicting voice in my too-full head.

"Sorry, but in the interest of time, can we talk about the app that's been developed for Strollfield Cultural Festival?" one of the journalists asked, derailing my train of thought.

I wanted to give the journalist a standing ovation, but I stayed put in my seat.

The announcer complied meekly. "Over to Mrs. Smith, the principal of Duckville High to present us the mobile application."

"Pardon my interruption, but shouldn't the leader of the app development team speak about it?" another reporter spoke up. "Where is she?"

Miss White and the Mrs. Smith gestured for me to come over fast. I got up from my seat, walked up to the stage, and took the announcer's position in front of the microphone. I'd prepared for this, even though it was not on the original agenda. From the podium, my eyes met my parents', who were beaming with pride. I was tempted to acknowledge their presence publicly and introduce them to the gathering, but I settled for a subtle smile and started my presentation.

For the next few minutes, I demonstrated the app that was being projected on a big screen behind me. Although I kept my eyes on anything but the chief sponsor's representative seated just steps away from me, I felt his fixed gaze boring into my skin. *Not now*, I told myself and plastered on a slight smile.

I showed the audience and the press members how users could navigate the app and register for the festival. I also portrayed the ease with which they could follow the event map so they would not get lost. I demonstrated a host of other features which were common to most mobile applications. The more I spoke about our work on the app, the more at ease I felt in my skin.

"Here's where our app stands out. When users point their phones at artifacts, such as paintings or sculptures, information about them will be displayed. Additionally, a user can access the menu of each food truck, including how many goodies are left for the day. For example, if your favorite ice cream is almost sold out, the app will let you know before you lose your last chance to grab it," I continued. "After all, isn't food the main reason we attend SCF in the first place?"

Everyone in the audience laughed in agreement with my rhetorical question and broke out into applause. The enthusiastic response to my app made my heart soar, and I glowed internally with a quiet pride.

"I request permission to video call my teammates, without whom this wonderful app wouldn't be possible," I added, wrapping up my presentation. "We burned the midnight oil for weeks together to get the code right and make things work. Please say hello to my team." I introduced everyone on-screen by their name and role, as they huddled together in Strollfield.

"Thank you, Tina," the announcer said. "That was very thoughtful of you to introduce the team. Before we go on to the addresses by the Duckville High principal and other guests, I would like to take this opportunity to thank the Strollfield Cultural Society for the opportunity for Duckville to host the festival this year. Our county is proud and honored for this chance, and we promise not to let you down."

I was about to get down from the stage when Miss White stopped me. "Tina, you need to be on the stage in the limelight."

And just like that, I came crashing down from my high.

"But, Miss White, I'm not comf—"

"Go on, Tina," Miss White interrupted. "This is a great opportunity."

Reluctantly, I went and sat on the chair that was reserved for me—next to Nicholas Parker. I moved my seat closer to Mrs. Smith, who was addressing the audience.

Nicholas smirked at me. "We meet again, sweetheart."

"What do you want from me? Why don't you leave me alone?" I whispered to him, annoyed.

"You intrigue me, Tina Lauren," Nicholas hissed back.

I didn't say anything but sat uncomfortably in my chair with both my legs angled away from him, lest he try something inappropriate.

He pulled his chair toward mine and leaned close to me. "See, this is why I can't let you go. So feisty, so serious. You put ideas into my head with your actions. You want me, too, don't you?"

I didn't respond, and he sat back normally, still close to me.

I need to get up from here, right now! Should I make an excuse? I heard the voice inside my head.

He won't try anything else now. After all, we're in public. Just don't react. I heard another voice counter the first one.

I hated the two contradicting voices inside my head. It was always like this. Discreetly, I reached under my shirt sleeve to use my secret technique, the only way to shut them up.

Suddenly, I felt a hand graze my thi— my upper leg. I froze, startled at the unwanted touch. As the principal droned on, Nicholas's hand continued to stroke my leg, traveling up toward—

"Hands off, you sick pervert!" I screamed, slamming my elbow into his face as hard as I could. I jumped to my feet.

There was pin-drop silence in the room as everyone in the audience and onstage looked at me, shell-shocked.

Uh oh. Did I say that out loud?

CHAPTER 2

A commotion broke out as all my teachers hurried to attend to Nicholas Parker's bleeding nose, pushing past me with accusatory looks. The room was being vacated by the organizers.

"How could you do this, Tina? This kind of outburst is not like you," Miss White reprimanded me.

"He…he was touching me inappropriately, Miss White," I blurted out to deaf ears. "I was only protecting myself."

"She's imagining it, Miss White. She's been coming on to me all day!" Nicholas snarled venomously, clutching his nose. He fished something out of his pocket. "Look, she even gave me her scrunchie."

"He took it forcefully. I didn't give it to him," I weakly protested.

Miss White sighed. "It's okay, Tina. I understand. These things are common at your age. But there is a time and place for everything."

I couldn't believe what I was hearing. It was like this Nicholas Parker could do no wrong. I nodded and looked down, wishing I could disappear. "I'm sorry, Miss White."

"Don't apologize to me. Apologize to Nicholas," Miss White told me.

No way. I shook my head vehemently. "No, I refuse to do that."

"He is our guest, Tina. And you've injured him quite badly," Miss White insisted.

"He deserves it," I retorted. "He needs to learn how to behave."

Miss White looked angry. "Tina Lauren, if you don't apologize right now, you will lose your star student status."

"That's fine by me. I will *not* apologize to Nicholas Parker," I persisted.

Miss White shook her head and went away to discuss something with the principal. I got up to meet my parents, who had been asked to wait for me outside the room. As I headed toward the exit, the reporters swarmed me with questions.

"Is it true that the rich and good-looking Nicholas Parker tried to touch *you?*"

"Is it true that you have a crush on him?"

"Why did you attack and humiliate the guest of honor?"

I glared at them and rushed over to Harriet and Laila without answering any of them.

"Tina, are you sure you didn't imagine Nicholas's touch? After all, you are sensitive about these things," Harriet tried to reason with me as soon as I had successfully escaped all the reporters.

"How could you punch him in the face like that? In front of everyone?" Laila joined her.

Why is everyone taking his side? Why does no one care if I'm alright?

Was Nicholas just being friendly? Maybe I was imagining his inappropriate touch.

Of course not. I know—more than anyone—what an unwanted touch feels like.

But I didn't have the right to hurt and insult him, right?

I tried to ignore the contradicting voices inside my head, but it was getting harder.

Thankfully, my mother intervened in our one-sided conversation. "Girls, we would like to take our daughter home now," she asserted with a stiff smile.

Feeling extremely grateful, I followed my mother. She placed a hand on my shoulder as she led me away silently. Out of earshot from everyone else in the parking lot, she asked, "Are you alright?"

Finally, someone cared to ask.

I nodded, my voice trembling. "I'm okay, Mom."

She nodded back, clearly grateful to drop the subject. I looked at Dad, who was avoiding eye contact with me. He simply patted my back reassuringly, if awkwardly.

On the drive home, no one talked, and the silence hung heavy. I was too tired to start the conversation and hoped my parents would initiate it. I wanted them to ask me what actually happened and why I had lashed out at Nicholas like that. But no one said anything—not a word.

I sighed inwardly and decided to take a nap until we reached home. My phone buzzed with a text message.

Rory

T, you did the right thing today. I saw what happened. I'm proud of you.
I'm always on your side.
I wanted to say this to you in person but didn't get a chance.

Me

Thanks, R. That means the world to me.

Rory

Of course. Parker gives me the creeps.

Me

He is a creep.

Rory

You won't meet him again. Don't worry.

Me

I hope so.

Me

By the way, I'm no longer the "the star student."

Rory

Their loss, T. You're awesome.

Me

No, you're awesome.

I felt slightly better after texting my best friend. At least he got it.

I was about to fall asleep when my mother spoke. "Tiar— I mean, Tina, have you considered therapy?"

I was instantly irked at her carelessness but responded as calmly as I could. "Why are you asking me that?"

"It'll help you, dear. I think you should consider it. Even I—"

"She's fine, Kiba," Dad interrupted. "She doesn't need a psychiatrist. She is not mentally ill."

Mom sighed. "There is nothing wrong with seeking help. It's not about being mentally ill."

"I don't need it, Mom. I'm fine," I said.

Mom continued. "Tina, what you went through as a child is—"

Of course, Dad didn't let Mom speak the unspeakable. "Kiba, don't unnecessarily bring up irrelevant matters."

"I'm over what happened back then," I reiterated my father's statement.

But I knew as well as they did that I was lying through my nose. I closed my eyes, wishing for the silence to return.

***

I tossed and turned in bed that night, trying to sleep, but there was a cacophony of voices inside my mind.

Mom is right. I need to see a therapist. It will help me.

No way! What if anyone in my class finds out? I will be the laughingstock.

Why should I care about what anyone thinks? I should focus on myself.

And what if the therapist laughs at me? Besides, I hate advice.

But it's been proven to help. That's why there are all these initiatives to remove mental health stigma.

Then why is mental health still a taboo? Besides, what's wrong with my mental health?

I can't look into a mirror. I can't wear what I want. I have an irrational fear of touch. I—

Okay, okay. So what?

I get nightmares. I can't forget the past. I need secret methods to—

"Alright, that's enough!" I said out loud, slamming my hand on my mattress to stop the pesky voices. It was no use trying to sleep.

I got out of bed. Strapping on my Rollerblades, I carried my skateboard and skated toward the park nearby.

I inhaled the fresh night air deeply, enjoying the feel of the cool breeze on my face. I looked up at the clear cloudless night sky, delighted to see the full moon shining. Though the town was quiet, Duckville was too brightly lit to spot any twinkling stars. A wave of nostalgia hit me when I recalled Rory's and my stargazing adventures with my grandparents. I was tempted to call Rory to join me right now but decided against it, as I didn't want unpleasant conversations about the press conference earlier today to ruin my mood.

I stopped for a while and listened to the soothing sounds—crickets chirping, cats mewing, and leaves rustling. I spotted security guards and sped away on my skates, not wanting to answer awkward questions about my night adventures. I silently thanked them for protecting our town, making it possible for people like me to wander outside without any fear. I wouldn't have dared to step out alone past dusk if I lived away from Duckville.

A few minutes later, I reached the skating park—my personal paradise past midnight when no one else was around. I swiped my membership card and entered the indoor rink. I secured my Rollerblades in my locker, wore my protective gear, and walked down the long corridor that led to the massive skateboard area, with its polished, smooth floors that glistened a golden color under the lights.

The skateboard section of the rink had high slopes and steep curves of all types, suitable for practicing stunts. I had mastered most of them in the past five years and had advanced to more dangerous moves, such as skateboard flips.

For the next perfect couple of hours, I glided on the slopes of the park on my skateboard, trying to complete my back flip. I couldn't do it like an ace yet, but I wasn't one to give up. I had fallen many times over the past five years while trying this stunt, but I continued to do it. That's how much I loved skating.

I laughed out loud as I leaped in the air and landed right back on the board. I kept increasing my jump height, and each time, I was safely back on the wheels. I stretched my arms out and felt like a bird soaring through the air, all my tensions from earlier melting away.

Once I felt calmer, I let my mind wander back to the events of the day. Only this time, I thought about never again wanting to feel confined like that.

What if I can't escape the next time?

I had to learn how to protect myself.

CHAPTER 3

On Sunday, the next day, Rory drove us in his mother's car to Strollfield, an hour away from Duckville, to look for a house. We both had got into Strollfield University and planned to become roommates starting this fall.

"Let's look for an economical place. I don't mind an old building, but it needs to be in a safe and well-lit area," I specified.

He chuckled. "The landlady I spoke to on the phone said this first condo was the 'perfect' place for all university students. So let's see if she's right. I doubt it, though."

I laughed with him. "Why do you say that?"

"They're all salespeople. We need to do our research and find out about everything ourselves—bedbug infestation and rodents, among other things," Rory pointed out.

I nodded. "That's correct. Let's see how this house is."

I marveled at the buildings and skyscrapers as we approached the downtown area. We had only one mall in Duckville, but there seemed to be a mall at every corner in this city. I felt like a small speck in a large ocean and wondered if I could adjust to this life.

"Look, there's a sidewalk connecting this condo and Strollfield University. You'll be able to skate or bike during the warm months," Rory told me.

I smiled. "I hope we like this place. That sounds exciting."

"The biggest thing I am looking forward to is seeing people minding their own business. Word spreads like wildfire in Duckville," Rory said.

"Exactly. I want peace and quiet in Strollfield—not people who speculate I had a teen pregnancy when I was fourteen," I replied.

Rory didn't say anything. No one—not even my best friend knew what really happened on my fourteenth birthday. But Rory was aware that it was something extremely painful for me and never brought it up.

I mentally kicked myself from taking up the topic. It was unnecessary right now.

"How about we stop somewhere for an early lunch?" I suggested, changing the subject.

"Sure, what are you in the mood for?" Rory asked. "Every third shop here is a diner. It's hard to choose."

I fished out my phone from my pocket and typed "restaurants near me." A place called Recharge Café stood out among all the options that popped up. The diner had a stellar rating of 4.8 stars and over a thousand reviews.

I showed Rory my phone. "This place looks interesting. Want to try it out?"

Rory pulled over at the parking lot. "Sounds good. But you'll drive after lunch. I'll be too full."

I laughed. "Sure thing."

We entered the casual eatery, which was relatively full, though it was not even noon yet. There were cozy booths with soft, dark brown, cushioned seats separated by glass sheets for privacy. The tables at the center were round and matched the color palette of the rest of the furniture. On one side, there was a display board with drawings, notes, and photographs of cheerful café customers. On the other, the walls were made of glass.

"They've used the old mirror trick to make this place look bigger than it is," I commented as we took our seats at a booth.

"Look closely. Those aren't mirrors. There are private eating areas that look like..." Rory trailed off with a puzzled look on his face.

"Conference rooms?" I finished his statement with a question mark because I wasn't sure.

What a unique idea. Students could complete their projects in this eatery, while grabbing a bite. Office-goers could have a semi-casual working business meal.

Rory nodded and showed me the menu card. "See, there are details about reserving the project rooms. It's even got projectors, whiteboards, and other fancy stuff."

"Wow," I exclaimed. "Let's hope the food impresses us as much as the ambiance."

Rory and I browsed the menu to order our food. The café had dishes from all over the world—most of which I had never heard of. Duckville had less variety when it came to cuisines, but my father was an ardent home chef. So I could recognize one or two items.

Our food arrived, hot and fresh, smelling divine. I had ordered a Mediterranean shawarma roll, and Rory had ordered an Ethiopian injera meal.

I hungrily bit into the tender, juicy meat, marinated in the right variation of Middle Eastern spices, blanketed in soft pita bread. I smacked my lips at the taste of the tangy hot sauce and the chili hummus. However, the flavor that stood out was the creamy garlic sauce, which I licked off my fingers.

I was lost in the heavenly taste of my wrap when I heard Rory calling out to me. "T, we decided to *share* the roll. Almost nothing is left for me now."

I laughed unapologetically. "I'm sorry, sir. Do I know you?"

Rory stuck his tongue out. "Ha ha. Very funny. Wait till I get back at you."

I laughed again, trying to reach his plate for a piece. "How's the injera?"

Rory slapped my hand away. "Strangers can't share my food." He took a bite of the flatbread. "It's the most unique thing I've ever eaten. It is slightly tangy and so spongy it melts in your mouth. When you eat it with the accompanying stew, there's a burst of flavors and spices that—"

"Yeah, yeah, I got it," I interrupted, jealous of his appetite. I was so full from the large roll, I couldn't eat an entire plate on my own. "Mine was better."

"How's the food? Sir? Ma'am?" our server asked us.

"We're new to this city, and we plan to try every single dish on the menu," I exclaimed as Rory nodded in agreement, his mouth full. I read his name plate. "Thank you, Mr. Okoro."

Mr. Okoro bowed slightly. "It's our pleasure, ma'am. Sir. Enjoy your meal."

"Dessert?" Rory asked me after our server left.

I looked at him in disbelief. "Aren't you full yet?"

"I have a separate stomach for sweets," Rory said, tapping his belly.

"Aren't you banned from eating them?" I teased my swimmer best friend.

Rory scoffed. "I'm not in Duckville. So to heck with rules."

I laughed and wiggled my eyebrows playfully. "Aren't you afraid I will tell on you?"

Rory looked at me with a puppy-dog expression. "Will you?"

I shook my head. "Of course not. Order all you want. It's on me."

When the dessert, kanafeh, arrived, I was tempted to try it myself despite being full. The cheese oozed from what looked like a warm, crispy, flaky pastry. When I heard Rory's crunch and saw the stringy cheese pull when he bit into the Mediterranean pie, all my resistance went down the drain, and I dove for the last piece before it was gobbled up.

After our scrumptious lunch, Rory and I were too full to move. We trudged back to his mother's car.

"R, you drive. I ate too much," I told him, giving his car keys back.

Rory grunted something I couldn't comprehend. He tugged at his pants to loosen their grip on his stomach. I laughed inwardly, grateful I was wearing overalls and didn't need to worry about that.

More than that, I was thankful to have Rory Matthews as my best friend. I always had a great time with him.

***

"Three students can share this condo. It's almost like each of you has your own place, because there are attached bathrooms in all three rooms. The only shared areas are the kitchen and living room. The bedrooms are spacious and equipped with small walk-in closets," the landlady said, as she showed us the apartment. "It's on the fourth floor, so it has a great view."

"What if we find rodents or bedbugs? It is an old building, after all, and the rent is unusually reasonable," Rory pointed out.

"We've never had complaints from our residents in the last thirty years," the landlady informed us. "There is a check every six months for pests."

"But if we do?" Rory pressed. "Would you compensate us?"

I admired Rory's negotiation skills. I was the type to accept the terms and conditions placed before me without bothering to see if they could be changed. But Rory ensured he got the best out of any opportunity.

"If it comes to that, I'll think about it," she said hesitantly.

We went around the house, inspecting it for any apparent damages. Everything looked intact and met most of our requirements. The place wasn't fancy or beautiful, but it had the bare minimum necessities. Most importantly, it was within a university student's budget.

"Why is there no padlock on the outside of the room doors?" I asked the landlady.

She gave me a puzzled look. "Why do you need to lock the room from outside? Do you have valuables?"

I shook my head. "No, but it's mandatory for my room door to have a lock on the outside and inside."

The landlady looked reluctant and began to fiddle with the keys nervously. My eyes met Rory's. He nodded in agreement and gave me a reassuring smile. He was the only one who knew about my habit of locking my room every time I entered or exited it.

Back when we were fourteen, Rory's family had come to visit us at my grandparents' farm which was about a half an hour drive from Duckville. He overheard me demanding that my maternal grandparents—whom I called Grammy and Gramps—install a lock for my room door. When Rory questioned me about this later that day, I told him, "That's the only way I'll feel safe." He hadn't prodded further and had even diverted his sister's attention the next day when she was puzzled to see a padlock installed only on one door in the entire house.

"I will pay an additional deposit if you give me permission to install my own lock," I offered the landlady now, encouraged by my best friend's assurance.

"That works for me," the landlady agreed.

I raised my eyebrows at Rory as if to ask, "Can we finalize this place?"

Rory gave me two thumbs-ups, our faces cracking into identical grins.

"Then, we're ready to sign the lease and make our deposit now," Rory said.

The landlady led us to her office. "I have already leased one of the rooms. They are from Duckville too." She rummaged through her papers. "Here it is. Laila Yousuf, your third roommate."

I gasped, delighted that I was going to be roommates with two of my closest friends. How exciting was that?

Rory looked happy, as well, and high-fived me.

The landlady smiled at us. "It looks like all of you know each other. Well, that's good for me, because I won't need to look for new tenants for a long time."

After finalizing our lease, Rory and I headed back home to Duckville. I drove, while Rory slept in the passenger seat. I thought about buying my own car once I started university. The Strollfield Cultural Society had paid me for coding the mobile app, and I expected my final installment to come through when the app development was complete at the end of the year. I would be able to afford a ten-year-old used car with both the installments.

I was excited to live independently and step into adulting. I knew it would be difficult, but I felt ready. I had always been a reclusive student in school, with few friends. In college, I wanted to expand my social circle, join clubs, meet new people, and maybe give romance a chance.

But would a big city like Strollfield accept me? Would my fashion sense repel them? I've been unpopular in Duckville, mostly because of the way I dressed. I didn't look like a teenager as much as a *grandmother*.

And romance? How was I supposed to find love when I never let anyone close to me?

Ha. Who am I kidding? I am going to remain the same, boring Tina Lauren.

Thoughts about a not-so-fresh start clouded my mind as I drove on to the oddly pleasant background score of Rory snoring softly. Despite realizing that I would never be a social butterfly, I couldn't help but feel hopeful about starting the next chapter of my life with my best friend. Maybe it would turn out okay after all.

Once in our town, I drove to my house, waking Rory up, and then he switched to the driver's seat and headed home. Back in my room, I unlocked my room door and locked it from inside. Exhausted from the day, I fell asleep the minute I hit the sack.

CHAPTER 4

"Princess, where are you, my princess?" called a creepy voice.

No, I am not getting back into their clutches. I am safe here behind the wine shelf; they can't see me.

"I can see you, princess. You can't hide from me," the other demon sneered, his breath hot on the back of my neck.

No. No. No. Their voices made my skin crawl. My stomach churned at their evil laughter.

Please, I'm begging you. Please. No.

"Caught you, my darling princess," they snickered. "Now, look at us."

They placed one filthy hand on my shoulder, turning me to face them.

Before I could see the faces I had seen a million times before in my nightmares, I woke up hyperventilating, sweat beading my forehead.

I sat up and tried breathing to a count to calm down, but that didn't help. My heart palpitated faster in my chest, and I started coughing.

I cannot wake up my parents.

I need help.

No, I don't. I'm fine.

No, I'm not. I can't do this anymore.

"Oh, shut up," I whisper-yelled at the annoying voices in my head. "Shut the heck up, please."

Rocking back and forth on my mattress, I pushed up the sleeves of my sweatshirt. Only my ultra-special method could unclutter my mind tonight.

***

"Tina Lauren whacked Nicholas Parker in the face. Can you believe it?"

"She's weird, but he shouldn't have got handsy with her."

"Methinks she was overreacting. That girl flinches if you place a hand on her shoulder."

"You're right. Ugh, that girl is so freaking abnormal."

Unsurprisingly, I had become the talk of Duckville High following Saturday's incident of me elbowing Nicholas Parker in the press conference. Part of me had hoped people would come to me and ask me questions about the Strollfield Cultural Festival mobile app, but, of course, that was forgotten.

"Do you have a crush on Nicholas?" one of the students asked me at lunch in the cafeteria.

I made a distasteful face. "Ew, no way."

"Why not? He's so rich and handsome. And you're so plain."

I walked away, ignoring him.

"I think Tina came on to Nicholas, and he refused. So, she took revenge. That's what he said," another student speculated.

Today is the last day of high school. In just a week, when we graduate, I reminded myself, I wouldn't need to bother about these people anymore.

I spotted Laila and Harriet and escaped from my nosy classmates to meet them.

"Rough day?" Harriet asked, greeting me with a high-five.

I sighed and nodded. "You know how it is."

"Don't worry, we will be university students soon," Laila said.

Harriet gave her a bitter look. "And you'll be roommates."

"Har, I offered to be your roommate first, but you refused," Laila pointed out to her. "You didn't like the area or the apartment. It's just a coincidence that I'm rooming with Tina."

Ouch. I felt hurt that neither had offered to stay with me, but I didn't say anything. It was worse that Laila considered living with me a mere coincidence when I was so excited.

"But I'll be the odd person out in the group," Harriet complained. "You'll all have fun without me."

"I'll give you a key to our place so that you can come to hang out whenever you like," I reassured Harriet.

"Thanks," Harriet said.

"As her boyfriend, I'm supposed to do that," Rory chipped into our conversation.

He greeted Harriet with a kiss, but the tension between the two was palpable. I had seen them fight many times over the last two years since they became a couple. But today, something seemed off—*way off.* Rory looked pleadingly at Harriet as she responded with a cold expression. Dejectedly, Rory sat down next to me.

I could feel Harriet's glare boring through me, though I didn't dare make eye contact with her. She always thought I sided with Rory because we had known each other for the longest time in our group. Rory and I had been best friends since we were toddlers, and our families had been thick for three generations. Laila, Harriet, and I became close during the first year of high school, and Rory joined us when he started dating Harriet.

Laila rolled her eyes at Rory. "Give her your room key. But don't tell us."

Harriet changed the topic. "How about we all head to Adopt-A-Friend today? My parents got me a new car, and I can't wait to show you guys."

After school, our group headed over to the dog shelter we all loved. Laila drove us there in Harriet's car. Laila had begged Harriet for the keys, because she didn't have a car of her own and wanted to test drive Harriet's new one. Harriet was about to get into the passenger seat in the front when I beat her to it. I didn't care where I sat, but I wanted the two lovebirds to sort things out.

Rory mouthed "thank you" to me, while Harriet looked angry.

Laila was oblivious to the atmosphere and talked about her "star student" speech. "Tina, aren't you upset that I'm giving the speech instead of you?" Miss White had informed her that morning that she would take the coveted position in my place.

I shook my head, though I felt my chest tighten. "You have a higher GPA than me, and you're the baseball team captain. You deserve this opportunity. It was yours in the first place."

"Oh, please, if that was the case, why didn't you decline earlier?" Harriet questioned me. "Miss White asked you if you wanted to address the graduation day audience, and you said yes, even if you didn't deserve it. You're not even ranked in the top five students of our class and have never won any big competitions."

My GPA is only 0.1 points below Laila's. Besides, I tutored more than half the students of our class, including Laila, in calculus, two days before the mid-term tests. That counts for a lot, I wanted to say but I decided it was best not to argue.

No one countered Harriet's statement either. I wished Rory would say something in my favor, but he was always tongue-tied in front of his girlfriend.

We reached the venue, and I ran to meet my favorite German Shepherds—Ribster and Dexter. They had served in the police force until a year ago but had now retired. I wanted to adopt them, but my parents' place wasn't big enough. If they didn't have a home in a few months, I planned to take them with me to university.

Harriet, Laila, and Rory were with the other dogs while I played with Ribster and Dexter. We played fetch and ran around in the park. When we were exhausted, we sat under a tree as I stroked their backs and chatted with them.

"Do you think it was wrong of me to whack Nicholas Parker in the face? I would still have my chance to deliver the graduation day speech that everyone dreams of, wouldn't I? I might not have the highest grades in my class, I am a true all-rounder. I can skate, code, and I even tutored more than twenty of my classmates in math by simplifying the subject for them. That's why I *deserve* to be the 'star student.'"

Ribster and Dexter barked in response.

"You think I did the right thing, don't you? You are such good dogs. Oh, how I wish you could be with me always."

Ribster licked my hand while Dexter snuggled close.

"I hate how everyone is saying that I overreacted because of my fear of touch. No one wants to believe me. Do you know what I think? I think

Nicholas Parker is vile and that I should be given a bravery award for setting an example for everyone else, not punished."

Ribster and Dexter barked again, and that felt like music to my ears.

"You're the only ones that don't judge me when I boast about myself. Have I told you both how much I love you?"

***

When Harriet dropped all of us home that night, there was an awkward silence in the car. As I waved goodbye to my friends, I contemplated whether or not to talk to Rory about his girlfriend. I didn't want to seem nosy. Both of them had done a great job hiding their fight. It was just obvious to me because I noticed these things. Though I sometimes wished I didn't.

Back home, I took a shower and changed into my long-sleeved shirt and pajamas. I plopped on my futon and played with my phone.

I heard a knock on my door. I got up and unlocked it for my parents.

"What's up?" I asked.

They didn't usually come to my room unless it was something important. My mother held out an article in the *Strollfield Times* that had two photos—mine and my team's.

High School Student and Her Team Impress at Press Conference

Tina Lauren, a senior at Duckville High, presented her team's Strollfield Cultural Festival mobile app and its fancy features. Not only have the young group of talented teenagers included the usual features to improve attendees' experience at the annual event, but they engage users before and after the occasion.

Our favorite part is the virtual tour of the festival that will give us information about the exhibit artifacts or menus of food trucks. We quote Miss Lauren here: "If your favorite ice cream is almost sold out, the app will let you know before you lose your last chance to grab it."

The app prototype looks promising, and if we can plan our food truck tours and not miss out on goodies, we are here for it.

My father hugged me, his hazel eyes twinkling with pride. "Congratulations, Tiar— I mean, Tina."

My mother put her arm around me, her eyes crinkling like mine as she grinned widely. "We are proud of you."

I beamed. "Thanks, Mom and Dad." Indeed, this was a pleasant surprise.

My parents had barely mentioned the press conference in the last two days. It was nice to be appreciated, even if they continued to avoid any mention of the confrontation. I was disappointed, but I didn't want to broach the topic either. I'd take what I could get.

My parents kissed me goodnight on my cheek. "Get some rest, now."

I read the article over and over before I fell into an uneasy sleep. It didn't last long. An hour later, awake again and tired of tossing and turning, I sat up in bed and wondered what to do.

I could read textbooks in any state of mind. "But all my exams are over," I said out loud. "What else?"

I nervously fidgeted with my pen, clicking it open and closed. I contemplated refining the fest app code, but I had already completed what I needed to for my meeting in Strollfield later this week. I felt too lazy to go out skating.

I browsed my streaming video platform for something to watch to pass the time. I stumbled on an international young adult romantic comedy. A few minutes into the show, I was hooked. The male lead wasn't a bad boy like in most teen movies but a nice guy. He was respectful toward the female lead and knew when to back off. A cherry on top was his extremely good looks.

I scoffed. "The writers need to be sued for creating too-good-to-be-true characters. They don't exist in real life." I sighed. "Who wouldn't fall for such a wonderful person?"

The trait I liked most about the male lead was his trust in his girlfriend's strength. When she was stalked by her ex, he didn't mansplain to her or take over her life. Instead, he told her he would be by her side if she ever needed him.

That's my ideal partner.

Ha, what's the use? I can't even shake hands with a boy without trembling and making a fool of myself.

I was distracted by my phone beeping.

Harriet

Are you awake?

Me
Yes, what's up?

Harriet
Why did you make Rory and me sit together in the car today?

Me
Both of you are my friends. I wanted you to work things out.

Harriet
Don't interfere between us.

Me
Alright, sorry. I won't.

Harriet
Let's switch to group chat. Laila wants to join.

Me
How about we talk on the phone instead?

Harriet
Sounds good.

Laila yawned as she greeted Harriet and me. "Hello."

I giggled. "Hi, sleepyhead."

"Why did you say you'd join the call if you can't keep your eyes open?" Harriet asked her.

"I'm too tired to sleep. I was preparing for my star student speech," Laila answered.

My chest ached with disappointment. That speech should have been mine.

Harriet chuckled. "Maybe Tina can help you. I'm sure she prepared hers way in advance."

I clenched my fists, feeling my nails dig into my palms, but I spoke calmly. "Sure, Li. I could share my ideas if you like."

"I hope you're not expecting her to give you credit. Because she can't," Harriet said.

I sighed inwardly. "No, Harriet. I'm not expecting anything."

"Good. So, help me with how to start," Laila instructed me. "Because what I decided sounds boring."

For the next hour, I helped Laila with the speech with input from Harriet.

Laila is going to deliver my star student speech. It's not fair.

Well, I lost my chance like an idiot. Serves me right.

No way. I did the right thing by protecting myself.

"What's the use? What's done is done. I shouldn't have acted so hastily at the press conference," I blurted out, forgetting that I was still on the phone with my friends.

Harriet giggled. "Did you realize that only now? You did the wrong thing by provoking Nicholas Parker."

Sadly, I couldn't argue with her, because, deep down, I agreed. I was suffering the consequences of my reaction.

CHAPTER 5

I yawned for the umpteenth time while riding the bus to Strollfield the next morning. High school was officially over, and I was free from my gossiping classmates. I tried hard to stay awake, but my eyes drooped. I didn't want to fall asleep on public transportation because I feared missing my stop, but what I hated more was letting my guard down in public.

I mentally kicked myself for staying awake all night studying anyway after I hung up the phone call with my friends. I was too preoccupied to watch anything, so I did math, even though I didn't have a test. Math problems calmed me down, along with coding.

When I finally reached my stop, I got a hot chocolate at Recharge Café, where I met with my mobile app teammates to catch up on our progress. After our brief, but productive, meeting, feeling doubly energized from the sugar rush, I headed to my destination of the day: the karate institute in my new neighborhood in Strollfield. It was run by Dr. Mio Nakamura, who was also a physiotherapist.

"Hi, I'm Tina Lauren, and I have an appointment with Dr. Nakamura," I informed the red-haired guy with light brown eyes at the entrance.

"Sure. Can you wait a moment?" he asked.

As I waited, I saw that the kids addressed the red-haired guy as "Sensei," meaning teacher in Japanese. I watched the burly instructor in awe as he taught the children some tough karate moves. There were four other classes being taught simultaneously by different instructors around the room. All the students and teachers wore the traditional white uniform, or "gi," pronounced as "ghee." I knew about this because I had come prepared for my first class.

My eyes wandered around the spacious and brightly lit dojo, which had soaring ceilings and could accommodate over a hundred students.

"Tina, Dr. Nakamura will meet with you shortly," one of the instructors informed me, leading me into an office that looked like a museum.

I sat down and curiously explored the tiny bright room from my seat. Dr. Nakamura's table was squeaky clean, with only her laptop, a photo frame, and a pen stand on it. At the sides of the room were wooden shelves with glass doors. Inside these were rare Japanese puzzles that I had only read about in manga comic books.

Fascinated, I continued to look from item to item in the locked glass cabinet. I squealed silently when I recognized the Japanese daggers from my favorite anime and wondered if Dr. Nakamura had inherited them from her ancestors. Maybe her great-great-grandparents were real samurais, who used these very weapons during a battle.

"Hi, Tina. Sorry to keep you waiting," Dr. Nakamura's voice interrupted my fantasy.

I was mesmerized by Dr. Nakamura's aura as soon as she walked through the glass doors. She was about the same height as me but leaner. I had read in many reviews online that, when Dr. Nakamura was in the room, all eyes were on her because she commanded respect.

She was a physiotherapist by profession who ran a karate institute because she was passionate about martial arts. Her students praised her patience and encouragement while teaching, even when they didn't get the moves right numerous times. Further, Dr. Nakamura's objective to focus on mental well-being through martial arts drew me to her classes. Therapy seemed like a long shot, but I was glad to take a small step toward uncluttering my mind.

I agreed with everyone's praise of Dr. Nakamura and noted that she seemed humble and approachable, making me feel at ease with her instantly.

I bowed to her in the way I had practiced by watching online videos. "Dr. Nakamura, please accept me as your student."

Dr. Nakamura smiled at me. "Why do you want to learn karate?"

"I want to become stronger and defend myself physically when required," I answered her. "I also want to strengthen my mind and improve my overall health."

Dr. Nakamura's eyes twinkled with amusement. "I see that you have studied our website well. Welcome aboard." She turned to the red-haired instructor I had seen earlier. "Pete Hilton will help you in the first few weeks, to learn the basics, and then I will be your trainer."

Pete gave me a tour of the institute. Most of the students were young kids, but there were a few who were older. Pete told me he worked part time at the organization, while being a student at Strollfield University, where he majored in law.

"What's your major?" Pete asked. "Any interest in studying law? If yes, I can help you."

"I'll be majoring in business studies and my minor is computer science," I informed Pete. "My mother is in law, though."

"So, that's why you look familiar. You're Kiba Lauren's daughter. I know Crown Counsel Lauren. She's my role model," Pete told me. "She's put some of the toughest criminals behind bars."

"Do you know my mother well?" I asked. My mother traveled to Strollfield often on cases and trained many interns fresh out of the university.

Pete shook his head, looking amused. "I haven't actually officially met her yet. But I have been to a few of her court proceedings. She's a powerhouse."

I smiled proudly. "Thanks, I'll let her know that."

"Hey, wait a minute. Aren't you the girl who whacked Parker in the face at the press conference?" Pete exclaimed out of the blue. "Your photo was on social media recently."

"Yes, and I'm proud of what I did," I said, a little more defensively than I meant to.

"You should be. That guy gives me the creeps," Pete replied. "I admire your guts."

Oh! I was taken aback by Pete's response. I'd been expecting him to lecture me or ask uncomfortable questions, but this was a nice surprise.

I gave Pete a small smile. "Thanks."

Maybe my life at Strollfield University would be better than I thought.

***

"So, Tina, are you ready for your first class?" Pete offered enthusiastically. "Let's start with some warm-up exercises."

Pete stretched his arms, and I followed his lead. We did the same with our back and leg muscles. Next, we warmed up our other joints, such as shoulders, elbows, and knees. I could feel the tension in these melting away.

"These exercises are mandatory to prevent injuries," Pete informed me, swinging his arms.

I nodded in agreement and repeated Pete's actions. I couldn't help but notice the differences in our moves; his were more well-defined, while mine were shabby.

It's just my first day of karate class. I need to stop being hard on myself.

We warmed up for fifteen minutes, after which Pete proceeded to show me some basic karate moves, such as choku-zuki straight punches. I could do them slowly, but when we picked up the speed, it was challenging to maintain the pace and concentrate on my breathing.

"Increase your speed slowly," Pete told me, seeing me struggle. "Focus only on your breathing. The rest will follow."

"My punches look nothing like yours," I complained.

Pete took a step closer to me, and I froze.

Is he going to touch me to demonstrate?

But he didn't. "Watch my fists carefully," Pete instructed, standing next to me. "Notice the difference in the force of my punching actions versus the others."

This time, I got the punches right, and my heart sang with joy.

Pete's face cracked into a wide grin. "That's great progress."

I smiled back at him. "Thank you, Sensei."

"Just call me, Pete," he said. "After all, we will be attending the same college."

"Sensei means teacher in Japanese, and you're my teacher right now," I said.

"Pete is fine, Tina," he insisted.

I nodded. "Alright, *Pete.*"

For the next hour, Pete taught me various punches, kicks, and pushups. I thoroughly enjoyed learning these moves, and it helped that my instructor was patient and encouraging. After class, I changed back into my overalls and went to thank Pete for the first class. He was packing up to leave for the day as well.

I waved. "Hey, Pete. I'm headed to catch the bus, but thanks a lot for your time and patience today."

He smiled. "How about I walk you to the bus stop? It's in the same direction as my place."

"Sure," I said. "Let's walk together."

"When are you starting classes at Strollfield U?" he asked as we started out.

"In September," I replied.

"That's exciting. I remember my first day vividly. I was so excited to realize my dream of becoming a lawyer. I have wanted to be one since I can remember. I got accepted to almost all the law schools in the country, but I chose Strollfield U because it's the best." He paused for a moment. "Of course, I still regret that I didn't get to experience living with my friends. My family has been in Strollfield since before I was born. So, I haven't really got to travel much. Will you be staying with friends?"

"Yes, that's the plan," I answered.

"Oh, you're so lucky," Pete exclaimed. "Welcome to college life."

"Thanks, but I need to wait until fall. I'm focusing on enjoying the summer break now," I said.

Pete fished into his pocket and brought out a hand-written Post-it Note. "Here, have this. It's my phone number. You can contact me any time you need something."

I accepted the note politely, though I was slightly confused by the gesture. "Thanks. I appreciate it."

We reached my bus stop, and I was about to say goodbye, when he spoke first.

"Um, Tina?" Pete paused. He fiddled with his green earring nervously.

"Yes?" I prompted.

"I was wondering if you'd like to meet for a cup of coffee sometime?"

"Thanks. But, um, I politely decline your offer. Sorry," I replied, glad my voice didn't quiver. I was stunned by being asked out so suddenly but didn't want to let it show on my face. "I'll see you next class."

He shook his head nonchalantly. "Never mind. Have a good night."

CHAPTER 6

I changed into my jumpsuit in the restroom of the girls' locker room on graduation day. My friends always told me how weird I was for doing that, but I didn't care. I would never, ever undress in front of anyone. I quickly brushed my hair, applied lip gloss, and texted Rory that I would meet him in a few minutes.

Rory greeted me at the entrance of the open-air theater. "Thanks for helping me set up everything today, T. I know I asked you at the last minute."

I smiled at my best friend. "No problem. I had fun."

Rory stepped closer to me and whispered, "Miss White ignored you blatantly today. That wasn't right of her. She could have at least thanked you."

I shrugged. "Whatever."

Though I pretended not to be affected by my teacher's behavior, I was hurt by how she was singling me out. I had received good grades in all other subjects in my high school final tests, except AP English, taught by Miss White. When I asked her why she had barely passed me, she gave me a vague answer about my critical analysis of the literature piece not being "up to the mark."

"Don't worry. University life will be better," Rory reassured me.

I smiled, feeling a little reassured. "Thanks. I feel the same way."

The graduation ceremony started off boringly with speeches from our principal and many other people I didn't recognize. I fell asleep on my chair, with Harriet nudging me awake every few minutes. They giggled at my droopy eyes while Miss White glared at me. I straightened myself in my chair at my teacher's stern look and forced myself to focus on the stage.

"I now request our chief guest, Dr. Mi-Seon Kim, to say a few words," Laila, the master of ceremonies, announced. "She is a psychologist and therapist—"

I switched off at the mention of "therapist" and didn't listen to the rest of the introduction. However, when a black-haired woman about my height walked to the center of the stage, exuding an aura of confidence, I couldn't take my eyes off her.

Dr. Kim smiled at everyone in the auditorium and made eye contact with all of us. "I can see all of you inwardly sighing and saying to yourselves, 'Why is a shrink at our graduation ceremony? How boring!'"

Everyone laughed with Dr. Kim.

"I blame the movies for making us so irritating. Either we are portrayed as know-it-all people who fix the protagonists' lives at the drop of a hat. Or we are seen as the annoying creatures who read the main character's mind against their will."

I nodded in agreement.

"The ones who see a therapist in real life never accept it because of the stigma around mental health. 'People will label me as crazy,' 'I will be judged as a freak'—these are the thoughts that come to our minds when we think of seeing a counselor."

I closed my eyes and sighed silently, relating with every word Dr. Kim said.

"Don't raise your hands when I ask these questions. Instead, take a moment to think about them. How many of you have felt the need to talk to someone—an unbiased person—about what you're going through but have been scared to take the step?"

I took a deep breath. *Me.*

"How many of you are curious about therapy but don't accept it because you're afraid of being shunned?"

Me.

"How many of you have felt that your issues would be dismissed as 'too small'?"

Me. Me. Me.

"All of us have these thoughts at some point in our lives. However, very few of us take action because of our fears. I'm here today to remove at least a small percentage of your uneasiness so that, the next time these questions come to your mind, you can take the step to try therapy. Let's start with this generic question—what thoughts keep a high school student up at night?"

For the next half an hour, Dr. Kim conducted an interactive session with the audience, concluding that there was no such thing as a "big" or a "small" issue. I learned that anything that affected us in our lives qualified as a reason to seek help if we wanted to.

I liked Dr. Kim's approach of asking us questions and helping us come up with our own answers. Further, she added "if you want," "if you feel the need," and "whenever you feel ready" when she spoke about therapy, making me feel at ease.

When her session ended, everyone clapped and cheered for her as she beamed at the audience.

"Thank you for attending my session today. Maybe you'll be less hesitant to try a one-on-one with me if you ever feel the need."

My palms were red from clapping hard, and my throat was hoarse from cheering loudly. When my teachers distributed Dr. Kim's business card with her contact details to everyone in the audience, I didn't hesitate to take it. Dr. Kim's session felt like a sign just for me.

By the time Laila was reading her star student speech, I was back to struggling to stay awake. Not only did she sound monotonous, but the flowery language made no sense. I turned to check my parents' reaction. They were sitting behind me, and I laughed silently when I saw them stifling their yawns. My father was almost asleep, but my mother made eye contact with me and mouthed, "That should have been you."

I nodded slightly and smiled, grateful that she was on my side.

Harriet nudged me. "Li is torturing everyone. Why did she change everything that we had decided?"

I giggled. "Maybe she is avenging our teachers for their boring lectures."

Rory laughed. "This *is* good payback."

"And now, we would like to show everyone a short video to relive our high school memories," Laila announced.

"Thank goodness, the torture is over," Harriet exclaimed to me in a whisper, and I chuckled silently.

A moment later, the shocking image of two half-naked people in a compromising position was splayed across the big screen, sending hoots of laughter and cheering all through the auditorium. I immediately averted my eyes, not wanting to watch two people who had probably been filmed without their consent. The teachers scrambled to stop the indecent show.

"Hey, isn't that Nicholas Parker?" one of the students shouted above the smutty audio blaring from the speakers.

"Yes. And the brown-haired girl making out with him is Tina Lauren," someone else screamed.

I was rooted to my seat at the mention of my name. Yet I could not bear to glance at the screen.

"Wow. What a hypocrite! She made a show of shoving him in public and accused him of molesting her. But, the truth is, she was screwing around with him."

"She has a smoking hot body. Look at those boobs in that bra." What was happening? That wasn't me! But it didn't matter, because everyone else thought it was.

I must go and stop this video right now!

Why should I do that? That's not me. I don't have a birthmark below my neck.

I'm publicly shamed. I can't show my face to anyone again.

Why should I feel ashamed when I have done nothing wrong?

As if in a trance, I got up from my chair and walked to the stage. I heard Rory calling out my name to stop me, but I kept going. I didn't look at my parents, not wanting to see the disappointment in their faces.

At the podium, two teachers were scratching their heads over how to stop the video.

"The footage is being played from outside the premises; it's impossible to stop it."

"I can't pause or stop the video on this device!"

In a rage, I picked up the laptop and was about to slam it onto the ground when I heard a long buzzing sound before the video on the big screen cut out.

"Why did the video stop playing?" one of the students asked.

"Darn! We were getting to the juicy part," another said.

I must not act out. I need to remain calm and focus on proving my innocence. I heard a single rational voice inside my mind instead of the usual cacophony of contradictory statements.

I calmly set the laptop on the table and turned to face two furious people—Miss White and our principal, Mrs. Smith.

"What's the meaning of this, Tina? You should be ashamed of yourself. Let's have a chat in my office right now," Mrs. Smith said.

I looked her in the eye and spoke loudly. "The person in the video is not me. I have nothing to be ashamed about. I did not do anything wrong."

Miss White raised her voice. "That's enough. Don't create a bigger scene, Tina. We all saw you."

"What scene did I create? That wasn't me!" I fought back. "It is obvious that Nicholas Parker is trying to take revenge on me for whacking him in public. But he deserved it for behaving inappropriately with me."

"Tina, if you say another word, I will make sure you never set foot in a university. If you care about your future, keep quiet and follow me. Now," Mrs. Smith threatened.

I followed our principal into her office, mortified and numbed by the sound of silence—this time, it was my own.

***

"Mr. and Mrs. Lauren, Duckville High is terribly disappointed in your daughter. It's hard to believe that a former 'star student' would do something so shameful," Mrs. Smith lectured my parents and me in her office.

The room was dark and suffocating, despite its significant size. My parents and I sat on plastic chairs facing the principal, seated on a luxurious leather swivel chair. Her table was piled with files and papers, with some of it scattered on the floor carelessly. The musty scent of the office made the already grave situation worse.

"With all due respect, ma'am, we need to investigate the truth first. The footage might have been a conspiracy against my daughter," my mother said.

I was grateful to my mother for standing up for me.

"I know you're a prosecutor, Mrs. Lauren. But everybody saw Tina with their own eyes," Mrs. Smith argued.

"It's a piece of cake to fabricate any video," I countered. "If I can have the file, I can prove it to you. Besides, I don't have a birthmark below my neck like the girl in the video."

Mrs. Smith looked at me angrily. "I can't believe you still have the nerve to speak."

"I'm not guilty, and I'm ready to prove that," I insisted.

"Please find out the source of the leak," my father urged. "We will cooperate with the investigators as required."

"The school will not take any effort to be involved any further in this," the principal informed us. "You can try talking to the Strollfield Education Council Chairperson for help."

Noooo, not the chairperson of the Strollfield Education Council. Please no.

"Why do we need to involve the education council? Shouldn't Duckville High take responsibility for letting a student's modesty be compromised publicly?" my mother demanded, refusing to budge from her seat. "We will sue the perpetrators who framed our daughter. If the school is involved, the law will not spare you."

Mrs. Smith raised her eyebrow. "Are you threatening me, Mrs. Lauren?"

My mother shook her head. "No. I am reminding you of our rights and the law."

Mrs. Smith sighed and got up from her seat. "Alright. Let's drop this matter altogether. I will ensure this doesn't spread on social media, if you promise there will be no lawsuits."

My father placed an arm on my mother's shoulder to stop her from saying anything further. "That works for us, ma'am. Thank you."

We left the principal's office without another word. Unsurprisingly, the car ride back home was quiet. I wanted to thank my mother for supporting me today, but I was too tired to say anything. However, I still wished my parents would say something like, "We trust that you wouldn't get involved with a creep like Nicholas Parker, Tina."

I sighed silently and closed my eyes.

Thank goodness, it's the end of high school. Tomorrow, I'm off to Grammy and Gramps's farm for the summer holidays. After that, I will be a college student.

CHAPTER 7

You're a slut. Die.
You lying ho, you accused Nicholas for no reason.
You're such a fucking hypocrite, Tina Lauren.
Leave the boys alone, bitch.

I sighed when I saw the hate notes in my locker again. It had been a week as a freshman at Strollfield University, and my college life was no better than my high school days. I had had a peaceful break at my grandparents' farm, where I spent my time baking, cooking, eating, and relaxing. I had switched off from the online world and felt rejuvenated when I came back to Duckville. No one in my family had spoken about the graduation day incident, and I was coming to terms with that slowly.

But I missed hanging out with Rory, who was supposed to come to the farm with me but canceled at the last minute. He told me that Harriet wanted his help remodeling her new room in Strollfield. She felt left out for not rooming with the rest of us, so he wanted to make it up to her.

When I was back in Duckville, Rory, Laila, Harriet, and I packed for our move to Strollfield together. Dad had spoiled us all with homemade snacks. My parents drove me to the city and helped me settle down. They even became friends with my neighbors in our building when my father presented them with his famous baked scones.

But I was in for a rude shock on the first day of college when my classmates gave me stern looks, refusing to talk to me. Some of them glanced at me with pity and looked too scared to approach me. I also started receiving hate notes in my locker and on my phone. I had thought everyone had forgotten the fateful incident three months ago, but I was wrong.

Nicholas Parker goes to Strollfield U too. That's why the bullying continues.

I hid the anonymous notes in my locker when I spotted Rory.

"Hi, T," Rory greeted. "How was your day? Did you get assigned a project partner yet?"

I shook my head. "No."

Rory sighed. "I can't believe everyone is abandoning you for no fault of yours."

You only know half the truth.

I changed the topic. "How was your swimming tournament?"

Rory's face fell. "I don't know. I am just not up for it; I don't feel like doing anything anymore."

"I'm sorry to hear that. Do you want to talk about it?" I asked.

"Classes are a chore, swimming is overwhelming. Everything is just bleak," Rory said.

"What about Harriet?"

He looked down and didn't say anything.

I opened my notebook and scribbled inside it: "I have saved some mango cheesecake from Recharge Café for you."

Rory mouthed, "Really?" and I nodded.

"Let's go, but my coach can't know," Rory whispered.

Both of us went to the secluded emergency stairwell, and Rory gobbled up the sweet treat within seconds.

"What would I do without you? You're the best," Rory said between mouthfuls.

I laughed and high-fived him. "*We* are the best."

"Hey, do you want to go for a picnic lunch today, just the two of us?" Rory asked.

My eyes lit up instantly at the prospect of hanging out alone with my best friend. We hadn't done that in a long time. But Rory got a call from Harriet, and I knew our plans would be canceled again.

I headed to the cafeteria to save seats for my friends while Rory attended to the phone call. The massive room was busy during lunchtime, like always. My classmates talked and laughed in large groups and shared their food. I enjoyed watching everyone experience each other's cultures and cuisines and wished I could be a part of them.

I observed the other students while waiting for my friends, when something caught my eye. I saw a slim student wearing a black cap crouched over a corner table. He had his face in his hands, and he was shaking. I tried to avert my eyes, because it was rude to stare, but I couldn't get him off my mind.

I snapped out of my reverie when I heard my friends talking animatedly.

"Hey," I waved. "Over here."

Laila and Harriet waved back without looking at me and took their seats continuing their conversation. Rory mouthed a "hi" to me as he listened.

"I never thought we'd still be playing baseball in university," Harriet said. "Ror, we can travel together for tournaments if our schedules clash."

"And I got selected as the captain," Laila announced.

"Congrats, Li. Great job, Har," I said.

"Thanks," Harriet replied. She turned to Laila. "Hey, Li, do you want to go shopping after classes today? And Rory, you're coming with us."

Rory nodded. "Sure. I want to check out the new photography store at the mall."

Harriet shook her head. "No. You're only going to carry our shopping bags today. Maybe next time."

Rory didn't say anything. I felt hurt that they didn't invite me on their shopping trip, but I let it go. In fact, I could barely participate in all their excitement, so I listened mutely.

"Nicholas Parker is throwing a party for all the first-year students at his mansion this Friday. Are you going?"

I froze, looking up at Laila.

"Of course, we're going," Harriet exclaimed, ignoring me. "The whole university will be there."

"I can't go. I'm traveling for a tournament," Rory informed us.

"It's unfortunate that you'll miss the biggest event of the year," Laila told him. She turned to Harriet. "I heard it's a costume party. Have you decided what you're going as?"

Harriet shook her head. "Not yet. How about you?"

"Me neither. We can decide together this evening," Laila said.

I could not stomach my friends discussing a party thrown by the person who had tried to wreck my life. It felt like I was all but invisible to them, my closest friends. I expected at least Rory to say he wouldn't go to Nicholas Parker's party, even if he *was* in town, or at least throw me a sympathetic look. But he never supported me in front of his girlfriend.

Without a word, I got up from my seat, tears threatening to spill from my eyes. I didn't want to cry in front of anyone, so I walked out of there. Rory gave me a puzzled look as I got up but didn't stop me from leaving. I glared at him angrily before I ran to the ladies' room.

Maybe I should swallow my pride and apologize to Nicholas Parker before he ruins my life further.

Why should I do that? I have done nothing wrong.

But I don't want to be slut-shamed. After that video was aired, everyone is spreading rumors that I was sleeping around.

Even if I was doing that, it's none of their business. No one has the right to slut-shame anyone.

Maybe I asked for it. Just like I did back then.

"Shut up. Please shut up," I pleaded.

Inside a grimy stall, I pleaded with the cacophony of voices inside my head for a long time, tears streaming down my face. But they got louder and louder. I couldn't stop them. I didn't even care if someone came into the bathroom. I was powerless to stop.

Finally, when it was all too much, as if on autopilot, I retrieved my pocketknife and dug it as deep as I could into a tender patch of skin on my right arm, already pink with past lacerations.

***

"Hi. Tina Lauren, right?" someone asked me when I walked out of my afternoon class for a short skate session.

I nodded uncertainly.

"You're bleeding. Are you alright?" the blond-haired guy asked, his ocean blue eyes showing genuine concern at the spot of bright blood on my shirt sleeve.

Uh oh, busted. I tugged it out of sight. "I'm fine, thanks. How can I help you?"

"I'm Aiden Wilkins, Rory's friend. I-I wanted to apologize to you," he stammered.

I gave him a puzzled look.

Aiden continued. "Everyone is spreading false rumors about you being involved with me. I'm sorry on their behalf."

I gave him a small smile. "I appreciate your apology. But I don't care about what other people say about me."

"I know. I admire you for that," Aiden said. "And I appreciate your courage for standing up to Nicholas Parker."

I didn't respond to that statement.

"Alright, see you around, Tina." Aiden waved to me and left.

I felt slightly better after Aiden's unexpected apology. At least someone was on my side, even though he was a complete stranger.

I skated across the massive university campus, enjoying the cool breeze against my face and the vibrant colors of fall. It was like a picturesque painting had come to life with shades of green, yellow, orange, and red splattered on a canvas. Perfectly in contrast, the hundred-year-old main building was sandy brown with carved stone pillars at the front. At the center was a serene fountain where the ducks and the geese enjoyed a refreshing shower.

Suddenly, a few droplets of water splashed on my face. My lips curled up slightly when I saw the culprit, a mallard shaking himself dry after his bath. The geese followed suit, and soon all the birds were spraying each other and me as if we were in a friendly water fight. Not wanting to get drenched before my next class, I skated off reluctantly.

On my way back, I spotted the guy with the black cap from lunch, still crouched, but this time on the steps outside the cafeteria. The other students were either glaring at him or laughing at him, or completely ignoring him. He was in the same boat as me.

Empathizing with him, I approached him and sat down. "Hey there, would you like to share some cheesecake with me?"

The boy didn't look up at me but spoke in a feeble voice, "Why?"

"I've had a terrible day, and I was hoping for some silent companionship," I answered him. "And who doesn't like cheesecake?"

The boy seemed to relax a bit, but he still didn't look up. "You mean the *silent* bit?"

I nodded. "Trust me. I am in no mood to talk."

He nodded slightly. "I'm game, then."

We enjoyed the scrumptious, silky, and soft cheesecake together in comfortable silence. And strangely, I felt a connection with this stranger more than with any of my friends in a long time.

***

I was still wrapped up in thoughts of the awful day by the time I got back to our apartment later that evening after karate class. I planned to go over the Strollfield Cultural Festival app before my meeting with the team tomorrow. I was on probation from the organizers after all the negative publicity caused by the scandalous graduation day incident and couldn't afford *any* mistakes. I expected to be alone at home and had bought myself a microwaveable dinner. But hearing Laila and Harriet's animated voices in our living room, I stopped at the door.

"I still can't believe the Duckville High principal let Tina go. Wasn't the footage we created believable?" Harriet asked.

"I don't know. I thought we did a good job tampering with the original," Laila answered. "But I was shocked when the video disappeared altogether after graduation. We still don't know who stopped it abruptly either."

"You both were careless and stupid." On the speaker phone, I heard a male voice I knew all too well. "I should have never worked with both of you."

I froze. Laila and Harriet had worked with Nicholas Parker to frame me?

"The Strollfield Cultural Festival organizers have warned her that they'll expel her if there are any other controversies regarding her. So, what we did affected her," Laila argued.

"That's not enough. I want to ruin her life. She dared to publicly humiliate me—a Parker. She has to pay for it!" Nicholas yelled into the phone receiver. "I will ruin both your lives if you don't do something fast."

"Nick, we have a trump card. Trust us. This will break her," Harriet pleaded with him.

"You have two days," Nicholas said and disconnected the call.

My body shook with anger at my so-called friends' betrayal. It took every ounce of my willpower to not barge into our living room and confront them. I knew I would break down if I faced them now, and I had too much pride to let that happen.

Instead, I sat on the stairs outside our apartment with my face in my hands and wept silently until my tears dried out.

CHAPTER 8

The next morning, I reached our college campus early because I didn't want to face Laila or Harriet. I grabbed a hot chocolate and a breakfast sandwich at the university café. As I ate alone in one of the booths, my friends' betrayal slowly sank in. Why did they try to frame me? Was Rory involved too? What was the trump card they had that would help Nicholas succeed with his revenge? The questions multiplied in my head by the minute till it was fit to burst.

When it was almost time for my first lecture, I made my way to the classroom, which was abuzz as soon as I stepped inside. As I took my seat, people around me whispered, stealing glances at me every now and then. Some seemed to look sympathetic, while others glared. Hisses and murmurs of "fucking freak!" made the rounds. I was used to the subtle unfriendliness of high school, but this kind of open hostility was starting to wear me down.

For the rest of the lecture, I resolutely kept my head down, avoiding eye contact.

After class, I got a message from one of the organizers of the Strollfield Cultural Festival.

Organizer

Meet me at my office today, as soon as you can.

Me

I will be there by noon if that works.

I also received a money transfer notification—a part of the remaining amount for the Strollfield Cultural Festival mobile app. I was confused at the sudden payment but decided to ask the organizers directly during our meeting.

After class, I was glad to get out of campus to meet the festival organizer.

I heard someone call out my name. "Hey, Tina."

I turned to see that it was Aiden, the boy who had introduced himself to me yesterday.

"Are you alright?" he asked.

I nodded. "I'm fine. Why do you ask?"

Aiden looked at me with concern. "Um, are you aware that there is a video circulating about you?"

I sighed with irritation. "Yes, I am. It's been ages since Duckville High's graduation—can't you just leave me alone?"

Aiden shook his head. "No, not that one." He handed me his phone. "I meant this."

My eyes widened in horror. Someone had taken footage of me in the university bathroom without my knowledge yesterday. They had clearly stood on the toilet in the adjoining stall and recorded me from above.

I couldn't bear to look at it further, because I knew what it would show.

So this was Laila and Harriet's trump card.

That's why the students had called me an effing freak.

That's why the witch hunt had only gotten worse.

I started spiraling right there in the university quad.

Why did I have to do that in the university bathroom?

They're right. Doing that is freaky. Period.

But that's the only way I can calm myself down. It's been hellish lately. No one had the right to invade my privacy.

But is self-harm really the answer? I need help, and I need it now.

The cacophony of voices inside my head became unbearable. Not realizing Aiden was still there, I screamed loudly with my eyes shut. "Shut up! Please! Just shut the heck up."

Aiden gave me a startled look but didn't say anything. He tried to place his hand on my shoulder in a comforting way, but I thrust his phone into his hands and ran away.

This time, Nicholas Parker had well and truly ruined my life, just as he said he would.

**

It was almost noon when I entered the elevator to the Strollfield Cultural Society office. I sighed when I was met with glares and disgusted expressions from people in the elevator. I pressed the button for the seventeenth floor and buried my face in my phone, avoiding everyone's gaze for what seemed like eons. Once off the elevator, I bent my head in silent prayer that the organizers of SCF would give me a chance to explain myself.

At the office, I was led to the same boardroom I was hired in six months ago. I remembered that day. I could hardly contain my excitement while waiting for the interviewers. I entered the familiar sophisticated space with a slightly oval, polished-glass table placed on a luxurious carpet. I sat on the same swanky swivel chair that I'd wanted to twirl around in when I was congratulated for being selected. I stared at the digital screen longingly, hoping I would get an opportunity to present the final version of the app to the organizers next spring if the meeting went well today.

When I heard the office door open, I got up from my chair, as if it was wrong of me to be seated without permission. Mrs. and Mr. Srinivas, the chief organizers of the festival, came in, dressed in crisp business attire, and gestured me to sit down. Both of them took their seats at the head of the table and rested their elbows in front of them.

"I'm sure you have an inkling as to why you're here, Tina," Mrs. Srinivas started, without any pleasantries.

"We feel you need to take time off and concentrate on your well-being," Mr. Srinivas added gently. "You're off the SCF app development team starting today."

"Please let me explain," I pleaded quietly. "Can't you give me another chance?"

Mrs. Srinivas's expression softened a bit. "We have already given you two chances. You're smart and bright, with great ideas, but we cannot excuse your behavior anymore. And we have already compensated you for your efforts so far."

They got up from their chairs, indicating that the meeting was over.

Mr. Srinivas shot me a pitiful look. "Good luck, Tina. We sincerely hope you get some professional help."

I left the Strollfield Cultural Festival organizer's office feeling hollow and dejected. I walked to the bus stop, not knowing how I was ever going to get over this. Maybe I could transfer out of the university? What if I got expelled? Was my future ruined?

I got a text on my phone from an unknown number, but I knew all too well who it was.

Nicholas Parker
You asked for it. All of it.

I broke down in the middle of the pavement, not caring anymore about the bystanders who looked at me like I was crazy. I started sobbing, sinking down onto the sidewalk and pounding my fists on the ground.

I was interrupted by a call.

"Tina, are you alright?" my mother asked me. "Do you want to come home?"

I wiped my tears with the back of my hand. "Did you watch the video?"

"Why didn't you talk to us?" my mother replied with a question.

I got angry. "How can you ask me that, Mom? When Nicholas Parker tried to molest me, and I whacked him in the face, not once did you or Dad bother to find out what happened." I took a deep breath. "Even back then, when—"

"Tina, calm down. Where are you? Can you come home?" my father interrupted me. They had me on speakerphone.

"Don't tell me to calm down, Dad. I won't. You never let me talk. You didn't then; you don't now," I lashed out.

"Tina, we have *never* stopped you from saying anything," my mother said.

"Well, you didn't listen either," I weakly argued. "And you did nothing about what happened back then."

There was pin-drop silence on the line. I thought my parents had hung up.

"Tina, we didn't know. Your dad and I did the best we could. He even gave up his position in the family business," Mom said, her voice breaking.

My eyes welled up again.

"Tina, my publisher is ready to take care of this bad publicity for us. My latest novel has become a bestseller, and we can use that to our advantage," my father told me. "Let's focus on removing that video first."

"Congratulations on becoming a bestselling author, Dad. I'm sorry I interrupted your path of success and fame," I retorted and disconnected the call.

The text from Nicholas and the phone call with my parents had replaced my tears with a quiet rage. I was furious that my father was more interested in his reputation than me.

Gathering myself, I bought a pass to travel the city on Strollfield Transit, the city's public bus, because I didn't want to go back to the university. I went around the town on the bus until my ticket expired in the evening.

***

By the time I got down from the bus, the sun had almost set. On the way home, I stopped at the karate institute, hoping to meet with Nakamura Sensei. Maybe doing some karate would calm me down. I did not want to go home and face Laila and Harriet tonight. Rory had sent me multiple text messages, even though he was on his swimming tour, but I didn't respond to any of them. I had also ignored all his phone calls.

At the karate institute, the door was open, but the lights were out inside, as if they were getting ready to close up, and everyone had left for the day except Pete. Not seeing Dr. Nakamura anywhere, I was heading toward the exit, when Pete called out to me, "Hey, Tina, did you come to meet with Sensei?"

"Yes, but I can meet with her some other time," I replied.

"Why don't you wait for her inside?" Pete suggested. "She's in the restroom."

I entered the empty dojo hesitantly and sat in the near darkness on the stool Pete brought me, fiddling with my bee pendant nervously. He also got me a glass of water that I didn't drink, even though I was parched. I wasn't going to trust anyone anymore.

As Pete was about to sit next to me, his cell phone rang, and he stepped outside to take the call. I got up to use the restroom, but it was latched from outside. I panicked realizing Dr. Nakamura wasn't inside.

Pete lied to me that Sensei was still in the office.

Panicking, I ran toward the main door, only to collide with Pete.

He put his arm around me. "Don't worry, Tina. Everything will be fine."

I freed myself from his sudden embrace. "Where is Dr. Nakamura? Why did you lie to me and say she was in the restroom?"

Pete reached for my hand, but I slapped it away. "Forget Sensei, Tina. Let me comfort you tonight."

I was flabbergasted and shook my head vehemently. "No way."

I frantically opened the door and exited the karate institute as fast as I could.

"You didn't have a problem sleeping with Parker. Why are you insulting me?" Pete demanded, but I ran out of the building toward the main road without responding.

My head was reeling, and the cacophony of voices inside my head chanted the same thing.

I asked for it.

I asked for it.

I asked for it.

I shouldn't have gone in the dark building. I should just have left instead of trusting someone I hardly knew.

Unable to take it anymore, I held out my left hand and folded the sleeves of my shirt up to my elbow.

Stop. I must not do this. I heard a loud and clear voice inside my mind.

I waited for the contradicting voice, but I heard nothing.

Ignoring my inner voice, I thrust my right hand in my bag to fish out my knife, but my fingers closed around a small piece of stiff paper instead. Pulling it out, I saw it was Dr. Kim's business card. I had forgotten all about it.

"Tina?"

I spun around to find Dr. Nakamura walking toward me, a cloth shopping bag in her hand. I glanced behind her and noticed there was a small grocery store on the corner down the street from the dojo. That must have been where she'd been.

I hastily pulled down my sleeve, so she wouldn't see the scars on my arm. "I-I came to see you, but the dojo is closed," I told her, unnecessarily, not quite meeting her eyes. I couldn't say anything to her about Pete. It would be mortifying.

"Have you had a bit of a bad day?"

My gaze shot to her face. She'd seen the video. I could tell by the look of pity in her eyes. My face grew hot. I couldn't speak.

She gestured at the card I still held in my hand. "What's that you have there?"

I looked at the card and then silently handed it to her. I couldn't possibly get any more embarrassed than I already was.

"I would choose Dr. Kim, always," she said kindly. "And I am not just saying that because she's my wife."

That was a surprise, but I couldn't even think about that. "Sensei," I said plainly, "it's too late for me for therapy now. My future is already ruined."

She pointed to the message on the cover of my cell phone, which was sticking out of my overalls pocket—"Today is a gift." Ironically, Laila and Harriet had given that to me as a birthday present. "Think about today. Now. This moment."

I sighed and shook my head. "I can't."

Dr. Nakamura took a step closer to me and smiled. "You already did."

I frowned at her in confusion.

She bent and picked up my pocketknife, which had fallen to the ground without my knowledge. She secured its blade in its safety nest and handed it to me.

I smiled feebly, but genuinely, for the first time that day.

Dr. Nakamura was right.

I had already made my choice.

CHAPTER 9

Feeling slightly better after my conversation with Dr. Nakamura, I went home straight to my room and locked it from inside. I called Dr. Kim's clinic and set up an appointment for the next day.

Determined to get out of this apartment immediately, I searched for rental listings nearby. There were some options available, but I needed a roommate as the rates were too high. I applied to the available ads and printed out a "roommate wanted" advertisement though the chances of finding one seemed bleak. Exhausted from the day, I fell asleep instantly.

The next morning, I saw over twenty missed calls from my parents, but I was in no mood to reconcile with them. I sent them a text that I was okay and had to get ready for my classes. When I saw the appointment confirmation message from Dr. Kim's clinic, I developed cold feet about therapy again. I took a deep breath and typed "YES," and pressed send before I could change my mind again.

Feeling more confident about my step toward my mental well-being, I discarded my pocketknife and all the other objects I used to harm myself. I trimmed my sharp nails, took a relaxing shower, and got dressed for school. It was still too early, so I sat at my desk and looked for a new job to pay for rent and therapy. I did not want to depend on my parents and aimed to start adulting for real. I got an email response to one of the real estate listing applications, letting me know that the apartment was available to view this weekend. But I had to bring my roommate along. Having lost hopes of finding a new roommate with such short notice, I started typing a reply that I wanted to cancel my application but couldn't bring myself to send the email.

Please. I need to get out of here. I can't stay with these traitors anymore.

But who will want to room with an effing freak?

Before the voices in my head could consume me any further, I skated to the university cafeteria, pinned my roommate ad on the notice board, and got myself a cup of hot chocolate. When I was engrossed in a contemporary coming-of-age YA book, *Young or Adult?*, by my new favorite author, Enida W. Alexander, when I got a call. It was from an unknown number.

"Hello?"

"Hi, Tina. This is Aiden."

"How did you get my number?" I asked, knowing I sounded rude, but I was cautious of everyone since yesterday.

"From your advertisement," Aiden answered. "You're looking for a roommate, aren't you?"

Someone saw my ad so soon? It's barely been an hour.

"I'm not interested, thanks," I told him. "The ad specifies I need a female roommate. Bye."

Aiden interrupted me. "Wait, Tina. This is for my friend. Ex-girlfriend, actually."

"Let me guess. You want to take revenge on your former girlfriend by making her room with a crazy freak like me," I said coldly.

Aiden sighed. "Madison lost her father recently and is moving to Strollfield. She needs a roommate urgently. Besides, I think you and she would be great roommates."

I softened a little. "Is she free this weekend to view the apartment? Hold on. Let me give you the details."

While I searched for the ad listing, I could hear Aiden's friends in the background.

"Hey, Wilkins, is that Lauren on the phone?"

"His coach warned him not to talk to her," another voice said. "We don't want FF's influence on the basketball team's star player."

"Why do you even talk to her, man?"

I hung up the call before I could hear the response and texted Aiden the address instead.

Tears stung my eyes, but I blinked them away. I thought I had gotten used to being called an effing freak, but it hurt like crazy. I instinctively reached into my pocket, but the knife wasn't there.

I would have to make a tremendous amount of effort to stop my terrible habit.

***

"Hello. You must be Tina. Please take a seat," Dr. Kim greeted me, her smile reaching her warm dark brown, almost black eyes.

I didn't take a seat. "Dr. Kim, I'm here because I need help. But the past few weeks have been rough on me, and I'm afraid to show you my vulnerable side."

Dr. Kim gave me a document, still standing herself. "Here, this is the doctor-patient confidentiality form. I've already signed it. The minute you do, whatever we say will not leave the four walls of this room."

"And what if you judge me for being a freak *inside* this room?" I questioned her, still standing.

"Then I am not fit to be your therapist," she answered me.

I almost smiled at her statement but didn't budge from my position. "There is a stigma around mental health. People who go to shrinks are made fun of."

"If you're physically ill, you go to a doctor for treatment. If you don't feel alright in your mind, you go to a therapist to get better. That's all there is to it," Dr. Kim stated.

Is it really so simple? "You mean to say your advice will make me feel better?" I asked.

Dr. Kim shook her head. "No. I will not give you advice. I will provide you with an unbiased perspective of your issues that will help *you* work on your problems."

"Okay, I'm convinced. Let's begin."

I finally took a seat on the cozy couch-like chair while Dr. Kim sat on a bean bag. I noticed that the room was not intimidating like I had imagined it. The walls were painted the lightest shade of lavender, while the furniture was a contrasting dark orange that was pleasing to the eyes. Soft music played in the background, which could stimulate conversations instead of being distracting. A subtle but fresh fragrance of mint filled the air, making it easier to take deep breaths. Dr. Kim helped calm down her patients' senses during therapy.

After my first session, which was comprised of the preassessment and the prescriptions for meds, I sat at the packed healthcare center café, sipping a hot chocolate and replaying my first session with my therapist.

When Dr. Kim discussed the results of the psychological tests with me, she had been objective instead of feeding me jargon. When I talked to her openly about my addiction to self-harm, she reassured me that I could overcome it if I helped her help me. The key was, I had to work on myself to heal.

The prospect of unearthing my buried past scared me, but I was willing to take any step necessary to unclutter my mind and life.

"Hi. Do you mind if I take this seat?" a slim guy, a few inches taller than me, with short black hair and glasses, asked me.

I shook my head. "Please go ahead. Take the *chair*."

He sat down across from me instead. We drank our beverages in silence. He wasn't playing with his phone but looking around. A few minutes later, the people at the next table left.

"You can take the other table now, it's fine," I told him.

He grinned at me, his smile lighting up his face. "I'm good, thanks." He paused for a moment. "You seem familiar. Are you from Duckville?"

"No," I lied.

"I'm from Strollfield, but my boyfriend is from your town," he continued.

I didn't say anything. I didn't want to talk to anyone.

"Ah, now I remember. You're Ken's tutor," the guy exclaimed, making me jump.

I was thankful my hot drink didn't spill all over me.

"I'm so sorry," he apologized. "But I was excited to meet the hero that made Ken's life again."

I gave him a blank look. I had no idea what he was talking about.

"You're Tina Lauren, aren't you? Last year, you tutored Kenneth and Keith, now known as the famous MyWay twin popstars, in mathematics. I met you once after one of those sessions," he explained. "Both of them had low grades and were banned from continuing in their band until you stepped in. Ken even got an A after you taught him."

I smiled, remembering whom I was talking to. "Jai Rao? Sorry, I didn't recognize you. Wow, you're already in college. I remember Ken telling me you were going to advance a year. The twins are still in their final year of high school, aren't they? I know they transferred to Strollfield High after they became popstars."

"That's correct," Jai said. "Nice to meet you again. How have you been?"

I didn't answer his question. "How are Ken and Keith?"

"They're doing well," Jai replied. "I think you know that MyWay is a big deal now. Neither can stop singing praises about you."

"I did nothing. They were good students, who weren't given a fair chance at math by their teachers."

He shook his head. "You have no idea how much it changed their lives. They rave to everyone about their high school tutor, who made them fall in love with math."

I smiled at the compliment. "Thanks."

"No, thank you. You have a gift of teaching. I hope you pursue it in the future," Jai said.

"I'll keep that in mind," I replied.

Jai gave me his card. "If you're here again, just text me or call me. I work part time at the pathology lab here at the healthcare center."

I hesitated. "I don't think that's a good idea."

He smiled at me. "It's up to you. But I would really like it if you would."

I shook my head. "You don't want to be seen with me. I'm called an effing freak by the other students at the university."

"That's all the more reason we should be friends," Jai stated. "The students call me a mute monster."

"Oh, I'm sorry to hear that."

Jai smiled and shook his head. "Don't be. I like monsters. I used to search for them in my closet when I was a kid…to befriend them."

"That's so cute." I laughed for the first time in weeks. "Alright, Fellow Monster. Don't regret it later."

Jai laughed with me. "I don't think I will, Little Monster."

CHAPTER 10

One year later

"Yes, Mom, I promise I'll be home for Thanksgiving," I told my mother on the phone. "It's more than two weeks away."

"I still don't understand why you didn't visit us even once in the last year," my mother replied.

"I wasn't ready to face you, or any of our relatives. I had already disappointed you," I said in a quiet voice.

"But you haven't harmed yourself in six months, right?" my mother asked, relief evident in her voice.

I nodded. "Yes, that's correct. And it's all because of Dr. Kim, therapy, and you. Thanks, Mom."

"Are you thanking me before I say 'I told you so'?" my mother asked in a teasing tone.

I laughed. "No, I genuinely mean it. I went to therapy because you urged me to go."

"No, the credit goes to you. You have worked hard on yourself."

I sighed. "But I have a long way to go."

It was hard to believe that it was already a year since my life had turned topsy-turvy. I realized a lot had changed since then: I had started working as an online tutor, which kept my evenings busy. I ate lunch with Jai Rao—the only person I trusted—in the emergency stairwell, and I had a decent roommate with whom I spent a lot of time, albeit quietly.

"Tina, did you zone out again?" my mother asked.

"Sorry, I was just thinking about how much my life has changed over the last year."

"Don't worry about the past, dear. Remember, today is a gift," my mother added after a pause.

We chatted for a bit about the upcoming break. After I hung up, I thought about how "Today is a gift" reminded me of the two people I had tried to avoid this past year: Harriet and Laila. I still got tongue-tied when I saw them on campus, and I cowered and ran away. Seeing them still hurt, and I was afraid that I would burst into tears in front of them.

Not much has changed over the last year, has it?

Of course, it has. I sleep better at night.

True, but the nightmares haven't stopped completely.

"I have made significant progress, but I have some things I still need to work on," I concluded aloud.

I heard a knock on my bedroom door.

"Tina, are we still on for movie-binge Friday night?" my roommate, Madison Narine, asked.

"Sure! I'll be out in five minutes," I replied.

I changed into my full-length pajamas from my shorts before heading to the living room. Even now, I could wear shorts only when I was alone. Hesitantly, I hooked my fingers into the waistband of my pants to change back to the comfortable Bermudas. Finally, I decided against it and unlocked my room door behind me.

Madison and I watched a suspense series that kept us on the edge of our seats. She and I sat on opposite sides of the loveseat. We sat facing a 30-inch television with a sound bar mounted atop a coffee table. We had purchased everything from a local thrift store and shared the costs. Though it wasn't a rule, neither of us watched anything new without the other. I was glad that we both enjoyed our entertainment time together and looked forward to it every time.

I appreciated the space that Madison and I gave each other, but also yearned to talk to her at times. I didn't know anything much about my roommate, other than the fact that she studied dance at Strollfield Dance Academy, part of Strollfield U, and was currently persevering to qualify for a country-wide contest, "Dance Divas." She lived and breathed dance and was one of the three scholarship students at the academy. Despite her hectic schedule, she made time for her boyfriend, Darma Pranadipa, who attended college an hour away from Strollfield.

I had never asked her any personal questions and had made it clear that I wouldn't answer anything either. However, as I got to know her, I wished we talked beyond, "I got some milk for you at the store today" or "Don't wait up for me for dinner." Whatever we knew about each other was either through observation or what we'd heard in college.

Right now, I could feel Madison looking at me from the corner of her eye, wanting to say something but hesitating. I paused our movie, turned toward her, and smiled, encouraging her to talk.

"Are you alright, Tina?" Madison asked.

I nodded. "Yes, I am." I frowned slightly, puzzled. "But why are you asking me that?"

"I heard that your project group pulled you out of their team, making you work alone again," she said, sounding concerned.

I waved a dismissive hand, ignoring the pang in my chest. Even though it had been a year, being isolated still hurt. "Oh, that? Yes, but I'm used to it."

"I think Nicholas Parker had something to do with it. Otherwise, there's no way everyone would treat you like that after a year," Madison reasoned.

I flinched a little at the mention of the name Nicholas Parker but shrugged nonchalantly. "Maybe."

"I'm sorry I started the topic," Madison said quietly.

I shook my head. "Don't be. Thanks for showing me your concern. It feels good that someone cares." I mentally kicked myself for saying that and embarrassing myself.

"Of course, I care. You're a wonderful person and don't deserve to be boycotted by your classmates." Madison took a deep breath. "Look, Tina, I'm going to let out everything I've kept inside me for a year. First of all, kudos to you for shoving that creep, Nicholas Parker. I wish you had broken his teeth. Next, those who fabricated that scandalous sex video should be punished. Not you, who did nothing. Further, as for the self-harm video, everyone should have empathized with you instead of isolating you."

I stared at my roommate, gobsmacked. I had always wished someone would take my side. However, now that it was happening, I had no idea how to react.

"Say something, please?" Madison urged me. "Your silence is killing me."

"How I wish I had heard that a year ago," I said, my voice almost breaking. "But thank you. That means the world to me."

Madison smiled a little, looking relieved, before turning serious again. "It was about time. One of my classmates transferred out of the university because of that sicko, Parker. I felt guilty for not comforting her when she was nice to me. Then I realized that I hadn't even once asked if you, someone I see every day, were alright." She paused for a moment. "I haven't been able to make new friends since my dad..." Madison trailed off and got up from the couch, tying her long, wavy black hair up into a ponytail nervously. "Anyway, it was nice talking to you."

I don't want this conversation to end on such an awkward note. Madison opened up to me a little bit, even though she was uncomfortable. I need to show her that I appreciate the gesture and reciprocate.

I took a deep breath. "I overheard my former friends and that pervert, Parker, discussing how they faked the scandalous video. Since then, I've had a hard time trusting anyone."

Madison's eyes grew wide in horror. "Oh, my goodness, that's horrible. I'm so sorry to hear that. You should lodge a complaint against them."

"I don't have any proof though," I said. "I could have tried to search for the obscene video and proved that it was fabricated, but I feel for the *actual* person in the footage who was dressed as me. She probably got recorded without her consent. So, I decided to let go."

Madison sat next to me on the couch. "Can I hug you?"

I nodded. I was getting better with touch these days. I put my arms around her petite, slender body awkwardly.

She patted my back. "You deserve better friends. Maybe someone like me?"

My face broke into a wide grin. "Definitely." I placed my hand on hers. "How about we talk each other's ears off the next time, instead of watching a movie? After all, both of us have a year of catching up."

Madison's honey brown eyes twinkled in delight. "I would love that, Teensy."

"Is that my new nickname?" I asked with a smile. "I am taller than you, though."

Madison laughed. "True, but doesn't it have a nice ring to it? Besides, you have tiny hands."

I giggled. "Then, you're Mads."

That's how we became Teensy and Mads to each other.

Back in my room, I sat at my desk and admired my personal paradise before my online tutoring session started. Compared to a year ago, it was no longer boring and bleak. My pale pastel clothes were gone, replaced by vibrant colors. I had filled the walls with display boards—inspired by the Recharge Café—and pinned photographs and notes on them. My favorite part of it was the "thank you" messages from my students when they did well. When I needed a boost of confidence, I would read everything on there to make me feel better.

After the class, I opened my journal to write three good things that happened to me today. Dr. Kim, my therapist, encouraged me to jot down the positives in my life. At first, this was a herculean task, but it was getting easier every day. I smiled and scribbled in my diary, because today, I had a lot to fill in.

***

The following Monday, Jai and I ate lunch in silence at our usual spot in the stairwell. It was a secluded spot, just outside the cafeteria, but without the hustle and bustle. Occasionally, we saw a couple enjoying their privacy or quarreling with each other, but most times, it was just us. Though it was not ideal for university students to eat here, it was a good place to enjoy a quiet meal in peace.

I was upset, and I could see Jai noticed. But we concentrated only on our food while we ate. We had prepared lunch for each other. Jai had made me a bowl of Indian rice vermicelli noodles, which was still warm after reheating in the cafeteria microwave oven.

I slurped the noodles from my chopsticks and smacked my lips. The sauce was a perfect balance of spicy, savory, and tangy. The vegetables were perfectly cooked and retained a bite, just the way I liked them. I closed my eyes when I felt the pleasant taste of mustard seeds coat my mouth with their nutty flavor.

Jai was enjoying the Bhutanese dish I had made for him—ema datshi. The standard version had yak's cheese, but my mother's recipe contained goat cheese and a blend of other types of locally available cheese. I smiled as I watched Jai gorge on the comforting veggie stew with pieces of meat that melted in the mouth. I wasn't a great cook, but I had mastered this delicacy.

"What should we make for each other next?" Jai asked, smacking his lips.

I chuckled. "I can make you my favorite momos—dumplings with succulent meat and juicy veggies. But that tastes better when piping hot."

"My mouth is watering at the sound of it," Jai said. He picked up his ringing phone. "I need to take this call. I'll be right back."

My mind wandered back to this morning when Rory had come to my class unannounced, and I had run to the ladies' room to avoid him. A flood of mixed emotions flowed through me. I was angry to see him but glad he was alright, despite his breakup with Harriet. Rory had texted me every once in a while over the past year, but I had not replied. I held a grudge against him for not being on my side back then.

That was a year ago, Tina. Besides, Rory did not betray me.

But it was because of him that—

"Tina, my roommate wants to talk to you. Is that okay?" Jai broke into my thoughts, handing me his phone.

I gave him a puzzled look and took it. "Hello?"

"Hi, T."

I froze when I heard the voice. Then I glanced up at Jai. Rory was his roommate?

Rory spoke in a quiet voice. "I hope we can talk. I am at the university cafeteria."

I saw Rory waiting for me at a corner table a few minutes later. He was unshaven, and that stubble didn't look groomed. His eyes had lost their liveliness, and he looked pale. His mouth curled up in a smile when he saw me.

"Hi, T," Rory greeted.

"What do you want from me?" I asked, sounding curt.

"It's been over a year since you moved out and stopped talking to me," he answered me. "I miss you."

"Are you just remembering me, now that your girlfriend ditched you?" I retorted.

Ouch, that was harsh.

But it is the truth.

I softened a little. "Sorry, that was rude."

Rory shook his head. "No, I deserve it. I've been a terrible friend."

Oh, so you realize that now?

I shrugged. "I've moved on, and so should you."

Rory took a deep breath. "I'm sorry for not being there for you when you needed me the most. I wish I could go back in time and mend everything—"

"There's no point dwelling on the past."

There was an uncomfortable silence, and I was about to get up when he spoke again.

"T, can we give our friendship another chance?" Rory asked quietly.

I could see he was remorseful, but I didn't want to get hurt again. At the same time, I didn't want to regret missing this chance to mend our friendship.

"I'll try, R, but don't expect us to get back to being best friends again," I replied.

Rory nodded. "Trying is good."

CHAPTER 11

"The nightmares still haunt me at night, Dr. Kim. They haven't stopped," I informed my therapist during my session the next day.

"What do you do when you get them, Tina?" Dr. Kim asked.

"I tell myself that I'm safe in my room and that they can't get to me."

Dr. Kim smiled. "See, that's progress."

I shook my head. "I'm still afraid of touch. I was awkward when I hugged Madison the other day."

"Isn't that progress too? Would you have hugged her at all before?" Dr. Kim questioned me gently.

"But what if I relapse? What if I harm myself again?" I let out the storm of questions haunting my mind.

"What have you done when such thoughts came to your mind in the last six months?" Dr. Kim questioned me back.

"It wasn't easy. I used to harm myself every time I heard the clutter of contradicting voices inside my head. Now, I cry and write down everything on my mind to let those pent-up emotions out. When I do that, I hear a loud and clear voice inside my mind that says, 'I'm going to be alright, I will get through this, and I'll be there for myself even if no one else is,'" I replied.

"Your inner voice," Dr. Kim stated.

"My inner voice," I confirmed. "But it's silent sometimes when I need it the most. It's frustrating. For instance, I shudder when I think about getting tongue-tied when I meet Harriet or Laila."

"Have you met them recently?" Dr. Kim asked.

I shook my head. "No, I always run away."

I told her how terrified I was to meet my former friends, along with my other fears.

"It's been a year since I started therapy. Sometimes, I feel I've progressed a lot. Other times, I feel stagnant." I sighed. "I want to reduce the frequency of our sessions and become more confident to handle things on my own, though."

"How about we do this? Let's book an appointment three months from today to assess your progress. And if you feel the need to see me before that, simply call in," Dr. Kim suggested.

I smiled at her for the first time that day. "Thanks, Dr. Kim. That would be great."

I left Dr. Kim's office with a wide grin on my face as I thought about how far I had come. When the self-harm video had leaked a year ago, I thought I would never get over my habit or the humiliation that ensued. But now, even if I still worked alone on all my school assignments, I had people in my life who cared about me. I had made a new beginning and was taking baby steps toward rebuilding my life, a few bricks at a time.

I had come to this clinic completely messed up. Six months later, I was now a little less messed up. And that felt good.

I headed to the university to meet Jai, excited to give him the news.

I jumped up and down like a kid. "I'm done. No more monthly therapy." I opened a box from my bag and offered it to him. "And I got cheesecake from Recharge Café."

"Wow. Look at you. Anyone would have thought you were *forced* to meet Dr. Kim," Jai teased me, helping himself to the sweet treat.

"Hey, I survived. I'm proud," I said, licking my spoon. "I'm less of a freak now."

"I am proud of you too," he replied. "And you were never a freak. Ever."

I smiled at him gratefully. "Thanks, Jai."

Jai patted me lightly. "A year ago, you smiled through a lot of your difficulties. Now your smile is effortless. That says a lot. I'm glad."

"Thank you. You know, I feel like I achieved the sun, the moon, and the stars." I giggled.

"It is a huge accomplishment, Little Monster," Jai agreed with me.

I smiled again. "Yes, Fellow Monster. And I am grateful to you for approaching me that day, after my first therapy session at the healthcare center."

Jai didn't say anything for a moment and continued to look down at his plate.

"Actually, *you* initiated our friendship," Jai said quietly. He chuckled softly and raised his cheesecake. "This is déjà vu to me. Ring a bell?"

I frowned at Jai, puzzled, and shook my head.

Jai hesitated a little. "I will give you a hint: mango cheesecake."

Suddenly, it struck me, and a shiver ran down my spine when painful memories of that day came rushing back—Laila, Harriet, and Rory treating me like I didn't exist. Me jabbing my pocketknife into my hand in agony in the bathroom stall, which got caught by a hidden camera unknown to me.

But my face cracked into a wide grin when I remembered enjoying the soft, silky, and scrumptious mango cheesecake in silence with the black-capped boy.

"Sorry, I shouldn't have brought it up. It's the past anyway," Jai apologized.

I moved closer to Jai and placed my hand on his shoulder. "You know, I was lonely and felt like I didn't matter to anyone that day, Fellow Monster. But the universe showed me that I was not alone. So, thank you."

Jai shook his head and placed his hand on mine. "No, thank *you*. If not for you, I would have quit college that day. I had had enough of my classmates bullying me."

I squeezed his hand lightly. "Well, I am glad we both are still here."

Jai nodded. "Yes, I am grateful for that too."

We ate our sweet treat in silence for the next few minutes.

"Hey, Jai, if it's okay to ask, why did your classmates bully you?" I asked, wiping my mouth with a paper napkin after I finished my dessert.

Jai sighed. "I get anxious when talking to strangers." He added with a humorless laugh, "It's ironic that I want to become a doctor who will have to talk to patients."

"How do you manage assignments that involve public speaking then?" I asked.

"I can manage public speaking because I am not speaking to anyone directly. Besides, I rehearse thoroughly. But if it's people I've never met before, I can't even open my mouth," Jai answered. "On the first day of college, it was bad that I was younger than my classmates but worse that I went mute when they tried to talk to me. And they refused to give me a second chance."

"It's your classmates' loss for not befriending you. You're awesome," I said.

Jai smiled. "You're the second person to say that to me this week. The first was Rory."

"It's true," I insisted. "And I'm glad you're roommates with Rory. He is a great guy."

Jai told me that Rory had moved in with Jai after breaking up with Harriet a few weeks ago. A couple of days ago, Jai had mentioned he was going to have lunch with me, Tina Lauren, and Rory had told him he knew me. That we used to be best friends.

Jai hesitated for a moment now. "Are you going to give him another chance?"

I gave him the rundown of what had happened a year ago to make me stop speaking to Rory. When I finished, I asked, "What would you have done in my place?"

Jai thought for a moment. "I would wait and see if Rory deserved to be my friend again."

I nodded in agreement. "Great minds think alike."

Jai laughed. "Fools seldom differ."

When I got back home, I received a text from Rory.

Rory

How about we drive to Duckville together next weekend?

***

The day before Thanksgiving, Rory and I took turns driving my car on our way to our parents' houses. The drive was beautiful, and the colors of fall were vibrant. It was bright and sunny, with a clear cloudless sky. The highway didn't have much traffic, making it all the more pleasurable to drive. The familiar fragrance of wheat and corn fields made me nostalgic, and I was glad to go back home to my parents.

Autumn is my favorite season, not just because it's the season I was born. For me, fall is to let go of the past, forgive previous errors, and try to make amends.

I loved this used ten-year-old vehicle I'd purchased a few months ago with my savings. It wasn't a luxury ride, but it functioned well.

"When are your parents moving out of Duckville?" Rory asked me.

"Next week. This will be our last Thanksgiving there," I answered him. "They're moving to Birch Town, two hours away from Strollfield."

An awkward silence lingered between us, and I could see Rory was trying hard to keep the conversation going.

"Have you read Walt's latest book, *Relentless*, the one that's all the rage?" Rory asked, referring to my father's most recent novel.

I nodded. "I've read all my father's books. I like his new bestseller, but, to be honest, it's not my favorite."

"Hmmm. I always thought Walt would take over Lauren Industries," Rory stated. "He even went to an Ivy League business school for that. Didn't he?"

"Yeah, but he writes amazing, gripping thrillers," I replied, carefully evading his question. I never talked about why my father had chosen to become an author, despite being the heir to Lauren Industries.

"Of course, he does. I don't read the printed books, but Walt's audiobooks keep my interest alive," Rory said.

I wondered when Rory and I would stop pretending that things were perfectly normal between us. An honest talk was long overdue, and it would be better to address the unspoken sooner than later.

Suddenly, Rory pulled over at the side of the road. "T, I can't do this anymore."

"Do you want me to take over the wheel?" I asked. "We're almost there anyway."

Rory shook his head. "No. We're behaving like strangers and making small talk. I meant, I hope we can be honest with each other."

He read my mind.

I crossed my arms across my chest. "What do you want to talk about?"

Rory took a deep breath. "I know that Harriet and Laila are Parker's underlings. I accidentally saw their text conversations on her phone a few weeks ago. That was one of the reasons for our breakup. Why didn't you tell me?"

I shot him an angry look. "Why didn't I tell *you*?"

Rory's eyes widened in horror. "Do you think I was also involved?"

I shook my head. "No. Because we wouldn't be having this conversation if I was suspicious of you."

Rory raised his voice. "Then *why*?"

"When Laila and Harriet..." I started, then stopped. "Forget it. The damage is done, anyway."

"Please, T," Rory requested. "I want to know why you ghosted me for a year. Five years ago, when you took a break from school, you stopped talking to everyone else, but not me."

"Why did it take you a year to come and find me?" I shot back. "Why did you remember me only after breaking up with Harriet?"

"I was furious that you left our apartment without discussing it with me. When I texted you numerous times to see if we could meet, you didn't reply. At that time, I didn't know that Harriet and Laila had forged the video they played at graduation. Why didn't you respond to my messages even once?"

"Did you ask me *even once* if I was okay?" I asked, my voice barely a whisper. "You kept saying you wanted to meet or rambled on about your coach. Did you care to check on me *at all* in the past year?"

Rory looked at me guiltily.

I sighed. "You never stood up for me in front of your ex-girlfriend, time and time again, but especially that day. I blamed you for hurting myself at the university that day, when all three of you behaved as if I was nonexistent. The same day, they caught me cutting myself on camera. I would have never done that if you had been on my side. I doubt you remember that."

"Of course, I remember," Rory exclaimed. "I'm so sorry, T. Harriet gave me a hard time whenever I took your side, and I noticed she doubled down on you too. So I tried to remain neutral. I was wrong."

"It devastated me," I informed him. "During my therapy sessions, I realized that I blamed you for that incident because I felt betrayed by you. However, I'm alright now, and don't hold anything against you anymore."

"I'm extremely sorry for hurting you. I won't give any excuses or justifications. I wish I could turn back time and make everything right. But, unfortunately, I can't do that," Rory said.

I gave him a small smile. "Apology accepted."

Rory gripped the steering wheel, his eyes blazing. "You didn't do anything wrong. Parker deserved to be hit. Now, Laila and Harriet should pay for what they did."

I shrugged. "I don't have any proof against any of them."

"I promise, I will make it up to you," Rory vowed. "I won't let you down this time."

***

"Surprise!"

I jumped, taken aback at the yelling. I had gone to the skating park to practice my stunts for the upcoming holiday fundraiser and had come back home to a party. My parents, Rory, Jai, Madison, and the MyWay band twins, Keith and Kenneth Wright, were all here.

"Happy birthday!" everyone wished me.

My birthday fell on Thanksgiving this year, and I thought no one had remembered. After dropping Rory at his parents' place the day before, I had had dinner and plopped on my bed at home. I was fast asleep when my parents came back home later that night. This morning, no one had wished me happy birthday, and I assumed they were busy with the festive preparations.

"Th-Thank you so much, everyone," I stuttered. "This means a lot." I was genuinely moved but not very good at handling all the attention.

After a quick change, I cut my birthday cake as everyone sang to me. Later, MyWay played live music.

"Happy nineteenth birthday, T," Rory said.

"Thanks! You planned this, didn't you?" I asked.

"Madison helped," he replied.

Madison scoffed. "It was Jai's idea. Rory didn't come up with it. Besides, I did most of the work."

I laughed. "Thanks a lot. All three of you."

Madison pulled me into a hug, and I didn't resist. "No problem, Teensy. You deserve to be happy."

I smiled. It felt good to hug my friend and not feel icky. I still felt a little awkward but was slowly getting over it. I gave Jai and Rory awkward side hugs to thank them as well. They were surprised by my gesture but accepted it graciously.

The MyWay twins were the highlight of the party. They had become stars on social media, and it was a big deal that they were here. My relatives flocked around them, gushing over their good looks and music. They didn't seem to mind the attention at all. They smiled, waved at me, and mouthed "Happy Birthday." I thanked them and gestured for them to continue entertaining the party guests.

I went to find my parents. I wanted to patch things up. After my outburst a year ago, I hadn't seen my parents in person. We had spoken over the phone and texted, but I was too scared to face them.

While searching for my parents, I spotted a slightly stocky guy, a few inches taller than me, attending to everyone at the gathering. I went over to him. This person had single-handedly assembled the refreshments and served everyone.

I recognized him instantly. "Mr. Okoro, you work at the Recharge Café, correct? Thank you so much for taking time out to help us out today."

He smiled back at me. "Oh, it was my pleasure."

His smile was so infectious that even my paternal grandmother, who was always grumpy, was grinning ear to ear.

"The cake was so delicious, I wished I didn't have to share it with any of the guests. Please tell your chef how much I loved it," I said.

He beamed. "That would be me. I'm glad you enjoyed it."

"Are you a chef at Recharge Café then?" I asked him.

He nodded and smiled politely.

"I am addicted to your food," I told him. "I hardly go anywhere else for a bite when I'm in that area. I wouldn't eat desserts before, but now I am obsessed with everything at Recharge. You're a magical chef."

And your eatery got me through my worst days.

Chef Okoro smiled again, blushing slightly this time. "Thanks. That's really high praise. I will convey your feedback to my boss."

He has a great smile, and that blush is cute.

Has my face gone red too?

One of the guests called the chef, requesting for him to get them more cake, and he excused himself.

Thank goodness, he didn't see my face just now.

I could have got lost in his eyes—those decadent pools of chocolate.

Did I notice him before today?

"Tina, happy birthday," said Keith Wright, one of the MyWay twins. I was grateful that someone had interrupted my thoughts.

"Hey, Keith, Ken," I greeted them. "Thanks for coming today despite your crazy schedule. And congratulations on the success of your latest album."

"It's our pleasure," Kenneth said. "We owe you big time for continuing our musical careers. We thought we were goners after flunking math in our first year."

"Well, I only remember both of you doing well in the re-test and all subsequent ones," I replied with a reassuring smile. "You both are smart. Just believe in yourselves."

"Thanks, Tina," they said in unison. "We should all plan to hang out together sometime. It's not fair that only Jai gets to eat your delicacies," they added, pointing to the person who had just joined our conversation.

Jai stuck his tongue out at the twins. "Well, Tina is my best friend, and I'll decide if we should include you *mere high schoolers* in our sophisticated lunch parties."

Kenneth shoved Jai playfully. "Please. It's hardly a party. You guys eat in the emergency stairwell."

Jai rolled his eyes at his boyfriend. "You're such a snob. MyWay fame is spoiling you."

Jai and Kenneth continued their love banter. I excused myself and continued to search for my parents.

I finally saw my father talking to my paternal grandmother, whom I called Grandma. I didn't get along well with her because she didn't like my biracial origin. Today, she was bickering with my father about the same thing as every year.

"We should have celebrated Thanksgiving in style. This house doesn't compare to the Lauren family mansion. That's where we should be celebrating, just as we always have. There's no reason to have changed to your house, when we are right across town. Your wife is responsible for brainwashing you into abandoning our family heritage. You're even following her to a godforsaken town far away—"

Dad interrupted her. "Mum, we have spoken about this multiple times. Please, let's change the subject. It was always our plan to move out of Duckville after Tina left for college. Besides, Birch Town is just a three-hour drive from here."

She put her palm on her forehead. "I want to spend one holiday in my own home before I die. Just one. Is that too much to ask?"

How melodramatic. But no, I am not stepping into that place, not in a million years, even if it is just across town.

Am I still scared that the mansion would unearth the buried memory of my demons?

My dad raised his voice, and I turned my attention back to their conversation. "Mother, you're fine. You are not dying anytime soon. Could we please just enjoy *this* holiday?"

I escaped from the unpleasant atmosphere, because I didn't want to ruin my special day. I tried to divert my mind and noticed my parents' packed boxes that had been moved to the side to make space for the party. There were no decorations this year, but I spotted the familiar kitchen cart with the food spread prepared by my father. I smiled as I recalled an incident from when I was a kid.

I'd sat nestled between my parents on our favorite reclining, faux leather couch, where we argued about what to watch together. Dad chose a reality TV show on the Food Channel, while Mom and I wanted to enjoy a crime series. My father was adamant about his choice, despite being a thriller author himself.

"Walt, don't you want inspiration from other writers for your work?" my mother asked.

Dad shook his head. "I have to think about crime all the time when I write. I need to unwind now with something different."

"Dad, let's watch *anything* else, not this reality show," I pleaded with my father.

"I will prepare Thanksgiving dinner this year, and every year, if you let me watch this," Dad declared.

My mother scoffed. "You haven't even peeled potatoes before. How will you be able to handle an entire menu?"

"Actually, I'm interested in learning how to cook," my father revealed to us. "Mum never allowed me in the kitchen because I'm a boy."

Mom reached out and squeezed Dad's hand. "Then, I can't wait to taste your dishes." She added, reading my father's hesitation, "It'll be our little secret."

We huddled in a tight family hug as I complained about being smothered by my parents but secretly loved it.

The memory made me miss Mom all the more. I bit into one of my father's scrumptious cranberry scones and wondered where she was when I felt a hand on my shoulder.

I immediately turned and hugged the person tightly. "Mom, where were you? Thank you for today."

"No problem. I was right here, but you didn't see me in front of your friends," she teased me.

I was glad to see her smiling. I reached out for another embrace when I felt a pat on my back.

I turned toward my father, who engulfed me in a hug. "Tina, it's so good to see you."

I was surprised, because my father rarely embraced me. It felt wonderful. I got emotional when my mother slipped her arms around my waist, and I was engulfed between my parents, just like back when I was a little girl.

The three of us held each other for several minutes in complete silence— one that spoke a thousand meaningful words.

CHAPTER 12

That evening, I helped my parents clean up and pack after the guests left. It felt too strange to enter what used to be my room for the last time. The space didn't look any different than when I used to stay here, even if it was empty. All it was missing was my futon and my desk. I hadn't decorated this place or bothered to add color to it at all. I shuddered when I recalled the grim, gray teen years my room reflected.

Memories of my high school days, particularly the hours I used to spend coding at my desk, flooded my mind. I also remembered the long late-night phone conversations I had with Rory, Laila, and Harriet. I closed my room door and left it unlocked for the first time since I had stepped into this house.

Goodbye, Duckville. The bittersweet memories of my life here will remain with me.

I hugged my parents goodbye and picked up Rory before heading back to Strollfield. I went back to my routine the next day and the rest of the week with classes, assignments, karate, online tutoring students, and skating practice.

On Saturday morning, I nervously entered the Strollfield Cultural Festival fundraiser at McCormick Park on my Rollerblades. The fundraiser was held in November every year, five months before the main festival. It had taken me immense willpower to come here. After being fired from the fest's mobile app team a year ago, I had stopped coding. My beloved hobby brought back unpleasant memories I didn't want to face, so I quit. I had also skipped the fundraiser last year and stayed at home, feeling sorry for myself.

This year, I was determined to face the public again and signed myself up as a volunteer and a performer at the fundraiser. I tried to ignore the butterflies in my stomach and focused on the event. The venue resembled a fair and was bustling with activity. Families with young kids enjoyed themselves at the various stalls. I laughed silently when I saw a couple walking out of the haunted house, hand in hand, trying to hide their amusement when a child asked them about their experience. I recalled a time when I had been inside, a few years ago, with my parents, and how I had been unimpressed by the plastic "ghosts."

The most attractive stalls at the fundraiser were the food trucks. I tried not to get tempted by the ooey-gooey, stringy cheese on the piping hot, wood-fired pizzas, baked fresh to perfection. I averted my eyes, only to get a whiff of juicy pieces of marinated meat barbecuing on the grill. I held my breath to stop the aroma and proceeded toward the eatery I'd been assigned to volunteer at.

I need to stop thinking about junk food. I have to perform skating stunts this evening.

Outside my destination, I saw that children had gathered to watch something. They were gaping in wonder as a guy prepared cotton candy by pulling sugar with his hands. He had his back to me, and I watched as he swung his arms from one side to another adeptly. I panicked, wondering if I'd need to repeat his actions as a volunteer.

He held up the white candy that glistened in the sun. "There we go, we have 32,768 strands of this special candy. Who wants to try it?"

The kids ran toward the food truck. "Me. Me."

He laughed. "There will be more for everybody. Give me a few minutes. Now, let the counting begin once again. How many strands do we have? 2... 4... 8... 16... 32... 64... 128... 256... 512... 1,024... 2,048... 4,096... 8,192... 16,384. And 32,768."

I couldn't help but admire him flexing his small-ish, but well-defined, biceps under his shirt.

What a show-off.

The children clapped. He rolled up the cotton candy strands and placed them in serving bowls, and they disappeared from the counter within seconds.

"Alright, kids, the live candy show will be back after fifteen minutes," the guy announced.

As soon as the kids had dispersed, I stepped up to the truck. "Um, hi. I'm supposed to help out at the cotton candy store," I said to the guy's back.

He turned around. "Oh, hi. Tina Lauren, right?"

"Birthday cake," I blurted. I went red in my face in embarrassment. "Sorry, Chef Okoro."

He smiled and offered his hand. "It's Ekon Okoro. You can call me Ekon."

I shook his hand. "Nice to meet you again, Ekon. How can I help? I see this place is packed already."

"Can you be the cashier?" he asked. He pointed to another chef, wearing an apron. "Sharon will help you settle in."

I stood in front of the checkout counter. "Sure. On it."

For the next three hours, Sharon, Ekon, and I worked in sync. Ekon attracted customers with his live show, Sharon prepared the machined cotton candy, and I was the cashier. Sharon and Ekon were speedy, and I struggled to catch up. Having an app would have made this process easier. I froze at the thought of coding for a second, but there was no time to ponder about anything now.

After shutting down the candy truck, Sharon, Ekon, and I cleaned up. Ekon handed me some handmade cotton candy. "Here you go. Try some. You worked hard today. We raised a lot of money."

I took some strands of the white sugar and put them in my mouth. "This is so good. No wonder they sold like hotcakes."

Sharon pitched in. "It's not easy to make. The technique originated from Ancient China. Ekon learned it from me in less than a week."

"Why didn't you just take care of the live counter instead, Sharon?" I asked.

Sharon chuckled. "I thought people would come for the eye candy and stay for the cotton candy. I was right."

I could totally see her point.

Ekon blushed. "Oh, please. Sharon is the real expert. She just doesn't like the attention and made me do it."

"Anyway, I don't think I formally introduced you to Sharon. She is my boss and head chef at the café. Tina, the base of your birthday cake was Sharon's recipe, with some touches from me."

"Thanks for the introduction. And belated happy birthday, Tina," Sharon said. "I've got to run now. Maybe I'll catch you sometime."

"Sure. See you later," I replied.

"Sharon's daughter isn't feeling well," Ekon offered once she'd left. "She needed to leave early. Without her, I'll have to opt-out of the games this afternoon. She was supposed to be my partner."

"How about *we* partner up for the games?" I suggested on a whim.

"That's a great idea," Ekon agreed.

"Are you sure? I heard the games were terrible last year," I joked.

Ekon laughed. "You only heard it, but I experienced it."

I laughed with him. "Maybe we should skip them then."

"I'm only here for the escape room," Ekon replied. "That's always fun."

We stood in line and waited for the organizers to register the participants one by one.

We should have created an app to expedite registration.

"They should have digitalized this process," Ekon echoed my thoughts.

I smiled. "Great minds think alike."

"You could have probably whipped up an app fast," Ekon said, snapping his fingers.

I laughed. "It's not so easy," I added after a pause. "How did you know I code?"

Used to code.

"I read an article about a year ago about your prototype for the SCF app. I thought your innovations were pretty cool," Ekon answered.

"Thanks."

"Hey, how come you're majoring in business instead of something tech related?" Ekon asked.

"I aspire to start my own tech company someday and wanted to learn the skills to do that," I replied.

Though my dream seems too far away, now that I have lost my ability to code.

I tried to shake away my negative thoughts. "Besides, my minor is computer science, so it's still relevant. How come *you're* majoring in business studies instead of culinary arts? I saw you in our campus the other day and Strollfield U doesn't have a culinary school."

Before he could respond, it was our turn to register. Ekon and I showed the organizers our IDs and filled out forms to enter. We hurried to find seats at the packed venue and managed to find two vacant ones in one of the middle rows. On the stage, the speakers boomed with loud music that made my head ache, and I wanted to get out of there.

"Good morning, ladies and gentlemen, and welcome to the fundraiser games. Our first game for today is—know your partner," the master of ceremonies announced. "It doesn't matter if you've known your teammate for a few minutes or many years. This game is going to be equally tough for all of you. Are you all ready?"

The crowd screamed, "Yes!"

The MC continued. "Each of you will be given a venue, where you will perform a list of tasks in a particular order. Your partner will then guess what tasks you did and repeat them in the same order. Any questions?"

"Will we know what tasks our partner performed, at least?" one of the audience members asked him.

The announcer shook her head.

Ekon and I looked at each other with the same expression—what nonsense was this?

"You need to think like your partner. The team that manages to do that wins," the announcer declared.

I was about to leave this ridiculous game when one of the volunteers called out to me. He wore an SCF fundraiser volunteer shirt and a pink wristband. "Are you performing today?"

I nodded. "Yes."

"There's a performers' meeting going on right now," the volunteer informed me. "Can you attend? It should take only a few minutes."

I told Ekon that I'd be back and followed the volunteer. He gave me directions for how to get to the meeting, and I followed his instructions.

When I reached the destination, it looked like a swimming pool that was under repair. There was no one else at the site.

Am I lost? Did I get the correct location?

This was the place the volunteer marked on the map.

Something doesn't feel right, though, I heard my inner voice speak up.

I had just decided to leave the place, when suddenly someone tried to grab me from behind. Instinctively, I ducked. However, a pair of strong hands held my shoulders firmly.

"You're a feisty one, sweetheart. I can't believe you had the guts to show your face here after everything that happened."

Nicholas Parker.

I tried to fight him. "Let me go. You can't touch me without my consent."

Nicholas sneered at me. "Or else what?"

"I will scream and report you to the police," I said, struggling to free myself from his grip.

Nicholas snickered loudly. "Try. You'll fail."

He pressed on my shoulders with force and made me kneel. He yanked my hair and forced my face into the water. With the other hand, he groped my breas— chest.

Swallowing chlorinated water, I kicked him with all my might. When he jerked back in pain, I brought my face out of the water and gasped for air. "Damn you! Is this what you want? Do you want to kill me?"

"Don't worry, Tina Lauren. I won't let you die just yet. I will squeeze the life out of you, bit by bit, and you will beg me to kill you."

Never. I will never give in to Nicholas Parker.

Before I could get up, he caught hold of me again. I was still panting and feeling lightheaded, but I refused to give up. Using some of the skills I'd learned over the last year with Nakamura Sensei, I headbutted his nose with all my strength, then tried to escape.

But the stubborn creep was much stronger. He caught both my hands with one of his hands and pinned them behind my back.

With the other, he roughly pulled my hair. Then he bit the exposed area between my neck and shoulder, sucking the skin.

He smirked. "There, I have branded you with my mark. You're my pathetic prey. Don't you ever forget that."

I am neither pathetic nor prey. And I will fight back.

CHAPTER 13

"Tina, where are you?" I heard a voice.

Ekon?

"Why are you in an employee-only area?" someone else asked.

Hearing the voices, Nicholas released me from his grip and took off.

I tried to get up, rebuttoning my overalls and smoothening my shirt, but winced in pain, shuddering about what could have happened if no one had come.

Hot angry tears streamed down my cheeks, despite my fiercest attempts to stop them. I pounded my fists on the ground in frustration. How did I fall prey to this perverted creep again? I had avoided him successfully for a year. Did I ask for it?

I did not ask for it. Not then, not now.

Ekon appeared around a corner, finally noticing me. "Are you okay, Tina?" Ekon asked, still panting from running to me. "Just a second." His eyes darted toward the bushes near the pool for a moment. He turned back to me. "Are you alright?"

How did he know to come here?

I nodded.

I tried to stand up again, but my legs gave away. Ekon held out his hand, and I took it reluctantly.

"Can you walk? Do you need help?" Ekon asked.

I shook my head, and Ekon waited as I tried to take a step forward.

"Why are you both here?" a pool employee asked us. "Did you miss the no-entry sign? This pool is closed for repair."

Parker and his underlings even removed the sign to set me up.

"Someone must have torn down the no-entry sign, and my friend lost her way," Ekon answered for me. I was grateful that he pitched in but embarrassed that I couldn't speak for myself.

The employee muttered under her breath and left. I trudged beside Ekon in silence, limping slightly. I expected him to ask me a ton of questions, but he didn't. Instead, he gave me some water and asked if I wanted to sit down for a minute.

We sat on a picnic bench, and I took my phone out of my pocket and tried to take a photograph of the wound on my neck.

"Do you want me to help you with that?" Ekon offered.

I handed him my phone to take pictures.

When Ekon returned my phone, he asked me to wait for a few minutes. I was puzzled as to why, but before I could ask, he was gone. When he came back, he gave me a Band-Aid. I peeled the cover and applied it to my neck.

"Thanks," I said, opening my mouth for the first time since the horrible incident.

"Are you alright? Do you want me to drop you home?" Ekon asked, sounding concerned.

"I'll be okay," I answered. "I have a performance scheduled this evening."

"Okay, get some rest then," Ekon said. "Do you want me to stay with you? Should I get you anything for lunch?"

I shook my head. "No, but thanks for the offer. I'll see you during the escape room challenge."

***

I trudged to the park exit, trying to shake off the feeling of Nicholas Parker's slimy hands on me. Before it could haunt me further, I focused on my task at hand and got a taxi to the nearest police station that was five minutes away. I barged into the building and walked to the information desk as fast as I could with my hurting leg.

"Hi, my name is Tina Lauren, and I want to lodge a complaint for se-sexual assault."

The officer led me into a room with glass doors but no windows and asked me to wait for another officer who would help me. I played with my bee pendant nervously as I waited. I stood rooted to my spot, staring at the table and two chairs that were placed at the center of the room. There was nothing else on the table other than a landline phone and a pen stand. The walls were gray, the same gloomy color as the concrete floor. There was an eerie silence in the room except for a large gray clock's second hand ticking loudly. For a space that was meant for assault survivors to talk about their experience, it felt too intimidating.

I heard the door open, and a policewoman walked inside with a laptop. "Hello, I'm Officer Lee, and I will be helping you file a complaint today. Please take a seat."

I sat down across from her obediently, unable to even greet her.

"Let's start with some personal information to fill these forms," Officer Lee said.

I nodded in response.

"What's your name?"

"T-Tina Lauren," I replied.

I clenched my fists and closed my eyes tightly to stop myself from stuttering. I was struggling even with monosyllable responses to the questions, but Officer Lee didn't seem to notice my difficulty and continued typing on her laptop.

"Where and how did the perpetrator sexually assault you today?"

"Uh... Um..."

Officer Lee looked up at me from her laptop and gave me a tight smile. "It's alright. Take your time."

My mind went numb.

It was blank.

It refused to remember the assault at the SCF fundraiser today.

I could only hear the wall clock ticking away.

Tick tock. Tick tock. Tick tock.

"Why don't you try writing down what happened instead?" Officer Lee placed a sheet of paper and a pen in front of me. "I will be right back."

I nodded and picked up the pen with trembling hands, watching mutely as the police officer left the room. I tried to rack my brains on the details of the incident earlier, but I got nothing.

No memories. No inner voice. Not even the usual annoying cacophony of pessimistic voices inside my mind.

Only tick tock. Tick tock. Tick tock.

I threw the pen in frustration and ran out of the police station, embarrassed at my inability to press charges. No, it was worse than that. I couldn't speak. I opened my mouth, but no words came out.

Desperately, I fished around my overalls for my pocketknife, but it wasn't there.

I thought I was over that phase of hurting myself.

But that's the only thing that can calm me down now.

I wouldn't be resorting to my old methods if I hadn't gone blank in there.

I am so pathetic.

Nicholas Parker is right. I am his pathetic prey.

No. No way. I am not *his pathetic prey. And nothing, absolutely nothing is worth harming myself.* My inner voice finally spoke up, loud and clear.

I collapsed on a sidewalk bench and let my tears flow. I wept silently with my head bent, holding my face in my hands.

Finally, I felt someone tap my shoulder gently, and I got up with a start.

"Sorry I startled you. Are you okay?" Officer Lee asked, looking concerned.

I shook my head but still could not speak.

"I know it's really hard to talk about a sexual assault experience, and it's alright if you're not able to press charges against the perpetrator today. You can do it any time in the future, because there is no statutory limit for sexual crimes in Strollfield," Officer Lee explained.

I nodded, grateful that I had another chance to get justice.

"Also, you can get a sexual assault evidence collection kit at any of these healthcare centers." She handed me a sheet of paper that had a list where this service was available. "These centers have trained sexual assault nurse examiners, who will collect samples that can be used as evidence against the perp. But remember, you need to press charges within the next six months to use the samples in court. Otherwise, the centers will discard them."

A light of hope stirred in my heart, and I smiled hopefully. "Th-Thank you."

CHAPTER 14

I breathed deeply and calmed myself down, feeling a little better that I still had ways to nab Nicholas Parker. I skimmed through the list of healthcare centers where the kits were available and was relieved to see the one Jai worked at. Luckily, it was only a two-minute walk from my current location and it was almost lunch time. I tried his number, and he picked up on the first ring.

"I need your help. It's urgent. Can we meet?"

"Tina, what happened? Are you alright?" Jai asked, sounding worried.

I shook my head. "No, I am not alright."

Jai met me at the café outside the healthcare center. He had bought me a hot chocolate and was waiting at a corner table. I sat down and took a long sip of the hot beverage, closing my eyes as the liquid comforted my throat.

"Are you feeling better now?" Jai asked me in a soothing voice. "Can you tell me what happened?"

Slowly, I peeled the Band-Aid on my neck to the side and showed him the bite mark. "Nicholas Parker."

Jai clenched his fists. "That sicko should be in jail."

I laughed humorlessly. "He said so himself. 'Try. You'll fail.'"

Jai shook his head. "I wish I could rip that smug smirk off his face."

"That's why I'm here," I stated. "I went to the police station to lodge a complaint, but I couldn't even utter a word. My mind went blank."

"What you went through was a lot. Give yourself some time," Jai said, squeezing my hand reassuringly. "I can come with you the next time you want press charges, if you like. Just to be with you."

My eyes welled up. This was why Jai Rao was my best friend.

I blinked back my tears. "Thanks. That would mean a lot." I unfolded the sheet of paper Officer Lee had given me and pushed it toward Jai. "Actually, can you accompany me now?"

He glanced at the paper, and once he understood what it was, Jai got up from his seat immediately. "Let me inform my supervisor that I'm taking an extended break. I will be right back."

When Jai came back, I followed him to the room where se-sexual assault examinations were conducted. I felt dizzy as I fretted about the procedure, half-wishing to run away, but my legs blindly fell in step behind Jai's, affirming my determination to nab the abuser.

At the entrance, I was asked to fill a form with all my personal information and details of the incident. I breezed through most of the form, reassured by my best friend's presence.

When I had to fill in the "nature of assault," the seriousness of the criminal offense registered in my mind as I wrote slowly, "a-t-t-e-m-p-t-e-d r-a-p-e."

My fear was replaced by an overpowering rage. I clenched my fists as I headed to the changing room to get ready for the examination.

"Here, change into these." A lady handed me two hospital gowns outside the changing room. "Remove all your clothes, including your underwear first."

I unfolded the two gowns and frowned. "This won't be enough to cover me up. Can I have a shawl please?"

The lady snickered. "*Now* you want to cover up? What's the use? If you had done so earlier, you wouldn't be in this situation in the first place."

Her words stung, even though they were untrue. Couldn't she see I was in overalls, covered from head to toe? Even if I was scantily clad, how was my outfit an excuse to be assaulted? But I had no strength to argue.

I sighed and changed into the gowns, shuddering at the thought of the snide remarks this woman may have made to other survivors who were in worse pain than me. Not only did we have to deal with the trauma of the incident, but we had to face insensitive people who blamed us victims for the abuse.

I peeked out from the changing room to check if the nurse examiner was there yet. There was no way I was going to step outside in these clothes. One of the gowns was open at the back and the one that went on top of it wasn't enough to cover my body. I tugged at the ends of the "coat" gown to conceal my chest.

"Are you here for the sexual assault forensic exam?" a woman in scrubs asked, spotting my face peeking out the changing room door.

I nodded in response.

"Why aren't you in the examination room yet?"

"Can I get something to cover myself?" I asked.

The lady opened a set of drawers and pulled out a blanket. "Here you go. Do you need anything else?"

I shook my head. "Thanks."

"I'm Nurse Johnson, and I will be conducting your forensic exam today," she said, walking with me down the corridor leading to the examination room. "Nurse Tremblay will be joining us shortly. Let's get you comfortable first and then we can go over the procedure. Sounds good?"

I hesitated a little. "Um, my case is attempted ra-rape. Can I still get an exam?"

"Yes, you can get a forensic exam for *any* type of sexual abuse in Strollfield."

I nodded, relieved that Nurse Johnson seemed approachable. The examination room had a bed, a table, and a lamp. The walls were gray and so was the floor, but I didn't feel intimidated or suffocated, unlike at the police station.

I climbed into the bed and Nurse Johnson adjusted the backrest so that I could sit upright.

"Are you okay? Let me know if you need any more blankets."

I nodded. "I'm good, thanks."

"Alright, let me go over how we'll proceed with the examination today. We'll get your consent at every step, and you can stop us at any time if you don't feel okay," she explained. "We'll ask you about the incident and take down notes first. Next, we will take photos of all the bruises and wounds, if any. Finally, we will take samples from your body for DNA. All three will be admissible in court as evidence *only* if you're alright with it. Any questions?"

I shook my head. "No, I'm ready to begin."

Nurse Tremblay entered with the equipment for forensic testing, along with cameras. The examination went on for an hour, and this time, I was able to speak about the incident. Both my examiners were patient and empathetic, which helped immensely. They were even impressed that I had been brave enough to take photos of the wound on my neck before coming here.

When we were finished, I felt like a heavy weight had been lifted off my shoulders. I thanked the two nurses profusely for helping me feel confident about pressing charges against Nicholas Parker the next time I went to the police station.

I changed into my skating body suit, because my overalls and shirt were handed over as evidence. When I went to the waiting area, Jai got up from his seat and came rushing toward me. "Are you okay?"

I nodded and smiled. "All thanks to you. I knew I could count on you."

Jai smiled back at me, looking relieved. "You'd do the same for me. Do you want me to drop you home? You didn't get your car today, right?"

I shook my head. "No, I'm going back to the SCF fundraiser now. I have a performance to complete."

"Here, then take this at least," he said, giving me a box. "I know you skipped lunch."

I squealed and threw my arms around Jai, seeing the pillowy soft rice cakes soaked in warm spicy lentil soup. "Idly sambar, my favorite Indian delicacy. Thank you. You're the best."

Jai returned my embrace laughing. "Enjoy the food. And you'll rock today, skater girl."

CHAPTER 15

"Presenting, Strollfield's very own Fire on Wheels," the announcer said as the audience cheered, and I appeared in the skate park wearing a helmet and safety pads on my shoulders and knees. In my hand was my prized possession—my skateboard. Butterflies fluttered in my stomach as I looked around. I had practiced here at the park over a dozen times in the last week, but today with the glitz and glamour, this place seemed totally different.

I took a deep breath and concentrated on the slopes and the curves of the stunt area, ignoring the pain in my body from the horrible encounter earlier.

Kick me all you want, Nicholas Parker. I will bounce back and soar high.

I rolled the skateboard on the floor and jumped onto it as the crowd cheered me on. I skated across the park as if I was on a rollercoaster and glided through the slopes like a bird. I flipped my board with my foot multiple times, jumped into the air, and landed gracefully right back on it. Next, I zoomed past obstacles in the park in a zigzag motion, enjoying the spectators turning their heads, following my movement.

Toward the end of my performance, I attempted something I had never succeeded in before. I rolled the skateboard from the top of the ramp and did a backflip from the same position. If I fell, I would be the laughingstock of the entire city, because my failure would go viral on social media. But I was used to it, and I had nothing to lose.

I landed on the skateboard at the perfect time, and the audience erupted with a standing ovation, chanting, "Once more! Once more! Once more!"

My heart burst with a sense of achievement. Every bone in my body ached, and I knew I would limp for many days to come. But it was worth it. I took quiet pride in my own resilience.

Because I have shown the world what Tina Lauren is made of. And that nothing, absolutely nothing, can keep me down.

I removed my protective gear and limped to the fundraiser entrance, still in my skater outfit. Ekon was waiting for me.

Ekon gave me a piece of paper and a pen. "Autograph, please? Your performance was breathtaking, Tina."

I blushed at his compliment. "Thank you, but an autograph is too much. I am nowhere as good as professionals."

Ekon smiled. "You're too modest. Is there anything you can't do?"

"I can't draw," I answered seriously.

He laughed. "You're cute."

No one had called me cute before, and I hoped I wasn't blushing.

I signed on the paper: "Thanks for my first autograph, Ekon. - Tiara."

I froze. *Why did I sign my real name? It's Ekon's fault. He distracted me.*

Ekon examined my autograph. "Tiara? Is that your alias? It suits you."

Thankfully, our conversation was interrupted by strangers gushing about my performance before we could go into the details about my real name. Some took selfies with me, while others shook my hand. I felt awkward at the attention but continued to smile. Ekon waited patiently for me to finish talking to everyone.

At a distance, I noticed Nicholas glaring at me. I ignored him but felt triumphant.

Don't you dare mess with Tina Lauren, Parker. You will always lose.

Ekon and I walked to the escape room that was a few blocks away. It was the last event of the fundraiser.

"Have you been to the escape room before?" I asked Ekon.

He nodded. "Yes. It was a part of the fundraiser last year as well."

"I haven't been here before," I told him. "It sounds like fun, though. Anyway, when did you start working at the Recharge Café? And how on earth do you get time to attend classes and do school stuff?"

"I started working at the café right after high school, about two years ago. I'm on my own, so I need to survive," Ekon answered.

"It's amazing how you managed on your own," I exclaimed.

Ekon frowned for a second but composed himself immediately. "It wasn't a smooth journey, but I somehow managed." He changed the subject. "How about you? When did you start skating?"

"I started when I was twelve," I answered. "I'm into all types of skating, on ice and land."

"Wow," Ekon exclaimed. "You should teach me sometime."

"Sure! We can start with roller skating. It's the easiest."

Ekon and I reached the escape room, and the organizers gave us a brochure with the rules. We would play against four other teams, each with two people. The ten of us would be locked inside the room, and the objective of the game was to solve a series of puzzles and find the key within an hour. The group that escaped first won.

All the teams entered the area that looked like a historical movie set. There was intricately carved, hefty, wooden furniture, with bulky brass handles everywhere, with little room to walk. The shelves were packed with books, treasure chests, showpieces, and other antique artifacts. All the items had complex patterns and designs on them that were jarring to the eye. On the walls, there were cobwebs, which looked real but were made of plastic.

"They do a great job of confusing participants," Ekon said, chuckling softly. "It's challenging to find clues in here."

I nodded and laughed with him. "I feel like I've traveled back in time to an ancient castle."

"You have an hour to escape from here," said the voice-over. "Follow the clues and solve the puzzles to escape. Good luck."

A few minutes later, it hit me that we were in a dimly lit room, and it was locked. I was claustrophobic. How could I have forgotten that? I was about to start hyperventilating when I recalled Dr. Kim's words: "When you're in a fearful situation—ask yourself three questions."

What's the worst that could happen? *I might suffocate in this horrible room full of strangers.*

Are your fears reasonable? *No. The room is air-conditioned, and it's safe. Besides, Ekon is a decent guy.*

What are your new thoughts? *I want to forget the horrible events of the day. Solving puzzles is a good way to divert my mind.*

"Are you alright?" Ekon asked.

I smiled. "Absolutely. Let's do this."

"Okay, I'll look on the left and you look on the right side of the room. Let's pick anything that we find and put it in our bags," Ekon instructed.

I nodded. "See you at this point in fifteen."

Fifteen minutes later, Ekon met me with four pieces of paper that fit together. I had a hammer, a magnet, and some pins. I'd had to open numerous doors and dig through many artifacts to find these clues.

I arranged the pieces like a jigsaw puzzle. The four pieces were the key to the combination of one of the drawers, which contained more clues. We worked in tandem to decrypt coded messages and other riddles until we were left with some strange objects.

"The magnet can attract these pins. You think that'll do something?"

Ekon used the magnet to attract the pins carefully, but nothing happened. "I'm sure there was some clue there."

Suddenly, the lights went out, and Ekon clasped his hands together. His breathing pace quickened, and he was clearly fighting hard not to make his fright obvious. I held out my hand, and he instinctively wrapped his fingers around it. He tried to release it immediately, but I held on gently. I didn't say anything, because I knew he'd be embarrassed by his fear. Instead, I squeezed his hand lightly to show him I was there.

A few minutes later, the lights came back on.

We heard the voice-over. "Sorry, there was a power cut."

We let go of each other's hands with shy smiles and got back to the task at hand.

In the next fifteen minutes, we figured out more clues—all of them leading to more puzzles. Finally, we only had a hammer.

The voice-over activated. "Please don't use the hammer on anything except the target. The target light will become green when you approach it."

We had gone around the room five times, and the "target" wasn't turning green. We didn't even know what this target was.

I sat down on the floor, exhausted. "I give up."

Ekon examined one of the treasure chests to see if we'd missed anything. "It's tough, but we're almost there."

I took a glimpse at the other teams and saw that they weren't too far behind. Two other groups were sitting next to the bookshelf like us, wondering what to do next. Absentmindedly, I removed a book from the bookshelf.

"Wait a minute. All the other books on this shelf are in Latin except these three books in English," I whispered to Ekon.

"Part 1 is on the bottom-most shelf, part 2 on the middle shelf, part 3 on the top shelf," Ekon concluded in a quiet but excited tone.

When we pulled out the three English books, the shelf moved aside like a cupboard, giving us access to a new passageway. Startled by the sudden change, and with a glimmer of hope, I took the hammer and stood near the passage. It turned green.

Ekon and I started jumping like two excited kids, high-fiving each other to the envy of the other teams. "It worked. What a stroke of luck."

He took the hammer and hit it on the target, which was a wooden box. It broke open, leading us to the key.

The door to the escape room opened, and in excitement, Ekon and I hugged each other. "We won."

I realized his proximity and pulled away immediately. My heart was thumping loudly as we awkwardly walked outside the room together in silence. I looked at him from the corner of my eye, and I noticed that he was handsome and had long eyelashes.

Why am I paying so much attention to this good-looking guy? Why can I still hear my heart beating?

As winners of the competition, we received free ice cream coupons that expired the next week.

"Do you have plans now, or are you game for some ice cream?" Ekon asked.

I shook my head.

He laughed. "I don't get you."

"Let's go some other day," I mumbled. "I need to go home now. It's late."

"Let me walk you to the bus stop then," Ekon offered.

I shook my head again. "I'm good, thanks. I had fun today."

Ekon smiled. "I had fun too. We should do this again sometime."

Don't smile. It's only making my heart race more.

I waved to him. "Sure. Bye."

I bolted before I could embarrass myself further.

This attraction was the last thing I needed right now.

CHAPTER 16

That night, I sat at my desk, unable to sleep because I was seething in rage from the day's events. Nicholas Parker's words, "You're my pathetic prey," rang in my ears. I was furious that I hadn't been able to press charges against the sicko. I completed my schoolwork, which wasn't due until the following week, to stop thinking about the events of the day, but I couldn't get that creep Parker off my mind.

The past year, I had laid low, hoping I wouldn't run into him again on campus, but I was done hiding and cowering in fear. Even though I had shown him that he could not pull me down, it wasn't enough. I wanted him to pay for his crime. I wondered if I did some detective work myself, would it be easier to press charges against him the next time I went to the police?

There must be some way to catch him.

I retraced my steps at the fundraiser earlier today and wrote down the sequence of events and the people I had seen. Who was the volunteer who sent me to the abandoned swimming pool area? Who removed the no-entry sign from there? Were there any witnesses who saw Nicholas Parker there, and would they be willing to testify?

Let's tackle one thing at a time, Tina.

I surfed the internet for photos and videos of the fundraiser to find a picture of the volunteer. My plan was to confront him and make him expose Nicholas. That sounded too far-fetched, but I was ready to try *anything* to catch the sicko.

I zoomed in on every single photograph of the event and marked the ones that had the volunteer's face in the background. In one of the pictures, I saw a familiar face with red hair and green earrings, shaking hands with the person in question.

Pete Hilton.

***

On Monday, during lunch, I headed to the cafeteria to find Pete. He sat at his usual table with his friends, talking animatedly about something. I had hardly spoken two words to Pete at the karate institute since he tried to take advantage of me a year ago. Thankfully, he was no longer my instructor, and I didn't need to interact with him. I only said a hello, or occasionally bowed to him at the dojo, since he was still a teacher.

"Hi, Pete. Can I have a word with you?" I asked him, shooting an apologetic smile at his friends for interrupting their conversation. "This will take only a minute."

"What do you want?" Pete asked with a cocky grin on his face as he and I sat at an empty table in the corner with our beverages.

I showed him the volunteer's photo on my phone. "Do you know him?"

He raised an eyebrow and gave me a smug look. "Why are you asking me that?"

"I need to talk to him about something."

Pete smirked with an evil glint in his eyes that sent a chill down my spine. "About what?"

Was Pete involved in Parker's devious plan too?

"Never mind," I said, realizing this had been a terrible idea. I placed my phone back in my pocket.

"No, no, tell me. Why do you want to know who *he* is?" Pete sneered.

"Your friend gave me wrong directions to a no-entry area at the festival, and now I need to pay a fine," I lied.

Pete snickered. "That's hardly the truth." He leaned forward. "I saw *everything* that happened there. He let you go with only a scar. If it were me, I would have made you beg for mercy and still not released you from my clutches, you weak slut. I would have taught you a lesson that you would never forget in your life. You wouldn't have the audacity to show your face in public ever again."

Pete stood and walked out of the café before I could react. I sat rooted to the spot, my blood chilled to the bone by the violence implied in his horrific threat. There were genuine tears of shock in my eyes, but I blinked them back and composed myself.

Well, at least I recorded the threat.

***

That evening, when I was about to head back home, someone blocked my way in the parking lot. "We meet again, sweetheart."

Please, not Parker again.

I ignored him, pretending to be engrossed in my phone and quickened my pace toward my car which was just a few steps away.

He smirked and snatched my device from me. "So, you're asking around about my people now, huh?" He reached out and ripped the Band-Aid off my neck. "Haven't you learned your lesson already?"

I shoved his hand away and tried to get my phone back from him. "Don't touch me."

He grabbed my other hand tightly and twisted it. "Then, *you* don't try to act too smart." He released my hand, still snickering. "I'm willing to let everything go if you publicly apologize to me."

I scowled. "For what?"

"Everything."

"Or else?" I challenged.

"You don't want to mess with me, sweetheart," he hissed. "I'm warning you."

"Okay. But first, give my phone back to me," I said.

Nicholas shook his head and held the device out of my reach. "No. First, apologize for ignoring me earlier when I was talking to you."

"Fine. Sorry."

"Good girl."

He tried to place my phone in the front pocket of my overalls, but I snatched the device and pocketed it, swatting his hand away.

He smirked. "Apology not accepted. Let's try again. Follow me."

I crossed my arms and leaned against the hood of my car. "No, thanks. I'm staying right here."

"As you wish, sweetheart."

Nicholas clapped his hands, and three teenagers arrived. Two of them had cameras, and one of them had a microphone in her hand. They gestured for me to stand in front of the camera. Reluctantly, I took a few steps toward them.

The girl pointed the microphone toward me. "Why did you hit Nicholas in the face at the press conference in Duckville High last year?"

Because he deserved it for molesting me.

"Who are you?" I demanded, instead.

She looked shocked. "I am the social media influencer, Ina. Haven't you heard of me?"

I shook my head. I was clueless.

Ina rolled her eyes. "Anyway, this is your opportunity to apologize to Prince Parker for your reckless actions. Now, please answer the question."

"Because he did not respect my personal boundaries," I answered, knowing I couldn't escape this madness now.

"He didn't rape you. Why did you have to get so over dramatic?" the influencer prodded me.

I flinched at the R-word but stayed calm. *That's exactly what he attempted at the fundraiser.*

Instead, I put my arm around her and pulled her close until our faces were almost touching.

"What are you doing?" Ina asked.

"Let's continue the interview like this," I answered her, hating the proximity but determined to prove a point.

She tried to move away from me. "This is making me uncomfortable."

"Why?" I asked her. "Am I assaulting you? Why are *you* overreacting?"

"No, but I don't like it," she replied.

I pulled away from her immediately. "Exactly. I didn't like it either. It was against my consent."

I smiled secretly to myself when I saw Nicholas Parker blowing a chewed piece of his nail on the ground. He glared at me. I smirked internally when I saw him stamp his foot furiously. When he went berserk and got violent with the influencers, I got in my car and drove away from the commotion.

My phone vibrated, and it was a text from an unsaved number. It was obvious who the sender was.

I will make you pay. This is not over.

Later that evening, unsurprisingly, there was a social media reel starring me, crying in front of the camera, apologizing for my "bad deeds," and begging everyone to spare me from bullying. I rolled my eyes at the terribly edited footage and reported it as fake. I uploaded mine from my car dash-cam—that I had activated from my phone when Parker approached me at the parking lot earlier today—from a newly created handle @tinaaaLauren, and challenged the viewers to compare the two to find the genuine one.

Exhausted because of lack of sleep over the weekend, I fell asleep the minute I hit my bed.

***

The next morning, during breakfast, Madison thrust her phone into my hands excitedly. "Teensy, you've become famous. Your interview with 'influencer' Ina went viral."

I laughed at Madison's air quotes on the word influencer. I expected the fake video to have become famous, but it was the footage from my car dashcam.

"How did this one get so many views?" I wondered aloud.

Madison scrolled on her phone and showed me another post. "Because of this."

I watched the reel where the uploader @aasquad had proved, through digital forensics, that my video was authentic. They had dissected both pieces of footage, frame by frame, and shown evidence of the other one being fake.

"Well, someone is sensible," I said, handing Madison's phone back to her.

"Do you feel like a star?" Madison teased. "Or is right the word 'influencer'?"

I laughed. "No way. I want peace in my life."

"Seriously, though, great job, Teensy. I'm proud of you," Madison said, giving me a side hug.

I beamed at her compliment. "Thanks, Mads."

"Look, even the Strollfield Education Council chairperson, Wilbur Lauren, is talking about you. He commends you for standing up for yourself against your bullies and says he's proud of you."

I froze. *No. Not him. No way.*

"Wait, is he your *uncle*? How come you've never mentioned him before? Are you going to reply to him?"

"He's just a distant relative. And we haven't spoken in years," I said with a shrug, ignoring my stomach convulsing at the mention of *that* name. I prayed Madison wouldn't ask me any further questions about my blatant lie.

Please, let my dark secrets stay buried forever.

"He probably just wants some publicity at your cost. The council has only a handful of followers on their social media handle," Madison reasoned, and I nodded.

I clenched my fists until my nails dug into my palms to overcome the nausea at the pit of my stomach.

Is this a sign that my buried demons could be unearthed soon?

No way. I'm not ready for that.

Uh oh," Madison said suddenly. And I was grateful that she changed the subject. "Someone has leaked private information about you on social media: your phone number, our address, and other details."

"What the heck?" I exclaimed. "Are you serious?"

Madison and I reported the post as a privacy violation, but there were many comments on it already.

"Be careful today," Madison said, getting ready to leave for her classes. Her face showed her concern. "Do you want me to come over during lunch?"

"I'll take care of myself, Mads," I assured her. "You practice for the national dance contest during lunch. That's more important."

At school, students waved at me and smiled because of my five seconds of fame. I acknowledged them but refused to get carried away. They were the same people who'd abandoned me in the past when I was down in the dumps. I wasn't going to support internet trials—even if they favored me.

"Hey, Tina, would you like to partner with me for the holiday assignment?" one of my classmates asked me.

"Thanks, but I already completed it," I told him with a smile. "Maybe, next time."

That is, if you don't get influenced by Parker again. He's definitely going to get his revenge.

After class, on my way to lunch, I felt a thump on my shoulder. "So, Tina, you've become a star. Congratulations."

I flinched at the voice. It was Harriet. Laila was with her.

I nudged her away with my elbow. "I need my personal space, Harriet. Haven't I made it clear several times?"

Laila snickered. "Don't build castles in the air, Tina. These five seconds of fame are not going to last."

"I'm not bothered about the fake fame, Li. But I do care about my precious time. Now, if you will please excuse me," I replied politely.

I enjoyed watching Laila's nostrils flare in fury.

Harriet looked like she would burst but continued to speak. "We just came to ask if you would like to give a speech about consent at our sorority—"

I didn't let her finish. "I practice, I don't preach, Har," I added with a fake smile. "Thanks for the opportunity, though."

I walked away from there with my head held up high. When the two were out of sight, I danced in joy at the way I had stood up for myself. I had not got tongue-tied, and I told them off like I'd always dreamed. I ran to the stairwell and narrated everything to Jai.

"You're so cool, Little Monster," Jai exclaimed. "You finally told the traitors off, like you wanted to."

"Now, my next goal is to make Pete and Nicholas pay," I said.

Jai frowned. "Why Pete?"

Uh oh, did I say that out loud? I don't want to burden my best friend any further.

I played the voice recording of Pete's offensive threat, and Jai looked astounded. He placed his hand on top of mine comfortingly. "You don't deserve this."

I nodded. "And this time, I want to put an end to it."

"Of course," Jai said. "How can I help?"

I hesitated. "You don't have to get involved. It's dangerous."

Jai squeezed my hand and looked me in the eye. "I already am. We are in this together."

I smiled back at him gratefully. "You're the best."

I opened my lunchbox and served Jai some of Madison's mother's special Caribbean roti curry. In exchange, Jai handed me a box with my favorite chitranna lemon rice and kosambri salad. Usually, we exchanged our lunches, but today, I had saved some roti curry for myself.

"By the way, we're not alone in our battle. I found somebody who can help us," Jai said.

"Help with what?" I asked, picking up some rice with my chopsticks.

"Ensuring Nicholas gets charged," he whispered.

My ears perked up at that. "How? Do you know any police officer who can help us?"

Jai shook his head and continued in a quiet tone. "No. But I know a group that can. Let's talk more when no one else is around."

I nodded and lost myself in the delicious food. The lemon rice was delightfully spicy and tangy, with crispy roasted peanuts. This was perfectly accompanied by the refreshing kosambri that had crunchy cucumbers and yellow lentils with fresh cilantro.

I licked my spoon clean before digging into the roti curry. The roti bread was wrapped in a flavorful meat and vegetable curry. I was pleasantly surprised by the taste of mashed lentils inside the roti, which provided the unique aroma of the dish.

"How did Madison's mother make this?" Jai wondered aloud. "It looks so complicated. Look at these intricate layers. Just wow!"

"Food is magic," I replied. "It can melt away the worst worries of one's life."

"Even for an influencer?" Jai teased me.

I laughed and stuck my tongue out at him. "Yes, and the influenced."

CHAPTER 17

When I went home in the evening, I saw people outside our building with cameras. I was contemplating walking past them, covering my face, when someone pulled me to the side.

"Teensy, let's go out for some rolled ice cream." Madison tugged at my arm. "Everyone should have left by the time we get back."

I'd been looking forward to a quiet evening, but I followed my roommate to her car and buckled up. "Where are we going?"

Madison didn't answer my question. "Did anyone bother you at school today?"

I shook my head. "No. I attended classes and went to lunch as usual." I added with a smile, "Thanks for the roti curry, Mads. Your mother is a magician."

Madison laughed. "I almost didn't want to share the dish with you this morning."

I giggled. "I don't blame you. By the way, Jai loved it too."

"I haven't met your friend, but tell him he owes me big time," Madison said, and we laughed.

Madison pulled over at the Recharge Café. "We have reached our destination."

"I'm not going there," I protested.

Madison looked surprised. "Why not? You love Recharge Café."

Because of a certain someone named Ekon Okoro.

"I do," I mumbled. "But there are so many other ice cream parlors in Strollfield."

Madison didn't budge, and I got out of her car reluctantly.

"Reserve a seat for me. I'll park the car and join you shortly. Be right back," Madison said, zooming away before I could protest.

Inside the café, I sat in a booth, waiting for Madison, when I heard a male voice. "You need to wait to get a seat. There are people waiting in line."

Ekon.

I didn't look at him, but got up from the seat. "Sorry, I wasn't aware. I just came to get some of your rolled ice cream. I wasn't planning to sit here for too long."

Ekon sounded annoyed but spoke in an even tone. "There's a sign at the entrance that says 'please wait to be seated.'"

I nodded without saying anything. I cursed Madison under my breath for suggesting we come here. People in the line glared at me for cutting.

Madison called my phone as I stood waiting. "Sorry, Teensy. Darma had an emergency. Can you wait at the café?"

"No, I can't," I replied curtly. "I'm going to take a bus back home. You take your time."

"Stay there and order for us. I will come as soon as I can," Madison pleaded.

"Whatever," I said and hung up, instantly regretting my attitude but still annoyed at my roommate.

I went outside the café and sat on a bench on the sidewalk. I wasn't interested in the rolled ice cream anymore. And I couldn't go home without being spotted by the people waiting outside our building.

"Looks like you got stood up," Ekon said.

"Do you have a problem if I sit here, as well?" I retorted. "This bench does not belong to the café."

Ekon chuckled. "No. I'm not here to make you get up again. I'm just taking a break."

"I thought your café was busy. Is it alright for you to take time off now?" I asked.

Ekon sat down next to me with his hot drink. "I have a great team helping out." He added in a teasing tone, "Do I need *your* permission to take a break?"

I shook my head. "Of course not," I added in an even tone. "Sorry, my irritation is not directed at you. Madison, my friend, ditched me, and I can't go home. I was really looking forward to try your café's famous rolled ice cream today." I looked up at him for the first time since I arrived. "And I apologize for not looking at the sign at the entrance."

Ekon smiled. "It's alright. I can't be partial to my friends, even if I want to. I might lose my job."

I grew more self-conscious by the second. I was acutely aware of the faint fragrance of cinnamon—from his beverage or clothes, I couldn't tell. Looking down at my hands, I worried if I sat too stiffly or breathed too heavily or seemed too flustered. *But why do I even care?* This was a strange new feeling for me.

"Do you want me to get you a coffee or a hot chocolate? Sorry. It was rude of me not to offer," Ekon broke into my thoughts.

I shook my head again. "No, thank you. I'm good."

I racked my brain to say something to him.

Maybe I should leave. No, that would be rude. I have to wait at least until he goes back into the café after his break.

"Why don't you at least try the rolled ice cream you came for?" Ekon asked. "At least something good will come out of your friend not showing up."

"I don't want to stand in the line," I said, immediately regretting my words because I sounded snooty.

"How about I make you a special rolled ice cream sundae?" Ekon offered. "You don't need to stand in line then."

"What do you mean by special?"

"I've created a new flavor and would like to know what you think of it. It's special because it's not for sale yet," Ekon replied. "Can you wait for forty-five minutes, until closing time?"

I hesitated, not wanting to be in a secluded café alone with a near-stranger after hours.

I got up from the bench to go back inside the eatery. "I'll have the regular rolled ice cream instead."

When I was about to enter, Sharon hung a board on the front door: "Rolled ice cream—sold out."

I sat back on the bench next to Ekon. "Wow, your ice cream is in demand. I'm all the more curious to taste it now."

"My offer still stands," Ekon told me. "Just wait here, and I'll bring your ice cream outside after we close. I need to get back to work now."

Oh, he meant outside.

"Sounds good."

Ekon went back into the café, and I relaxed my back against the bench, enjoying the cool breeze hit my face. I was annoyed earlier at the change of plans this evening, but now, this didn't seem that bad anymore.

"Tina, I'm back," Ekon said, taking a seat next to me. "My boss let me go early today."

"Did you forego an hour of pay to spend more time with me, Chef Okoro?" I teased, surprising myself. "I'm flattered."

Ekon laughed and shook his head. "I've worked overtime the past few days to perfect my new rolled ice cream recipe, the one I'm getting you to try. Sharon was more than happy to let me off early today."

"How about we take a walk until your café closes, then?" I asked.

Ekon and I started roaming down the sidewalk side by side. Both of us had our hands in our coat pockets, and we were enjoying the cool pre-winter breeze. It was the first time I had company on an evening stroll in Strollfield's downtown area. Usually, I skated all the way from home to this part of the city for a bite at the Recharge Café because the food was irresistible.

Like always, this was the busiest part of downtown, and people flocked to the numerous eateries and shops in the area. We walked past the biggest mall in the province and the other skyscrapers in the heart of Strollfield. I remembered being mesmerized by these tall structures when I was new here a year ago, having lived in a small town all my life.

After our "date" in the escape room, I had looked Ekon up online and learned that he was also from my hometown, Duckville, and moved to Strollfield during his high school years. He was a year senior to me, though he was older than me only by a few months.

Did I just say date?

I turned to Ekon, hoping he hadn't read my mind. His handsome face glowed in the city lights, and a day-old stubble was visible. From the corner of my eye, I noticed a slight, hardly visible, dimple on his left cheek when he smiled at someone's pet dog.

I need to stop checking him out.

"The downtown area is really busy," I stated out of the blue to break the silence. "But Bunny Creek that's close by is a perfect getaway from all the hustle and bustle. It's one of my favorite places in the city."

Ekon gave me a surprised look. "You know Bunny Creek? Not many people know about the picnic spot. I am pleased that someone shares my love for the place."

I nodded. "I go there during the winter for ice skating."

"That sounds like a lot of fun. Have you heard of the Landfill Hill?" Ekon asked me.

I shook my head. "What's that?"

"It used to be a landfill area for waste; however, a few years ago, it was cleaned up, and it's now a spot to watch the sunset. It's a twenty-minute drive from here," Ekon explained.

"Wow," I exclaimed. "We must visit sometime. By the way, have you seen the sunrise at Strollfield Beach? It's picturesque."

Ekon shook his head. "I haven't had the chance to do that. I am glad you're interested in the road less traveled, like me."

I smiled. "Thanks. It's a wonder you've traveled around the town despite being busy with the café and school."

"Well, the café is closed on Sundays, and they don't make me work *every* day, so I try to enjoy natural beauty during my time off," Ekon replied.

For the next half hour, Ekon and I talked about the various places to visit in Strollfield. I noted Ekon's suggestions on my phone and liked it when we made casual plans to visit these spots together. Like me, Ekon was also interested in wildlife; however, he had never been to Adopt-A-Friend.

"I so badly want to adopt a dog, but my roommate is allergic to dog hair," Ekon complained.

"That's just like my mother," I replied. "That's why I spend time with dogs when I get a chance. I don't mind cats, though I prefer dogs."

Ekon laughed. "I like both as well. I can't decide which I like better, though, so you can't categorize me specifically as a cat person or a dog person."

I laughed with him. "I love lions. They are from the cat family, right? I guess I'm both too." I looked at my watch. "It's been forty-five minutes. Time flies when I'm talking to you."

I was not supposed to say that out loud.

Ekon smiled. "Yes, it's time to head back."

After heading back to the bench outside the café, Ekon went into the now-closed café for a few minutes, then brought out a tray with two bowls and one plate. "Here you go, cold apple pie ice cream with freshly baked cinnamon rolls."

"This was so worth the wait," I exclaimed, enjoying the aroma of the sweet treat. "I would have regretted not having this."

Ekon laughed. "You're the first person to have this combination. What do you think?"

I took a bite of the cinnamon rolls. They melted in my mouth. They were just the right amount of sweetness, and the cinnamon wasn't overpowering. The icing was light and had a hint of lime. The rolls were like a warm blanket, perfect for the weather. I closed my eyes and got lost in the bliss. "Mmm, yummy. These are heavenly." I looked at the bowl of ice cream and frowned. "Where's the spoon?"

"Here, you eat it with chopsticks. That way, you get the taste of the layers of the rolled ice cream. Spoons destroy its taste," Ekon explained.

I tried to pick up a roll with the chopsticks, but it slipped. As a part of my culture, I could pick up even the smallest morsel of rice with the cutlery, but I couldn't tackle the ice cream without breaking it.

Seeing me struggle, Ekon took the chopsticks from me, picked up a roll, and gently put it in my mouth.

Why is my heart racing from such a simple gesture? This feels like a date.

My thought was interrupted by the burst of flavors in my mouth. It was a cold apple pie. Never in my life had I dreamed that I would enjoy the classic dessert in icy form. I didn't even like the sweet taste of pie, to people's horror, but this was perfect. I was speechless.

"Ekon, I'm sorry, but I'm going to have to use my fingers to finish this."

Ekon laughed. "You didn't tell me how it is."

I picked up another roll and bit into the ice cream. It gave me a brain freeze but I didn't care. The flavor bomb was worth it. With my other hand, I took another bite of the cinnamon roll. "I am eating like a cave person. That should be your answer."

Ekon looked amused as he watched me eat in the most uncivilized way. Unlike me, he used chopsticks for his ice cream and a fork for the roll.

"You're cute," Ekon said.

Again.

Immediately, he avoided my eyes, and I could see him blush.

No, you're cute.

"Who else has tried this combination?" I asked Ekon, trying to divert his mind from my flushed face.

"No one. Not even my fellow chefs," Ekon replied.

I laughed. "So, I wasn't the 'special' person to try this but the guinea pig for your experiment?"

Ekon looked at me seriously with his chocolate brown eyes. "Not everyone has the privilege to be my guinea pig, Tina."

I was expecting a cheesy response, but his honesty made my heart beat faster.

"As a reward for today, how about I add some games in the café's mobile app for customers to play while waiting in line?" I offered before I could stop myself. I knew I had to find an excuse to see him again. "Fewer people will dine elsewhere during busy times if you offer discounts for the game-winners."

Ekon's warm eyes twinkled. "Would you do that? That would be wonderful. Let me talk to Sharon about it."

***

Later, in Madison's car, I sat in the passenger seat, still trying to process my unexpected evening with Ekon.

"Someone's smiling a lot. It looks like you're not mad at me anymore," Madison interrupted my thoughts.

"Well, I wanted to kill you at first, but then, I was glad that you ditched me."

What am I saying? Zip it, Lauren.

"Oh, did something good happen?" Madison teased.

I put on a straight face. "I took a nice walk in the cold night breeze. It was lovely."

Madison muttered something under her breath.

"Did you say something?" I asked her.

She shook her head, suppressing a smile. "Nothing at all."

CHAPTER 18

"Sensei, I need to discuss something privately with you," I told Dr. Nakamura after karate class the next evening.

She led me to her office and closed the door. "What's the matter, Tina?"

"How long have you known Pete Hilton?" I asked.

"He's been working here for the last couple of years," she answered me. "Why?"

Without explanation, I played the voice recording with Pete's threat. Dr. Nakamura had a bewildered expression on her face for a minute but quickly regained her composure. It was enough to tell me she'd believe me.

"Is that really Pete?" Dr. Nakamura asked.

I nodded and told her how he had made a move on me a year ago, the same night she caught me on the sidewalk and told me that I could make different choices. "Back then, I didn't complain to you because I managed to escape. Since then, we've been civil with each other. I hadn't even imagined he might be a criminal's accomplice. He's dangerous, Sensei."

"You will never have to worry about him here again, Tina." Dr. Nakamura leaned forward in her chair and looked at me with a concerned expression. "How are you holding up? By your own account, you have been through a lot in the past year."

"I'm doing my best to keep fighting," I replied honestly. "But it's getting difficult, and I'm scared."

Dr. Nakamura gave me a reassuring smile. "You will not lose, Tina. You have done nothing wrong and do not deserve this. You'll have your classes with me now. I will help you fight, in body and in spirit."

I smiled back at Dr. Nakamura and repeated her words with conviction. "I will not lose, Sensei."

I skated back home, feeling relieved that I'd be able to finally sleep better tonight. Parker's and Pete's threats had haunted me all these days, and I felt anxious that they would get away with everything.

Back home, I took a relaxing warm bath, had dinner, and sat at my desk to code the games I had promised Ekon. I didn't have online students today, and I looked forward to a quiet evening engaged in my beloved hobby. I opened my laptop and studied the programs I had worked on in the past. My chest ached at the unpleasant memories of being ousted from the SCF app team last year, and I shut down my computer with a dejected sigh. I just couldn't do it yet.

Just then, my phone rang.

Saved by the bell.

"Hi, Mom," I greeted her. "What's up?"

My mother and I exchanged pleasantries for the first few minutes, and then her tone changed. "Um, listen, Tina, what are your Christmas holiday plans?"

"I'm coming to Birch Town to spend them with you and Dad," I replied. "I thought you already knew that."

"Can you drive to Duckville instead...for the Lauren party?" Mom asked, and I froze. I knew she meant that we would spend the holiday at my paternal grandparents' mansion.

Can't the universe cut me some slack? Have I not been through enough already?

"It's just for a day. After that, your father and I need to travel for work," Mom tried to convince me.

"What if I say no?" I asked.

"We will be there for you," my mother said, her voice breaking.

I hated to hear the remorse in Mom's voice. Maybe it was time to do this. Therapy had made me stronger. I was working to be able to press charges against Nicholas Parker. Maybe I needed to face all my demons.

"I will be there."

***

For the next few weeks, I was busy with classes and work and didn't have time for anything else until D-day arrived. Reality hit me when I reached my dreaded destination.

I was tempted to take a U-turn back home to Strollfield. I sat inside my car and looked at the aesthetically pleasing house that stood tall and proud, despite the shameful secrets it kept buried deep inside it. The winter sun glistened on the Victorian windows, but only I knew that this was an optical illusion of all the darkness the place hid.

Sighing, I carried my luggage from the trunk and went inside. The door was open, and the house was decorated for the Christmas party tomorrow, but it still felt like a dungeon.

"Ah, Tiara dear, there you are," my grandmother called out to me. "Can you go to the cellar and get some aged wine? The cooks want it. I would have gone myself, but my knees hurt."

I froze. *I can't go to that place. What a welcome.*

My grandmother pushed me toward the stairs that led to the cellar. "Hurry now. Don't stand there like a doll."

Without a word, I went down the stairs, because I could feel my grandmother's eyes on my back.

I don't want to go there. I don't want to go there. I don't want to go there.

Go on, Tina. It will be alright. Besides, the two of them are not here. I heard my inner voice.

I took a deep breath and entered the cellar. I felt the wall for the lights and switched all of them on. I walked to the shelf and picked up the aged wine bottles.

Instantly, I heard the creepy voice from my nightmares…the one that never failed to make my skin crawl. "Princess, where are you, my princess?"

I clutched onto the bottles tightly and shook my head vigorously.

No. No. No. There is nobody here. I'm alright. I'm fine.

The voices continued, like I'd been transported back in time. "Princess, you know we don't like hide-and-seek. Come on out now. Come to us."

I felt nauseous and dizzy. I ran out of the cellar and up the stairs and thrust the bottles into my grandmother's waiting arms. Without another word, I ran to the bathroom and threw up.

What a horrible start to the holidays.

I started hyperventilating. I tried to use Dr. Kim's three-question method to calm myself down in this situation, but there was no point. I sat on the floor with my face in both my hands.

Maybe I couldn't do this, after all. Perhaps I was weak.

Still trying to catch my breath, I recalled my conversation with Dr. Kim.

"Dr. Kim, why me? Why did I let something like this happen to me? First, it was them, and now it's Nicholas. Did I ask for it?" I cried. "Parker even told me he approached me because I asked for it by dressing weirdly. I thought I would be bait for abusers for exposing my skin and started covering myself up. Then why am I still targeted when I am covered up?"

Dr. Kim, who was always calm, raised her voice. "No. You did not ask for it, Tina. Nobody ever asks for it, not by the way they dress, not by anything. So don't let anyone tell you that. And don't even let that thought come to your mind."

I looked up at her. "Why me, then?"

"All of us ask the question 'why me?' when we feel troubled. It's a standard question to ask when cornered. Unfortunately, that doesn't help us move forward," Dr. Kim continued in a gentle tone.

Now, I raised my voice. "Then what question should I ask?"

"Think about them for a second, even if it's tough. How do you feel?" she asked me.

"I feel fury. Anger. Hatred. Disgust. Rage. Frustration. Guilty," I replied.

"Why do you feel guilty?" Dr. Kim prodded gently.

I looked down. "Maybe if I had done things differently, this wouldn't have happened to me."

Dr. Kim leaned a little closer to me. "How could you have done things differently?"

I looked up at her with a serious expression. "I wish I hadn't shown my fear. I could have complained to my parents despite being threatened. I could have run away faster. If I was stronger, I could have punched or kicked them. Coming to Nicholas, I could have avoided sitting next to him on the stage that day. Then, he wouldn't have tried to molest me again, and I wouldn't have whacked him in the face…and he wouldn't have exacted revenge on me."

Dr. Kim continued gently. "Now, why do you feel frustrated?"

I pounded my fist on the table. "Because I know I can't change the past."

"How would you approach them if you saw them again? I know you don't want to, but let's say you did, what would you do?" Dr. Kim prodded.

I got up from my chair suddenly, my eyes filled with rage. "I will not let them come near me. If they do, I will not be afraid. Even if I am afraid, I will not let it show on my face. I will not let those sickos torment me."

In the present, I wiped my eyes and shook my head.

"You will not let them torment you, Tina," I told myself.

Feeling better, I left the bathroom. My grandmother was standing near the bathroom door.

"What happened? Were you throwing up and crying in there? Are you pregnant? Is that why you wanted to stay alone? With a mother like yours…"

I clenched my fists. I wanted to shout back, "Look at yourself first. Does your older son take after you? Are you a criminal like him?"

But I walked away, ignoring her.

"Come back. Show some respect," my grandmother called after me.

"I will, when you learn to do the same," I retorted and went to find my parents.

Despite my self-pep talk in the bathroom, my nauseous feeling persisted. I went up the stairs to what used to be my room and saw that it was locked.

"You'll be sleeping in my room tonight," I heard a calming female voice say.

"Mom!" I called and ran down the stairs to hug her.

She enveloped me in her arms. "It's so good to see you."

"Kiba, can you come here for a moment?" my aunt called her. "Oh, hi, Tina."

I greeted my aunt and let my mother get back to her work. I helped out with the decorations, grocery shopping, and running other errands for the rest of the afternoon.

Later, I entered the kitchen to place the grocery shopping bag on the counter. There I found two people having a serious discussion—Dad and Ekon.

I was glad Ekon and his team were handling the food for our party. In fact, I had been hoping that would be the case. In the evening, I sat back on the recliner in the living room, exhausted from all the chores. I soon fell asleep.

You think you can escape just because you've grown up?
Nothing can change your ill fate
Always remember, I am one level up
And you're my helpless bait

How long will you bury the memories?
Do you think they won't resurface?
How wrong you are, you shall see
My wrath and me, you will have to face

I may be your worst secret
That you're trying to desperately protect
Your cries and screams, you seem to forget
Are enough to make you totally wrecked.

I woke up sweating from the nightmare, which featured someone I despised, reciting my worst fears to me.

Just then, I heard the voice that made my skin crawl.

"Stop it, Mum. You fuss over me too much."

"Well, my son is the chairperson of the Strollfiled Education Council. He deserves all the attention and praise in the world," Grandma gushed.

I froze. Wilbur Lauren. Not only did he haunt me in my dreams, but he was here in person. The nauseous feeling came back.

"Tiara, come here and help your uncle with his luggage," my grandmother called.

It's time to get out of here. I can't stand to be in the same room as that child se-sexual abuser demon, Wilbur Lauren.

I had to listen to my inner voice. "Sorry, Grandma, I have an important errand to run." I walked out the back door at a regular pace before the new arrival could greet me.

"Walter, you need to teach your daughter some manners," I heard my grandmother tell my father.

I went outside but didn't go to the terrace or the garage. I didn't want to be in a place alone, where that predator could prey on me. I didn't want to walk straight into his trap.

I clenched my fists in anger.

Why is he here? Why did my parents agree to invite him, and why was... am *I still trembling in fear at the sight of him?*

There was no way I would sleep in this house tonight with him around.

CHAPTER 19

I shook my head, counting the number of enemies in my life as I sat in Duckville's only 24-hour diner, Burger All Night. It was starting to feel like all of them were ganging up on me at the same time. I buried my face in my hands.

As usual, countless what-ifs cluttered my mind. What if my father hadn't let his brother and the butler babysit me? What if I hadn't attracted attention to myself by wearing overalls all the time or fastening my collar button? What if I hadn't whacked Nicholas Parker and made him swear revenge on me? What if there was no scandalous video of Parker and me? What if I hadn't gone to the karate institute so late at night a year ago and allowed myself to be alone with Pete?

Would I still be in this situation—traumatized and tormented by the villains in my life?

None of this was my fault. I couldn't have controlled my abusers' actions. I could only control my actions, I retorted. *And I will not let them torment me.*

I thought of how I had lied to my parents about spending the night with Laila and Harriet tonight. It was easy, because they weren't aware of my fallout with my former friends. The truth was, this diner was my home for the night. I sighed at my situation and continued to read the e-book on my phone when it buzzed.

Pete Hilton

You bitch! How dare you get me fired from the karate institute? I will spread this and ruin your life.

I rolled my eyes at Pete's threat and opened the attachment. Though I was not surprised that he had recorded the assault at the SCF fundraiser, a chill ran through my spine at the prospect of this footage leaking to the public. It was shot at such an angle that you couldn't tell who was assaulting me. It only caught the back of Parker's black jacket and pants. Other than that, he wore a backwards cap with a bright green brim. But it was very clearly me. Everyone would see what happened to me. I shut it off, took a deep breath, and straightened.

I can use this as evidence against Pete Hilton and press charges against him. Pete is threatening me because he is scared of getting punished for his crimes. I must not back down.

My inner voice calmed me, but the nauseous feeling from the day's events lingered in my mouth. I ordered another cup of watery hot chocolate, when I saw a face I'd dreamed up in my mind all too often lately. I contemplated going back to my freezing car to escape from the situation. I was hoping not to run into anyone I knew here. But he looked distressed. He sat with his head bent and his hands covering his face—Ekon.

I was still pondering whether or not to take a seat at Ekon's table when I heard his order buzzer go off. Ekon got up from his chair to get his food and noticed me. I waved to him. He smiled and waved back.

"Hi, Tina," he greeted me. "How come you're here?"

I smiled. "I can ask you the same question."

Ekon laughed. "Can I safely assume that neither of us wants to answer that question?"

I nodded. "That would be great." I got up from my seat and walked over to his table. "I don't suppose you'd want to keep me company tonight, since neither of us seems to plan to leave this café any time soon? Unless I'm imposing on you, and you want me to leave."

Ekon smiled. "You're not imposing at all. Take a seat."

For the next few minutes, both of us sat in silence, sipping our drinks.

Ekon broke the silence. "So, what was your original plan tonight?"

"I was going to sleep in my car, but it's too cold outside. So I came inside to get warm. Then I was going to read this trashy novel all night in this café. What about you?"

"Honestly? I was thinking of driving back to Strollfield, abandoning the party at your place tomorrow," Ekon said.

I laughed. "I have no problem if you do that, but you won't be able to escape from my grandmother's clutches."

Ekon laughed with me. "Before that, I would need to face Sharon."

I took a sip of my drink. "I miss your café's hot chocolate. This is *not* good."

Ekon made a face. "This strawberry thing is worse. I wish I could barge into their kitchen and prepare my own drink."

I laughed. "Why are you pursuing business studies at Strollfield University when you should be going to a culinary school?"

Ekon's face turned serious. "I would if I could." He changed the topic. "So, what trashy novel are you reading?"

I made a face. "It's a terrible novel called *In Love with My Bully*, about a bullied boy falling in love with the girl who bullied him. The boy stands up to her, she realizes her 'mistakes,' and they fall for each other. The boy's best friend, who was there for him all along, watches in shock as the two of them get together." I rolled my eyes. "No one changes like that overnight. And I'm only reading it because I got it for free and I have already read all of my favorite author Enida W. Alexander's novels three times each."

"Do you think the boy is stupid?" Ekon asked me.

I shook my head. "No. I won't judge the boy. I still can't believe my former friends-turned-bullies betrayed me. But I don't think I'll ever be able to trust them again. That's why I find this whole trope ridiculous." I paused for a moment. "Sometimes, though, I can't help but hope that their betrayal was a lie. So, strangely, I can empathize with the bullied boy in the book."

"I'm sorry you went through that, Tina. You didn't deserve it," Ekon said. He spoke some more about bullying. "In real life, some of these bullies pretend to change, and then, when the time comes, they walk all over you. Such toxic and abusive relationships aren't good, but they're romanticized in books and movies all the time. The reality is, such relationships emotionally damage the person. I learned this the hard way."

From the way Ekon spoke about this topic, it seemed like he had also gone through something similar. But it wasn't like me to press anyone to divulge details. I knew I wouldn't like it myself.

"It's strange how bullies in books apologize for their mistakes, and everyone gets closure. My friends-turned-bullies would never accept they were wrong, even after committing a crime," I told Ekon.

"You're better off without such friends," Ekon replied. "When I dared to confront the person that tormented me, she slammed me with a false legal case."

My eyes widened in horror. "That must have been terrible."

Ekon nodded without saying anything and looked down at his drink.

Sensing that the conversation was becoming uncomfortable for him, I decided to change the subject. "I miss your hot chocolate. This is artificial syrup in adulterated milk."

Ekon laughed. "We will have to put up with it if we want to stay in this café the whole night. I'm going to get another drink."

I got up from my seat. "Let me get it for you. What do you want? I plan to try a juice or something. You can't screw up fruit and water, right?"

Ekon laughed again. "Thanks, strawberry lemonade for me, then. I will hold on to our seats."

I ordered our drinks, an apple juice for me and strawberry lemonade for Ekon. As I waited, I thought about Ekon's claim of being slammed by a false legal case.

Who could have stooped so low? That was scary. I wondered how Ekon dealt with that.

I took our drinks back to our table and took my seat. "I got you the strawberry syrup separately, in case it's unpalatable."

Ekon smiled widely. "Thanks! I didn't want to specify that, in case it sounded too picky."

"I got you. You have every right to complain about food if it tastes terrible. Your culinary creations are far superior, after all."

Ekon's grin grew wider. "Thanks. That compliment means a lot to me."

I sipped my apple juice, and it was too sweet. The only good thing about this diner was the fact that it was open twenty-four hours.

Ekon looked at me. "You don't need to hold back. It's clear from your expression that you don't like it. This strawberry syrup tastes like red plastic, and the lemonade has no lemon."

I laughed. "Should we get some midnight snacks at the convenience store?"

Ekon laughed with me. "Great minds think alike."

"And fools seldom differ." I concluded his sentence grinning widely.

Ekon and I walked to the convenience store, which was just across the street.

"Oh, this place is interesting. I didn't know they had ingredients from various global cuisines," Ekon said, taking a jar from one of the shelves. "You must try this Chinese seven-spice mix. It goes on everything."

"I already have. My father has used all the ingredients from this store for his culinary experiments," I replied.

Ekon looked impressed. "Wow. No wonder his scones were so good this afternoon." He added after a few seconds, "I hope you know that I *never* praise anyone's cooking unless it's exceptional."

I giggled. "I guessed that."

Ekon raised his eyebrow. "What do you mean?"

"Well, culinary snobs like you can't be chefs unless you're hoity-toity like the ones on the Food Channel," I teased.

"Hey, that's not true," he protested.

I laughed and nudged him. "It's a good thing you're cute." I couldn't believe how comfortable I already felt in his company.

Ekon didn't meet my eyes and muttered under his breath, "I'm not a snob."

I was enjoying joking with him. "Oh yeah? Then, I challenge you to eat two of these." I pulled the lowest-rated cup noodle boxes from the shelf. "If you eat them without any other ingredients, I will take back my words."

Ekon made a face and placed the boxes back on the shelf. "I accept that I am, indeed, a classy culinary snob."

We both laughed.

During the next hour, Ekon introduced me to a plethora of international foods as we walked among the shelves, with him explaining the history and origin of each. I listened to him intently, enjoying his anecdotes. His knowledge of global cuisines was impeccable.

When we finally paid and left the store, it was really late in the night. I hadn't realized how fast time passed when I was with Ekon. We walked back in silence, enjoying the snacks quietly.

Suddenly, I heard someone shouting on the road, and instinctively, my hand went inside my pocket to get my pepper spray. The drunk person just ambled past us without even a look.

I saw Ekon staring at the weapon in my hand, and I sheepishly put it back in my pocket.

"I guess I assume everyone is out to attack me," I feebly joked and laughed nervously.

Ekon didn't laugh with me. "Tina, I'm aware of what you've been through, albeit through everyone else's eyes. I don't talk about it with you because I don't want to add to your pain. But I want you to know that I'm on your side."

I was touched by his words and hoped my voice wouldn't break. "Thanks, Ekon."

He shook his head. "No, thank *you* for taking the initiative to spend the evening with me. I was having a tough time earlier, but I feel better now."

I smiled at him. "Likewise."

We munched on our snacks as we roamed the empty streets. It was strange how a dreaded evening had turned into one I hoped would never end.

"Hey, Ekon," I said. "Would you call me Tia?"

Ekon gave me a questioning look.

"Well, I accidentally revealed my real name to you when I signed that autograph for you, and I thought it wouldn't be a bad idea if you called me a part of it," I explained. I added after a pause. "Only when the two of us are alone."

Ekon smiled at me mischievously. "Are you suggesting we should spend more time alone together, Tia?"

I could feel myself blush, and my insides glow with an unfamiliar warmth, but I tried to hide it. "Maybe, *Eko*." I was taken aback by my own boldness.

Ekon looked surprised. "Oh, I have a nickname as well?"

"Why? Do you not like it?" I teased.

"I don't hate it," Ekon replied. "Maybe because it's you."

We walked in silence, enjoying the only sounds in the quiet winter night—of our feet falling in step and our hearts beating in sync.

CHAPTER 20

The next morning, I asked Ekon to go to the Lauren Mansion first. Both of us hadn't slept even a wink last night but had spent the time chatting and snacking. I was disappointed when it was time to leave the diner but looked forward to seeing him during the party. I pulled into the driveway of my least favorite place in the world with a sigh.

The house was decorated with colorful streamers, and lively music played in the background on my grandmother's prized gramophone. She was blatantly showing off her vast collection of exclusive antiques and posh furniture to our relatives. She gushed at my cousins' praises of her exquisite taste as I rolled my eyes silently.

What's the use of all the luxury? It still feels like a dreadful dark dungeon.

A wave of nausea swept through me when I ran my eyes across the room. Bracing myself, I ran to my parents' room to get dressed. I locked the door from the inside and stepped inside the closet, which barely had any space inside. Forcibly, I closed the door behind me, wincing in pain when the sliding door went over my foot. I threw on three shirts and two jackets, ignoring the stuffiness I felt in my chest. It was getting harder to breathe inside the cramped closet, but I pulled the zipper of my coat all the way to my neck.

There, now the demon will not come for me.

But I can barely walk in these layers of clothes.

It's okay. Anything to keep Wilbur Lauren away from me.

I started hyperventilating and opened the closet door, collapsing onto my parents' bed. I took deep breaths to calm myself down, the way Dr. Kim had taught me.

I'm alright. I can endure this. It's just a few hours before I will be back home safely in Strollfield.

My soothing inner voice helped in getting my breathing pace back to normal, and I removed the extra layers of clothes slowly until I had only one shirt on. I slipped my jacket on and zipped it up midway across my chest without choking my neck.

"I can do this," I whispered to myself, and stepped outside into the party room, forcing a smile on my face.

My grin grew wider when I spotted Ekon, who waved, looking equally happy to see me. Seeing he was busy, I didn't stop to chat with him and went to find my mother instead. I felt a tug on my arm and turned to find Grandma scowling at me.

"There you are, finally. Stop slacking off and hurry to the store to get me these," Grandma said, thrusting a list into my hand.

"Why did you wait until the last minute?" I grumbled. "This shopping list is too long."

"Do you need help?" she asked me. Without waiting for an answer, she called out, "Wilbur—"

Instinctively, I made a dash toward my car and drove away, to a store all the way across the town, lest the demon follow me. I pulled over in the parking lot and sat there for a few minutes, relieved that I had escaped from the clutches of the sicko. I fished Grandma's shopping list from my pocket and giggled to myself. "It's going to take me *forever* to get all this. Looks like I'll miss the party."

Humming happily, I went inside the store and examined every single item there and read all the labels. I had an excuse not to be at the dungeon and wanted to make the best of it. Some things on Grandma's list required preparation, and I had to wait for them. So, I got myself a cup of hot chocolate and sat at a table.

"Hi, Tina," someone greeted me.

"Hey, Dad." I smiled, surprised he was here. "Why aren't you at the party?"

My father made a face and placed his coffee cup on the table. "I...I wanted to be sure you were okay, so I followed you. And it wasn't my idea to host the holiday gathering."

His admission made me feel warm inside. "But you're the bestselling star author," I teased. "Your presence at the party is mandatory."

Dad shook his head. "Mum won't miss me. She's too busy being ostentatious."

I laughed again. "I can't believe Grandma took the pains to move all her furniture and antiques to an empty house just for this party."

Dad just shook his head and changed the subject. "How are you doing? Do you want me to take over Mum's shopping for you?"

"And give up my chance of missing that lame party? No way!" I exclaimed, and my father laughed.

It felt good conversing easily with my father like this, after a really long time. I hardly spoke with him over the phone and always called Mom if I needed anything. I was delighted that Dad had followed me across town just to make sure I was safe.

I got up from my chair and hugged my surprised father, whose face went red at the sudden contact. He wasn't one for public displays of affection, but he returned my embrace before pulling away quickly.

"Your mother and I really wanted to spend the holidays with you," my father said. "But unfortunately, we can't cancel this trip."

"That's alright," I replied. "I'll come over soon. How's Birch Town?"

"Oh, you'll love it," my father answered, his eyes lighting up. "Our building is surrounded by lush greenery, and the lake view, especially from your room, on the thirteenth floor, is gorgeous."

It warmed my heart to hear the words "your room," even though I had moved out. My parents had bought two apartments on the twelfth and thirteenth floors of a building in Birch Town.

"I can't wait to stay in my room," I told him.

Dad smiled at me. "Great. Then come soon." He added after a pause,

"And don't drive to Strollfield this evening. Stay with your Grammy and Gramps."

I nodded without arguing with him.

Dad chuckled softly. "You didn't get any sleep last night, did you?"

"L-Laila and Harriet wanted to catch up after a long time," I stammered, scared he would know I was lying. "We don't get any time together at the university."

"Sure you don't," Dad replied, trying to hide his smirk. He got up from his seat. "Why don't we finish your grandma's shopping together?"

I jumped up from my chair in excitement. "That sounds great."

For the next two hours, my father and I bought everything his mother wanted. When we were done, we drove back to the mansion in our respective cars. My nausea had subsided, and I was feeling relaxed after spending the morning with Dad.

A few more hours, and I will be off to Gramps and Grammy's.

At the party, I sat in the corner of the room, texting Jai and Madison. My cousins had flocked around Grandma, who was giving me the cold shoulder for running off earlier. My mother and her parents were talking to their friends. I was a part of their conversation for a few minutes before I excused myself and let them catch up. My father was surrounded by his fans, and I saw that he enjoyed the attention.

Though I was calm and composed, I was staying alert, ready to respond if I felt that the demon was close by. I knew the sly sicko wouldn't corner me in a crowded place, but I was determined to not let him bog me down. I was conscious of his whereabouts in the room and remained far from his clutches at all times.

To pass the time, I browsed my phone and looked at all my photos. I stopped scrolling when I spotted a particular picture. It was of a page of my diary that contained a poem.

The poem was meant for my eyes only.

Nine years old
Young and innocent
Did as she was told
Trusting one hundred percent

Mommy's little girl
And apple of Daddy's eye
She owned the world
As everyone's sweetie pie
She rocked, she ruled
As the reigning princess
Only to be fooled
Reducing her to nothingness
Those buried memories of demons
Often do they resurface
She feels hammered and beaten
And unlimited disturbance
That she is I
No, that's not a lie
I keep saying "she"
Hoping to distance her from me
This is not a phase
It's not going to disappear
But, something I face
Every hour, day, and year
May have happened to you too
You may be okay and free
But you're you
And I'm me
I'm fumbling in the darkness
It still haunts me
But this is my business
So please don't judge me

Blinking back my tears, I typed additional stanzas under the picture:

Fear still haunts me
But I won't let it get to me
I will not let them ruin me
I will not let them torment me

I shall make them pay
What they did was a crime
Their evil I shall slay
It's only a matter of time

Feeling satisfied, I went back to looking at more photos and delving into nostalgia. I smiled as I saw pictures of my favorite dogs, Ribster and Dexter, feeling proud of how much they had grown over the years. I felt bad for not visiting them this time and mentally promised myself to do so soon.

My stomach finally growled in hunger, and I realized I had skipped breakfast. I glanced toward the kitchen to check if the food was served, wondering where Ekon was. I hadn't seen him the whole afternoon.

"Tina, I'm sorry we left you alone, dear," I heard my mother's voice. "We're so glad you could make it."

I set my phone aside and squealed joyfully. "Mom."

She laughed and hugged me tightly. "Were you bored?"

I shook my head. "No. I was just—"

"She was just pretending to be on her phone while trying to check out that cute chef," Grammy said, her eyes twinkling in mischief.

"*Kuzu zangpo la,* Grammy," I greeted Mom's mother in Dzongkha, the native language of Bhutan, hoping to divert her attention from Ekon.

"Well, as a matter of fact, I saw Mr. Chef's eyes searching for our dear granddaughter a few minutes ago," Gramps added with a chuckle as he walked up and joined us.

"What? When? Where?" I asked, immediately regretting my words, as my face went red at the realization I had given myself away. I tried to justify. "I mean, I asked where the food is."

My mother laughed and patted me on the back as her parents reminisced about their own love story, speaking animatedly in Dzongkha. I smiled warmly, watching my grandparents' banter.

They really represent couple goals.

"Tina, we need to leave in a few minutes. Stay with your grandparents tonight," my mother said, pulling me aside. "And keep your promise of coming to Birch Town soon."

I smiled. "Did Dad tell you about our rendezvous today?"

Mom nodded and grinned. "Of course. Your father tells me everything."

I laughed and hugged her tightly. "I have two couple role models right here in our family."

My mother returned my embrace. "Take care, Tina. We will make it up to you for missing the holidays this time."

I pretended to wipe a fake tear from my eyes. "I hope so. It's going to take me a while to recover from this heartbreak."

My mother shoved me playfully. "Stop being a drama queen."

I spent the rest of the party chatting and catching up with Grammy and Gramps. We had a scrumptious lunch with a widespread of dishes from across the world. Later, I left with my grandparents to their place, two hours away from Duckville. The car ride and the rest of the evening were a blur as I slept blissfully, exhausted from the previous night.

***

The next morning, after a delectable breakfast at my grandparents' farm, I took a cab back to Duckville, where I had to pick up my car. My grandparents wanted to drop me, but I insisted that they rest after the previous day's party. I loaded my trunk with all the goodies they had packed for me and headed toward the driver seat. I was horrified when I saw that all four tires were completely flat.

Immediately I knew who the culprit was—Wilbur Lauren.

Who else would play this sick joke and puncture *all* my car tires?

I cursed myself for not letting my grandparents drop me off and shuddered in fright at the thought of him being close by.

How much more wrath was I going to face from my foes for trying to stand up for myself?

CHAPTER 21

I pounded my fist on my car, fuming that the sicko demon had got me. I'd felt proud of myself yesterday for protecting myself from his clutches, but today I felt frustrated and helpless. I sat in the driver's seat and took a deep breath.

I need to calm down and get back home to Strollfield safely.

I got out and opened the trunk to get my bag out, so I could take a bus back home…but then I saw the two huge bags of veggies and fruits from my grandparents' winter hydroponic garden. There was no way I would be able to carry those with me. I took my phone and called the person who could use them.

"Thanks for coming, Ekon. I would have had to throw these away if not for you," I told him when he arrived within thirty minutes.

Ekon laughed. "It's a crime to waste this fresh produce."

We loaded the boxes in his trunk, and I turned to leave.

"Are you heading to Strollfield? I'm going there too. Why don't we go together?" Ekon offered.

I hesitated. "It's alright. I can take the bus."

"But why? Think of the lift as thanks for the amazing present," he said, referring to the vegetables and fruits.

I laughed. "Alright. And thank you for the ride."

"Hey, it's a beautiful day. Would you like to go for a picnic lunch with me? It's just leftover food from yesterday's party, though."

I welcomed the thought of spending more time with Ekon and getting my mind off the unpleasant incident from this morning. "Sure, that sounds great."

The sun was shining brightly on the soft white blankets of snow that covered the fields. The tree branches, rooftops, and everything else were covered in feathery white, matching the fluffy clouds in the winter sky. I tried to search for animal footprints in the snow like I did with my parents as a little girl, and a wave of nostalgia swept over me. I missed my parents already, and it didn't help that everything in this town reminded me of them.

"You can skate and code. Are you interested in anything else?" Ekon asked.

"Well, I write poetry as well. I also read and binge-watch series. Plus, I recently started karate," I replied. "How about you? What are your interests other than your culinary creations?"

"School and being a chef takes up most of my time. I like rock climbing, but I am nowhere near a pro. Other than that, thanks to my roommate, I have started binging series too," Ekon responded. "What kind of series do you watch?"

"I like anything that catches my interest. Comedy and mysteries with a little bit of romance are my favorites."

"I, too, like both genres. As for the romance, my roommate and I secretly watch it. We claim it's for research purposes for future dates," Ekon told me.

I laughed. "There's nothing wrong with rom-com."

Ekon laughed with me. "They are cheesy. Though I like that new author Enida."

I squealed. "You like Enida W. Alexander too? She is my favorite!"

Ekon grinned. "I've read all her books. My roommate and best friend, Aat, recommended her novels to me. Now I'm hooked. But I prefer crime and action thrillers over romance any day."

I nodded in agreement. "I love those too. We should watch crime thrillers together sometime."

Did I just invite him on a movie date? I panicked. What if he thought I meant "movies and chill"?

"I mean, not together-together," I justified. "But together simultaneously, separately."

Now I was just spouting nonsense.

Ekon turned to look at me. "Together-together would be nice as well." When our eyes met, he looked away. "Maybe we could go out to the movies sometime."

Did Ekon blush just now, or is it my imagination? Why is my heart racing?

There was an uncomfortable silence for a few minutes. I racked my brain to say something to break the awkwardness.

Ekon spoke first. "Do you want to listen to some music?"

I nodded. "Sure. Let's play the radio. Here, try this homemade strawberry rock candy. They're Grammy's specialty and I'm addicted to them."

Ekon switched on the radio and lowered the volume. "I would never say no to anything with strawberries."

Ekon sucked the strawberry candy and made a slurping noise. He paused for a moment and looked at me. "Pardon my rudeness, but these are irresistible."

I handed him a tissue. "Feel free to lick your fingers. I know you want to."

Ekon laughed. "Thanks. I'm going to befriend your grandparents for these."

Within the next thirty minutes, we finished the entire box of candy. I turned up the volume on the radio when MyWay's new song, "Nostalgia," came up.

Ekon looked at me. "Do you like this band?"

I nodded. "Oh, yes, the twins from this group were my students. I tutored them in math."

"That's cool," Ekon said. "So that's why they were at your birthday party. I didn't know they were from Duckville before that day."

"I didn't know you were from Duckville either," I replied. "Didn't you go to Strollfield High, though?"

"You seem to have dug out information about me, Tia. I don't remember telling you that," he teased.

My face went red, but I continued talking. "I read it in your chef bio on your café website. Everyone knows that about you."

"I am originally from Duckville. I only moved to Strollfield during my senior year of high school," Ekon told me.

"I don't remember seeing you in Duckville High at all," I said. "It's such a small town."

"I was an invisible kid," Ekon replied with a shrug. He pulled over at a parking spot. "Here we are at Landfill Hill, our picnic spot. Let's walk around for a bit and then have lunch here. What do you think?"

I nodded. "Sounds good."

We took our backpacks and started climbing up the hill. Ekon slipped, and I caught hold of his hand to help him maintain his balance. A few minutes later, I slid down the ice, and Ekon held my hand. "Are you alright?"

I nodded. "I'm fine."

"Are you sure you didn't slip deliberately as an excuse to hold my hand? Aren't you an expert ice skater?" Ekon teased.

I immediately let go of his hand. "You were about to fall first. Besides, I am an ice skater, not an ice walker."

Ekon laughed and offered his hand again. I didn't take it. He extended his hand further for me to take it. "You're so cute when you sulk."

I bit back a smile and held his hand. "I'm only taking care of you because you have made food for me."

Ekon laughed again. "Thank you. I'm in your care."

"Do you speak Japanese or Korean?" I questioned Ekon. "It's not common to say, 'I'm in your care' in this part of the world."

"Dr. Kim and Dr. Nakamura are like family to me. They say this all the time," Ekon answered.

"You know them too? Dr. Kim is my therapist, and Dr. Nakamura kind of saved my life," I told him, immediately regretting oversharing.

"Mi-Seon and Mio saved me as well," Ekon stated, calling them by their first names. "I'm closer to them than my real family."

We walked the rest of the way in comfortable silence, still holding hands. When we reached the top, we saw a group of people skating. I turned to Ekon. "I would have brought my skates if I had known earlier. I could have taught you as well. Maybe next time."

Ekon chuckled. "We seem to be planning many future dates, Tia. I'm not complaining, though."

As if we are a real couple.

I looked away to hide my blush. "Well, I don't mind, as long as you treat me to your food," I joked.

Ekon laughed. "Come on, let's eat first. Can you heat the food in the microwave oven in the cafeteria?"

I stood in line to wait for my turn. I opened the box, my curiosity getting the better of me. My mouth began to water when I saw the quesadillas and the waffle sandwiches. By the time I'd heated the food, Ekon had set everything up.

"I'm digging in. Bon appétit," I stated.

"*Itadakimasu. Jal meokkesseumnida. Smaaklike,*" Ekon replied. "By the way, I said 'thank you for the food' in Japanese, Korean, and Afrikaans."

I shoved him playfully. "Show-off. Do you always do this?"

He laughed and took a bite of his quesadilla. "No, I'm trying to impress you. Did it work?"

I laughed. "No, but it was cute."

We ate the quesadillas, which were stuffed with turkey from the party. Ekon had shredded the turkey and added cheese, scallions, and other ingredients. I was surprised that the leftover meat was still juicy. I bit into the waffles that were made from mashed potatoes. They were crisp, and inside were veggies, pickles, guacamole, and sauces that I didn't recognize.

"I hate seeing food go to waste. These were actually for my friends," Ekon told me.

"I'm not going to apologize for finishing them," I said.

Ekon laughed. "No, I'm glad I could share these with you. I would have ended up eating all this alone because everyone's away for the holidays."

We concentrated on the food for the rest of the meal. While I said "delicious," "yum," "this is so good," and "I feel like a glutton right now," Ekon evaluated his culinary skills. "The ratio of avocado to the rest of the spices in the guacamole is off."

"I don't find anything off," I replied with my mouth full.

He continued criticizing all the dishes, picking on each, right down to the nitty-gritty, and I was fascinated by his knowledge of food.

"Do you always critique your food?" I asked him, wiping my mouth with a napkin.

"Yes, it helps me improve," he answered. "I know it can be a bit much. Is it bothering you?"

I shook my head and giggled. "No, but it makes you sound like you're fishing for compliments."

Ekon smiled. "My friends say that, too, but I'm not. I used to write down all the points during meals. I stopped after it drove my friends crazy."

I placed my hand on his. "I admire your passion for food. It's inspiring."

"Thanks." Ekon smiled again. "How about we take a walk? Or would you prefer getting back?"

"Let's pack up and walk," I said.

The white snow glistened in the sun, resembling powdered diamonds. The ice skating area looked like a mirror, and we could even see our reflections. Magpies flew close to the ground, their blue wings glowing.

The view from the crest was breathtaking. We could see the snow-covered tops of trees and buildings in the town that lay below, along with white, half-frozen lakes with puddles of pristine water and gray-blue outlines of the hills near the horizon. If I were a painter, this place would have been an ideal place to create my masterpiece.

I looked at Ekon. "This place must be more beautiful in the summer."

Ekon smiled. "Each season brings out Landfill Hill's beauty in its way. It wouldn't be fair to compare."

"I'm coming back every season," I stated.

"Oh, we definitely should," said Ekon.

Why did such a simple promise make me so happy?

"Do you want a picture with this background?" Ekon asked.

"Why don't we take a selfie together?" I suggested.

Then, I froze immediately in fear. I hated looking at myself in a mirror or otherwise. How was I going to pull this off without revealing my secret?

Ekon and I took a picture with our sunglasses on. I faced Ekon and avoided looking at the screen. Not wanting to let him out of my sight,

I forgot my fears and removed my sunglasses and put them in my coat pocket. "I want one without these."

Ekon removed his sunglasses, as well, and clicked a picture. I couldn't help but gaze into his eyes that were twinkling in the sun. As always, they looked like pools of decadent chocolate. I could lose myself in them.

Ekon held my gaze. "Tia, are you done checking me out?"

"Are your eyes chocolate brown or coffee brown?" I whispered, my breath caught in my throat.

"Coffee," he replied.

"Nope, chocolate." I inched closer to him. "I like chocolate better."

Ekon gently cupped my face. "How about strawberries?"

In response, I put my hands around his neck and kissed him. He kissed me back deeply. I could feel our hearts beating to the same rhythm.

It was electrifying.

It was wonderful.

It felt right.

I definitely like strawberries better.

But the most beautiful moment of my life was interrupted too soon by the sound of my phone ringing. I ignored it, but it rang again.

Groaning internally, I pulled away from our kiss. "I'm sorry. I need to take this call." I walked a little further out before answering. "Hey, what's up? Is it urgent?" I asked Jai.

Jai sounded furious. "Pete Hilton has been declared Strollfield University's brand ambassador for next year. That criminal who threatened to rape you is going to represent the college. Can you believe it?"

"What? That's awful news," I exclaimed.

"We need to do something about this," Jai told me.

I nodded. "Of course, we can't let Pete represent us. Let's meet up as soon as I'm back in Strollfield." I hung up the call.

I looked at Ekon, who had a concerned expression on his face. "Sorry, I need to leave now."

Ekon placed a hand on my shoulder. "Is everything alright, Tia? I can drop you."

"No, thank you. All is well, but I need to get back to my place urgently," I said vaguely.

I felt terrible for running away from Ekon abruptly, but I had more important things to do. I couldn't see my harassers bask in the glory that did not belong to them.

Ekon didn't press for details, but his face betrayed his disappointment. "Shall I at least drop you at the bus stop or the taxi stand? You have too much to carry."

"I'll book a cab on my phone, thanks," I replied without looking at him. "Can you open your car trunk for me?"

Without a word, Ekon walked to the parking lot, and I followed him, tapping in my information to the cab company on the booking app. I swore under my breath for this sudden turn of events and wished I could tell him how grateful I was for today. I had truly enjoyed the ride from Strollfield and our little picnic date but there was no time for romance. I had to face reality and get back to fighting my abusers.

By the time we'd reached Ekon's car, my ride had arrived. He offered to help me move my stuff out of his trunk, but I refused. I got everything except the produce and strawberry candy.

"You're forgetting something," Ekon said, handing me the bags that were meant to be his present.

"But these are for you. As a thanks for today," I replied.

Ekon shook his head. "I'm good, thanks. They're yours."

I thrust them into his hands, still not meeting his eyes. "Please."

I left without looking back.

I didn't want to feel guiltier than I already did.

I didn't want to see Ekon upset.

I didn't want to give in to my heart and lose sight of my goals.

CHAPTER 22

The next morning, I received a text from Pete Hilton

Pete
I told you so. You mess with me, and you pay.

The text had a social media link. The thumbnail read "Shameless Tina Lauren learns her lesson for being a whore."

It was the assault video from the fundraiser.

Without clicking on it, I blocked the number and pounded my pillow several times and screamed into it to vent out my frustration. Why? Why me? What had I done to deserve this nonsense?

Last night was terrible, and I hadn't slept at all. To distract myself from everything else in my life, I had tried to sleep with my room door open but had failed. I ended up completing all my holiday assignments since studying was the only thing I could do without driving myself crazy. Seeing Pete's message this morning was the last straw. I didn't care about fighting my abusers anymore. I wanted peace.

I had a sore neck from falling asleep on my study table but had no motivation to get up. My phone rang many times, but I let it go to voicemail. But Jai kept trying my number. I sighed and finally answered it. "Hello?"

"Are you okay?" Jai asked, sounding concerned.

I wanted to say, "would *you* be okay in this situation?" but he continued talking.

"Sorry, that was a stupid question. What I meant was, can I do anything to make you feel better?"

"I'm exhausted," I answered. "I'm sick and tired of this whole thing."

"None of it is your fault." Jai tried to console me. "Pete should be arrested for uploading that video on social media."

"I know," I said louder than I intended to. "But that doesn't make any of this better."

"Do you want me to come over?" Jai asked.

"You're at work," I replied. "We can meet later."

"Alright, I'll come over after I'm done for the day. I work morning shifts anyway. Let's have lunch together."

"Actually, let me come over to your place," I offered. "Grammy and Gramps have given me a lot of food. It's enough to last Rory and you at least until tomorrow."

"What about Madison?"

I laughed. "Of course, I saved some for her. Are you scared of my roommate?"

"Extremely," Jai replied, chuckling. "Especially when it comes to food."

I felt better after chatting and joking with my best friend. I showered and packed some of Grammy's dishes for Jai and Rory. Though Rory and I were still awkward around each other, I saved some food for him, knowing how much he loved Grammy's cooking.

After napping for a couple hours, I took a cab to Jai's house and called the Duckville mechanic on the way, hoping my car would be ready soon. I missed my vehicle, and taxi fares were really expensive.

I walked up the stairs of the building and knocked on the door, hoping I had the right apartment. Now that I thought about it, I had never hung out with Jai outside the university campus or the healthcare center cafeteria.

"Little Monster, welcome to our humble abode," Jai said, opening the door.

I removed my shoes and went inside the neat and tidy place. I felt a pang when I recognized some of the furniture in their living room: the walnut-colored coffee table that now served as a TV stand and the bean bags—Rory's.

"I like your cozy apartment," I told Jai. "Is Rory home today?"

Jai looked a little sheepish. "About that, actually, I wanted to tell you, uh—"

"Hey, Jai, I found it. Can you believe it? I told you I would, and I did." Rory burst into the apartment, sounding excited. His tone quietened after seeing me. "Hi, T."

"Rory and Aiden wanted to talk to you about something urgently, so I invited them as well," Jai finished. "I hope that's okay."

"Hi, Tina," Aiden greeted me awkwardly, stepping into the room behind Rory.

I was still trying to process what was going on and had too many questions in my mind. *Why is Aiden here? What does he want to talk to me about? What did Rory find?* My stomach growled, reminding me that I was famished because I had skipped breakfast.

"Have you all eaten yet?" I asked the three guys. "My grandmother packed me a lot of food, which should be enough for us all."

Rory's eyes lit up. "Has Grammy made momos?"

I smiled and nodded. "And thukpa, the noodle soup. She has also made ezay, her signature sauce, to go with the dumplings or momos. I'll reheat them right away."

The four of us ate without talking for the next few minutes, and the only sounds we heard were the ASMR-like slurping of the refreshing soup and biting into the succulent momos. I smiled secretly when I heard Rory panting because of the spicy ezay, remembering how he would continue to lick the sauce, despite its heat, even during our childhood. I snickered to myself when I saw Aiden struggle to pick up the noodles with his fork. Clearly, he didn't know how to use chopsticks.

I didn't feel bad for making fun of Madison's ex and basketball star Aiden Wilkins in my mind because this was a very small payback for how I had felt last year. The conversation I overheard between him and his team members had rung in my ears for weeks after it happened. I knew he was not at fault, but couldn't stop resenting him for not asking his friends to shut up.

I could feel Jai glancing at me guiltily for forgetting to mention Aiden and Rory were going to be here today, but I ignored him, still cross at the sudden turn of events. However, after Grammy's lip-smacking meal, I felt better and ready to face whatever these three had in store for me. I could see that everyone at the table shared my sentiment, because not even a single morsel remained.

When the four of us were clearing the table, the doorbell rang. Jai ran to open the door, and I wondered if more people were joining us. My lips curled into a smile when I saw the latest entrant—Madison.

"I can't believe you guys finished all that yummy food," Madison said without even greeting me. "I can tell everything was delicious from your satisfied faces."

I laughed. "Of course, I saved some for you at home."

Madison hugged me tightly. "I knew it. You're the best."

When the five of us finally sat down in the living room, there was an awkward silence. I had a puzzled look on my face while everyone else just looked at each other, avoiding my gaze. Madison squeezed my hand reassuringly but wouldn't meet my eyes. I knew what this was about—the assault video from Pete's phone.

"Guys, I've had enough of this silence," I said, finally starting the conversation. "Will you please tell me what's going on?"

Aiden cleared his throat. "Tina, we promise, whatever we talk about today will not leave this room because it's a sensitive topic." He took a deep breath. "Did someone try to assault you at the SCF fundraiser?"

Wasn't that obvious from Pete's social media post? Why was he asking me? I was so not ready for their questions and judgment about the crime.

"I heard Hilton and some other students talk about it in the men's locker room," Aiden explained. "He was gloating about tricking you into going to the no entry area and then watching when—"

Madison placed a photo on the table. "Look at this photo. Pete had both his earrings in the morning." She placed another one next to the first. "And in this, one of his earrings is missing."

"And I found this at the same McCormick Park swimming pool," Rory said, pushing a resealable plastic bag toward me on the coffee table.

I gasped at the contents of the cover. It was Pete Hilton's lost earring.

"How did you manage to find that tiny piece of jewelry?" I asked, my head still whirling at the reveal.

Rory shrugged. "It was the least I could do to catch that useless bastard. It took me hours, but I finally found it."

Without a word, I walked up to Rory and hugged him. "Thank you, R. What you've done for me is unbelievable."

Rory embraced me back. "I'm sorry. I'm really sorry for not being on your side earlier. I wanted to prove with my actions that I always am."

I blinked back my tears. "You don't need to apologize. You've more than made up for everything already." For several minutes, we held each other tight, never intending to let go again.

I was overwhelmed by the amount of support I was getting from my friends and felt guilty for believing the worst in them. I felt a glimmer of hope crop up in my heart again. Maybe I wouldn't need to give up my fight against the abusers now that I had these people on my side.

"Teensy, you absolutely have to ensure that horrible Hilton goes to jail or is at least expelled." Madison echoed my thoughts. "I received this text from him this morning." She showed me her phone.

Pete
Ask your friend to stay put or else you will also pay.

"I'm so sorry, Mads. You've been caught up in the middle of this nonsense," I said.

Madison shook her head. "No way. We are all doing the right thing by getting this guy punished." She clasped her hands and sat upright. "So, let's review all the evidence we have. First, Pete's lost earring; second, Aiden's witness testification; third, his text sent to me. Anything else?"

"Four, voice recording of Pete's ra-rape threat," I stated.

Everyone except Jai looked at me, horrified. I played it on my phone.

Madison clenched her fists. "How did this asshole become our brand ambassador?" She squeezed my hand. "I'm really sorry that you're going through this. You don't deserve it."

Aiden nodded. "We're all on your side, Tina. Let's submit these as evidence against Pete to the dean. Does anyone have anything else?"

I wondered if I should bring up the social media post that Pete had uploaded this morning. Had these people not seen it yet? Even though it was evidence, it was hard for me to even imagine my friends watching the footage. I looked at Jai, who seemed to understand my dilemma and he shook his head slightly and gave me a reassuring smile.

"No, I think we have enough," I replied. "Thanks, guys. I'll go to the dean's office tomorrow and submit all the evidence."

"Alright, then, let's wrap up," Aiden said. He got up from the couch and turned toward me. "Hey, Tina, may I have a word with you please?"

"I need to run a quick errand," Madison informed me. "I will come back in a few minutes to pick you up. Let's go home together."

Jai and Rory went inside to give Aiden and me some privacy to talk. I patiently waited for Aiden to speak. He shook his legs and bit his lips nervously. "Um, I've been wanting to say this for a really long time but never had the courage."

"Go on, Aiden."

"Well, remember when we met for the first time in freshman year? I hadn't come to apologize to you for people spreading rumors about us. I wanted to say something else," Aiden said. "I had heard Nicholas Parker threaten students into bullying you and making you an outcast. He also boasted that he had taught a student a 'lesson' at a party for trying to complain against him. It was so bad that she dropped out of college. That's why I didn't have the courage to speak up against him or admit to you that I was on your side." He paused for a moment. "That guilt has eaten me up since last year, and I'm glad that I did the right thing this time. I am really sorry for being a coward. You didn't...no, do *not* deserve any of this crap from Parker or Hilton or the other students."

I stood silently for a moment trying to process this. Were there other students like Aiden, who were aware I was being wronged but who chose to stay silent out of fear? Would I have done the same thing in their place? I wasn't sure.

"Thank you for sharing that with me. I appreciate it." I finally said, not knowing what else to add.

Aiden nodded. "I just had to let it all out." He bent his head and avoided my eyes. "And I need a favor."

"Sure."

"My sister, Amanda, wants to contact you. She's currently out of town for the holidays but she said it's important. Is it okay if she calls you?"

I nodded. "Sure. Do you know what this is regarding?"

Aiden shook his head. "I'm not sure. But she insists *only* you can help her."

"You can give her my number, and I will talk to her."

Aiden looked relieved. "Thanks, Tina."

When Aiden left, many thoughts clouded my mind.

Why did Amanda want to contact me?

And how could *only* I help her?

Was I even in a position to do so, considering how I was struggling with my own stuff?

CHAPTER 23

I went to Jai's kitchen to help him with the dishes. I picked up a pair of gloves. "Let me do that."

"Little Monster, it's alright. I can manage on my own," my best friend said when we were alone in his spotless kitchen.

"Oh, come on, Fellow Monster, I know how much you hate washing the dishes," I said, putting on an apron he handed me.

I rinsed the dishes, and Jai placed them neatly on the rack.

"Thank you for arranging this meeting. I was feeling discouraged about fighting back earlier, but now, my motivation is back."

Jai shook his head. "I can't take any credit for that. Rory, Madison, and Aiden did everything." He sighed. "I just listened mutely as usual. You know that I find it hard to speak with strangers."

"But *you* stopped me from bringing up Pete's social media post. I thought everyone else would know about that, but I was surprised—"

Jai raised his voice. "It's illegal to upload assault footage in public." He added in an even tone, "It was reported to the police earlier today."

"Who reported it?" I asked.

Jai wiped his hands on his apron and showed me the social media posts on his phone.

@aasquad
10:17 AM

Hi Strollfield Police @stfPolice, we are reporting an illegal and offensive sexual assault video uploaded on social media this morning by Pete Hilton, a law student at Strollfield Law School and newly appointed brand ambassador of Strollfield University. We request you take necessary action against the perpetrator. Thank you.

@stfPolice
03:28 PM

Thank you @aasquad. It's commendable that you did the right thing. It's indeed illegal to upload such content in public. We will take care of it.

"Oh wow, aren't they the same people who validated my post earlier using digital forensics? The one with the interview with Ina?" I asked.

Jai nodded.

"Interesting. So, are you a part of the squad too?"

Jai looked at me, surprised. "How did you decipher that?"

"Because you're awesome." I pointed at his phone. "And these are direct messages to the Strollfield Police. They aren't public and no one else can see them. This means you need to be logged in as aasquad. That's only possible if you're a member. Elementary, my dear Jai."

Jai laughed. "That's great detective work. Would you like to join us? I've been meaning to ask you, but you already have so much going on."

"Tell me more about the squad."

"What did you wish for the most when you were outcast for no fault of yours?" Jai asked.

I giggled. "You sound like Dr. Kim, my therapist. She always answers my question with a question."

Jai smiled. "That was the question AA asked me when I asked her what the squad does."

"AA? Is that the founder's name?"

"Well, she goes by AA. None of us have ever seen her. She attends all meetings on the phone," Jai replied. "So, answer my question: what did you wish for the most when you were out cast for no fault of yours?"

"For someone to be on my side and support my fight against the abusers," I said.

"Exactly. That's what the members of AA Squad do for each other. We are all survivors of bullying and abuse who have come together to fight."

"Wow, can anyone join your squad then?" I asked.

"We aren't a secret group per se, but we aren't out in the public either," Jai answered. He added with a laugh, "None of us are social butterflies. I doubt too many people would want to hang with us. But you'd fit right in, which is why I'm inviting you."

I smiled. "Thanks for the offer. I will think about it."

"Great, let me know," Jai said. "By the way, MyWay is throwing a year-end party on New Year's Eve. Ken and Keith have told me to drag you there if I have to."

I groaned, removing the dish gloves and placed them back on the rack neatly. "I was planning to get cozy on my couch and read Enida W. Alexander's latest novel. It's finally out."

Jai chuckled. "You can do that for the rest of the holiday break. No excuses."

I sighed. "Fine, I will be there."

***

I drove Madison's car back home because she was exhausted. She had gone to her hometown only for Christmas and had returned early for the next round of the Dance Divas contest that was being held in a town two hours from Strollfield. Her team had qualified, and she was leaving this week. She had rehearsed all night last night, and I expected her to fall asleep during our ride, but she browsed on her phone.

"I'm watching your Fire on Wheels performance video at the SCF fundraiser. I can't believe I missed your spectacular performance. Oh my, that back flip—I had my heart in my mouth while watching it. Unbelievable," Madison said.

I made a face. "It was a fluke, Mads. I could never repeat that stunt again."

Madison raised an eyebrow. "You mean, it was adrenaline? I can clearly see the pain in your eyes in this video. Was this after the...?"

"Mads, I'm sorry I couldn't tell you earlier about—"

"Don't you dare apologize for anything." She cut me off firmly. Her tone softened immediately. "Oh, Teensy, my heart broke when I heard about the rape attempt at the fundraiser. I felt like an idiot for not noticing your pain. But not once did I blame you for not telling me." Madison paused before she continued. "What you went through was unfathomably traumatic. No one can expect you to share something like that."

I pulled over at the side of the road, unable to control my emotions. I spoke quietly, without meeting her eyes. "I thought I would lose you as a friend for keeping secrets. My former friends hated it when I didn't share."

Madison shook her head vehemently. "No, you will *not* lose my friendship. It shattered me when I realized how lonely you must have felt. You were alone through it all—when you punched Parker because he deserved it, when you were framed for a false sex tape, and when your most unfortunate moment of self-harm became the laughingstock of the entire college. How could I have expected you to confide in me or anyone?"

Tears welled up in my eyes. Madison placed both her hands on my shoulders and looked at me, her eyes brimming with tears. "It's not your fault. I am sorry on behalf of everyone who deserted you when you needed them the most. I don't expect you to trust me after what you've been through, but I'll prove that I am not like your former false friends."

Madison's words made me bawl like a baby, uncontrollably. She held me in her arms as we cried, stroking my back reassuringly.

I wiped my eyes with the back of my hand. "I'm really lucky to have you in my life. I love you so much, Mads. I mean it."

Madison raised an eyebrow. "Do you love me even more than Rory Matthews and Jai Rao?"

I laughed. "I love all of you equally. I don't know what I would do without the three of you."

Madison sighed melodramatically. "Oh well, I guess I should just be happy being the third-best."

I giggled again, starting the engine. "You're being a drama queen. No, you're first. Always."

Madison tilted her face and batted her eyelids. "Always? Are you sure?" She wiggled both her eyebrows and smirked. "What about Ekon Okoro, then?"

I got back on the road and continued to drive, looking straight ahead, my face probably red as a tomato as Madison continued to giggle.

"What? How did you—? I mean, why would you think that?"

Madison's eyes danced in mischief. "It's written all over your face." She added with a smug smile, "Who do you think set you both up? Remember your rolled ice cream date?"

"Who told you that was our first date?" I challenged her, enjoying the surprised look on her face.

"Teensy, it's not fair. I need *details*!" Madison wailed like a child.

I guffawed loudly, enjoying her discomfort. "Keep guessing."

***

That night, I tossed and turned in bed, unable to sleep. I was alone at home because Madison had left for her dance rehearsals. The events from the past few days flashed before my eyes like a movie. The Laurens' holiday party, Ekon's and my night out, our romantic picnic, our kiss…

But I ruined the perfect moment by running away.

Ekon's hurt look was etched in my mind, and I couldn't get rid of it. I took my phone out of my pocket and thought about calling him.

Realizing it was a terrible idea, I threw the device on my bed. I got up to get a late-night snack and opened the refrigerator. My eyes fell on a box of strawberry-flavored rock candy that reminded me of Ekon again.

I sighed, closed the fridge, and went into the kitchen. I found a bag of roasted nuts and began munching on them, trying to divert my mind off Ekon. I worked on documenting all the evidence for my upcoming meeting with the dean. I went over everything to be submitted multiple times until I was convinced that nothing was missing.

Later that night, still unable to sleep, I sat at my desk, bored. I had completed all my holiday homework and didn't feel like reading any novels. I sighed and opened my diary to the page where I had the list of fears I wanted to overcome. I felt overwhelmed at the number of bullet points, my stomach convulsing at the thought of most of them. I finally decided on the seemingly simplest ones: Leave my room door open while in the living room or kitchen and sleep in my room, keeping it unlocked. I had tried this earlier but failed.

I left my door open and went to our living room and plopped on our couch. I switched on the television and watched skating stunt videos. I had chosen a position from which I could see my room, and every few seconds, my eyes fell on the ajar door. It took every ounce of my willpower to stay rooted in my seat and not jump up to close it.

I rewound the skating stunt video multiple times, because my mind was on the darn door. I sighed and opened a timed game on the TV, hoping the interactive activity would help me concentrate on something else. However, I failed because, after a few minutes, my opponent was playing all alone.

Frustrated, I got up and stomped my feet. My stomach growled in hunger, and I decided to make myself some food. I found some leftover bruschetta topping in the fridge and some fresh bread. I hummed to myself as I toasted the baguette to a perfect golden brown and spread the tomato-basil mixture marinated in extra virgin olive oil evenly on the surface. I took a big bite of my snack, relishing the tanginess of the tomatoes and the crunch of the baguette.

I took my plate and went back to my room to get a novel to read, when I shrieked in delight suddenly. "I did it. I stayed outside my room with the door open, without thinking about it."

I danced around the house, still munching on the yummy bruschetta, feeling immensely proud of myself. I finished the rest of my snack, washed my plate, and entered my room confidently, keeping the door wide open. A few seconds later, I closed it, but left it unlocked.

Let's do this and cross it off the list, Tina.

With my stomach full and a satisfied smile on my face, I fell into a blissfully dreamless sleep.

And this time, not once did I think about the darn door.

CHAPTER 24

The next day, I filed a complaint against Pete Hilton and submitted all the evidence at the dean's office at the university, as planned. As my online tutoring classes were closed for the holidays, I got a new temporary job as an ice skating instructor at the local rink during the break. The kids were a handful, and I returned home exhausted the next few days, but I was grateful that the time flew.

My car had been dropped off during the week by an old family friend from Duckville, and I was elated to have it back. The mechanic had informed me that my spare tire had also been flat and all of them had to be replaced. I was furious that Wilbur Lauren, that *demon,* had gone to such extents to torment me again, but there was nothing I could do about it because I didn't have any proof against him.

On the morning of New Year's Eve, I was glad that Madison was home for breakfast but felt guilty that I hadn't prepared anything elaborate. Feeling too lazy to cook, I had been surviving on cereal, toast, and boiled eggs in her absence. She didn't seem to mind though and helped herself to an egg.

"Teensy, Pete Hilton has been expelled from the university," Madison informed me.

"Really? That's great news," I exclaimed.

She smiled but didn't seem as happy as me. I decided not to ask her about it and thought that she was probably tired.

"Do you know why he got appointed as Strollfield U's brand ambassador in the first place?" she asked.

"*Former* brand ambassador," I corrected her. "Why though? I'm curious too."

"Apparently, he defended a student who was wrongly accused of a crime at the university student court," Madison replied. "How ironic."

"Wow, I had no idea that such a 'court' existed. Let's look it up," I said. I pulled up the info on the university website. "It seems like a platform to provide justice to Strollfield U's students. A victim of bullying, abuse, or any other crime can file a complaint, and the perpetrator will be tried in this mock court. Law school students will play the roles of lawyers and prosecutors, while a group of students who don't know either the perp or the victim will form the judges' panel. For each case, the panel will change. Of course, the final decision of expelling the perp if found guilty is in the dean's hands."

"That sounds interesting."

I nodded. "Guess what its name is?"

"What?"

"Court Us," I said, trying hard not to laugh.

Madison burst into a fit of giggles. "Seriously? Why would they name it that? The name is so misleading. 'Court Us.'"

I wiped my own tears of laughter. "It says here they need an app developer on their team. If I'm accepted, the first thing I plan to do is suggest a name change."

"Please do," Madison agreed. "I will sign a petition if you want."

"Who came up with such a bizarre name? Anyway, on a different note, I wonder why Pete wasn't tried at this court. I am the 'victim' in this case, but I wasn't contacted," I said.

"Yeah, strange." Madison said. She changed the subject. "How's your new job?"

"Never mind that. Tell me all about your dance contest. Did you make it to the finals?"

Madison grinned widely. "Yes."

I squealed and hugged her, both of us jumping up and down like excited kids. "Congrats, Mads! Tell me everything that happened."

We chatted until it was time for me to leave for work. When I reached the parking lot, I realized I had forgotten my lunch and headed back to my apartment. When I was about to unlock the door and enter, I heard Madison talking to her boyfriend Darma on speakerphone.

"Tina doesn't know that I lost my scholarship. I didn't have the heart to tell her. I'm sure Nicholas Parker has a role to play in this. You know that his family provides a huge amount of funding for the university. Ironically, though, they cited 'shortage of funds' as the reason for my scholarship loss and that I have the lowest GPA of the three awardees." She took a deep breath. "What's strange though is that Rory Matthews got suspended from the university for two weeks for going to a 'no-entry' location, unauthorized. But he told me that his swimming coach had signed a permission slip. All this is so strange."

"Aiden got removed from the basketball team, too, right?" Darma asked.

"Yes. But he was planning to quit anyway," Madison replied. "It beats me how all three of us have faced actions against us on the same day. That cannot be a coincidence."

I clenched my fists and gritted my teeth in anger. Hot tears of fury sprang into my eyes, but I fiercely blinked them away.

I barged into our living room. "It's *not* a coincidence. It's Nicholas Parker and his underlings' way of showing me the price I have to pay for going against them."

Madison jumped, startled at my entry. "Teensy, what are you doing here?"

"I'm so sorry you all are facing his wrath because of me, Mads. None of you deserve this for standing by my side."

Madison shook her head vehemently. "No. If I had kept quiet, I would not have been able to live with myself. I did the right thing for *me* as much as for you. So, don't apologize. I am not worried about losing my scholarship, and I will work ten times harder to achieve my dance goals. This is not going to bog me down. So, please don't hold back on getting Parker and his underlings punished. I will stand by you as a solid support. No matter what."

I threw my arms around her, letting my tears flow. "Thank you. I am so lucky to have you in my life."

And I promise, I will not let anything else happen to you.

***

After work, I drove to the police station and pressed charges against Nicholas Parker and Pete Hilton. This time, I had zero hesitation and fear. I was even able to speak about the traumatic incidents coherently.

When I was done, I felt proud of myself, but there was a pinch of guilt still bothering me for dragging my friends into this.

I decided to go and check on Rory, feeling awful that he had been suspended through no fault of his.

As I was about to get into my car, I got a text from Jai.

Jai
Don't forget MyWay's New Year's party tonight.

I called him from my cell phone, realizing that I had completely forgotten about the event. "Hey, I'm not in the mood to party tonight. I'm heading to your place to be with Rory. Didn't you hear about his suspension?"

"That got canceled, though. He showed the university the required permission slip, and he is all set now," Jai said.

"That's great! Why did they suspend him in the first place though?"

I couldn't hear Jai's response because of the background noise. He was already at the MyWay party venue getting everything ready. I only heard him say, amidst the drilling and hammering sounds, "I'll see you and Rory soon," before hanging up.

I stopped at the mall and bought a blue jumpsuit for tonight's party. When I was about to leave the shop, my eyes fell on a beautiful yellow dress that looked like it was tailor-made for me. I ran my hand gingerly on the soft fabric, loving its feeling against my palm.

"Would you like to try it on?" the customer sales representative asked me.

I shook my head. "No, thanks."

"We have an offer going on right now. If you buy one dress or jumpsuit, you can get the second at half the price." She walked to dressing rooms, gesturing for me to follow her. "And we have a vacant spot just for you."

Before the sales rep could persuade me to get into a room full of mirrors—my biggest nightmare, I bought the yellow dress and bolted out of the shop.

Even if I might never ever wear it.

CHAPTER 25

I changed into the blue jumpsuit at home and went to pick up Rory. He waited for me outside his building, playing with his phone. On our way to the party, he answered my questions about his near suspension.

"I don't get it. Why did the university not check the admission slip before suspending you?" I asked.

Rory sighed. "Because my coach lied to them."

"How did they retrieve it later then? Did you give it to them?"

He shook his head. "No, I didn't have it. I had submitted it to the park security."

I frowned. "Why didn't they verify all the facts before accusing you?"

"The whole thing was really weird. My parents and I were summoned to the campus this morning. Dean Sibiya issued us a letter for my two-week suspension. He explained to us that Coach Dennis denied giving me permission to go to the swimming pool under renovation and that there was no record of an admission slip at the McCormick Park security desk either. I tried telling him that there must be a mistake and pleaded with him to reconsider, but he didn't budge."

"Oh, how did everything work out then?"

"When my parents and I came out of the dean's office, still shocked, we met Officers Hussein and Lee. They requested to speak with me regarding Hilton's crime. They didn't divulge details on the case but asked me to explain how I had found Pete's earring at McCormick Park. When I did that, they asked me if I had permission to enter the forbidden area. I said yes and informed them about the lost admission slip. Then, Officer Hussein asked me if I had taken my car and where I had parked it." Rory paused for effect.

"And?"

"I was puzzled at first and wondered why she would ask me that, but I answered that I had parked at the McCormick swimming pool."

I spoke excitedly. "Did you have the one-time parking pass with you? You can't park there without one. And you only get one if they permit you to enter the swimming pool."

Rory smiled and nodded. "Exactly. It was a stroke of luck that I had placed the pass in my car. I have never run so fast in my life the way I did to get it. I showed it to Dean Sibiya, as well, and he canceled my suspension… reluctantly."

"Wow," I exclaimed. "My head is whirling from all this information. Are you planning to sue the university for accusing you falsely?"

Rory sighed. "I haven't thought about it. I hope that they fire Coach Dennis, though. He shouldn't have lied and tried to frame me."

I squeezed his hand. "I'm on your side, whatever you choose to do. And thanks again for everything you did for me. And I'm sorry you and your parents went through such a rough day today."

Rory patted my hand. "None of this was your fault."

When I pulled over at Strollfield Convention Center, the venue for the MyWay party, I had a good mind to drive away aimlessly to escape from here. I hated loud crowded gatherings and Rory didn't seem interested either and was still buried in his phone. I sighed as we went inside the hall but cheered up when I spotted Jai waiting for us at the entrance.

Jai waved to us, grinning from ear to ear. "Little Monster, you came."

Rory cleared his throat and placed his phone in his pocket. "I'm here too."

Jai laughed. "Thanks for convincing her to come. As the head of the food committee today, here's your reward."

Jai gave Rory a pass for the food counters at the party.

I giggled. "Isn't it too early to stuff ourselves?"

"Who invited *you* to the buffet counter?" Rory retorted. "This pass is only for me."

Jai handed me another pass. "You better hurry, Tina. After five minutes, everyone will flock to the food, and you'll miss your chance. We decided to feed everyone first so there's no mess during the concert."

I followed Rory to the buffet counter containing various types of fancy appetizers from different cuisines. There were options for every kind of eater—dairy-free, vegetarian, vegan, nut-free, gluten-free, and even diabetic-friendly. No one would go hungry tonight. Only Jai could be thoughtful and inclusive of everyone.

I placed one piece of each dish on my plate. While Rory took photos of the food, I took my first bite of a cheese-filled snack called a "bird's nest." The crunch was so loud Rory placed his phone into his pocket and ate as well. While wolfing down the freshly barbequed pieces of meat, the first person I thought of was Ekon. I wondered if he would critique the dishes or if that was only for his own cooking. Besides, he would have narrated stories of each of the delicacies and how he would improve them.

The truth was, I missed Ekon terribly. And I was hoping he'd be in attendance tonight.

That's because I like Ekon Okoro.

I tried to ignore my inner voice and looked around. MyWay's production company had converted the city's most famous convention center into a party venue for teenagers. There was a bar, but with only nonalcoholic drinks. There were rumors that teens smuggled alcohol into such parties, but I was never a witness to this, because I hardly attended any when I was their age. But I was having a good time so far, and I turned to Rory to see if he was enjoying himself but found his face buried in his phone again.

"MyWay will be on the stage shortly. We request attendees to take their places. You can also dance in the discotheque area if you like," the organizers announced on the microphone.

"Tina, over here," someone called out to me. It was Jai. "Hi, Rory."

Behind him, I spotted Ekon with his friends. He stood with his back to me. I wondered if he had spotted me already. Immediately, I gravitated toward him.

"Aat, I don't want to go with you to the disco. I'm good here," I heard Ekon tell his friend, who I'm guessing must be his friend Aat. He'd told me about him on our date at Landfill Hill.

"You don't have a choice. Your girlfriend is here with someone else," Aat replied. "By the way, she looks beautiful in the blue jumpsuit."

"She's not my girlfriend, but, yes, she's always gorgeous," Ekon said.

I blushed. I wasn't supposed to eavesdrop, but I couldn't stop. Would I really mind being Ekon's girlfriend? And also, who did he think I was here with instead of him? Rory?

"Tell me the truth. You abandoned me for her the other day, correct? The day after the Lauren holiday party?" Aat accused Ekon.

Ekon evaded Aat's question and followed him to the dance area. "Happy? Now, stop giving me a hard time about her."

Jai tapped my shoulder. "Tina, the twins told me specifically to get you on the dance floor. Rory, you're welcome as well."

"I can't dance," I protested.

Jai shrugged. "I'll let them know that you refused. They will be so upset."

"You're emotionally manipulating me," I told him. "That's not fair."

Jai laughed. "Come on. It will be fun."

I sighed. "Fine. I give in."

Rory declined Jai's invitation. "You guys go ahead. I'm good here."

Jai and I headed to the dance floor. People stood in circles with their groups. Ekon's group had two guys and a girl. I stood awkwardly next to Jai, who was texting someone on his phone. A few minutes later, MyWay arrived on the stage. There were six of them, including Keith and Ken—three boys and three girls. Keith was one of the main singers, while Ken played the drums. The other guy was the lead guitarist. One of the girls was a lead singer, one was on the keyboard, and the other was the bass guitarist.

"Hello, Strollfield!" MyWay greeted the crowd. "Thank you all for coming today. It means a lot to us. Let's get this party going."

They started singing their famous song, "Young-ness," with a fast beat.

Everyone on the dance floor moved to the rhythm. Jai did his own thing, which looked easier to follow, so I ended up copying him. In Ekon's group, Ekon's friend Aat was dancing like a professional. Ekon and his two other friends were clapping and encouraging him.

Suddenly, I spotted a girl in the crowd who was trying to grab another student's bu—, I mean, behind, while he stood clutching his chest tightly and closing his eyes. Aghast, I moved a little so that I would come in between her and the boy. The girl promptly proceeded to grope someone else's behind. The guy spun her around, and they started making out. I was dumbfounded at this scene.

Couldn't she have asked the guys before grabbing them like that?

The student thanked me silently with his eyes, and I shot him a reassuring smile.

"Having fun?" Jai asked me, dancing obliviously.

"I'm copying you. You can sue me," I replied.

Jai laughed. "I think we both will be thrown out if we keep talking."

I laughed with him. "You started it."

During the break for dinner, everyone scattered. Jai went to meet his boyfriend. Rory requested that I give him my car keys and said he'd wait for me in the car. Someone tapped me on the shoulder.

It was Ekon.

"Hi, Tina. Can we talk in private?" Ekon asked.

"Sure," I replied, my heart doing a somersault.

We went to a quieter place and took a seat.

"So, I'm going to be honest with you, Tina. I'm interested in you as more than a friend. I know you have a lot on your plate, but I need to know what's on your mind. This ambiguity is not going to help either of us."

I wasn't expecting him to be so blunt. "I feel the same way about you, Ekon." I paused, deciding whether to be equally honest. "But you're right. I'm not ready for a relationship. I'm sorry for giving you mixed signals all the time. I really enjoy spending time with you...but..." I trailed off.

Ekon got up from his chair. "Okay. I'm glad we cleared this up."

I nodded, gulping down the sudden urge to cry. "Thanks for understanding."

When Ekon left, I felt a sharp pain in my chest—a pain more intense than anything I'd ever felt before. Tears rolled down my face despite my fiercest attempt to stop them.

So this is what a broken heart feels like.

It was the worst feeling in the world.

***

When I was about to leave the party, I saw Aiden and walked up to him. I wanted to ensure he was okay after being ousted from the university basketball team. "Hey."

"Hi, Tina. Happy New Year," Aiden said.

I smiled. "Same to you, in advance. Still a few hours to go."

Aiden nodded. "Yes, I know. But I wish midnight would come earlier. I was up all night last night and just want to sleep."

I laughed. "I'm sneaking out too."

Aiden made a face. "I can't leave until I drop my friends back at home."

I changed the subject. "How are you holding up? I'm sorry you're no longer a part of the basketball team."

Aiden waved a dismissal hand. "I'm glad I'm out. My parents are terribly disappointed, but I want to concentrate on my books now."

"Books? Are you an author?"

Aiden leaned closer to me and whispered. "It's a secret. I write young adult fiction under the pen name Enida W. Alexander."

I whisper-squealed gleefully. "OMG. I am a *huge* fan of Enida's, no, *your* books."

"It's a secret, though. I'm scared of being made fun of for writing 'girly' YA novels."

"My lips are sealed," I assured him. "And there's no such thing as 'girly' or 'boyish.' They are just stupid stereotypes. I think it's super cool that you're the best YA author *ever*."

Aiden smiled. "Thanks. I'm not that popular though."

"Yet. But it's just a matter of time before you get there," I said. "You've got over a hundred reviews already. And I presume at least a thousand sales?"

"Two thousand seven hundred," Aiden corrected me shyly.

"See? Don't forget us commoners when you become famous!"

After my conversation with Aiden, I walked to the parking lot, still trying to process his secret. It made perfect sense now. Enida was an anagram of Aiden.

A shiver ran down my spine from the cold wind, despite wearing my warm fleece-lined jacket over my jumpsuit. I called Rory to pick me up at the entrance but got his voicemail. I switched on my phone's flashlight as it was dark outside, and the streetlights were dim. The parking lot was deserted, as it was before midnight, and most of the partygoers were still inside.

All was still, yet I had a distinct feeling I was being watched.

Trusting my instincts, I walked faster, looking for my car. Why had I parked so far away?

Soon, I heard footsteps behind me. Fear engulfed me. I could run but wasn't sure how far I'd get. Keeping my pace up, I reached into my backpack slowly to take out my pepper spray without making it obvious.

What are my options?

Turn around and get back to the party? They could attack me before that.

Turn around and pepper spray them and run? What if I am overreacting and the person is just walking to their car?

Turning, I could now see the shadow of my follower. I could tell they were wearing a cap and a pink glow-in-the-dark wristband. And they were inching closer to me.

I dialed Rory's number again in vain. Panicking now, I held up my phone and flashed the light, waving frantically, praying someone would recognize my SOS.

Within seconds, I felt a blow to my hands. My pepper spray and the cell phone fell to the ground. Before I could even wince in pain, the masked attacker approached me, pinning both my hands with one of his behind my back.

With the other hand, he pushed me against a parked car and raised a knife.

I don't want to die.

CHAPTER 26

When my attacker tried to stab me, my survival instincts kicked in, and I quickly ducked. Kneeing them hard in the stomach, as Dr. Nakamura had taught me, I tried to free myself from their grip, but in vain. I wasn't strong enough.

They swore bitterly and raised the knife again. But before they could bring it down, two humongous shadows bolted toward us and tackled the attacker to the ground.

Ribster and Dexter!

The two dogs pinned him to the ground and started barking loudly. Finally free, I kicked the attacker's knife far from his reach. Next, with the dogs nipping at the person, their owner, a lady with long hair, and I dragged him to a pole nearby and tied both his hands with a scarf.

Before we could secure the attacker's hands, he slashed the side of my stomach with a pocketknife, and I winced in pain, forced to let him go free. Ribster and Dexter's owner knocked the guy unconscious with just one blow to his head.

Collapsing on the ground and clutching my side to control the bleeding, I watched as the wonder woman single-handedly tied the criminal's hands up with her scrunchie. She tied his shoelaces together as I called 911.

Next, she tied a scarf around my wound as we waited for help to arrive.

"Thank you so much," I said to my saviors.

Ribster and Dexter licked my hand lovingly in response.

"I'm glad you're safe, Tina," the lady told me with a smile that reached her striking eyes. "Take care."

"T, are you alright? What happened?" Rory came running, and I turned toward him.

I gestured for him to wait for a moment and spoke to the lady. "Wait, how do you know my na—"

"Who are you talking to?" Rory asked me. "There's no one else here."

"Where did my saviors go?" I wondered aloud. "If not for them, I wouldn't have survived."

Rory apologized profusely for draining his phone battery, but his voice was a haze, and the world around me went black.

***

When I woke up, I wondered where I was, as everything was a blur. I tried to sit upright, pushing the white sheets covering me slightly when I felt a faint pain in my side. I wrapped the thin blanket tightly around me when I realized I was at the hospital and wearing nothing but their gown.

My throat parched, I reached for a cup of water on the table next to my bed, but knocked it over, spilling it on the floor.

"Little Monster, are you alright?" Jai asked me, drawing the curtain aside and rushing to me.

I giggled nervously. "Sorry, I was thirsty and dropped the cup."

Jai poured some water for me in another plastic cup. "Thank goodness you're okay." He opened the small paper box next to it that read "Recharge Café." "Do you want something to eat as well?"

"Did you get this cinnamon roll for me?" I asked as I bit into the heavenly treat that was still warm.

Jai shook his head. "No, Ekon brought it. He's my friend."

My heart did a flip-flop. *Was Ekon here?*

"Rory informed your parents, and they'll be here as soon as they can," Jai said.

I was relieved that Mom and Dad would be with me soon. "Thanks."

Rory peeked through the curtain. "T, the police are here. They have some questions for you. Can you talk now?"

I nodded slightly, my head throbbing. Jai left as a lady officer stepped inside and smiled at me. "Hi, Miss Lauren. I am Officer Hussein. How are you feeling?"

"I don't know, Officer. Everything happened so fast. It feels like a dream," I answered.

"Don't worry, your attacker won't hurt you again. He's in police custody," Officer Hussein replied. "Do you know the person who tried to stab you?"

"I'm not sure. His face and head were covered. Even when I switched on the flashlight on my phone, I couldn't identify him," I said.

"Can you tell me more about what happened?" she asked.

I told the police what had happened, and she took notes intently. Reliving the horrifying experience sent a shudder down my spine, and I thanked God silently a million times for sending Ribster, Dexter, and the mysterious stranger to save my life.

"Do you know anyone who would want to hurt you?" the officer questioned. "We want to ensure that this wasn't a planned crime targeting you."

I felt the blood drain from my face when I realized I might have been attacked by Nicholas Parker or his gang. This hadn't struck me until now, and I racked my brain about how to answer Officer Hussein. Should I reveal the truth? Or hide some of it?

"There was a se-sexual assault attempt on me at the Strollfield Cultural Festival fundraiser. And I just gathered the courage to press charges against the perps today. One of them, who helped plan the crime, Pete Hilton, got expelled from the university, but the other who attacked me, Nicholas Parker, has not yet been charged," I explained to Officer Hussein.

I provided more details about the crime at the fundraiser and everything that happened after that. I told her everything, including how a stranger and her two dogs saved me tonight. I also spoke about my speculations of Nicholas's attempts to torment my friends. I didn't have proof, but if his team was involved in stabbing me tonight for pressing charges against him and his underlings, everything else fell in place logically.

"Have you registered for the victims' notifications service?" Officer Hussein asked.

I shook my head. "What's that?"

"The police will notify you about the investigation's progress via text." She gave me a business card that read "Special Victim Protection Services." "You can also call this number at any time."

After the police left, exhausted from the night's events, I drifted off to Dreamland.

***

The next morning, I was woken up in my hospital bed by a call from Madison. "Teensy, how are you? I heard everything."

I was glad to hear Madison's voice. "Mads, Happy New Year. How are your rehearsals coming along?"

"Let's talk about you first," Madison said, her voice breaking.

No, Mads. I want to know how you are. You lost your scholarship while trying to help me.

"I'm alright, Mads," I reassured her.

I told her what had happened last night as she listened intently.

"Well, thank goodness, you're not more hurt," Madison told me. "Have the police found out if it was a mugging attempt, or were you the specific target?"

I shook my head. "No, they haven't found out anything yet."

"I'll be back this evening. Until then, please don't go anywhere on your own. Jai and Rory will be with you at our place until I come," Madison said. "This is nonnegotiable."

I nodded. "Yes, ma'am."

In the afternoon, the doctors signed off on my discharge, and I was elated to get back home. Jai and Rory helped me get into my place and instructed me not to move from the couch. Both of them were gloomy and quiet the entire time. They had hardly spoken to me except that they had informed my parents, and that they would be here to see me later today. Rory pulled up a chair and sat on it, burying his face into his phone. Jai went to our kitchen to prepare food.

178

I tried to get up from my seat, but Rory's glare stopped me. A few minutes later, Jai brought me some oatmeal that warmed my soul and felt like a hug. He sat next to me on the couch with his own bowl of food but refused to look at me. Rory ate while browsing his phone.

"R, Fellow Monster, if you both are mad at me, please say something," I said. "Your silent treatment is driving me crazy."

"Why did you leave the party midway?" Jai asked, the hurt evident in his eyes. "I went to see the MyWay twins for a moment, and you were gone. Couldn't you have informed me?"

Rory sighed and placed his phone on the coffee table. "It's my fault. I was waiting for her in the car. But my phone was switched off because I had drained its battery."

I took a deep breath. "Neither of you had anything to do with this; it was the attacker's fault. Sure, I should have informed you before leaving the party, Jai. And R, I could have asked you to pick me up at the entrance. But there's no guarantee that, even if we'd been more careful, I wouldn't have been attacked." I paused for a moment. "I followed Parker's underling's instructions willingly and went to the abandoned swimming pool area at the fundraiser. Was that my fault?"

Rory and Jai shook their heads vehemently. "No way."

"Do you know how many times I have asked myself 'what if' questions about that day?" I asked my friends. "It never helps. The only thing that did was—it could have been worse, so I am thankful."

Rory and Jai nodded their heads in agreement.

"I'm sorry I made both of you worry, but can we please put this behind us and enjoy the first day of the new year?" I requested.

Jai smiled at me for the first time since last night. "Fine, but you better promise never to leave without informing one of us again."

I grinned back at him. "I promise."

Rory, Jai, and I played Scotland Yard, my favorite board game. Jai was new to the game, and I explained the rules to him.

"So, one of us would be selected as X, the convict. The objective of X is to run away from the other two police officers who try to catch them," I said. "The board is the map of Scotland. The officers and X have only finite bus, taxi, and tram tickets to achieve their respective objectives. If the police detect X's position, they win. Otherwise, it's X's game."

I won all games, whether I was X or the officer. Jai and Rory were bent on beating me, so I asked them both to be the fugitives and still won.

"Not fair, T. We're newbies, and you've played this many times before," Rory complained.

I laughed. "You've played Scotland Yard before with Mom and me. That makes you a little more experienced."

"Well, I played this for the first time, and it still took Tina nine moves to catch me," Jai added proudly. "Maybe I'm secretly a pro and will be able to beat both of you by the end of today."

"No way. It's impossible to beat me at this game," I boasted.

"Then show us by winning with only half the moves," Jai challenged me.

I smirked at my friends. "Challenge accepted."

Sure enough, Jai and Rory were still not able to beat me.

Rory threw his hands up in frustration as I guffawed loudly, mocking him. "I give up. This game is rigged."

I stuck my tongue out at him. "You are a sore loser. And I am a genius. Accept it."

"Yeah, yeah, beat me at *chess*, then I will accept your statement," Jai said, snickering.

"Don't ever play chess with Jai. He turns into a monster," Rory cautioned me.

Jai snickered at Rory's warning, but I flipped my hair mock-arrogantly, knowing chess was one of the most difficult war strategy games in the world, with intricate rules. "So what? You still can't beat me at Scotland Yard."

Our banter continued for some time when I suddenly started feeling drowsy and exhausted. I could feel the effect of the medication wearing off. I winced in pain, and my friends got up from their seats to make sure I was alright.

"T, please get some rest in your room," Rory suggested.

I went to my room without argument and plopped on the bed. I woke up with a start later and realized it was dark outside.

I saw that wristband in my dream just now. Was it really him?

Still groggy, I fumbled for a piece of paper inside my backpack. When I found it, I switched on the lights and examined the photograph carefully. It was the same picture that had led me to believe Pete Hilton was involved in the horrific crime at the fundraiser. Shaking Pete's hand was the person wearing a pink wristband.

He was the one who misled me by lying about a volunteers' meeting that day.

Parker's underling attacked me yesterday.

I dialed the number that Officer Hussein had provided me. "Hi, this is Tina Lauren. I was attacked last night at the MyWay New Year's party venue parking lot."

"Hello, Miss Lauren. How can I help you?" the police officer who picked up the call asked me.

"Actually, I called to ask if you found out who attacked me. Did they target me deliberately?"

"Oh, we found out that he was just a petty thief, who tried to mug you," the police officer answered.

Parker pulled strings again to hide the truth, huh?

"Did you want to report further information, Miss Lauren?" he asked.

"Yes, the person who stabbed me last night is the same one who misled me to the no-entry area at McCormick Park during the SCF fundraiser. He is a perp, along with Nicholas Parker and Pete Hilton, for the attempted ra-rape case," I replied.

"Thanks for the information. I have taken note of it and will inform the officers on this case."

I was gobsmacked after my call with the police, as it slowly began to sink in. Was this the price I had to pay for standing up for myself and fighting my abusers? Madison lost her scholarship, Aiden was ousted from the basketball team, and Rory was almost suspended from college. And I was almost killed!

Should I stop fighting altogether and succumb to my fate?

Absolutely not. I will fight back. No matter the consequences.

"Tina, are you awake? Your parents are here," Jai called out through my bedroom door.

I opened the door and gestured my best friend into my room.

"What's the matter, Little Monster?" Jai asked me. "You look like you saw a ghost."

"Fellow Monster, please introduce me to the AA Squad," I replied. "I can't sit idle doing nothing anymore."

CHAPTER 27

"Let's discuss this later, in private. I promise," Jai whispered to me as my parents entered my room. He greeted them and then left.

"Tina, you're awake." My mother rushed to my side and held me in her arms. "How are you feeling?"

"I'm much better, Mom. The sleep helped," I answered, hugging her back, loving the feeling of my mother's warmth.

"I'm so glad you're feeling better, dear."

"Why were you alone in the parking lot in the middle of the night?" my father demanded.

"Now, let's not interrogate her, Walt," Mom told Dad. "She's had a rough time already."

I smiled at her, grateful for the support. "Thanks."

"Fine. Both of you catch up. I will go and reheat dinner," Dad said, hugging me from the side.

After he left, I poured out my heart to my mother about everything from the assault at the fundraiser to the attack the previous day. My mother listened without interrupting, looking mortified. Once I was done, she took a long sip of water before speaking. "Wow. We had no idea that you were going through so much. Why didn't you confide in us?"

"I didn't want to worry you," I replied.

"You should move back in with us and transfer universities. I'm not comfortable leaving you here all alone," my mother said. "Let me discuss this with your dad."

I shook my head. "I want to stay and fight."

"But it's dangerous, Tina. And what you went through is traumatic."

"Mom, you're a prosecutor. You've tackled many such assault cases before," I pointed out.

"Yes, but you're my *daughter*," she argued. "It's different when it's personal."

I took both her hands in mine. "I need your help. I want all these perps sent to jail. I've pressed charges against them, but I know their lawyers will bail them out."

"Darren Parker will never ever let his son lose, Tina. The Parkers are too powerful and influential. I feel ashamed to say this, but it's best to let it go. You've done your best already by engaging the police."

I shook my head vehemently. "No. I will not give up until Nicholas Parker is punished for his crimes." I clasped her hands tightly. "Please, Mom. Is there nothing we can do?"

My mother's eyes welled up. "There is, but I'm scared of the consequences. It's not going to be an easy fight."

I smiled through my own tears. "I'm willing to do whatever it takes. Besides, haven't you put away worse criminals in jail?"

Mom sighed. "Yes, but my daughter was not involved then. That's why it was much easier."

"Dinner is served," Dad called out to us.

"Did you go to your therapist after that...that day?" my mother asked, referring to the SCF fundraiser. "I hope you didn't start—"

"I haven't hurt myself. I promise," I replied. "And I have an appointment with Dr. Kim tomorrow."

She smiled slightly. "Good."

My parents had brought ready-to-bake spanakopita from Recharge Café. I had tried the flaky Greek pastry filled with spinach, feta cheese, and other herbs before. It was one of my favorite menu items from the eatery.

"Not bad," my father said, with his mouth full. "I guess it lives up to the hype."

"Try this poutine," my mother told him. "It's delectable."

My father passed me our country's favorite crispy french fry dish, topped with the addictively flavorful gravy and stringy cheese curds.

"I have advised Tina against any fried food when she is on medication," Jai informed my parents. "Her stomach doesn't react well to strong pain killers."

"I ate only one spoonful, Mr. Future Doctor," I mumbled.

"Thank you for looking out for Tina when we aren't around," my mother said to Jai and Rory.

I beamed at my friends. "They both are the best."

"Hey, you forgot me," Madison said, bursting into the room with a bag from Recharge Café in her hands.

I squealed at the sight of my roommate and got up to hug her. "Mads, you're back."

Madison returned my embrace. "You better include me, else no dessert for you."

"Recharge Café again?" my father grumbled. "Don't you kids know any other place in Strollfield?"

I laughed. "Why did *you* go there, then?"

"Chef Okoro had given me a discount coupon the last time I met him," Dad answered. "But I see you eat there a lot. I see that half of your recycle bin is filled with boxes labeled 'Recharge Café.'"

We all laughed in response. Everyone talked and ate, but I couldn't help but let my mind wander back to my mother's worried expression when she implied that we might be making a mistake going against Nicholas Parker. I wished I had never whacked him in the face at the press conference in Duckville, even though he deserved it. Maybe then, I wouldn't be in this horrible situation.

No, I did the right thing by standing up for myself.

I forced myself to concentrate on the dinner table conversation. I could see everyone was making humungous efforts to lighten up the grim atmosphere. I owed it to my friends and family to participate.

"I don't want to go back to school. The holiday break was too short this year," Madison complained.

Rory groaned. "Tell me about it. I haven't completed my assignments either."

"Me either," Madison agreed. "Jai, how about you?"

Jai took a bite of his spanakopita. "I completed them the day before yesterday. What about you, Tina?"

"Don't ask her. She probably completed tasks that aren't due for another month," Madison answered for me.

I nodded and smiled.

"I hated holiday assignments during college, too, but Kiba here did everything in advance. That's where Tina gets it from," my father explained.

All of us talked more about our respective classes and interests. Even Jai, who was usually quiet around people, conversed easily with my parents. After dinner, Madison got dessert from the refrigerator. I felt a twinge in my heart when I saw the strawberry sorbet, because it reminded me of someone.

The feel of Ekon's lips against mine when we kissed—he had tasted like strawberries.

I mentally kicked myself for rejecting Ekon at MyWay's party. We could be together right now instead of me yearning for him. I told him I wasn't ready for a relationship. Why had I done that? The more I thought about it now, the more my reasons seemed weak.

Lost deep in thought, I analyzed my reasons, my inner voices battling it out:

Why am I not ready for a relationship?
One, I'm not comfortable with intimacy.
But I have improved a lot now. Besides, Ekon has always respected my personal space.
Two, I need to concentrate on making Parker and his underlings pay.
But what has that got to do with me being in a relationship?
Three, I'm afraid of betrayal and heartbreak.
But Ekon has shown me he's here for me. Not being with him is heartbreaking as well.
Four, I have a lot on my plate.

Like what? Just assignments, skating, coding, karate, online tutoring. That's usual stuff.

I sighed, spooning some strawberry sorbet into my mouth. These sounded less like logical reasons and more like lame excuses.

I hated my rational and analytical mind.

***

Jai and Rory left after dessert, and Madison helped my parents clean up. All of them ordered me to get back to my room and rest when I offered to help. I sat on my bed, clouded by pessimistic thoughts. What would Parker try next? He had already hurt my friends and me. What if he came after my parents as well? Should I isolate myself from everyone so that no one else is affected?

I must not let Parker get to me.

"Tina, are you awake?" my father asked, knocking on my bedroom door.

"Yes, I was planning to come and chat with you," I replied.

My mom followed him in, and my parents took a seat with me on my futon.

"You still didn't get a bed frame," my father pointed out.

I froze at my father's sudden statement, but I managed to mutter a response. "I haven't had the time."

My mother did not take the topic further. She placed her hand on my shoulder. "How is the pain now? Did you take your prescription?"

"It's better," I replied. "I got thirteen stitches, so it'll take some time to subside. The medication helps, though."

"Tina, have you considered moving to Birch Town with us?" my father asked me. He didn't meet my eyes, so it was obvious that Mom had told him about the assault. "You can get a fresh start there."

"I already spoke to her about it," Mom chipped in. "But she wants to stay and fight."

Believe me, I have thought about leaving the country, because that's how scared I am.

"What if I face the same thing in Birch Town again, Dad?" I asked. "I kept quiet when it happened in Duckville. Did it prevent anything?"

Dad sighed. "We just want you to be safe."

"The only way I can ensure my peers and I are safe is by getting the perps behind bars," I said. "I need your and Mom's support to do that."

"I'll talk to my contacts at the Crown Counsel that can help with your case," Mom said after a pause. "The police need to complete their investigation first, though."

"Thanks, Mom."

"And I'll see if we can hire you a personal bodyguard," Dad added.

"What? No way," I exclaimed. "That's completely unnecessary. I'm learning karate and will get better at defending myself."

Dad crossed his arms across his chest. "Fine. Then I have some ground rules. You will text us your whereabouts every two hours, you will be home by 10:00 p.m. every night, and you will not venture out alone in the dark or to isolated areas. And these are nonnegotiable."

I nodded. "Yes, sir."

"Good night, Tina. Get some rest now," my mother said. "We need to check into our hotel before the deadline."

I hugged both my parents tightly, and we didn't let go for several minutes. Though they didn't say it in words, I knew what their gentle patting on my back meant. "What happened was not your fault, Tina. And we are proud of you for fighting back."

Still, a part of me wished I had heard it out loud.

CHAPTER 28

The next day was the first day back at school after the holidays. Jai drove me to the university as I was advised to take it easy for at least a week. I had slept well last night and felt all geared up for the winter term. Having my parents over had cheered me up further, and I had almost forgotten about the attack on New Year's Eve.

It was bright and sunny outside. If not for the snow, anyone would have mistaken it to be summer. I craved to go ice skating again, but I couldn't, at least for a month, until my wound completely healed.

"So, I still don't get it," I said as Jai drove. "Rory, Madison, and Aiden helped me file a complaint against Pete at the university. But they faced the wrath for it. Then why did Pete get expelled? And why was he not tried at the student court?"

"The university, under pressure from the Parkers, was planning to brush the whole Pete issue under the carpet; however, the AA Squad complained to the police about the assault video. Hence, the dean was forced to expel Pete," Jai replied.

"Wow, you guys are incredible," I exclaimed. "I've thought about your offer. Can I join you? I'd like to help other people the way the AA Squad helped me."

Jai smiled. "Definitely. I already invited you."

"Isn't the AA squad scared of the consequences, though?" I asked. "Look at what happened to Madison, Aiden, and Rory for supporting me."

"Are you going to give up on your fight, then?" Jai asked back.

I shook my head. "Of course not. But I'm not involving my friends anymore."

Jai smiled. "Except me. Because we will fight Parker and his underlings together. You, me, and the rest of the AA Squad."

I grinned back at my best friend and comrade. "Yes, we will."

After chatting a little more, Jai left for his classes, and I walked toward mine. I got a call from an unknown number, and I picked it up.

"Hi, Tina. I'm Amanda Wilkins. I got your number from my brother, Aiden," the caller said.

I greeted her. "Hi, Amanda. How are you doing?"

Amanda sighed. "I wish I could say I'm alright, but I'm not. Can we meet sometime this week, please? There's something I want to discuss with you in private."

"Sure. I'm available this Saturday," I replied.

"Great, can you come to the Strollfield Drive-in theater at 5:00 p.m.?" she asked.

I nodded. "See you then."

In class, I doodled hearts around Ekon's name on the last page of my notebook absentmindedly, forcing myself not to worry about Parker's next move to harass me. I tried to concentrate on the class, but the professor was droning on and on, boring us all to tears. I had already completed all my assignments for this class for the next two weeks, and it was pointless for me to be here. But I was never one to skip classes without a valid reason.

I continued to play silly compatibility games with Ekon's and my name and wondered how to communicate with him. There was a high chance that he would refuse to date me, because I had hurt him multiple times, but I still wanted to tell him how I felt.

I looked at my page in horror when I saw the poem I had just scribbled.

Chef cutie

Eyes beauty

Strawberries tasty
Sexy booty

I struck the last line as many times as I could, aghast at the language.

Ekon Okoro, what have you turned me into?

CHAPTER 29

I was extremely embarrassed by my behavior in class that day and ate lunch quietly with Jai at our usual place on the stairs. I hadn't said a word all afternoon because I couldn't get that poem out of my mind. I felt guilty for objectifying a person and scared that I had such carnal thoughts. Anything related to se-sex frightened me, and I was unable to even utter that word without stuttering.

Thank goodness, I have an appointment with Dr. Kim this evening.

Seeing me in distress, Jai placed two extra deep-fried kodubales, or ring-shaped savory and spicy, crispy South Indian snacks, on my plate, and I smiled at him gratefully. We never ever pressed each other to share anything that we were not comfortable with, and yet, we disclosed secrets to each other first. Recently, Jai had confided in me that he wanted to try sitting in the cafeteria, but he needed time to muster the courage. Needless to say, I would support my best friend in his decision whenever he was ready.

After classes, Jai dropped me at Dr. Kim's clinic on the way to work. My therapist's room calmed me down instantly with the pleasant ylang ylang aroma and her amiable presence. I talked to her about the last few months and how I had overcome many of my fears.

"I'm glad to see that you're doing better, Tina. And you've made so much progress. I'm proud of you," Dr. Kim praised me.

I beamed at her compliment. It had been three months since I'd last had a session, and it felt good to evaluate how far I'd come. "Thank you, Dr. Kim. I, too, feel like I've made progress. And for the first time, I have a crush on someone."

Dr. Kim smiled at me. "That's wonderful."

"Actually, it's not just a crush. We both feel the same way," I continued.

Dr. Kim's grin grew wider. "I'm happy for you."

I sighed. "I kind of blew it, though."

"Why do you say that?" Dr. Kim asked.

"I thought I wasn't ready when Ekon asked me out. But now I miss him too much," I admitted, biting my tongue. "Oops, I wasn't supposed to say his name."

"Don't worry, what we discuss here is completely confidential," Dr. Kim reassured me.

I nodded. "I'd feel foolish initiating a relationship with him after saying no," I said.

"Why?"

I shrugged. "Won't he think I'm stupid to change my mind so many times?"

Dr. Kim leaned forward a little. "Wouldn't anyone be happy if they learned that the person they're interested in feels the same way?"

"Yes, I guess so." I smiled. I took a deep breath before broaching the actual topic that bothered me all afternoon. "Dr. Kim, like I have told you before, I have always attached negative connotations to attraction. How do I get over that?"

"What do you mean by 'negative connotations?'" she asked.

"Earlier today, I wrote a poem, which was, um, lewd. I've never had such carnal feelings before, and I got scared. I wasn't ashamed, and didn't feel dirty like I used to a year ago, but..." I trailed off.

"Describe your fears to me," Dr. Kim gently prodded. "What scares you?"

"What if the person I care about sees this side of me and turns into a se-sexual predator?" I stuttered. "I know it sounds illogical, but I can't help but worry. Up until now, I had no reason to fear this, because I thought I couldn't be attracted to anyone. But now..."

"It's not illogical. Everyone worries about their relationship taking an unexpected unpleasant turn," Dr. Kim said. "For you, this is especially difficult because of everything you've been through. You need to try to go easy on yourself and give yourself time to overcome these fears. Now, can you elaborate on how you felt when you had these desires? You don't have to get into details of the poem if you don't want to."

I could feel my face going red when I described my feelings. "I get stomach flip-flops and a warm fuzzy feeling inside my chest. I replay our kiss over and over in my mind and crave more intimacy. Later, though, all these fears cloud my mind."

"Do you enjoy all these feelings you just described?" Dr. Kim asked. "Other than the fears?"

I nodded. "Yes, when I feel this way, a happy grin is plastered on my face. I am more cheerful, positive, and *alive*."

Dr. Kim smiled. "Isn't that a good thing?"

I nodded again. "It is." I paused for a moment. "But I can't help but feel that I have many foes. I mean, isn't one antagonist enough in my life?"

"I wish life could guarantee that we will have only one problem or one person that causes trouble, but unfortunately, that's not the case most often," Dr. Kim replied.

I sighed. "I just feel I have too many to handle."

"It's okay to feel like that." Dr. Kim agreed with me. She added, "Don't you have a solid support system now, though, to help you handle it all? You told me you couldn't have made it this far without your family and friends."

I nodded. "That's right." I paused for a moment. "I know my parents love me and will protect me as best they can. But I really wish they would talk to me about...about the abuse I've faced. They came over, cutting their trip short when they heard I had been attacked. They are even supportive of my decision to put the perpetrators behind bars, but they never speak about what happened."

"What do you want them to say?" she asked.

I thought for a moment. "I just want them to be on my side. I mean, I *know* they are. But I want to hear it from their mouths. And I want to tell them I don't blame them anymore. But they change the subject whenever it comes up."

"Think of it this way," Dr. Kim spoke in a soothing manner. "None of it was your fault, Tina. It's not theirs either. And you're all hurting from it."

I sighed. "Am I wrong to feel this way about Mom and Dad, Dr. Kim?"

She shook her head. "No. You're not wrong. But we all are different and cope with things in our own way. For your parents, the method to deal with this is to try not to think about it. And that's okay too."

Dr. Kim made sense as usual. She rarely gave me answers about anything and made me think for myself, but her insight always helped me immensely.

I smiled at her. "You're awesome, Dr. Kim."

"Right back at you, Tina." She beamed back.

***

That evening, I sat at my desk in my room after my online tutoring sessions with my diary open. I jotted down game ideas for Recharge Café customers. This was my excuse to see Ekon again. After three hours of brainstorming, I had come up with two games—one for people to play anytime and gain points that they could exchange for discount coupons, and one for playing while they waited for a vacant table.

I opened my laptop and tried to type the code for the games, but my mind went blank as usual. I closed my eyes in frustration and clenched my fists, digging my nails into my palms. The disappointment and disapproving expressions of the Strollfield Cultural Festival's chief organizers when they fired me flashed in my mind.

I'm a really good coder. Just because I was unfairly ousted from the festival's team doesn't make me any less of a programmer. I love it, and I will not let an unfortunate incident make me quit.

I tried to listen to my inner voice, but I still couldn't type a single line of the code. I thought it would be magic. I would say "I can do it" and perform immediately. But that was not the case.

I sighed. *I need to find another excuse to meet Ekon. The café app cannot be it.*

But what if my application to be on the Court Us app development team is approved? I don't want to look bad.

I was about to give up and close my laptop when I decided to go through my old work to get some inspiration. I browsed all the programs I had written since I was ten. I smiled at the first game I had created. The hours of effort on these, and my improvement over the years, was obvious.

My heart soared when I saw the high school prom web application code I had written. The app helped plan and organize any school event in an efficient manner, which saved a lot of time and effort. They had even presented me with a trophy—even though I skipped prom—because the committee felt the app had revolutionized event management in Duckville High. One of the reasons I was chosen as the high school "star student" was because of how valuable my creation was.

What was the use? All that was in the past. Then, Parker came into my life like a parasite and ruined it.

I heard Nicholas Parker snickering in my mind. "You're my pathetic prey."

I clenched my fists under my desk and shook my head violently. No, I couldn't let him win.

I can do this. Even if it's one line per day. I will code again, because I love it, and I am excellent at it. No one can take that away from me. No one.

My inner voice was right. I copied my own code from a game I had developed when I was younger and tried to improve it.

It took me an hour, but I smiled when I had the new version ready, and it ran smoothly.

Baby steps, Tina. As long as I am making progress.

CHAPTER 30

The rest of the week breezed past as my routine resumed in full swing after the holiday break. I was exhausted at the end of each day, but still found time to code for an hour or so. I finished creating the games for Recharge Café and was now working on a new project. My application to be on the app development team for Court Us, the student court of Strollfield University, had been accepted, and I had loads to do every evening.

It was good that I kept myself busy, because otherwise I would have been a nervous wreck. It had been almost two weeks since I pressed charges, but the only message I received was: "The investigation is in progress, and we will keep you posted on any updates."

The only ray of hope I saw regarding my fight against Parker and Hilton was my meeting with the AA Squad later this week. I had circled the date on my calendar and waited anxiously for the day to arrive.

On Saturday morning, I drove to the address Jai had provided me. He had instructed me to wait for him outside. Jai arrived within a few minutes, and I followed him into a large glass building.

"I feel like I've entered Gramps's greenhouse," I said. "It's massive compared to his, though, and has so many more plants."

Jai nodded. "All this belongs to AA. You should see her garden during summer. It's spectacular."

"Wow!"

I continued walking behind Jai, mesmerized by the potted plants and smaller saplings. Each one of them was labeled neatly with the scientific taxonomy and the common name. They also had their native region, environmental requirements, and other facts. I could spend an entire day admiring this lush green museum.

I was almost disappointed when we exited the greenhouse through the back door and entered another heated shed. But I squealed delightfully when I heard familiar barks.

"Ribster! Dexter! My dearest friends, what are you guys doing here?" I squealed.

They licked my hand affectionately as I petted them.

"Had I known you'd be here, I would have brought you some treats. You both saved my lives."

"So, you both are ignoring me now that your new friend is here," Jai said, tickling the dogs playfully.

I laughed. "I've known them for over two years, since they were in Adopt-A-Friend shelter. *You're* the new friend."

Jai gave me a surprised look. "What do you mean?"

I told him about Adopt-A-Friend and how the two dogs had saved my life on New Year's Eve.

"Wow, it's a really small world," Jai exclaimed.

"But they love *me* the most, don't you?" a tall girl with wavy black hair said, her smile reaching her striking eyes. "That's because I'm their Mommy now."

Ribster and Dexter forgot Jai and me and jumped on the girl, who laughed and hugged them. She looked up at us and waved, her arms still around the two dogs. "Hi, Jai. Hey, Tina."

Jai waved to her. "Hi, Win."

"I like your luscious black curls so much," I said, forgetting to greet her back.

When I realized that I had uttered those words out loud, I wanted to bury myself right there. The girl looked amused, and Jai stifled his laughter.

"Sorry, I've always wanted curly or wavy hair," I clarified. I added sheepishly, "Anyway, it's nice to meet you. Are you Ribster's and Dexter's owner?"

The girl nodded. "I'm Winona."

"Wait a minute, was it *you* who saved my life during New Year's?" I asked, not realizing I was shouting.

"Ribs and Dex found you. So the credit goes to them," Winona replied. "And Jai and Ekon called the squad the minute they realized you'd left the party."

"How did you know I was in danger?" I pressed for details.

"Ribster and Dexter were relentlessly barking that night trying to release themselves from their leashes. They hardly ever do that. When I was forced to let go of them, they rushed to the Strollfield Convention Center parking lot," Winona explained.

"Wow, I'm speechless," I said, a shiver going down my spine recalling how I'd been almost killed that night. "I can't thank you all enough. I owe you, Ribster, Dexter, and Jai a big one."

Winona smiled. "I hardly did anything."

I shook my head. "You knocked my attacker out with a single blow. That was awesome."

"Win is an expert in Martial Arts and has a black belt in both taekwondo and karate. She is also an expert in okichitaw, the indigenous combat art system," Jai said. "That's super impressive but she's too modest to admit it."

Winona blushed at Jai's compliment. "That's not a big deal, though, considering that I started when I was still in my diapers."

"It *is* a big deal. Three martial arts? That's amazing," I exclaimed. "I started karate a little over a year ago and I know how tough it is. You're awesome, Winona."

Winona beamed at us. "Thanks."

"And um, sorry for commenting on your hair earlier. I didn't realize I was saying that out loud," I said.

She smiled. "I liked that you complimented my hair. No one has called it luscious before."

"I meant it. My stick-straight hair is boring," I said.

"No, yours is silky smooth. I want hair like that," Winona replied.

It was surprising how comfortable I felt with this stranger. It was not like me to discuss topics like hair with someone I barely knew. As we walked to the meeting room, Winona spoke about herself. She was a second-year student at the Strollfield Law School and had been a member of AA Squad since its inception two years ago. She helped AA start the group to support survivors to stand up against their abusers and bullies.

"And we've finally reached the venue," Winona said, unlocking the meeting room door. "The next time, I will remember to unlock the front entrance so that we don't have to walk through the whole greenhouse."

"I didn't mind it at all. Besides, I had a lot of fun looking at the plants in the greenhouse," I said.

"Let's settle down soon. We begin in a few minutes," a robotic voice said.

"That's AA," Jai whispered to me.

I took a seat between Jai and Winona in the brightly lit meeting room. It was empty except for a white table and six matching chairs. At the center of the table was a sleek silver conference phone.

I wondered why AA didn't join us personally when this was her place.

"Here you go. This is the access card to enter next time," a boy with brown hair said, startling me. He seemed to have appeared out of nowhere. He handed me a card.

Nicholas Parker.

"You. Why are you here?" I asked, getting up from my seat angrily. "Is this some kind of a joke?" I stared around the table at Winona and then Jai. How could they have set me up like this?

"Excuse me?"

"I'm sorry, I should have introduced you both, first," Winona interjected, standing between us. "Tina, this is *Nate* Parker."

I scowled. He could have been Nicholas's twin, they looked so much alike. "*Nate* Parker? Are you related to—"

"Sharing DNA with someone does not make me the same as them," Nate insisted.

I scoffed. "Oh please. How am I supposed to believe that? When you resemble that sicko so much that you could very well be the same person?"

Jai placed his hand on mine lightly. "Trust me, Tina. He's not at all like—"

"That's enough," boomed AA's robotic voice, silencing everyone in the room. "If you have a problem with Nate, leave. Now."

"AA, you can't blame Tina for feeling this way. Don't forget what she's been through because of Nicholas," Winona reasoned with AA. She turned to me. "Nate's not at all like Nicholas, Tina. Trust us on this."

Jai squeezed my hand reassuringly and nodded.

"Nate has done a lot of things in your favor," Winona continued. "He stopped the fabricated sex video of you and Nicholas from playing further at Duckville High graduation ceremony."

"That's right. And Nate was the one who tracked down Nicholas at the SCF fundraiser and sent Ekon to the no entry area," AA added. She paused for a moment and cleared her throat. "I'm sorry I was rude, Tina. It's just that I'm protective toward Nate. He is a cyber genius but the youngest member of our squad."

"I'm almost eighteen. Stop treating me like a child," Nate grumbled.

Winona reached out and patted Nate's hand in a caring way. She seemed like a mother hen of the group. "Did Nate prove that influencer Ina's social media post was fake and mine was real too?" I asked meekly.

Winona nodded. "That's correct."

Wow.

I sat in dumb disbelief, trying to process all the information I had just received. AA Squad had been secretly looking out for me for longer than I ever thought, and *Ekon* was a part of this group? A shudder went down my spine as I recalled the horrific assault at the fundraiser. Things could have been worse, much worse if not for the AA Squad.

I stood from my seat and bowed my head. "I'm sorry, Nate. And thank you all for looking out for me."

"Welcome to the squad, Tina. We are happy to have you on board," AA said. "I will warn you though, what we do is not easy. We've tried to catch Nicholas Parker many times but have never succeeded. A few times, we were almost close, but some of our previous members ran away like cowards scared of Parker's threats."

I felt that AA's words were unnecessarily harsh. Even though she didn't bracket me, it was uncalled for to refer to the other victims as cowards. Abuse is a traumatic incident, and each survivor can react to it differently. If they choose not to fight against the perp, it's their choice. We aren't to judge them.

"Not to say all other survivors are cowards," Winona clarified quickly, echoing my opinion.

"I know I sounded harsh. But I just wish they had a little more courage. Think about how many crimes we could have prevented if they hadn't run away," AA said. She added after a pause. "Anyway, Nicholas has gotten away way too many times for his crimes. We want to get him this time."

I nodded. "It's been two weeks since I pressed charges against him and Pete. I haven't heard anything from the police. It says the investigation is in progress."

Nate opened his laptop and attached three screen extensions. "I could find out what happened—"

"N, no hacking the police servers. We already talked about this," AA said. "We don't do illegal stuff at the squad."

I looked at Jai and gave him a "What the heck? Nate is a hacker?" look. Jai nodded and mouthed, "It's okay."

Being a coder, I had taken extra care to secure my devices against hacking and malware. Seeing how casually Nate was talking about hacking into a government website, I was unsure if my attempts were enough to protect my phone and laptop.

"What about the illegal stuff that Nicholas pulls off every time?" Nate exclaimed. "Is that okay? He has no criminal record, even after so many reports filed against him. Either he terrorizes his victims until they take the complaint back, or his lawyers don't even let the charges proceed to a court hearing by digging up dirt on the victims. I'm sick of following rules all the time."

"But if you get caught doing anything unlawful, your future will be ruined, Nate. You're still a high school student, a minor," Winona said.

Nate sighed. "I'm in my senior year, so soon-to-be major. Fine, I will stay put. But I never leave traces. I've been tracking Nicholas's phone for two years now, and he doesn't even have a clue."

"Are you tracking mine too?" I asked.

Nate shook his head. "No. Not without your permission."

"We all share our locations with each other most of the time. It helps keeping track of each other in case one of us is in danger," Jai said. "But it's not a rule."

"You can contact Nate after the meeting if you're on board too," AA told me.

"Okay, back to the subject of catching Nicholas. Tina, can you tell us more about the police reports you filed?" Winona asked.

I elaborated on the details of the charges I had pressed against Nicholas and Pete. "I couldn't find out details on who attacked me, though. It was the same person who lied about a volunteer's meet at the fundraiser."

"That was Sudesh. He used to 'run errands' for Nicholas to pay for his mother's expensive prescriptions. She is chronically ill," Nate said. "Nicholas has now cut him off because he was arrested."

I sighed. "Yes, the police told me that my attacker was just a petty thief and had no connections with any prior crimes."

"This always happens. The last time someone stood up to Nicholas, his father ensured the victim's parents were fired from their jobs. She and her family were forced to retract their police complaint against Nicholas and leave the city," AA said.

I gasped. "I feel so terrible for the survivor."

"Yes. And that was for rape," Winona stated, and my face fell.

I had heard people talking about a se-sexual assault incident at the freshman party last year. But I had paid little attention to it because I had hit rock bottom after my self-harm video had been leaked. As usual, the students had blamed the survivor. Some even said that she was dating Nicholas and had falsely accused him.

Winona turned toward me and placed her hand on mine, bringing me back to the present. "Tina, it's good that you pressed charges. But I'm afraid it's not enough to get Nicholas to jail."

I swallowed the lump in my throat. "I know. That's why I joined the squad."

"Yes, you're in the right place. And one day, we'll get him," AA said. "He's wronged all of us and deserves to pay for his crimes."

I wondered if anyone else would share how Nicholas Parker had tormented them, but the awkward silence that lingered in the room, and everyone's grave expressions, revealed the truth. Our wounds were deep, and the horrific memories were still fresh in everyone's minds.

But at least this was a safe space where we all could share each other's pain—without the need to utter even a single word.

CHAPTER 31

"Tina, why haven't you left?" AA asked in her morphed robotic voice. "The meeting is over."

I got up from my seat. "Sorry, I didn't realize that. Where's Winona?"

"Win had to leave. Ribster and Dexter had an appointment with their vet," AA replied.

"Are you okay?" Jai asked me.

I shook my head. "No. I'm not alright. I'm scared. I regret the day I stood up to Nicholas and got myself into this mess. And frankly, I just want to run away from all of this. Go ahead, AA. Call me a coward. I don't care."

"You're not a coward," AA said. "It takes a lot of guts to stand up for yourself. Even if there are terrible repercussions. It's been over a year since you hit Nicholas in the face at the press conference. Since then, you've been outcast by almost everyone at the university. But you have stood by what you believe without budging even once. That shows you're courageous."

Jai nodded. "AA's right. Even now, you work on all group assignments alone, Tina. And you're the only one in your class that does that. It's not easy."

I sighed. "I appreciate both of you trying to make me feel better but look at what happened to the assault survivor from last year's freshman party. You said so yourself that she had to leave everything behind when she did nothing wrong. How can I be sure that my plight won't be the same in a few weeks?"

AA scoffed. "You think you're the only one that's scared? Why do you think I morph my voice and keep my identity hidden, even from the squad members whom I trust the most? Why do you think Nate has spent a ton of money on cybersecurity? Why do you think Winona has learned *three* martial arts? It's because we all are afraid."

"Tina, do you want anyone else to suffer the same way you did at the hands of Nicholas Parker?" Jai asked.

I was taken aback by Jai's sudden question. I saw that his eyes had welled up and he blinked back his tears fiercely. I wanted to stand up and hug my best friend right then, but I didn't want to embarrass him in front of the others.

I shook my head vigorously. "No way."

"It's up to you, Tina. You're free to do whatever you like. Don't feel obliged to stay because we helped you. We didn't do it just for you. We did it for *us*," AA said. "We fight because we survivors deserve better."

AA's practical talk pepped me up.

I smiled. "I'm in. Let's work together to punish Nicholas and his underlings."

Jai high-fived me in response and Nate grinned.

"Okay, I'm glad to hear that," AA said. "I've got to go now."

"Um, AA, Before you leave, can I ask a question?"

"Yes, Tina?"

"Why did you choose the name AA?"

AA laughed with her morphed voice. "You really want to know?"

I nodded, wondering how AA's real voice would sound. Her robotic laugh had a cute ring to it.

AA giggled again. "The three founding members of the squad Win, N, and I argued like crazy about the name. We finally went with the first letter of the alphabet. Only 'A' sounded too boring, so we went with AA. It's a fond memory now. And it's just a coincidence that my real name has two A's in it."

I smiled. "Thank you for sharing that with us."

"Alrighty, bye squad."

I asked Jai to go on ahead as I wanted to apologize to Nate for my earlier behavior. It was wrong of me to speak to him so rudely just because he was related to Nicholas. After all, my dad and that child abuser demon Wilbur Lauren had *nothing* in common.

Nate still had his face buried in his computer. I knocked lightly on his laptop to get his attention when I noticed scars near his wrist. My eyes widened at the intensity of the pink bumps on his skin, but I composed myself immediately when I saw Nate pull his sleeves down to cover them.

"Nate, I'm truly sorry for being rude to you earlier," I said. "And thank you for everything you have done for me so far."

"It's fine," Nate replied. "Besides, I'd do it for anyone Nicholas tries to hurt. We can't let him get away with his crimes."

"I agree. Um, Nate, can you help me set up the location sharing feature, please? While you're at it, do you mind checking if my phone security is good enough?"

Nate examined my device. "Sure, let's see what you've got."

Nate connected my phone to his laptop and examined it for a few minutes. He nodded slightly and turned the device to me. "Okay, so your security layer isn't bad, but it's not the best either. Did you create it yourself?"

"I modified a popular app based on my needs. What's the problem with it?"

Nate explained to me in four sentences the risks I could face and the possible remedies. He was clear, crisp, and concise.

"So, if we add this code to your phone, it's harder for criminals like Nicholas to access it illegally."

I gave him a surprised look. "Does that sicko have the tech skills to do that?"

Nate shook his head. "No, but he has hired phishers and cyber criminals in the past."

"Whoa. But I am sure they aren't half as smart as you."

Nate cracked a small grin.

"Hey, can you help me with coding in the future, in case I have questions? I would love to learn from the expert."

Nate smiled at me, his eyes lighting up like a child's for the first time since we had met. "Sure. Feel free to text me."

Nicholas Parker and Nate Parker are not alike. At all.

***

Jai was still waiting for me at the parking lot. I smiled and ran toward my best friend, eager to chat more about the squad. "Fellow Monster, thank you for getting me on board the AA Squad."

"No problem. You're the right fit here, so we are grateful to have you on board. Doesn't it feel wonderful to finally be a part of a group where people empathize with you instead of shunning you?"

I nodded. "Yes. And the best part is, no one asks to share anything we don't want to and there is no judgment."

"True."

"So, how is Nate related to that sicko Nicholas? I didn't want to ask him directly."

"Half brother. They share the same father," Jai replied. "Nate never speaks about his mother. I just know that he doesn't live with the other Parkers. Other than that, it's all hear-say talk. There are all kinds of scandalous rumors about him and his family."

"It must be terrible dealing with that."

Jai nodded. "Unfortunately, all of us at the squad can relate to being judged all too well."

We stood in silence for a few seconds. My mind drifted back to my own painful memories of being treated like an outcast in the university. Now that I had people who got me, it felt worse to go back to that environment on Monday. I tried to shake my pessimistic thoughts away and focus on something else.

Ekon Okoro.

I was itching to ask Jai about Ekon's role in the squad but didn't want to reveal my crush on the handsome chef. Why was he not at the meeting today? He probably had work. Recharge Café was open on Saturdays. Was he an active member? Would I see him in future meetings?

"So, is this the usual meeting venue?" I asked Jai instead.

"The only other place we use is Recharge Café. It has conference rooms that we can rent for meetings. But we hardly meet in person. Most of the time, we interact on the AA Squad chat group," Jai answered.

I opened my phone and saw an invitation from Nate to join the chat group. I clicked on the link and was delighted to see Ekon's name pop up in the list of members.

Jai nudged me. "Ekon is an active member of our squad. You will get to see him next time."

"I-I never asked about him."

Jai grinned at me with a mischievous glint in his eyes. "Thought you might want to know."

CHAPTER 32

That afternoon, after the meeting with the AA Squad, I drove to Recharge Café to meet Ekon. My excuse was to show him the games I had developed for the café's mobile app, but my real reason to meet him was to ask him out.

I got out of my car, took a deep breath, and entered the café. A friendly cashier greeted me and asked me what I'd like. I looked around and saw the blackboard with Ekon's neat handwriting—"Today's Special—South African fried snack vetkoek."

"I will have one plate of that, please," I said, pointing to the board. "And could you please let Chef Okoro know that Tina Lauren is here to see him?"

I sat at a booth, my heart beating loudly. What if Ekon rejected me, or worse, laughed at me? Maybe I should just walk away. No one would know.

Before I could run away, though, my order was ready, and the deep-fried golden balls of dough made me change my mind. I tried to cut the vetkoek with my knife but was unsuccessful. I placed my cutlery to the side and dug in with my fingers.

The fritters were piping hot, but I managed to get a bite-sized piece in my mouth. The crunch was so satisfying I moaned softly. I spooned some curry onto the vetkoek and closed my eyes when the flavors and spices coated my mouth. The meat was so succulent it melted in my mouth. Without wasting a single minute, I dunked the entire ball into the curry and wolfed it down.

I blew on the next fritter to cool it down and bit into it. I was pleasantly surprised when a string of cheese erupted from its center. The more I pulled on it, the further it stretched.

"You wanted to see me, Tina?"

I looked up to see Ekon, who was trying hard not to laugh. I felt embarrassed for being caught amidst my wrestling match with the cheese.

I cut the string of cheese with the knife and placed the fritter back on the plate. I swallowed the piece in my mouth, though it burned my throat, and wiped my hands with a paper napkin casually.

"Hi, Ekon. How have you been?" I asked him calmly, though I wanted to mentally kick myself for not ordering just a drink. At least I wouldn't want the earth to open up and absorb me right now.

Ekon raised his eyebrows. "Did you come here to ask me that?" He immediately softened his annoyed tone. "I mean, I need to ask you that first, after what happened on New Year's Eve."

"I'm much better, thanks," I replied. "So…I came here because I developed these mobile app games for you and wanted to present them."

"You'll need to set up a meeting with Sharon for that," he replied.

I miss you, and I was an idiot for running away from you.

"How are Sharon and everyone else?" I asked him instead, unable to broach the actual topic I wanted to talk about.

Ekon got up from his seat. "You can talk to them anytime you want, Tina. I'm sorry, but I need to leave now if you don't have anything else to say. I have to work."

I raised my voice a bit to get his attention. "Wait. Give me two minutes."

Ekon looked startled but didn't say anything.

I put my hand into my bag, fished out a note, and gave it to him. "I just came to give you this. Read it when I leave."

I walked out of the café shaking my head, disappointed in myself. I was such a coward and couldn't even convey my feelings properly to Ekon.

I hoped my note got my feelings across to him.

There was once a girl who met a guy
She fell for him when he met her eye
She resisted, she denied
She ran away, she cried
But in her heart, she couldn't say goodbye

Will you go out with me, Eko?

***

After the awkward meeting with Ekon at Recharge Café, I drove to meet Amanda, Aiden's sister. I went to the drive-in theater and found an empty spot. A few minutes later, Aiden's car pulled up next to mine, and a girl in an oversized coat, with long blond hair and blue eyes, stepped out. The resemblance to her brother was uncanny. While Aiden had golden blond hair, Amanda's was darker. But both had the same eyes.

I opened the passenger door of my car for her so we could talk. Amanda took a seat, removed her sunglasses, and greeted me. "Thanks for meeting up with me today."

"Hi, Amanda," I greeted her back with a smile. "How are you doing?"

"What I am about to share with you is confidential. I feel I can trust you, and that's why I am opening up to you. Can you promise not to breathe a word to anyone?" Amanda continued without answering my question.

I nodded. "Yes, you can trust me. My lips are sealed. What do you need my help with?"

"I want to lodge a complaint against someone," Amanda answered my question. She continued. "There is this teacher in school, Ms. Shera. She is the principal's daughter. She doesn't deserve to be called a teacher at all because… because she touches us inappropriately and—" Amanda's voice broke off.

I felt nauseated in the pit of my stomach. I knew exactly what Amanda was talking about. I wanted to push Amanda from my car and drive away, but I would never be able to forgive myself if I did that.

I need to focus on Amanda and give her my full attention. This is not about me.

My inner voice was right. I waited for Amanda to continue, nodding slightly to show her that I was listening to her attentively.

"It's not just me. It's Affy and Yash, my friends in my band, who face this as well. It has been happening for months now, and we want to take action against this perverted teacher," Amanda went on. "I came to you because I thought you'd understand. I've seen your viral social media post so many times, and it was clear you're someone who empathizes with survivors like me. I didn't know who else to confide in."

My heart went out to the fifteen-year-old girl, whose blue eyes were filled with hope. But how could I be of any help to her?

"Tina, I'm sorry if I made you uncomfortable," Amanda broke into my thoughts. "I'll leave now."

"No, you didn't make me uncomfortable at all," I assured her. "I'm sorry that you and your friends are going through this terrible trauma. It's courageous of you to speak out about it."

Amanda covered her face with her hands. "It's getting too much. I can't eat, sleep, study, or practice music because the trauma of the abuse haunts me. My friends and I have started drinking to forget the pain, but it helps only temporarily."

I clenched my fists angrily, tempted to punch this perverted teacher, Ms. Shera, until she yelped in pain. But I had to control my own emotions and focus on Amanda's.

"You know, everyone loves Ms. Shera. No one would believe that she is a pedophile. She has my parents on her side and has promised them that she would recommend me to one of the best music schools in the world. In fact, she is the one who encouraged Affy, Yashpreet, and me to perform at the upcoming SCF this year. She tells us she loves us all the time."

I could relate to *exactly* what Amanda was talking about and my nausea intensified. But I let her continue without saying anything.

"But I read about people like her online and realized I was being wronged. I decided to report her to our school counselor, but Ms. Shera caught me before I could do that. She stroked my shoulder and quietly threatened me. 'Ammy, do you want to ruin your future? You know what will happen if you anger Ms. Shera, don't you?' Scared, I ran back to class. Since then, Shera has been more violent toward me. And I can't take it anymore. What do I do?"

My nails dug into my palm further. Abusers always do this. They emotionally manipulate victims to get away with their crimes.

"There are many things you *could* do, but only you know the extent of pain you're facing. It's not right for me to give you any advice," I replied, choosing my words carefully.

"What would you do if you were in my place?"

Keep my secret buried. Every time my traumatic memories threatened to resurface, harm myself until it stopped. Then one day, when my shameful truth is exposed—

This is not about me.

Focus on Amanda.

"I would talk to my family and convince them that I want to report Ms. Shera to the authorities. Then, I would seek the help of a support group or a therapist who would help me lodge a complaint against Shera to the police."

"But my parents are already upset about Aiden being kicked off the basketball team. Should I burden them with my problems as well?" Amanda whispered softly.

"You're right in wanting to punish Ms. Shera, Amanda. She is committing a crime against you and your friends."

Amanda nodded slowly. She unzipped her coat to reveal her clothes. She was wearing a loose shirt and baggy pants. She had fastened even the collar button of her shirt. She fanned herself with her hand and fiddled with her button, clearly contemplating whether or not to undo it. I reached over to the heater in my car and switched it off. I opened the windows slightly, so she'd stop feeling hot.

Amanda's hesitation in unfastening her button brought back a lot of memories. I did the same thing, even in summer. I was the laughingstock in school, but I couldn't stop. I felt unsafe without it.

"Thanks for switching off the heater. It was getting warm in here," Amanda said.

I smiled at her. "I was feeling hot, as well. Do you want to have ice cream after this to cool off?"

Amanda laughed. It was a genuine laugh, but it still didn't eliminate the expression of pain in her eyes. "It's too cold for ice cream, though."

I laughed with her. "I like ice cream, especially when it's freezing outside. Do you want one?"

Amanda shook her head. "I'm not that adventurous. I'd prefer a hot chocolate. Let me go get it."

"Nope. My treat. And I'll go get them."

I got Amanda her hot drink and a chocolate ice cream bar for myself. We ate and drank in silence, relishing our treats. The cold creamy dessert reduced my nausea a little.

Amanda finished her hot chocolate with a last long sip. "My strict parents were finally proud of me because our band was selected to play at the Strollfield Cultural Festival. High school students rarely get to perform at such a big event. I'm so scared that I'll lose this wonderful opportunity if I decide to fight against Shera. There's no way the principal would allow us to represent our school after we go against her daughter."

"It's your talent that has got you this far. Not Ms. Shera or your principal," I said.

Amanda frowned. "But if my band is banned from performing, won't it be my fault?" She added with a sigh, "Affy supports me in wanting to press charges against Shera. In fact, they are more determined than I am. Yash, on the other hand, isn't sure. He fears the consequences."

"What if we show everyone how good your music is? Maybe upload it on social media?" I suggested.

"We are not that influential, Tina. Can you help us? After all, your video went viral, and you have more followers than us."

"I'm not at all active on social media, but I'll give it a shot."

"Thank you. I knew we could count on you." Amanda looked at me, her eyes brimming with tears. "Tina, did I ask for this? Was there anything I could have—"

I raised my voice and interrupted Amanda firmly. "Of course not."

A few months ago, I'd been in the same place as Amanda—blaming myself for Nicholas's lewd advances toward me. Scratch that—on some days, I was *still* there. However, when I heard Amanda using that horrible phrase "ask for it," I couldn't stand it.

I continued in a gentler tone. "You did *not* ask for it. This sicko—Ms. Shera—she's a teacher and is supposed to protect you and nurture you.

Instead… It's not your fault at all, so don't ever feel that way or let anyone tell you that."

Amanda started sobbing. I could see she was letting her pent-up emotions out. I gently rested her forehead on my shoulder and patted her back.

Once she was done crying, she wiped her eyes and looked at me. "Thanks again. I mean it."

I placed my hand on top of hers. "Let me know if you need anything else. I'll be waiting for your band's music samples."

Amanda nodded. "I will send them over by tonight." She looked at her watch. "I need to leave now. I'm getting late for my band practice."

"Take care, Amanda." I waved to her. "Bye."

After Amanda left, I drove back home with a heavy heart. I played music full blast and bellowed along to stop myself from recalling my dark memories.

Back home, I took a long and relaxing shower. When I came out of the bathroom, I felt better. I inhaled and exhaled deeply.

All will be well.

Amanda will report Ms. Shera, and she won't be able to harm anyone else. We will not let the abusers win.

I completed my online tutoring sessions and saw that I had received an email from Amanda with their band recordings. I played the videos and saw the three band members: Amanda, Affy, and Yash. Their music had a catchy tune, and their voices had a lot of energy. Their music was classical and different from MyWay's pop genre.

In one of the videos, I saw a woman in a pencil skirt suit and straight black hair introduce the band. One of the boys in the video referred to her as Ms. Shera, and my blood boiled. She looked prim and proper and had a smile on her face. If Amanda hadn't told me that she was a child molester, I would have been deceived by her sweet voice and polished words. But now, I could see right through her. I forwarded the video, unable to watch this further.

As I sent the video, a moment caught my eye. The person that I had guessed may have been Affy earlier clutched onto their jacket, trying to cover themselves with it further, even though it was already fully zipped up. Their head was bent, but I could see them shut their eyes in silent prayer. At the opposite end was a guy about my age, who leered at them lewdly, smirking sadistically at their discomfort. He called out their name, and they lifted their face hesitatingly, the fear evident in their green eyes, half-covered by their short, red curly hair. He winked at Affy mockingly, and I saw them cringe.

Nicholas Parker.

What was he doing there?

CHAPTER 33

Seeing Nicholas leer at Affy in the video that Amanda sent was my final trigger. All my buried memories of those demons resurfaced, threatening to come back any moment. I shook my head vigorously, willing myself to think about something else, but I couldn't.

The memories, the thoughts, the anxiety—they all came back.

The pain, the screams, the evil laughter—they all came back.

The fear, the guilt, the feeling of being dirty—they all came back.

My struggle while dealing with puberty and my changing body while growing up—they all came back.

My hatred for touch, my loss of trust in everyone, my love for lying to protect myself—they all came back.

My inclination to wear only baggy clothes, my yearning to wear skirts and dresses but the fear of exposure—they all came back.

Sleepless nights, lonely days of wondering "why me?", being laughed at for the way I am—they all came back.

The horror on my parents' faces when they found out—it all came back.

I forced myself to recall a conversation with Dr. Kim.

"Dr. Kim, the false se-sex tape that got leaked at the graduation ceremony

wasn't the first time I was publicly humiliated. Nor was it the worst," I said. "I've refused to recall the incident that happened on my fourteenth birthday since that day, though bits and pieces of the memories haunt me now and then."

"Would you be able to speak about those memories with me now?" Dr. Kim asked.

I shook my head. "No. I've buried them deep in my mind. I'm scared to let them out. What if I can't handle them?"

Dr. Kim nodded in understanding. "What do you do when parts of those unpleasant memories come back to you?"

I shook my head vigorously as a demonstration. "I do this and try to think of something else. Sometimes I distract myself with something. When it's difficult to distract my mind, I tie a rubber band attached to a sharp metal object around my wrist and pluck it and release it so that it hits my hand. When it gets even more unbearable, I cut myself with a knife. The pain helps me forget these memories."

Dr. Kim sat up straight in her seat. "That's known as self-harm, and it is not a healthy coping mechanism. We will work on that separately so that you stop that habit and replace it with self-care. Coming back to your memories, what will you do if all of them come back at once one day and you're unable to stop them?"

I looked down. "I don't know, Dr. Kim. I shudder to think of such a day. What if I can't take it?"

Dr. Kim continued questioning me in a gentle tone. "Do you want those memories to disappear so that you can move on?"

I nodded my head slowly and looked at her, my eyes welling up. "Yes, I want to move on more than anything in this world. But it's so hard. I feel so weak and scared. I wish I could erase those memories permanently."

"Unfortunately, it's not possible to erase them or remove them from your mind. There are different ways people deal with this—either they bury it so deep in their minds that it gets lost forever, or they let it out once and then move on. Both ways are methods for us to cope with unpleasant memories. There is no 'right' or 'wrong' method," Dr. Kim explained.

"Are you saying that I can let it all out and then forget about them?" I asked her eagerly.

"*I wouldn't call it forgetting; I would call it removing them from your system. Like writing about it and tearing it up or talking to yourself and then never letting yourself bring it up again, or more rarely, confiding in someone, and then both of you don't speak about it again,*" Dr. Kim answered.

"*And what if the memories continue to haunt me?*" I asked.

"*The key is to tell yourself that it was in the past and that you're safe now. And all that matters is your present and future. And that you will not let your happiness be ruined because of your past trauma,*" Dr. Kim replied.

I frowned slightly. "*That's easier said than done. I think I'd rather bury the memories deep inside me forever.*"

Dr. Kim looked me in the eye. "*Tina, if the memories resurface, promise me you won't do anything to hurt yourself. It's not worth it. Your well-being and happiness are the most important things. Please remember that.*"

In the present, with trembling hands, I took a pen and a notebook and started jotting down my worst memories. At first, I couldn't write more than one line, because the events flooded my mind. I was overwhelmed with a mixture of emotions—anger that I had gone through something so horrible, pain that was both physical and mental, frustration that I couldn't keep the past events buried in my mind, and exhaustion from the effort of bottling up my memories for so long. Finally, I let it all flow—the tears and the words.

***

Five years ago

It is my 14th birthday party. I am wearing a gray pencil skirt with stockings and a baggy white blouse. My mother doesn't understand why I wanted to wear stockings, but I insisted. My paternal grandmother wanted me to wear a flowery dress that would make me look lady-like, but I refused. Though I yearn to wear pretty and colorful clothes, I don't, because I don't want them to leer at me.

I don't want them in my personal space.

I don't want them to tell me that I asked for it.

But I have no choice. One of them is a part of my so-called family, and the other is "almost like family," our butler. To me, both are demons that devour me at any chance they get.

To my dismay, Wilbur Lauren, my uncle, appears before me as soon as I enter the grand hall of the family mansion. He looks at me lecherously as he checks me out from head to toe. I want to bury myself somewhere deep and never come out. He has a large pink box wrapped with a purple ribbon in his filthy hands, probably my birthday gift.

I don't want a present.

I don't want his presence.

Then I spot the other guy, Frankenstein, known as Frank by everyone else. He is talking to the guests as if he cares about this family. He and Wilbur exchange a secret smirk. I hate it when they do that. That only means they will find an opportunity to catch hold of me when I am alone and then drag me to the wine cellar in the basement, where my screams and cries can't be heard.

"Shhh, Princess. Not a word to Mommy or Daddy. You don't want them to get hurt now, do you?" they say.

Frankenstein grins at me, and a chill goes down my spine. He looked at my breas—, I mean chest, lewdly, and licked his lips. Helplessly, I look down, wishing that my chest hadn't grown so much. Maybe then they would spare me. Every day, I want to cut off my chest with an ax. Yes, it would hurt, but less so than the abuse these demons put me through.

I try to ignore both of them, but I can't, because I can feel their eyes lingering on me. Oh, how I wish I could pull their eyes from their sockets. But

I am helpless. I have been powerless since it started. It's been so long that I can't even remember when that was anymore.

Today, on my fourteenth birthday, my grandparents insisted on inviting my entire class for my birthday party to show off their wealth. My parents weren't happy with this but went along, thinking that I wanted a lavish party. My classmates come to me one by one and wish me a happy birthday. Most of them have presents for me, and I feel terrible, because I don't know them well at all. I keep to myself at school, and Rory is my only friend.

When it's time for cake cutting, I am called to the stage. My heart stops when I read the words "Happy Birthday, Princess." I hate that word—princess, the one that the demons use to refer to me. Wilbur Lauren's filthy hands try to place a tiara on my head. I attempt to duck , but my grandmother holds me firmly by the shoulders. Instantly, the hours of abuse in the cellar flash before my eyes.

Their iron grip.

Their merciless laughter.

My cries of pain.

"Shhh. Be quiet, Princess. Else, something bad will happen to Mommy and Daddy."

I black out in front of my whole class as they sing the birthday song.

When I wake up in my bedroom, someone is stroking my back. Rough fingertips touch my chest, and I flinch.

Wilbur.

I get up with a jolt and push him away. He firmly holds my shoulder and hisses in my ear. "Princess, why did you pass out like that?"

I try to shove him again. "Don't call me that."

He snickers evilly and tries to grope my bottom. "You're a big girl now, but not changed at all. Still asking for it, I see. Your stockings don't cover you up. The outline of your arse is still visible. You're a dirty little slu—"

I scream as loudly as I possibly can, blinded by fear and rage. I have reached my tipping point. I start throwing things around the room. I fling the chair, pull down the curtains, throw some books from the bookshelf at Wilbur Lauren. He tries to catch me, but I am unstoppable.

Hearing the commotion, my parents come running. They look shocked at the state of the room.

"Tiara, what happened?" my father asks me.

"Don't call me that," I shout at him angrily. "I hate that name. I hate it."

My mother tries to calm me down, but I push her away. "Don't you dare touch me."

Wilbur Lauren has the guts to come near me, and I push him away too. "Especially you. Stay away from me, you child se-sex offender demon."

My parents are shocked when I reveal this information. The rest is a blur. All I recall is my father dragging Wilbur out of the room by his collar and my mother trying to calm me down as I continue to unleash my wrath on the objects in the room. When I am exhausted, I collapse on the floor and sob uncontrollably.

After this incident, I refuse to stay in this house. For a few months, I stay with my maternal grandparents. They don't ask me any questions and let me stay with them. I have panic attacks and lose my temper regularly but refuse to talk to anybody. I don't even want to consider therapy.

I try going to school in my grandparents' town, but the rumors that I aborted a teen pregnancy and that I am a slut are unbearable. Thus, I have been home-schooled for a year and have developed an interest in coding and skating—both loner activities. I interact with my coding club members, who speak only on text, which makes me feel comfortable with them.

As an aftermath of the horrific incident, I develop many habits that seem unreasonable to others around me. I start locking my room when I am inside, and I put a padlock on it when I am not around. I am paranoid about finding the demons in my room without my knowledge.

Even though I have tried to dress modestly for a few years now, so as not to "ask for it," I now take this to the extreme. Because I don't want to feel exposed or attract attention, I start covering myself from head to toe. I wear high-necked and long-sleeved blouses with full-length overalls. If I wear a shirt, the collar is always buttoned. I wear leotards with my swimsuit, even during summer, so I'm fully covered. My breas—, I mean chest, and bu—, I mean, behind, are never visible. I refuse to change in the girls' locker room in the school and insist on using the bathroom. And most of all, I hate anyone coming too close.

During the time I stay with my grandparents, my parents move out of the Lauren mansion and rented an apartment. My father quit his position in *the family business and focuses on becoming an author. My mother, a public defense lawyer, is the sole breadwinner of the family. We distance ourselves from the Lauren clan. Frankenstein quit his job at my grandparents' place a few years later, after my grandfather's death. I wish that it was he who died instead. I still have to see Wilbur Lauren at family gatherings, but I do my best to stay away.*

Despite the far-reaching changes in our lives, on the surface, my parents behave as if they have forgotten the incident because they never bring it up again. Either they don't notice, or they choose not to question, the changes in my outfits and behavior.

When I return to high school, my unusual attire starts attracting unnecessary attention, and I become a target for people like Nicholas Parker. With my childhood snatched away by Wilbur Lauren and Frankenstein, I am left with a lifetime of darkness to reckon with.

CHAPTER 34

In the present, I closed my pen and let my tears flow. I sobbed for an entire hour, feeling sorry for myself and expressing my anger at my abusers. I tore the pages of the notebook and shredded them with my bare hands. I imagined the papers were Nicholas Parker, Wilbur Lauren, and Frankenstein. I wanted to rip them apart in the same way.

It is the last time I will cry because of them. Next time, I will make them cry.

Feeling better after letting it all out, I took another long shower. The hot water felt heavenly on my body, and for a moment, I forgot about the Wilbur Laurens and Nicholas Parkers and Pete Hiltons of the world. I used the hand shower like a microphone and started singing loudly. There was no one at home. Even though Madison would be back home any moment now, I wanted to continue to bellow at the top of my voice because it felt good.

After my shower, I looked at myself in the mirror. I had always avoided doing that because it scared me. But today, I noticed every little detail of my face. Miraculously, there were no blackheads on my nose, and my face was acne-free. I'd had pimples when I was in high school, but they'd subsided when I turned nineteen. I realized my brown complexion was flawless.

I leaned closer and examined the reflection of my sparkling hazel eyes. Even though they were swollen from all the crying, I saw the determination in them—to overcome my past trauma.

I will not live with a lifetime of darkness. There is always light at the end of a tunnel.

When I looked at the reflection of my neck and chest, I averted my eyes and could feel myself panicking. I distracted myself by practicing winking in front of the mirror. I couldn't wink; I could only blink. I closed only my left eye with a lot of effort to avoid wrinkles on my eyelid. I looked like a scary pirate without a costume.

"Teensy, I'm back. Have you had dinner yet?" Madison called out to me.

"No, Mads. I'm still in the bathroom. I'll come out and make something for both of us. You can relax for a while," I yelled.

I got dressed in the bathroom and went out. I had never stepped out after a shower with only a towel wrapped around my body. I was paranoid about someone attacking me if I did that.

Today, I admired my face in the mirror. I would be able to appreciate the rest of my body sooner or later.

Let's take baby steps, Tina.

Yes, even baby steps meant moving forward—toward accepting, loving, and pampering myself.

Later Madison and I sat down to a simple dinner of mixed fried rice at our dining table.

Madison smacked her lips. "This looks so good, Teensy."

I picked up a spoonful of rice. "Let's eat it while it's piping hot."

We ate in silence because both of us were hungry. The only sounds were the sounds of our spoons on our plates. Though I'm not a chef like Ekon, I cook decent food. Today, the fried rice balanced savory umami flavors from the oyster sauce and heat from the Sichuan peppers. We finished the entire dish until not even a morsel was left. After dinner, we had fruit for dessert, cleaned up, did the dishes, and plopped on our couch.

Madison patted her belly. "I had planned to go on a low-carb diet. But I told myself I needed the energy."

I gave her an "oh, please" look. "You have flat abs and no extra flab. You have a typical dancer's body. Now stop body-shaming yourself." I got up from the couch and pinched my hips through my shorts. "Look, I'm pudgy and have a muffin top, and I'm proud of it."

Madison squealed. "Teensy, I just realized you're in shorts for the first time. You look so good. I want to take a picture."

I pretended to resist her attention but was secretly pleased Madison had noticed. "You're making an unnecessary fuss."

Madison whistled. "Look at those skater legs. Next time, you should wear tighter shorts. I'm sure those will suit you as well. They'll accentuate your lovely curves."

I shook my head. "Comfort over cute any day."

"You can get well-fitting clothes that are comfortable," Madison replied. "Only if you want to, though. Now, let's capture you in these lovely shorts first."

I posed for Madison as she clicked photos. I was stiff at first but loosened up with her instructions. We both sat together and took several selfies where we smiled for the first few pictures. For the rest, we made funny faces and silly hand gestures. By the end of it, both of us were rolling on the floor laughing.

Madison tried to catch her breath. "What was that? A wink? I have never seen anything like it in my entire life."

I demonstrated my scary wink to her again and she burst into laughter. "It's my secret weapon, didn't you know?"

Madison clutched her stomach as I winked several times with both eyes.

She yelled, unable to take it anymore. "Stop! Show me some mercy. I will blame you if I die laughing today!"

"Alright, the show is over. You can now pay me for entertaining you," I joked.

Madison beamed and took out her phone. "I'll pay you back, Teensy. Do you want to look at my dance routine for the finals? This time I'll be performing, as well as choreographing."

I nodded. "Of course, I do."

Madison cast her phone on our television. We watched her dance routine on the big screen. All the dancers were good, but I couldn't take my eyes off Madison. She was mesmerizing. Her movements were graceful, and her expressions were on point and in sync with the song. She did the lifts so effortlessly that it looked like she was gliding in the air. When it was her turn to carry another girl on her shoulder, she made it look like she was holding a feather.

"Wow, Mads, you're awesome," I exclaimed. "No wonder you're one of the best dancers at the university."

Madison beamed at my compliment. "Thanks. Do you think we'll win the Dancing Divas contest?"

I placed my hand on hers. "Of course. You guys are too good."

Madison squeezed my hand. "Thanks, you're the best." She got up from the couch and stretched her arms and legs. Then she looked at me with a puppy-dog expression. "Do you think it's okay for us to have a teeny bit of ice cream?"

I laughed. My roommate had a sweet tooth. "Do you want me to say yes so you can blame me later when you regret your decision?"

Madison laughed with me. "You know me well."

I opened our freezer and served us each two scoops triple-flavored ice cream. It had chocolate, strawberry, and vanilla in one tub.

Madison licked the back of her spoon. "Hey, I love those addictive games you've created on the Recharge Café app. Thank you for appointing me as the first person to try them."

I smiled. "Thank you for your encouraging feedback."

"When are you presenting them to the café?" Madison asked me.

"Soon," I answered, not wanting to divulge details of my meeting with Ekon earlier today.

"Cool. I'll email Sharon my feedback about your app before I leave. She'll get some views directly from a customer," Madison said.

I beamed at her. "Thanks, Mads."

Back in my room after dessert, I opened my notebook and went through the list of things I wished to do, striking more items off it.

My wish list:

- ~~Hug my friends without hesitation~~
- ~~Keep my room door unlocked~~
- ~~Code again without recalling unpleasant memories~~
- ~~Wear shorts~~

- ~~Look at my face in the mirror~~
- Be comfortable with my body
- Wear a dress
- Use words like breast, buttocks, and sex without hesitating
- Be comfortable with intimacy
- Flirt without inhibitions
- Don't feel guilty about adult thoughts
- Stop having nightmares about the past
- Buy a bed frame
- Change my name back to Tiara Lauren

CHAPTER 35

On Sunday, I lazed around the whole day with Madison watching TV and ordering food from our favorite fast-food joints. It was the last day she could relax before her dance contest. She was going to be away for the next few weeks, and I wanted to spend as much time with her as I could before she left. In the evening, I helped her pack and get ready for her big trip.

Before beginning my hectic schedule the next week, I uploaded the music from Amanda's band, "Soul," on my social media account. However, it hardly got any views or comments. I tried to contact MyWay to help promote the classical band's music, but they were away on a tour.

I was disappointed that the Soul music posts didn't gain any traction online but something else constantly haunted my mind throughout the week—Nicholas leering at Affy, and their distressed expression.

Was Affy alright? Should I approach them? But what would I say? And was I allowed to talk to them directly since they're a minor? However, if I let this go, would I lose an opportunity to get Nicholas? I needed to talk about this with Jai. He would know what to do, but he'd been busy the whole week, too, and we hadn't eaten lunch together even once.

On Friday evening, I finally caught hold of Jai at the university parking lot. His tired eyes lit up when he saw me, and he waved. "Hi, Little Monster."

"Fellow Monster, I missed you," I gushed with a wide grin. "I hope your assignment went well."

Jai made a face. "I'm glad it's over. Anyway, what's up? Your text sounded important."

"Let's go to someplace private," I suggested.

Jai and I drove to Recharge Café in our respective cars. I followed him to one of the conference rooms in the eatery, which I'd always been curious about. There was a long oval wooden table and colorful chairs placed neatly around it. At the center of the table were stationery items of different kinds, such as markers, highlighters, and crayons. On the walls, there were three different types of boards: a whiteboard, a chalkboard, and a display board with pins.

"What a fun little space for working," I commented, taking a seat.

"And it's safe, private, and free for students," Jai said. "So, what's up?"

"I have something big to show you." I hesitated for a moment. "The person sent it to me confidentially, though."

"But you feel that the squad can help?" Jai asked me.

I nodded. "I wanted to talk to you before approaching anyone else."

"My lips are sealed," Jai assured me. "I won't breathe a word of this to the squad unless I have your permission."

I told Jai how I had met Amanda last week and how she and her bandmates were getting molested by their music teacher. I showed him the footage that Amanda had sent me, pausing at the part when Nicholas Parker appeared.

Jai's eyes turned red with rage. "He doesn't even spare minors."

I sighed. "So, what do we do? Neither can we ignore this, nor can we go ask Affy about it."

Jai thought for a moment. "Can we get the squad's opinion? Is it okay if I post this on the group chat? I promise, you can trust them."

I nodded. "Let's do that. But can we please not mention Ms. Shera or Amanda?"

"Don't worry. I'm posting only the parts of the footage with Nicholas and Affy."

Jai uploaded the video on the squad group chat and explained to the members about Nicholas's involvement. Responses flooded in the chat room from everyone.

Winona
A minor. Nicholas is disgusting.

Nate
The footage is genuine.

AA
But it's useless as a piece of evidence against Nicholas.

Me
I'm worried about Affy. They look so distressed.

Winona
Yes, but we can't approach Affy. None of us know them.

Nate
I can snoop around our school records. They're three grades behind me in school.

AA
Fine. But no hacking into any other website.

Ekon
Aren't these students the ones performing at SCF this year? They rehearse at the café sometimes.

Me
Yes, the band's name is Soul.

Ekon
Suits them. Their music is soulful.

Jai
Ekon, Tina and I are at the Recharge Café. Pop in when you sign off for the day.

In a few minutes, we heard a knock on the conference room door and Ekon stood outside. Jai opened the door. "Hey, Ekon."

"Hi, Jai," Ekon greeted him, stepping inside with a tray of snacks: a bowl of freshly baked chocolate chunk cookies and cactus cut potato chips with Ekon's special curry powder, a cup of coffee, and a mug of hot chocolate. He shot me a dazzling smile. "Hey, Tina."

My heart skipped a beat, but I waved to the chef and flashed him a fake grin. "Hello."

I was angry with Ekon for not bothering to respond to my note asking him out. It had almost been a week since I expressed my feelings, and couldn't he have said yes or no? Why leave me hanging?

"Thanks for getting us refreshments," Jai said, taking a cookie and his cup of coffee.

Ekon offered me the tray with goodies that looked amazing, but I was determined to remain cold toward him. "I'm not hungry, thank you."

Jai looked at me, surprised. "You never say no to hot chocolate."

I glared at him and gritted my teeth. "I said I'm good."

Neither pressed me further, and we got busy talking about the issue at hand. All the squad members had gathered together anyway, so we decided to speak on a conference call.

"N, did you find anything about Affy?" AA asked Nate in her morphed robotic voice.

"Full name: Affy Rodriguez. Their biological parents are deceased. There isn't any other information available about them other than a piece of identification information: a birthmark below their neck. Affy is currently under the care of child services, and there are no records of adoption," Nate replied. "And they are moving to a new foster home next month."

"That's next week," Ekon pointed out.

"When did Affy change their pronouns? Do we know?" Jai asked.

"Last year," Nate answered. "It's here in the notes."

"Nate, did you find their birth certificate?" Winona asked.

"Nope, not here."

Winona swore under her breath but didn't say anything.

"Nothing else helpful here," Nate said. "If we need further information, I need to break more rules. I could check Nicholas's messages and see if he has contacted Affy."

AA raised her voice. "Absolutely not. You're not hacking into Nicholas's phone. That's way too risky."

Nate sighed. "Fine."

"On a different topic, Tina, has a member of the Crown Counsel contacted you yet?" Winona asked.

I shook my head. "Not yet. The investigation is still in progress."

"We can do a mock trial at the next squad meeting," Winona suggested. "That will help you prepare for the real court hearing. But only if you're comfortable."

"Nicholas's lawyers will be ruthless in court, so you'd need to be prepared for the worst. And Win here is the right person for that," AA added. "I'll be the judge, Winona will be the defense lawyer, Nate will act as Nicholas, the defendant. Ekon will be himself, since he is a key witness, and Jai will play the roles of all other witnesses. You will be the prosecutor for your case *and* the victim. You would need to submit all the evidence to the court, that is me, in advance. Any new evidence during the trial is not permitted."

I gasped. "Winona is going to eat me alive."

AA chuckled. "It's better than Nicholas Parker's lawyers bringing you to your knees."

I nodded. "I agree. Anything else?"

"You have to disclose *all* the evidence in advance. You may not provide any new evidence during the trial," Winona said.

I nodded again nervously at Winona's sudden seriousness. Her usual friendly demeanor was gone, replaced by a no-nonsense tone.

"Tina, let us know if you need a safe word, in case you're unable to take it. Things will be intense at the trial, even though it's just a practice one," AA offered.

"Honeybee," I said, playing with my pendant. "That's my safe word."

"Alright. You say the word, and we stop. No questions asked," Winona reassured me.

"Great, I've got to go now," AA said. "Bye, squad."

After we hung up, Jai left in a hurry, saying he had to run an errand. It was strange seeing him run like that without even saying bye to Ekon and me.

Great, now I was left alone with Ekon Okoro, the one person I was trying to avoid.

How awkward!

***

I exited the café without acknowledging Ekon's presence and walked to the parking lot and got into my car, slamming the door behind me furiously. I expected him to call my name or come after me, but he didn't. Shaking my head, I started my car, but then decided to confront him and get my reply once and for all.

If Ekon's answer was "no," I needed to know that right away.

I swung open my car door and walked to Ekon's vehicle. He was at his trunk, loading some bags.

"Hi, Ekon. How was your day?" I asked him.

He frowned, looking confused. "It was good. How was yours?"

"Are you heading home now?" I questioned, not answering him.

Ekon nodded. "Yes."

"Oh, so you *do* know how to answer questions," I said sarcastically.

Ekon closed his trunk and turned toward me. "What do you mean?"

I shook my head and started walking back to my car. "Forget it."

Ekon caught up with me. "Forget what? Just come out with it. I don't like this indirect communication."

I stopped and looked at him. "It took me a lot of courage to give you that note last week. The least you could do is respond. Even if it's to say no."

Ekon took out the note I had given him from his bag. "You mean this? I don't see any question here."

I looked at the piece of paper Ekon was holding, and my face was flaming hot in embarrassment.

No. No. No.

There is no way I gave him the doodle from the last page of my notebook. That is the wrong *note.*

Did he see his name written all over? The compatibility games I had doodled? The hearts??

OMG! Did he read that silly poem with his boot—, um behind, as well? Nooooooooooo!

I tried to snatch the paper from Ekon's hand, but he held it over my head, out of my reach. I jumped several times, but he ensured I couldn't get hold of it.

"Give that back to me right now, Ekon."

Ekon laughed. "No way. Catch it if you can."

"That note does not concern you," I lied to him weakly.

Ekon held it up against the street light. "Even though you crossed out the name, the imprint reads Ekon. See? E-K-O-N."

I looked away so that the blush on my face wasn't noticeable. "That's some other Ekon."

Ekon looked hurt for a second, but he quickly regained his composure. "Oh, I see. Here you go. I guess you gave it to me by mistake. Bye then."

He started walking away, but I ran after him with the right note in my hand. "Ekon, wait. I wanted to give you this. The papers got mixed up." I unfolded it and showed it to him. "Look here…it's your name."

Ekon stopped walking, took my note, and pocketed it. "Ah, alright, thanks."

I sighed exasperatedly. "What? That's it? Are you not going to give me a reply?"

"Sorry, no can do. I don't have a pen," Ekon answered me.

"Suit yourself. I don't need your response," I said and strode off angrily toward my car.

I sat in the driver's seat, and Ekon got in on the passenger side. "Hey, it's not fair that you're getting angry. You're the one who brought someone else between us. Don't do that again."

"Haha—you know it was a joke. Look, I'm embarrassed for baring my soul in that note, okay? And now you're torturing me. Don't do *that* again," I snapped back at him.

"Well, who keeps running away and raising doubts in my mind?" Ekon retorted.

He was right. I was running away all the time, without considering Ekon's feelings.

I sighed. "I'm sorry. I won't do that again."

"Do you have a pen?" Ekon asked.

"There's one in the glove box," I told him.

Ekon scribbled something on the note I had given him earlier and passed it to me. It read:

Yes, Tia Lauren. I will go out with you.
PS: Can we kiss again?

I smiled when I read the last line. In response, I turned toward Ekon and leaned forward. He cupped my face, and we kissed.

Strawberries really are the best.

CHAPTER 36

After we pulled away from our kiss, Ekon and I looked into each other's eyes, blushing slightly, without saying anything.

Ekon broke the silence. "Tia, you need to return something that belongs to me."

"What?" I asked him.

"The other note, the one you gave me first."

I pinched his cheek lightly. "You're cute for believing you'll get the note back."

Ekon gently removed my hand from his face and leaned close to my ear. "I will steal it."

I blushed so hard at his comment that I was sure my ears also turned red. His breath tickled my ear, and his stubble brushed across my cheek. His proximity intoxicated me, and my heart was threatening to burst out of my chest.

Ekon chuckled at my flushed face and got out of the car. "Talk to you soon, Tia."

It was past midnight when I got done with my tutoring sessions. Ekon called me. I smiled and picked it up.

"Are you done with your tutoring yet?" Ekon asked me.

I nodded. "Yes, a few minutes ago. What's up with you?"

"I was catching up on schoolwork," Ekon answered. "How come you tutor students so late at night?"

"I have students from different parts of the world. When I started, no one wanted to join my classes because of my ruined reputation, so I had to get international students. And that has continued," I explained.

"I'm sorry you had to go through that."

"It's alright. It all worked out well," I said. "It feels good to have rave reviews from across the globe."

"Cool, I'm glad to hear that." He changed the subject. "So, we need to discuss the thing you stole from me."

I laughed. "Your heart?"

"Nope, my note," Ekon said.

I played dumb. "What note?"

"The one that was meant for me but was ruthlessly robbed from me," Ekon replied.

"I already gave you the other note," I argued. "That was the real one."

"I like the first one better," Ekon stated. He added after a short pause. "Especially the poem."

I could feel my face turning red at the fourth line of the poem mentioning Ekon's behind. I felt flustered and could feel a mini panic attack brewing. Did he think I was a pervert?

I'm not a pervert. There is nothing wrong with having adult thoughts.

"I don't remember any poem," I lied.

"Chef cutie, eyes beauty, strawberries tasty..." Ekon recited the poem he had clearly memorized. "What is the last line?"

I heaved a silent sigh of relief. "Why don't you guess, chef cutie?"

I could sense Ekon's embarrassment on the other side. *Ah, gotcha!*

Ekon continued. "You even scribbled on the backside of the note. I couldn't even read the imprint."

I laughed. "Well, it's for me to know and for you to guess."

"Oh yeah? I thought you didn't remember the poem, you lying beauty," Ekon teased.

"I didn't. But your husky voice brought back my memory."

"Oh, you mean my sexy voice?" Ekon asked, his voice laced with mischief. "Like my booty?"

My heart stopped for a moment. *How did he interpret that?*

I felt my body trembling with nervousness because of the nature of this talk, but I faked confidence. "You wish. Keep guessing!"

"I need the note for that," Ekon said.

I laughed. "No, you don't. You have etched the poem in your memory."

"Not just the poem," Ekon replied. "I studied that piece of paper the whole night—" He added after a pause, "I wasn't supposed to reveal that."

"No, thank you," I told him, floored by his sincerity. "I was feeling embarrassed that I bared my soul on that page. But if it made you think about me the whole night, it was worth it."

"It did. And it confirmed that you felt the same way about me." He hesitated a little. "I was really hurt when you kissed me at Landfill Hill and ran away like it was a mistake. I spent days wondering what I did wrong."

I took a deep breath. "Eko, I'm sorry I gave you mixed signals when I obviously felt the same way about you. But that had nothing to do with anything you did. You're simply wonderful. I already had too much going on that day, and Pete being declared the university brand ambassador was my final trigger. That's why I didn't want to hurt you and decided not to pursue this further. But I should have communicated that better. I apologize for leaving you hanging." I paused for a moment. "But I missed you too much and didn't want to let you go."

"Wow, Tia. I had decided not to forgive you. Ever. That's how angry I was. But I'm grinning like a goofy idiot right now. Can you say that again? That I'm wonderful? Then, maybe, I'll let this go."

I smiled. "How about I say that in person the next time we meet?"

"Deal. And you give me the doodle dedicated to me."

I laughed. "Ha, in your dreams."

"Come on. It has my name, so it's mine."

"Eko, I already gave you a nice limerick. *That* one is yours."

"Fine. But just so you know, I like the doodled poem better," Ekon grumbled.

I laughed and changed the subject. "So, are you free next Saturday or Sunday? Want to go anywhere? Maybe we could go rock climbing."

"Or you could teach me to ice skate."

"Oh, you need an excuse to hold my hand," I teased.

He chuckled. "You mean like the way you couldn't let go of mine at Landfill Hill?"

"Yeah. That *was* an excuse to hold your hand," I admitted. "I can balance well on ice."

"Wow, Tia, I was not expecting you to be so direct," Ekon said, his voice light.

"I'm going to be honest and sincere with you from now on. Just like you've always been with me."

"Tiara Lauren, I would like nothing more," Ekon said. "And we are on for next weekend."

I was surprised that I hadn't flinched when Ekon called me by my real name.

"Great, can't wait. It's a date."

CHAPTER 37

After we hung up last night, Ekon and I had chatted over text for some time, which had led to another phone call that went on forever. The next morning, I picked up my phone groggily when it rang. "Hi, Eko."

"What's Eko?" the voice asked me. It was not my boyfriend.

I sat up on my bed with a jolt. "Mom?"

My mother giggled and teased me. "It looks like you were expecting someone else's call."

I pretended to yawn. "I was studying all night and fell asleep at dawn."

"If you say so," my mother said, her tone light. "Is your wound completely healed now?"

I nodded. "It stings a little at times when I do karate, otherwise, I'm fine."

"Great. Take care."

"Um, Mom, I haven't heard from the police or the Crown Counsel yet regarding the cases against Nicholas Parker or Pete Hilton," I said. "How long is it going to take?"

Mom sighed. "These cases take time to investigate. I'm talking to my contacts to get the best prosecutor assigned to them."

"Would it be any faster if there were multiple charges against the perps?" I asked.

"Possibly. That depends on the severity, though," my mother answered. "Please don't do anything dangerous. Let the law take its course. Your safety is extremely important."

"I understand."

"So, we look forward to your visit during spring break. You're coming right?"

I nodded. "That's the plan," I added with a laugh. "Unless you and Dad decide to ditch me again."

"You aren't going to let that go, are you?" my mother asked me.

I shook my head and chuckled. "No. But I am really looking forward to spending the whole week with both of you."

"Us, too, Tina." My mother cleared her throat. "So, what else is new with you?"

"Nothing."

"Nothing at all?" my mother pressed.

"Nope," I insisted.

"You've never called me Eko before," she pointed out.

"I'm trying to be more eco-friendly, Mom. I use that word a lot these days," I told her, knowing it was the lamest excuse on earth.

"Funny. It's also the perfect nickname for *Ekon*," my mother went on.

I almost had my heart in my mouth for a second and felt my face going hot. *How does she know?*

"I...um," I stuttered. "I don't know who you're talking about."

"I see," my mother said. When I thought she might let it go, she added. "Then who did your father and I see at Burger All Night in Duckville the night before the Christmas party?"

I laughed, giving in to my mother. "Fine, you got me. Ekon and I started going out yesterday. And keep it a secret from Dad, please."

"Just yesterday? Not since last month?" she asked.

"And why should it be kept from me?" I heard my father ask over the speakerphone.

"Dad, you need to announce your presence," I protested.

"If you weren't going out with that chef earlier, why did you spend the whole night with him?" Dad interrogated me, ignoring my words.

"We met at the burger joint by coincidence," I clarified in an irritated tone. "I didn't know where else to go during the party with that demon—"

"Okay, okay, calm down," my father interrupted.

"We're happy for you, Tina," my mother told me.

"But if he dares to hurt you, I'll shred him to bits," my father added. "And when can we meet him?"

"You have already talked to him, Dad," I said, secretly pleased my parents had my back.

"Officially," my father persisted.

"Walt, she just started dating yesterday. Let's give them some time," my mother reasoned with him.

Dad sighed. "Fine, but I have my hawk eyes on him. Remember that."

After we hung up, I laughed while replaying my conversation with my parents in my mind. My sharp prosecutor mother and brilliant crime novelist father had known about Ekon all along. I was amused that my father was vocal about "shredding Ekon to bits" if he hurt me but wouldn't let me broach the topic of the thing that really bugged me—the abusers.

That's their way of coping with the horrible memories, Tina.

Before, I would have been upset after such a conversation with my parents. But today, I felt alright. I had learned to accept them and let my grudge against them go. They were hurting from my childhood abuse as much as I was, but their way of coping with the trauma was to bury the horrifying memories deep within and pretend it never happened. And that was okay.

I looked at the time and decided it was too late to go ice skating today. Besides, I was feeling too lazy to leave the house. So, I took a nice long warm shower, humming to myself.

When I came out, I realized I'd forgotten to take my clothes to the bathroom. I panicked and sat on the tub edge in my bathrobe, cursing myself. This had never happened before, and I was terrified to go back to my room. I fumbled around the cabinet for extra towels and wrapped them around myself.

Slowly, I took small steps toward my room, chanting to myself, "I'm safe. There's no one else here," the whole way. Once in my room, I slammed the door behind me and locked it, taking deep breaths to calm myself down. I threw on my clothes, a pair of jeans, and a sweater, as quickly as I could. After getting dressed, I sat at my desk with my head in my hands.

Why did these unreasonable fears still haunt me? Why couldn't I get over them? Why?

I have overcome a lot of things these past few months and need to stop being harsh on myself.

My inner voice was right. I had made considerable progress and worked on myself to overcome the past trauma. Patience was key to continuing to move forward.

My stomach growled, and I decided to fix myself something to eat. When I got up from my chair, I realized that I was wearing outdoor clothes and went back to my closet to change into my shorts.

When I pulled the shorts from a shelf, I saw the full-length mirror I hadn't used in ages hidden behind all the clothes. I dragged it out and stood nervously in front of it.

I let my eyes move down to look at my chest. My colorful blouse was loose but not baggy. The neck length was high. I saw that the outline of my breas— I mean, my chest was visible. I examined my hips and thi— upper legs. They were covered entirely by my shirt. I began to feel short of breath, but before it could turn into a full-blown panic attack, I averted my eyes.

Then, with trembling hands, I removed my shirt and stood in front of the mirror in my camisole. My reflection stared back at me like a stranger, but I continued. I unzipped my jeans and stepped out of them. I didn't know how long I'd stayed in front of the mirror. After what seemed like an eternity, I closed my eyes and took a deep breath. It felt like coming home.

My body is my temple. It does so much for me. It's been through more. Isn't that worth cherishing and celebrating?

I slowly opened my eyes and looked at myself in the mirror. In front of me stood a girl who was in no way perfect, but that didn't matter. The girl had wounds that only she could feel and scars that were visible only to her. But what mattered the most was the fact that she stood straight and proud, despite everything she had been through.

"My body is beautiful, my body is good," I said aloud to myself. "And I am not ashamed of it."

Tears welled up in my eyes, because I had finally managed to forgive myself for sins that were not my own. I ran my hands over my body tenderly. I cupped my breasts with my palms. I stroked my stomach. I grazed my buttocks. Bit by bit, I explored all the parts of my body that I had loathed earlier—the precious parts that made me who I was.

"I'm sorry I blamed you for whatever happened. It's not your fault at all," I said out aloud.

My eyes fell on a bag that I had stashed at the back of my shelf. With trembling hands, I pulled it out and carefully opened the paper bag. Inside it was the beautiful yellow dress that I had bought during New Year's, with no hope of ever putting it on, not even in the dressing room.

I ran my hands gingerly over the soft material of the sleeveless dress, touching the handmade tassels that ran along the knee-length hem. It would expose my arms and legs. Would I ever muster the courage to wear it?

Surprisingly, the old urge to take a pair of scissors and snip this dress to pieces—like I had done to my wardrobe at fourteen, before replacing it with baggy clothes, long sleeves, and muted colors—did not return.

I unzipped the outfit slowly and put it on, without daring to stand in front of the mirror. I could tell it fit me perfectly, accentuating my curves. I was almost afraid I would *like* the way I looked—and break down at the thought of not being able to wear it outside the four walls of my room.

Taking a deep breath to slow down my palpitating heart, I stepped in front of the mirror with my eyes closed.

Come on, Tina. I can do this. I saw my naked body for the first time in years today. This is nothing.

I opened my eyes.

A beautiful girl in sunshine yellow looked back at me. I felt a rush of emotions all at once—relief that I finally wore the dress without collapsing like I thought I would, amazed that it had taken me so much effort to take this step, hopeful that this was only the beginning, and ready to give myself the time and space to take the next one.

This was no simple task, Tina Lauren. And it's only a matter of time before I let the world see Tiara *Lauren. Until then, I will celebrate her today.*

I smiled proudly at the mirror one last time before I changed into my home wear.

CHAPTER 38

On Tuesday the following week, after classes, I drove to a café near Strollfield High to meet Amanda's bandmates, Affy and Yash. Amanda had informed me on the phone yesterday that she and Yash had pressed charges against Ms. Shera, with the help of their school counselor, Ms. Walker. Amanda had taken Aiden along, because she didn't have the courage to talk to her parents yet. Yash had brought his older sister. Affy didn't go along with them because they had no family to accompany them. Ms. Walker had offered to stay with them during the process, but they had refused.

Amanda was keen to introduce me to her friends, particularly Affy. She felt that Affy would open up to me, as they hadn't said a word to Amanda or Yash since yesterday. It had been Affy's idea to file a police complaint against Ms. Shera, but they ended up not going. I was hesitant to go along with Amanda's plan, but she had pleaded with me until I agreed.

I pulled over in the parking lot and went inside to find a booth to wait for the other three. At one of the tables, I spotted Nate, sitting alone and sipping a hot beverage. When he saw me about to wave to him, he shook his head slightly, indicating that I shouldn't acknowledge his presence. I noted with my eyes that I understood and took a seat at the corner.

Amanda, Affy, and Yash arrived a few minutes later. They greeted Nate with a quick wave—they must have recognized him from school—and walked to the table I was sitting at.

"Hi, Tina," Amanda greeted me with a smile. "This is Yash. And this is Affy."

I held out my hand to Yash and Affy. "I'm Tina. Nice to meet you."

"Likewise," Affy said.

"Same here. And I'm Yashpreet, but I go by Yash."

There was an awkward silence, and we just sat there smiling at each other.

"So, what's good here?" I asked. "Order whatever you want. It's on me."

"Nope, I'll pay for my coffee," Affy said.

Amanda frowned at them. "Affy—"

"It's fine. I just offered to pay because I'm the oldest."

"Thank you, but maybe next time," Yash said. "If we end up performing at the SCF, you can treat us."

I smiled. "Sounds good."

We got our beverages to our booth. The café was massive, but there were no vacant seats left. They were all occupied by high school students. Nate was still here, his head buried in his phone. He had given up his table to someone else and stood leaning against the wall near the window. His unfinished cup of coffee on the sill had probably gone cold. I wondered why he hadn't left yet.

"Back to the SCF topic, thanks for uploading our music on your social media account, Tina," Amanda said. "We haven't been removed from the fest yet, but it helps to build fan following."

"What fan following? Her post hardly got any views," Affy pointed out.

"Well, I'm not as famous as I thought, after all," I joked, embarrassed at Affy's comment.

Yash laughed politely. "Do you know any influencers though?"

"I can ask around," I said, thinking about MyWay. "But I don't get why your school would stop your performance. Ms. Shera is the one who is wrong here. What has that got to do with you? You're officially on the list of SCF performers, aren't you?"

"There's a high chance that our school would back out from the fest once Ms. Shera is arrested. That's why we want to see if we can make it to SCF on our own, without the school's help," Affy explained. "And that's only possible if the public demands it."

"I see, that makes sense."

"Nicholas has promised to help us, as well," Amanda said.

I saw Affy flinch at his mention.

"He is our mentor and has said that he would put in a good word for us to the SCF organizers."

Mentor? Tormentor suits him better.

"He's changed, Tina," Amanda added, looking at me. "He maintains a respectful distance from us during our rehearsals. Your viral video must have taught him a lesson."

"Who wants a refill?" Affy asked suddenly, getting up from their seat. "The best part about this café is that it offers two free refills for any hot beverage."

"I want one. Let me come with you," Yash said.

"I'm sorry Affy is being so rude to you," Amanda said when both of them left. "I shouldn't have asked you to come today."

"I understand. Affy is going through a lot right now. You all are."

"But they can't take it out on us," Amanda said. "It's not fair."

I didn't respond to Amanda, because I was busy staring at Affy. They stood in line behind Yash, with their hands in their pockets, staring into space. They seemed so preoccupied that the cashier had to snap his fingers twice before he got their attention.

"I still think you should talk to Affy. Yash and I will leave now so you have some privacy."

"Amanda, that's not a good idea," I protested. "We mustn't force Affy to speak against their will."

But Amanda had left the table anyway. And two minutes later, she and Yash exited the café.

I sighed and got up to leave as well. Affy's voice stopped me. "So, this was Amanda's plan the whole time. To get you to lecture me for not going to the police station yesterday. Well, no amount of nagging is going to convince me."

I turned to see them looking at me defiantly with their arms crossed.

"Are you okay? Is Nicholas Parker bothering you?" I asked in a low voice.

Their eyes grew wide for a moment, but they quickly looked away. "Why are you asking me that?"

"I just want you to be alright."

Affy turned toward me, softening their expression. "Both of us are going to get into trouble if we continue this conversation. Let's never bring that subject up ever again."

I nodded in understanding.

"And Tina, I'm sorry for being rude to you today. I really thought you came here to give me a bad time. And thank you. For asking if I was okay."

Without waiting for my response, Affy left the café.

I just sat there, my eyes welling up.

Earlier today, a small part of me had hoped to convince Affy to help me strengthen my case against Nicholas Parker. But now, I felt really small for being so selfish.

Affy had too many battles going on in their life right now.

And it was their choice on how to fight them.

I had to find an alternate way to strengthen my case against Nicholas.

**

Still feeling terrible about myself, I drove to Recharge Café hoping to see Ekon during his break. Just fifteen minutes with him could cheer me up. When I pulled over at the parking lot, I was ecstatic to see him sipping his decaf coffee and browsing on his cell phone.

"Eko," I called out, getting out of my car.

He flashed me his dazzling smile and set his coffee cup aside. "Tia. What a wonderful surprise."

"I'm so glad I could catch you during your break," I gushed, taking his hands in mine, ready to hug him. I let go suddenly. "Sorry, I forgot we were in a public place."

"So, what brings you here?"

"I was having a bad day and needed cheering up," I said.

He took my hand in his. "Is this better?"

I giggled. "Yes. Much better."

"Do you want to talk about your bad day?"

I shook my head. "We've just got fifteen minutes. I'll tell you some other time."

"What do you want to do then?"

"Nothing, I just want to stand close to my boyf—" I let go of his hand and looked up at him. "Wait. We need to discuss the nature of our relationship before I can call you that."

"Do you want me to go first and ask you to be my girlfriend? You know, because I'm the *guy*?" Ekon teased.

I punched his arm lightly. "You know that's not it. And I don't live in the Stone Age."

He laughed. "Alright." He added seriously after a pause, "Casual relationships are not for me. And I would really like us to be exclusive, if that's okay with you."

I smiled and took his hand again. "I was hoping you'd say that. Because I really like you and feel the same way."

Ekon blushed and squeezed my hand tightly. We were lost in each other's eyes, thinking the same thing. If only a million people couldn't see us right now...

I leaned toward him. "By the power bestowed by myself, I now pronounce us boyfriend and girlfriend."

Ekon let out a snort while guffawing. "You're too funny."

"And you're cute. Even when you snort-laugh."

He caressed my cheek. "This feels like a dream."

I smiled. "Yeah. Who knew the outcast of Strollfield University would end up dating the hot chef?"

"You're not an outcast. A-And my past is not too rosy either."

I squeezed his hand. "Well, you know mine, and you're still here. When I learn yours, I'm not going anywhere."

"Even if it's worse than yours?"

I intertwined my fingers in his. "Try me."

"I could teach you a thing or two about courts, Tia. I have been in a *real* trial before."

"As a witness?"

Ekon paused for a moment. "No, as a defendant. I was falsely accused, of course."

"Oh, my goodness. I'm so sorry you had to go through that. Wait a minute. Did that bully you told me about earlier do this to you? That's terrible."

Ekon nodded. I didn't press him further for details because he didn't seem to want to talk about it.

"Can I give you a hug?" I asked.

Ekon chuckled. "Tia Lauren, this is a public place."

I pulled him by his waist closer to me in a side hug. "This will have to do for now, then."

CHAPTER 39

I hummed to myself as I got ready for karate class on Sunday morning. Ms. Shera had been arrested yesterday. According to the news report, several students and alumni had complained against the music teacher during the investigation. They had all stayed quiet earlier because Ms. Shera had threatened to ruin their future. But Amanda and Yash's police complaint, and the resulting investigation, had made all the other previously silent survivors speak up at their school. Of course, the article didn't have her name, but Amanda had called me when the police had taken Ms. Shera. A glimmer of hope regarding my own battles had lit up my heart. Maybe, just maybe, I could get Nicholas Parker jailed and stop him from tormenting anybody else ever again.

Another reason I was on cloud nine was because of my date with Ekon. We had decided to go to the sports center in Strollfield, which had both rock climbing and ice skating. I applied my lip balm and winked at my reflection in the mirror before Rollerblading to karate class.

After class, I got back home, took a quick shower, and wore my favorite violet shirt and black jeans for the date. When I was about to get my car keys and leave, I heard a beep on my phone. My heart stopped for a second when I read the text from Aiden:

Aiden

Tina, Amanda is in Strollfield General Hospital. She's out of danger now
and is asking for you. Can you come and visit her today?.

I called Aiden immediately, and he told me that his sister had slashed her
wrists earlier that morning. He didn't know why she took such an extreme
step but was shocked to see her unconscious when he came back from practice.

I rushed to the hospital immediately, calling Ekon to inform him about
the sudden change of plans.

I pounded my fist on my steering wheel. Why? Why should we go
through this when we did nothing wrong? Why should Amanda decide to
hurt herself through no fault of hers? Wasn't the abuse that a survivor went
through punishment enough? Why did we need to suffer any further?

Tears clouded my eyes as the events of last year flashed past my eyes—
Laila and Harriet leaking the self-harm video, making me the laughingstock
of the entire college, the university students abandoning me, calling me a
freak, and everyone blaming me for hitting Nicholas Parker in the face when
I was just trying to protect myself. Even now, after more than a year, I was
still working alone on all group projects.

Why could no one see my pain? Why was I treated like an outcast for
something that wasn't my fault? Why did I have to resort to self-harm to
unclutter my mind in the past?

*But I sought therapy, worked on myself, and am much better now. I need
to calm down and focus on Amanda now.*

I pulled into the hospital parking lot and ran to Amanda's room but
stopped when I heard voices.

"I understand what you're going through, Am—"

Amanda interrupted him, scoffing. "No, you don't understand, Aiden.
No one does. Do you know how much I loathe myself for letting that pervert Shera molest me? Do you know how much I hate anyone coming near
me, even by mistake? I can't sleep at night without the horror playing in
my mind over and over again. And I'm supposed to pretend nothing happened in school, because if I utter even a single word about the abuse, my
friends will start treating me differently, like it's all my fault. No one can
even fathom the trauma that sexual abuse survivors like me go through.

My life will never be the same again."

"I am on your side," Aiden tried to console his sister.

"I appreciate your support, but it's not enough. I thought all this would be over when Shera was arrested, but I hate seeing Mom and Dad's disappointed expressions. Did you see how upset they were when our school decided not to participate in SCF this year? They asked me why I couldn't wait until our band's performance before pressing charges against Ms. Shera. They blamed me for ruining my future. They're right. My life is over, and I can do nothing about it."

Blinking back my tears, I texted Aiden that I was at the hospital, outside Amanda's room.

He met me at the entrance a few minutes later, and I squeezed his hand reassuringly.

"I can't calm her down, Tina," Aiden told me, looking dejected.

"She's going through a traumatic time. Let's give her some time."

"I'll be back in a while," Aiden said and left.

I went into the room, sat on the stool beside Amanda's bed, and placed my hand lightly on hers. She smiled at me, but her eyes brimmed with tears. I laid her head on my shoulder and let her cry as much as she wanted as I patted her back softly.

"Sorry, Tina," Amanda apologized, wiping her tears with the tissue I handed her. "I didn't mean to break down like that."

"Are you feeling better?" I asked.

She nodded. "Yes. I am, thank you."

I smiled. "Good that you let it all out. Don't be sorry."

Amanda grinned back at me. "Thanks. I didn't intend to commit suicide, you know," Amanda admitted. "I just cut myself deeper this time, accidentally."

"You've suffered immense trauma," I said as I helped her sit up on the bed. "Only you know what you've been through. And I'm no one to judge you." I told her that I used to do the same thing and showed her some of my scars.

"Um, how did you get over your self-harm habit?" Amanda asked. "How did you deal with being treated like an outcast?"

I sighed, silently recalling the toughest thing I had ever done.

"I can't, Dr. Kim. I just can't do this. I hide the sharp objects in the morning, but at night I have to use them. It is of no use. I'm a failure," I wailed to my therapist.

"Self-harm is not healthy, Tina. There are many other ways to cope," Dr. Kim tried to console me.

"I know that. But nothing else works for me. Absolutely nothing. Not even skating that I love so much." I sighed. "I'm going to cover my body up all the time anyway. So, who would see these scars? I just need to be careful not to do this at the university the next time."

Dr. Kim looked me in the eye and spoke in a gentle tone. "Tina, you told me you chose life when you tried to take the extreme step the other day, didn't you? That was the right thing to do."

I nodded. "I don't want to lose my life for those sickos."

Dr. Kim leaned forward in her chair. "Then why should you face any more pain for them? Haven't you suffered enough already?"

"But this pain calms me down," I tried to reason with Dr. Kim. "It's so intense that I forget the nightmare or the thing that made me go berserk in the first place."

"Does the pain really calm you down?" Dr. Kim questioned me. "Do you really think that?"

I nodded. "It's the only method that works."

"Then why do you feel guilty the next morning?" Dr. Kim challenged me with her tone firm, but she had the same kind expression in her eyes. "You just mentioned a few minutes ago that you did."

"Because I'm scared of harming myself in the university again," I answered her. "I don't like being called an effing freak. Maybe I should opt for completing my studies remotely—"

"So, have you decided to live with this unhealthy habit and let it rule over you?" Dr. Kim interrupted me, her tone still even.

I nodded weakly, blinking back my tears. "I have no choice."

Dr. Kim was quiet for a minute. I could see she was deep in thought. I clasped my hands nervously, hoping she wouldn't get angry at me. Deep down, I knew self-harm was wrong, and I wanted to stop. But my circumstances told me otherwise.

"Why do you think abusers and bullies harass others, Tina?" Dr. Kim asked.

I was puzzled at her question. "Because they derive sadistic pleasure from seeing others suffer."

"And what do you think is their objective in doing this?" Dr. Kim continued.

"To ruin the victim's life and show them their place," I answered with my fists clenched. "To never let them live in peace again."

"Is that what the survivor *should accept, though? The abusers ruining their life?" Dr. Kim prodded me gently.*

I shook my head. "No, of course not."

"Then what should the survivor do?" Dr. Kim asked.

"They should overcome their past trauma and try to live the life they want," I answered with conviction. "Survivors must not let abusers ruin them. And self-harm ruins us. I know that, but…"

I felt tears streaming from my eyes, but I made no effort to stop them. Dr. Kim offered me a tissue box and waited patiently until I finished crying.

"It's really hard to get over my terrible habit, Dr. Kim," I admitted to my therapist. "I don't think I can do it."

Dr. Kim leaned forward a little and gave me a reassuring smile. "Knowing that self-harm isn't the answer is the first step."

I nodded. "How do I get over it completely?"

"Why don't you try replacing the sharp objects with a diary and a pen?" Dr. Kim suggested.

"Do you want me to write down everything in my mind?" I asked. "But what if it's too overwhelming?"

"Isn't it better than the overwhelming guilt you face every morning?" Dr. Kim questioned.

I nodded and smiled slightly. "Yes. I'll try anything to overcome this terrible habit."

Back in the present, I snapped out of my reverie when Amanda tapped me on my shoulder.

"Sorry, I took an unpleasant trip down the memory lane," I told her, laughing nervously. "Overcoming my self-harm was an ordeal—the hardest thing I've ever done." I opened my backpack and handed her Dr. Kim's card.

"I went to therapy and worked on myself like crazy to quit reaching for the pocketknife. Writing down all my thoughts in a notebook and shredding them into bits worked for me, but Dr. Kim says each person has their own method."

Amanda placed the card in her wallet. "But what if people find out I'm going for therapy? Won't they think I'm mentally ill?"

"I had the same fear, which is why I stalled going to therapy for a long time," I said. I showed her the video of Dr. Kim's talk at Duckville High's graduation. "This convinced me to take the first step into her office. And I have absolutely no regrets."

Amanda watched the recorded footage of Dr. Kim's session, fascinated. Once it was over, she applauded and let out a delighted squeal. "This is amazing, Tina. It really seems like therapy helps."

I smiled back at her echoing the enthusiasm. "Yes, but working on ourselves is key."

CHAPTER 40

On my way back home, I tried Keith's and Kenneth's phone numbers, but they didn't answer. I hoped that the MyWay twins would be able to help with promoting Soul's music. I called Jai to see if he knew the twins' whereabouts.

"Their band is currently touring the country, Little Monster."

"But do you think the twins would promote Soul's music?"

"Unfortunately, they can't do anything without their producers' permission. Besides, it could take months for them to accept such a request."

I sighed. "I really wish I could help Amanda, Affy, and Yash somehow."

"Our squad could try uploading their music," Jai suggested.

"But wouldn't that look odd? The squad only posts content on abuse and bullying. We don't want Soul to receive pity-votes on social media. Their talent should stand out."

Jai sighed. "These are the times when I wish I was active on these sites."

"Same here," I agreed.

"One second, putting you on speaker. Rory is here."

"Hey, T. Why don't you come over if you don't have plans? I have something I want to share with you."

"Alright, I'll be right over."

When I reached Jai and Rory's place, I was greeted by the aroma of mouthwatering food. My stomach growled. Until now, I had forgotten that I skipped lunch. I was tempted to head straight to the kitchen, where I could hear the sizzling sounds of hot batter being spread on a pan, but I stayed put in their living room.

"We were just about to have lunch. Why don't you join us?" Rory offered.

"Here, serve yourself some set dosas," Jai said, placing a plate of pancakes on the table. "I'll be right back with the curry."

Jai brought a glass bowl of piping hot lush green curry and set it on the table. "Let's dig in."

For the next few minutes, we ate in silence, enjoying the savory pancakes that were crisp on the outside but soft and spongy on the inside, dipped in a flavorful curry filled with veggies.

"What's this curry called?" Rory asked, licking his fingers. "It looks like Thai green curry but tastes a little different."

"It's saagu," Jai replied. "Thai curry has coconut milk, but this has fresh coconut. Saagu has cilantro, while Thai curry has, uh, *Thai* herbs."

"I absolutely loved it. And I will get the recipe from you later," I said. I turned to Rory. "So, what's up with you?"

"I'm taking two weeks off and going on a trip," Rory answered. "To Hong Kong. To curb my mobile addiction."

Jai frowned. "What mobile addiction?"

"Haven't you seen my face buried in my phone all the time? Well, it's time I stop that."

"Good luck, R," I wished him. "Enjoy your trip."

"You deserve a break," Jai agreed. "When are you leaving?"

"Next Friday."

"I'll drop you at the airport," I offered.

"Thanks, T. And I'm not planning to tell anyone else."

"Our lips are sealed," Jai and I said in unison.

"Great, I'm going for a walk now. Jai, I'll wash the dishes when I'm back."

I got up from my seat. "No, I'm doing the dishes." I added after a moment, "Oh, by the way, I'm dating Ekon."

Jai chuckled. "Ah. Finally."

"Who's Ekon?" Rory asked. "That chef from Recharge Café?"

I nodded. "That very one."

"I've heard stuff about him. Be careful," Rory warned. "He has a criminal record."

I scowled. "It's not right to judge anyone without knowing the truth."

"I'm just looking out for you, T."

"I appreciate that. But I really like him and don't want to hear anything against him."

"Point noted. See you on Friday," Rory said and left.

"So, when did you start seeing each other?" Jai asked. "After our squad meeting last week?"

"How did you know?"

Jai laughed. "Why do you think I left Recharge Café early that day? My errand was just an excuse. I wanted you lovebirds to work things out. There was an intense chemistry between the two of you."

I blushed hard. "Stop it, Fellow Monster."

"When you said no to Ekon's hot chocolate, your favorite, I knew something was up with you two," Jai continued. "Tina Lauren saying no to hot chocolate is otherwise impossible."

I shoved him playfully. "Ha ha ha. Very funny."

"Seriously though, I'm happy for both of you. Ekon is great."

I smiled happily. "Thanks. He is."

After washing the dishes, Jai and I sat in his living room, waiting for AA and the others to join the conference call.

"Guys, it's Sunday. I was sleeping," AA complained.

"At four-thirty in the afternoon?" Ekon asked.

"I repeat. It's *Sunday.*"

"Strollfield High has decided not to participate in SCF this year. So, Amanda's band can't perform," I said, getting straight to the point. "Unless the public demands it. Do you all know any influencers who can help promote their music?"

"Sorry, I don't know anyone," Winona said.

"I have no personal accounts on social media. Only the one for the squad," Nate said.

"I'm a part of a plant lovers group with a lot of followers. If their music is soulful, I can post it on my account," AA offered. "But only if the sounds help my plants grow."

"That would be fantastic. Thanks, AA. I'm sending you their clips right now."

"Cool," AA replied. "Anything else or can we all get back to Sunday mode?"

"Uh, I found something," Nate said. "Tina, this might bring back unpleasant memories. I'm sorry about that. But this is really important. Is it okay if I continue?"

I felt my heart pace quicken. *What now?*

"It'll help us with the case against Nicholas," Nate prodded gently when I didn't say anything. He added after a pause, "And I've made sure that what I'm about to show you will never be viewed online by anyone else ever again."

I nodded reluctantly. "Alright. Let's continue."

"Thanks," Nate replied. "Can you get your laptops for a screen sharing session please? I have to show you all something."

When all of us were ready, Nate spoke again. "This is one of the videos I found online. It was the same one that was played at Duckville High graduation ceremony. We all know that Tina's face was swapped with the original person's."

"Nicholas's face has been blurred here," Winona pointed out.

I clenched my fists under the table while Jai placed his hand on mine in a comforting way. Even though I knew that it wasn't me in the scandalous footage, it was hard to see my face there.

"That's right, Win. The asshole protected himself before making it public," Nate replied. He shared another video on his screen. "Now, look at this other one I found. Nicholas's face is not visible in this either. This one's really hard to watch, but try to examine it closely as I zoom out and zoom in again."

I gasped out aloud, shocked and looked at Jai. He mirrored my exact expression.

"It's Affy," AA finally spoke out loud. All of us knew that too but were too tongue-tied to open our mouths. "That's Affy in both the videos. The one with Tina's face has Affy's body with the birthmark under their neck."

"When you zoomed out, it was clear that Affy's hands were tied. And they were screaming," Ekon said. "It's obvious they were forced into this."

Nate switched back to the first video. "In this, since it's a close-up, the tied hands are not obvious." He paused to zoom in the screen. "But now, you can faintly see the rope." He placed the second video next to the first one and pointed to the similarities one by one. "See, Nicholas's hand positions, the clothes, and everything else is the same." Nate closed everything and stopped sharing his screen. "Sorry for making you watch that. But that was the only way I could prove my point."

"Nicholas Parker has stooped to the lowest depths possible by raping a minor and recording it," Winona stated. "This is disgusting beyond limits."

"So have Laila and Harriet," I added quietly. Their betrayal still hurt me like crazy. But it was much worse that they tampered with a ra-rape footage.

Jai pounded his fist on the table, startling me. "We need to report this immediately to the police."

"But Nicholas's face is blurred," Ekon pointed out.

"And the sicko's lawyers will try to prove it's not him," Winona reasoned. "If this ever gets to court."

"I could try to snoop around a little more and find the video which shows Nicholas's face," Nate said. "Besides, it would be a piece of cake to unblur his face."

"Evidence sought by illegal hacking won't be admissible in court," AA pointed out. "And you do *not* have the authority to unblur anyone's face. Affy will need to file a police complaint against Nicholas Parker."

"But Nicholas and his underlings have threatened them not to press charges. If they do, the video will be used against them to ruin their reputation and a chance to be adopted by a decent family," Nate explained.

"How do you know this?" Ekon asked. "Did you hack—"

"No, I've witnessed Affy being followed by Nicholas's underling," Nate justified. "Tina, they were there at the café that day when you met the Soul members."

"Did I end up making things more difficult for Affy?" I asked.

"No. They seem to look up to you," Nate said. "Check out their thank you note on your Soul post."

I opened the post and read the comment out loud. "Thank you @tinaaaLauren for your support. We promise you we will not give up. #SCF, here we come." I added in a voice barely above a whisper, "That's why Affy backed out of going to the police station with Amanda and Yash. Nicholas was threatening them."

"Nate, you implied you corrupted *all* the online copies of Affy's video. You wouldn't have done that unless you've already located the original, knowing it's solid court evidence," Winona pointed out. "You wouldn't have stopped at guessing it exists."

Wow, soon-to-be Attorney Winona is sharp.

Nate sighed. "Fine. You got me. Affy has the original. I know this because I hacked into Nicholas's phone and found that he sent it to them. That's why they've kept mum."

"You've got to stop doing this," AA scolded him. "AA Squad doesn't do illegal stuff like hacking."

"Alright, alright. I promise never to hack into or track anyone's phones again without permission. Except Nicholas's. I will continue tracking his device. That's nonnegotiable."

"Fine. But please be careful," AA and Winona said in unison.

"I promise I will," Nate replied.

"Tina, can't you add defamation in your charges against Nicholas now that you have proof?" Jai asked. "That's a huge offense. And you can file a complaint against Laila Yusuf and Harriet Shelby as well. They, too, committed a crime against you."

"I will, only if Affy goes to the police first though. It's not right for me to pull them into this without their knowledge," I insisted.

"No, the right thing to do is report it to the authorities," Winona replied. "You're putting away a criminal and helping Affy. Why don't you look at it that way? Besides, it is our duty to report abuse against minors. The police will take action even if the victim does not press charges. That's the law in Strollfield."

I thought for a moment as Jai squeezed my hand reassuringly and whispered, "Win is right, Little Monster."

"Okay, it's decided then. I'm going to the police station again tomorrow with these videos to file more complaints against Nicholas, Harriet, and Laila. Thanks, squad."

***

When I got back home, I was exhausted from the events of the day. I ordered a pizza for dinner and ate it groggily on my futon, staring at my phone, willing it to ring. Ekon had texted me earlier this evening that he had to go out on some personal work but would call me after he was back.

When my phone rang, I greeted the caller. "Hello?"

"Hey, Tia, you sound sleepy," Ekon said.

"Uh-huh," I replied. "But I want to talk to you."

Ekon laughed. "It's fine. Let's talk tomorrow."

"Five minutes, Eko," I replied. "What's up?"

"I wanted to speak with you about Soul," Ekon said, and I sat up straight at the band's mention. "They just booked a gig for this Friday at Recharge Café. And I thought I could help them in another way."

I was totally alert now. "I'm listening."

Ekon sounded shy. "Um, this is a secret, though."

"My lips are sealed," I assured him. "Go on."

"Do you know the influencer JustCooking?" Ekon asked.

"Sounds familiar. My father mentioned the name once or twice," I said.

"That's actually me," Ekon revealed.

"Wow! That's awesome." I shrieked in delight. "Will you share Soul's music then?"

"I was planning to use their instrumental music in my next video, providing them a shout-out," Ekon suggested.

"That's a brilliant idea," I exclaimed, jumping up and down. "You have our full permission."

"Tia, no one can know my social media identity," Ekon repeated. "If anyone else finds out, I'll be in trouble with my family. They don't approve of me being a full-time chef. They only agreed to let me work at Recharge Café part-time temporarily until I graduate."

"You can trust me," I reassured him. I added in a light tone, "I can't believe I am dating an influencer."

Ekon chuckled. "Would you have agreed to go out with me earlier if you had known?"

I laughed. "No way. Ekon Okoro is much more special to me than the world-famous JustCooking chef with almost a million followers."

"Tia, stop saying things that make me want to run to you right away," Ekon said.

I blushed at my boyfriend's heart-fluttering words. "I can't wait to see you again in person."

"Me neither," Ekon replied. "And Tia, I'm glad I trusted you with my biggest secret."

CHAPTER 41

On Monday, I pulled over at the university parking lot, excited and nervous about the launch of our new app for "Are you okay?" formerly called "Court Us." My name probably wouldn't even be there on the flyers, but knowing my work was going to be available for people to use very soon made my heart soar. I felt proud of finally overcoming my fears and launching my first coding project in months. My phone beeped in my pocket. It was a text from Jai. He had sent me a picture of the full app poster near his classroom and another one with my name in extremely small print at the bottom.

I called him right away instead of texting him back.

He picked up on the first ring. "I spent an eternity searching for your name on this thing. Finding a needle in a haystack would have been easier."

I laughed. "I'm just happy it's there. You know, it's actually good that it's not that apparent. I won't get unwanted attention again then."

"Congratulations, Coder Queen, you've done it again."

I smiled. "Thanks. But what do you mean again?"

"You're going to knock the socks off Sharon with the Recharge Café games you've developed. I'm not even into mobile games, and I loved them. Aren't you presenting them to her tomorrow?"

"Yes, after my classes in the evening," I replied.

"I'm so glad you're coding again, Little Monster. I wish I could at least sit in the cafeteria with others. I chicken out every time."

"You will, Fellow Monster. I promise. And I will be with you when you do. Whenever that is."

"Thanks. My professor is here. I will catch up with you at lunch."

I ran my fingers over the letters of my name on the photo of the flyer gingerly.

Well done, Tina. Good job.

***

Still high from my success earlier that morning, after classes, I drove to the police station to press more charges. I filed complaints against Nicholas, Harriet, and Laila, and submitted the video evidence. It was the same gray and gloomy room with the annoying, ticking clock as earlier, but I answered Officer Hussein and Officer Lee's questions confidently.

Since it was confusing, I explained to them that there was a vulgar video with Nicholas and someone else. Laila and Harriet had worked with Nicholas to replace the other person's face with mine. Then they had played this during the Duckville High graduation ceremony to humiliate me. I wanted to report it earlier, but I never found the footage. Recently, I had found it online while searching for "Duckville High graduation video" and was shocked.

"And here's the original non-fabricated video," I said, submitting another flash drive to the officers. "I know the survivor. They're a minor."

"You did the right thing by reporting this to the police," Officer Hussein said.

"Yes, it was really brave of you to come to us," Officer Lee agreed. "It must have been terrible to see illegal videos of yourself and your friends online."

"Thank you."

When I left the police station, I hoped that this would expedite the investigation and the perps would pay for their crimes soon.

Though it was not my fault, I couldn't help but worry about the number of people who had watched the video online. I knew it was fabricated but the thought creeped me out. The fact that Affy was being threatened for no fault of theirs sickened me further, and I started getting nightmares again with Wilbur Lauren chanting, "Princess, you asked for it." My inner voice helped calm me down every time, but it was hard to get a full night's sleep.

To make things worse, nothing had changed at the university either. I wasn't expecting an applause for developing the revolutionary "Are you okay?" app, but I definitely did not want to be removed from the committee. But there it was, the cancellation of future meeting invitations on my calendar with the note: "Since your work is done, you don't need to be on this anymore." I sighed and navigated to the app reviews, content that the students thought it functioned well and was a great initiative.

At the end of the day, what mattered the most was that if someone in the university was being wronged, they had a platform to report it and obtain justice.

But my other app presentation with Sharon at Recharge Café went extremely well. She was so impressed that she paid me a large sum of money for my effort though I wasn't expecting anything. When I declined, she insisted, saying that I deserved it and earned every cent of it. It felt wonderful that my work was acknowledged, and I truly felt like a coder queen.

On Friday evening, I picked up Rory from his place to drive him to the airport. He had one bag, a book, and no phone. I was surprised to see him with a book, since he never read. He either listened to summaries of novels or waited for them to be turned into movies. I was curious to see the title, but he had covered it with his large hands. So, I decided not to ask him about it and drove.

"Jai can't make it today," I informed him. "He had to cover a colleague's shift at work."

"I'm aware. He's my roommate, remember?"

I didn't speak further and drove quietly, seeing that he was not in a good mood.

But he broke the silence. "So, Jai has replaced me as your best friend, eh?"

I was taken aback by the question. "What do you mean?"

"I never see you anymore. Neither on the campus nor during the weekends. But you both seem to be involved in a lot of stuff together. That's why I got out of your hair the other day and lied, saying I wanted to go for a run. It was obvious that the two of you wanted to be alone. At first, I thought you were ditching me for your new boyfriend. But no, I seem to be the only one you're not talking to," Rory continued. "Are you still angry with me?"

I shook my head. "Of course not." I placed a hand on his lightly. "Look, hanging out with me almost got you suspended. I don't want that to repeat. That's why Jai and I don't let you join our stairway lunches. You have friends and a life outside of us that must not be affected by being seen with me."

"Thank you for looking out for me, but you don't have to. I can take care of myself. And I would really like it if I could join you for lunch or just hang out sometime. I miss you."

I smiled. "I miss you too. I promise we'll hang out more when you're back."

"Great." He added after a pause, "And um, I threatened your boyfriend not to hurt you the last time I was at Recharge Cafe. He asked me to mind my own business."

I laughed. "I'm not taking your side for that."

"You're too smitten," Rory grumbled. "Just don't regret it later like me."

Hey, Ekon and Harriet are nothing like each other. I wanted to say, but I didn't want Rory to feel bad.

"Thanks for looking out for me, R."

I hugged Rory at the airport and wished him a good trip. It felt good to be R and T again, just like the old times.

"I'll call you," he said, before entering the airport. "I don't have a cell phone, but maybe through a payphone."

"Take care and enjoy your trip. I'll look forward to your call."

***

Back home from the airport, I stuffed my face with some leftovers and studied until I dozed off on my desk. I had a nightmare about the court trial for Nicholas Parker's case. His lawyers defended him so well, denying every single bit of evidence, one after the other.

"Your honor, the final evidence against the defendant is also false. The person in the pornographic videos is not my client at all. Someone fabricated the video, framing Mr. Parker, making him the victim in this case. Hence, we request you to set him free, as he is not guilty."

"No," I said, waking up from my horrible nightmare. "That can't be true."

I clenched my fists and blinked back my tears furiously. Nicholas could not get away with his crimes. The violence and the sadism in the footage should be enough to jail him. I could not forget Affy's screams, even though I had seen only a few seconds of it. It was horrible enough that they had to go through the pain and trauma of abuse. But now, they were being threatened? Why? How was it their fault? It was not fair.

Nicholas, his accomplices who recorded the footage, the people who uploaded it online, the company that allowed the illegal video to be watched by millions of people across the world, and every single person who watched it should pay for their crimes. Not Affy, who did absolutely nothing wrong.

I tried to go back to bed but I couldn't stop wondering how to make Nicholas's face visible in the videos that could be clear evidence against him. I researched online about unblurring faces and saw many websites and apps that could do this. But I decided to ask the expert before taking any step.

Me
Nate, you still up?

Nate
Yes. What's up?

Me
Why did AA and Win warn us against unblurring Nicholas's face in the video?

Nate
Why do you think?

Me
I really don't get it.

Nate
Do you want to be accused of fabricating the evidence? Then it will become useless.

Me
But I'm only looking at the copy.

Nate
Right, but if the defense lawyers find your modified copy on the servers when it's been uploaded, they will argue that the original was tampered with too.

Me
OMG. Thank goodness I asked you before doing anything stupid.

Nate
No, thank Win and AA. I would have done the same if not for them.

Me
I had a nightmare that Nicholas's lawyers proved it wasn't him in the footage and that he was a victim, not the perp.

Nate
That seems like a premonition, not just a dream.

Me
Don't say that!

Nate
They are going to do that though. Why do you think we have the mock trial set up with the squad next weekend?

Me
To prepare me. I know.

Nate
It's really commendable that you've come this far against Nicholas.

Me
There's always a possibility that he may retaliate against me. To get revenge.

Nate
He wouldn't dare try anything against you. You have multiple charges against him.

Me

You want to talk on the phone instead? Might be tiring to text.

Nate

Na, I prefer texting. Talking is tiring.

Me

LOL. Okay. I can't believe I'm chatting with you (who is going to be Nicholas during the mock trial) about him.

Nate

Haha. You want me to go easy on you?

Me

No way. Come at me with all you've got. I want to be prepared for the real thing.

Nate

Okay I promise. You know, you could ask Aiden if he heard any guys talk about recording the video they played at your graduation. That one has Nicholas's face. Many Duckville High alumni go to Strollfield U. Besides, Aiden owes you a favor for what you're doing for his sister.

Me

Aiden and Amanda don't owe me anything. I'm just there for a fellow survivor. Besides, I'm not involving Aiden or anyone else in this. He already got removed from the basketball team for helping me earlier.

Nate

Wow, you put everyone before yourself first. Just like Ekon. No wonder you're dating him.

Me

Are you close to Ekon?

Nate

He's my bro. If you ever hurt him... Wait, you would never dare to mess with a hacker now, would you?

Me

ROFL.

Nate

It was a real threat.

Me

I know. But it's too funny. The way you said it.

Nate

The consequences of hurting him won't be. Good night.

I set my phone aside and continued to laugh, tears streaming down my face. What was up with these people and their threats? First, Rory, and now, Nate? Well, it was nice that Ekon and I had people who cared enough to threaten anyone who would hurt us.

At that thought, I fell asleep blissfully.

CHAPTER 42

On Saturday, I spent the whole day working on my school assignments and tutoring sessions. Exhausted, I plopped on my couch and fell asleep. When I woke up, my stomach was rumbling in hunger. I peeked at my phone to check the time, and it was quarter past ten.

I grabbed a snack from the kitchen while going through my phone and saw a missed call from Ekon. I called my boyfriend, stuffing my face with the trail mix. "Hey, what's up?"

"Tia, I was just about to call you again," he replied, sounding excited.

"See, we have a couple telepathy," I joked, settling myself on the couch and munching on my snack. "What's up?"

"I'm about to go aurora hunting and was hoping you could join me," Ekon said.

"Do you mean the northern lights?" I shrieked, delighted. "I've always wanted to see them."

Ekon chuckled. "Yes. So, are you in?"

I nodded. "Yep. See you soon."

All my tiredness had disappeared by the time Ekon came to pick me up. I got some of my special hot tea ready and packed it in a Thermos. While waiting for him downstairs, I had a minor panic attack, realizing the two of us would be alone in a secluded dark area. I calmed down when I recalled the late-night stroll in Duckville and other times when I felt safe around Ekon. Besides, my boyfriend was scared of the dark himself.

When Ekon arrived, I got into the passenger seat and secured my seat belt. He greeted me with his dazzling smile and held out a paper bag. "This is for you. Careful, it's still hot."

I pulled out an orange-colored spiral goodie that glowed in the dimly lit car, examining it carefully, making sure the sticky sugar syrup didn't spill. "What's this?"

"Try it," Ekon urged.

I bit into the sweet, enjoying the satisfying crunch from the delicacy. It was delightfully sweet with a hint of tangy lemon juice to balance the flavors. "Isn't this jalebi, the famous Indian dessert?"

Ekon nodded. "You got that right. I'm impressed you knew."

I laughed with my mouth full. "Of course, I know. There are songs dedicated to this delectable dessert, and now I know why. Thanks, Eko."

Ekon smiled at me and squeezed my hand. "No, thank *you*."

I had no idea what Ekon was thanking me for, but I was too busy enjoying the treat. I polished off the entire bag within minutes, and it was too late by the time I realized I hadn't saved any for my boyfriend. "Sorry, I finished the whole thing without offering you even a small piece."

Ekon laughed. "That's fine. I heard you gobbling something on our phone call and figured you were hungry."

"I was ravenous," I told him, wiping my hands with a wet tissue. "I fell asleep on my couch the minute I plopped on it after completing all my work this evening."

We drove in comfortable silence as I enjoyed the night view of Strollfield. It was a clear, cloudless, starry night with an almost-full moon. The city lights became fainter as we approached the lake area. Snow-capped trees laced around the still-frozen water, despite it being almost spring. I whisper-squealed when I suddenly saw something cross the road. "Eko, look. A coyote."

Ekon laughed. "The animal is too far away to hear you. You don't need to whisper."

I giggled. "I know, it's just a habit. On our nature walks, we were taught to be quiet and not disturb the wildlife." I sighed. "I wish I could go on more such trips now. Every year, my family used to travel to the goose sanctuary near Strollfield University. After moving here, I haven't been there even once."

"How about we go sometime on a weekday?" Ekon suggested.

My eyes lit up. "That sounds wonderful. It's best to go in the morning, though."

"Let's go before classes," Ekon said. "Afterward, I'll take you to the best breakfast joint in Strollfield."

"Recharge Café?" I teased, nudging him lightly.

"No. We have a long way before we become the best, but we'll get there," Ekon said, not getting my joke. "This place really deserves the 'best' title."

I smiled at Ekon's cute, honest response. "Can't wait."

We pulled over at Strollfield Beach and got out of the car. Ekon and I held hands, using our phones as flashlights. I could feel that Ekon was stiff because he feared the dark. I intertwined my fingers in his in reassurance and held him close.

I turned to Ekon. "Can I ask you a question?"

Ekon nodded. "Sure."

"You can choose not to answer if you don't want to," I said. "I'm just surprised you're an aurora watcher despite your fear of the dark. I wondered why."

"I got interested in the northern lights to conquer my fear. When it's pitch dark at night and Lady Aurora dances in the sky, I feel reassured that there is nothing to be afraid of. It's like a sign from the universe that there is always light in life. And we just need to look for it."

"That's beautiful, Eko."

Ekon smiled. "Thanks."

We sat huddled next to each other on his car hood. When we looked up, the mesmerizing night sky presented itself in full glory. It was illuminated by the soft moonlight and millions of twinkling stars. Hand in hand, Ekon and I gazed at the stars and made up constellations. Suddenly, we saw a faint green light near the horizon, close to the North Star.

I squeezed Ekon's hand in glee as the ribbon of light started rising higher. Slowly, they started appearing in all directions, and sparkling green lights glowed across the sky. Every time Lady Aurora changed her path, she became more radiant. We photographed the dancing lights, stunned by the breathtaking beauty.

After witnessing the celestial spectacle, Ekon and I pocketed our phones, sat up on the hood of his car, and smiled at each other happily. A cold breeze made me shiver a little, but I felt warm and fuzzy inside just being with my boyfriend. Ekon took off his jacket to give it to me, but I held up a hand and jumped off the car, slipped my backpack off my shoulder, and pulled out my hoodie in one smooth motion.

He looked at me, bemused.

I swung the jacket, continuing my little show, and put it on. "Thanks for the offer. But smart girls bring their own jackets." I took my hair out of the collar, flipping it.

Ekon started laughing at my antics. Before we knew it, we were both guffawing loudly.

"Tia, that was—" Ekon paused, clutching his stomach. "I can't even."

I shrugged. "Well, I have always felt bad for the guy who is chivalrous in movies. I understand that it is sweet, but doesn't *he* feel cold too?"

Ekon stroked my cheeks. "You're so adorable."

I lightly pinched his nose. "So are you."

He leaned close to me and whispered in my ear. "Do you want to make out under the stars?"

"I thought you'd never ask." I surprised myself by putting my arms around Ekon's neck and pulling him closer without a second thought. I inhaled his intoxicating fragrance as I brushed my lips against his. We kissed passionately for a long time, savoring every second of our intimacy.

Consent is lovely.

So lovely.

CHAPTER 43

It was past three in the afternoon when I woke up on Sunday. Ekon loved the tea I had made. Not only did it have zero caffeine, but it was also refreshing and tasted good. He guessed all the ingredients: ginger, palm sugar, a dash of lemon, and a pinch of cinnamon. After watching the lights, and still feeling cold, we got hot soup at an all-night eatery on the highway to warm ourselves up. After our midnight meal, we had talked until early morning and watched the sunrise before heading back home. Still giddy from the wonderful date, I had tossed and turned in bed until I finally fell asleep.

Until Thursday, the following week, I had absolutely no time for myself. I had collapsed on our couch when I received a video call.

"Teensy, we made it to the final round. Our hard work paid off," Madison told me, looking excited.

"I'm so proud of you, Mads. Congratulations."

"Thank you. Oh, I am so happy. I can't believe we have a chance to win a huge cash prize. That sum will mean a lot to Mom," Madison said.

I smiled. "I know you'll win. Your team is talented, hard-working, and perseverant. It will pay off."

"Thank you so much, my dearest roommate," Madison gushed. "I will be back in a few weeks. Miss me until then."

"Trust me, I do," I replied. "Good luck."

I pumped my fist in the air and danced, happy that Madison had made it. Deciding that it was an occasion to celebrate, I got the ice cream tub from our freezer and scooped large scoops onto a bowl. With my two left feet, I twirled around, enjoying my treat and making kewa datshi, one of my favorite Bhutanese dishes with potatoes and cheese for Jai and me.

The next day, Jai and I sat for lunch at our usual spot on the stairway. He was delighted that I had made lunch for him.

"This is so yum. The spiciness, the creamy texture, the gooey cheese… Just wow. Everything's still warm. And where did you get datshi from?" Jai asked. "I've searched for it all over Strollfield and couldn't find it."

"My parents brought some during their last trip. Mom knows I die for this yummy cheese."

"Sorry to eat and run but I need to finish something before my next class," Jai said, closing the insulated lunchbox.

When he was about to leave, we heard someone storm into the stairway, yelling. "Tina Lauren, you bitch, where the fuck are you?"

I froze. Nicholas Parker.

This is not the time to panic. I need to act fast.

Listening to my inner voice, I gestured for Jai to take everything, hide, and call for help.

I ran toward the cafeteria door, but Nicholas caught up with me. He clutched my chin and shoved me on the wall. Still holding me by my neck, he reached to switch off the light as I swore under my breath.

"Let's see how you'll report me to the police again, now," he sneered, hurling my phone down the stairs.

"I will use anything you say or do to me as evidence against you," I fired back and kicked him between his legs with my knee.

He winced in pain for a moment, and I tried to escape. But he held both my hands with his and stamped hard on my feet. He yanked my shirt so hard it tore.

When I tried to head butt him like Dr. Nakamura had taught me, he slapped me hard, leaving me stunned.

"Thank you, Officer, please get here soon," Jai spoke in a loud voice.

Furious, Nicholas banged my head against the wall, over and over, tightening his hold on my neck. "How dare you call the police?"

Jai hurled his backpack at him. Nicholas let me go and clutched the back of his head.

I twisted his arms behind him, as I'd learned in karate, making him scream in pain. "I'm not afraid of you, Nicholas."

He kicked Jai's shoulder as he was trying to get hold of Nicholas's feet. When Nicholas tried to kick again, Jai ducked and kicked his knees, while I twisted his arms further. Jai managed to tie Nicholas's shoelaces together when he was still in pain.

"Fuck you both," Nicholas swore. "I swear I will get you for this."

"Try," Jai and I said in unison.

When we heard the police siren, Nicholas slipped out of his shoes and our clutches and ran away. I collapsed on the floor from pain, relieved that it was over.

Jai wrapped his jacket around me and held me in his arms. My body was trembling, while my head and face throbbed.

Medical help arrived first. They wrapped me up in warm blankets and attended to the wounds on my face, head, and feet. They did the same with Jai, who was also injured.

The police were there shortly, along with Dean Sibiya. Many curious students tried to come to the stairway, but the dean stopped them from entering.

"Officer, I'm sure it was just a fight between two students. There was no need to trouble you," Dean Sibiya said.

"I was physically assaulted by Nicholas Parker. He slapped me, stomped on my feet, and banged my head against the wall. My injuries are proof of this," I countered.

"Assault is too strong a word—"

"No, Dean Sibiya. I saw it all. I'm a witness," Jai cut him off. He turned to the officer whose badge read "Jenkins." "I was the one who called for emergency help."

"Why were the two of you eating lunch in this secluded area?" Officer Jenkins asked.

I scowled. "How's that related to the physical assault?"

She moved my blanket to the side and exposed my torn shirt. "This would not have happened."

"I request you to please move your hands away from me." I spoke in an even tone, though I was livid. "I deserve to be treated with respect, and I refuse to speak with you further."

"Miss Lauren, you're overreacting," Dean Sibiya said. "Officer Jenkins is just trying to help."

"With due respect, sir, I know my rights. I can request another officer if I'm not comfortable with the current one. Could you please leave, along with Officer Jenkins?"

They left reluctantly, and I gestured Jai to hand me his phone and called the special victims' protection services number that I knew by heart. I told them everything that happened. Luckily, Officer Hussein came on the phone and assured me she'd be there soon.

The medical responders asked me if I would like to go to a hospital, but I refused to budge until Officer Hussein arrived. After half an hour, she came with another officer whose badge read "Bennett." Jai and I talked about the incident and answered their questions. We submitted Nicholas's shoes as evidence. They were custom-made with a unique logo that had a crown on top of the N in green.

"I'm sorry one of our officers didn't treat you with respect," Officer Bennett said, handing my phone back to me. "You did the right thing by calling the special victims' protection services' number." He turned to Jai. "We'll ensure you'll be provided the appropriate witness protection, sir."

I smiled. "Thank you, Officer."

"Miss Lauren, you need to go to the hospital now and get treated," Officer Hussein said. She leaned closer and whispered. "I brought my boss along, so people think twice before messing with you again."

Officers Bennett and Hussein marched into the cafeteria, as Jai and I followed in our stretchers. It was way past lunch, but students and professors were still in the cafeteria, curious about the commotion. They watched in awe as Officer Bennett walked to the center of the room.

I could hear him speak as we left the cafeteria. "There was an unfortunate incident of physical assault today in the cafeteria stairway. We request witnesses who are willing to testify to come forward and do so."

I grinned widely, even though my face hurt like crazy.

We were one step closer to getting Nicholas Parker.

***

Ekon picked Jai and me up from the hospital that evening and drove us to Jai's place. Winona and Nate were coming over later for an AA Squad sleepover. They were bringing Jai's and my cars. AA said that her virtual self, a.k.a. her robotic voice, would be present.

"How did your tests go?" Ekon asked. "Nothing to be concerned with, I hope."

"All good, thanks for asking," Jai answered. "Just a second. I need to take this call."

We heard Jai speak with his parents in Kannada. It sounded musical and sweet.

"My parents are really glad I'm not staying alone tonight. They say hi to all of you," Jai said after hanging up. "They'll be here tomorrow evening."

"Mine wanted to come over, too, but there is a snowstorm expected this weekend. So, I told them not to travel," I said.

When we reached Jai's place, walking up the stairs was an ordeal for me. Ekon offered to carry me, but I refused.

"Can you hold onto my waist and climb?" he asked. "Is it okay if I put my arm around your shoulder for support?"

I nodded, feeling my face grow hot.

I slipped my hand around his waist and felt his arm around me. As I climbed up the stairs slowly, I wished Jai lived on the twentieth floor and not the second floor. Ekon must have felt the same way because he didn't let go of me either when we reached Jai's apartment. Until we heard someone clear their throat.

"Is this how it's going to be the whole time we're together? Your PDA?" Nate teased.

"Ekon was just helping me climb the stairs," I replied defensively. "I got attacked by Nicholas today remember?"

"No more Nicholas talk today," Winona said, waving to all of us. "Save that energy for the mock trial tomorrow."

We got inside Jai's apartment, settled down in his living room, and ordered some pizza. While deciding on what game to play or which movie to watch, our conversation kept drifting to the events of the day and Nicholas Parker. Finally, after dinner, we decided to hold the mock trial right away since we were talking about the case anyway.

Jai brought his whiteboard and markers from the room. He wrote "Victim (survivor): Tina Lauren role-played by herself," and "Defendant: Nicholas Parker played by Nate Parker."

AA started first. "First, we will write down the "evidence" and "witnesses" that we have so far. Obviously, all of the original evidence is with the police, and we might be missing some additional things they might have found during investigation, so we go by the ones we already know about. What are those, Tina?"

"First, we have the possible evidence from the sexual abuse forensic exam: Nicholas's DNA sample, the photographs of my wounds, and my clothes. Next from Pete's phone, we have the video of the attempted rape incident that shows Nicholas's back. Then we have the videos we found online with Nicholas's blurred face—one fabricated, one original. And finally, his shoes from today's assault," I replied as Jai listed them on the board.

"Next, let's go to the witnesses," AA said. "These will now be played by Ekon and Jai. Both of you can decide who would take whose role."

"Rory Matthews: alumnus at Duckville High. Ekon Okoro and the workers at McCormick Park from the SCF fundraiser. Laila Yusuf, Harriet Shelby, Sudesh, and Pete Hilton, Nicholas's underlings. The nurses who conducted the forensics. Officers Lee, Hussein, and Bennett. Jai Rao. Any Strollfield U student who was at the cafeteria today…" I trailed off.

"Affy Rodriguez," AA finished my sentence.

"Is it okay?"

"We'll go with the assumption that they'll testify. They're a minor, so they can choose not to appear in court. If they choose to testify, their anonymity, safety, security, and comfort will be ensured," Winona assured.

"Okay, now, finally, court roles. Judge: AA; prosecutor: Tina; defense attorney: Winona." Jai wrote on the board. "Let's begin."

Most of the mock trial proceeding was a recap of everything that had happened since the press conference at Duckville High when I had met Nicholas for the first time. However, there were some surprising things that were revealed.

"So, Mr. Okoro, are you sure you saw the defendant's cap and watch at the SCF fundraiser last year?" Winona asked.

Ekon nodded. "Yes. I did."

"Can you describe what you saw?"

"I saw Nicholas extend his hand to pick up his fallen cap. It had a fluorescent green brim that was hard to miss. I also got a glimpse of the large silver dial studded with diamonds on his watch." Ekon answered.

"How can you be so sure it was Nicholas?" Winona asked. "It could have been anyone else."

"I have seen Nicholas wear the cap before," Ekon responded.

"He could have lent the cap to one of his friends," Winona countered.

"But it's highly improbable that he would give his expensive watch to anyone else," Ekon replied. "It's too expensive. Besides, I doubt anyone else has the same custom-made watch."

Winona continued to badger Ekon and the other witnesses, twisting everything completely. She was a pro at playing the defendant's attorney. Nate was even better at being the defendant. He spun a story about being in love with me since the first time he saw me, and claimed I was framing him because I hated him. But the one whose performance surprised me the most was Jai's. He was despicable as Pete, Laila, and Harriet, who denied all charges against them, giving the falsest, but the most believable, excuses.

"Your Honor, my client Nicholas Parker has been in love with Tina Lauren in the purest way. Even after she hit him publicly at the press conference, he pursued her. She finally started reciprocating his feelings, but not for too long. She broke his heart and he found solace in Affy Rodriguez. They told my client that they were over sixteen, the legal age for sexual consent in our country. Jealous of their relationship, Miss Lauren fabricated an intimate video of the two and publicized it to play the victim. Further, her victim mentality was established at the SCF fundraiser where she staged an attempted rape and even got a forensic exam done. Yes, my client and Miss Lauren got intimate that day, but no, he did not sexually assault her. Finally, at the university, Nicholas went to the stairway only to see why Miss Lauren screamed, because he still cared about her. But she and her friend removed his shoes forcefully, tore their own clothes, and fought each other to create more false evidence. Your Honor, the defendant is the actual victim here. All he wanted was love."

Wow, there was no way I would win this case. This trial proved that every single piece of evidence we had worked so hard to obtain could be destroyed within seconds.

"Prosecution, provide your closing statements," AA called out. "If you don't say anything, the judgment will be provided without it."

But the truth is, Nicholas is a criminal and he deserves to be jailed. He and his lawyers can twist all the facts, but the truth will remain the truth.

"Your Honor, the victim was minding her own business as a high school student when the defendant came into her life out of nowhere. He harassed her and expected her to bear it quietly, but she stood up for herself by asking him to lay off. He should have stopped then, but he vowed to take revenge on her and ruin her life. First, he tried to ruin her reputation by fabricating a pornographic video and playing it publicly. When that did not work, he tried to rape her at the fundraiser. The defendant and his co-perps lied to the victim about a nonexistent meeting, removed the no-entry sign so she would be tricked, and attacked her in an abandoned area. Though his face is not seen in the video taken by Pete Hilton, the cap matches the defendant's, exactly as described by the witness Ekon Okoro. And it's clear that the defendant is wearing the same watch that Mr. Okoro saw from the fundraiser photos."

"Coming to the incident at Strollfield University, the defendant stormed into the cafeteria stairway, furious that the victim had pressed multiple charges against him. He assaulted her yet again and ran away before the police arrived. Again, we have his shoes as solid evidence. Finally, if you examine the illegal pornographic videos, it's clear that it's not intimacy footage but that of abuse. Sexual abuse. Rape. That's the category it was under on the website. Your honor, the victim has done everything by the law—pressing charges, sexual abuse forensic exam, submitting original untampered-with evidence, and contacting the special victim services protection unit. She did this, braving injuries and dangerous situations multiple times. That is not victim mentality but a survivor's hope for justice. And all the evidence points toward the defendant that he is guilty. Therefore, the defendant deserves to be punished for rape, attempted rape, physical assault, and defamation."

Everyone gave me a standing ovation, beaming at me proudly, and my eyes welled. Winona hugged me tightly, trying hard to blink back her own tears. "That was amazing. It's not easy to stay focused when so many people twist the truth like that."

I smiled. "Thank you."

Thank you, my inner voice, for helping me snap out of it in time.

"Have you considered taking up law?" she asked. "You'd be good at it."

I shook my head. "No way. I'm happy where I am, thanks. One case in my life is more than enough."

All of us laughed at that.

"Hey, don't you all want to hear the verdict?" AA asked.

"Guiltyyy!" everyone, including her, screamed.

CHAPTER 44

After the initial excitement of my explosive speech died down, we realized that the chances of winning the actual case were still low. We analyzed every single thing that could possibly go wrong—witnesses could go missing because of threats, cops could change sides, evidence could be tampered with or be made to disappear... And the probability came down to less than 50%. Clearly, all of us had watched way too many crime dramas.

We sighed, dejected at the low percentage, until Ekon got up and erased the number. He wrote "Reasons why we shouldn't give up – 100% hope." Winona added a +1 next to it and added "100% legal" below that. All of us followed one by one, and soon we had a positive list of 100%: hope, legal, truth, honesty, transparency, and AA Squad.

"Tina, 100% AA Squad doesn't make sense," AA said, laughing.

"It totally does. I wouldn't have made it this far without you all. Thank you."

We all cheered for our squad and celebrated our teamwork with chocolate brownies we got from the pizza place. They weren't that good, but we still enjoyed ourselves, chatting and laughing together.

"Hey, AA, why don't you join us in person next time? You're really missing out on all the fun."

"Tina, I..." AA trailed off.

"It's alright if you aren't comfortable. It's just that we miss you."

I looked at the others to add something supporting my statement, but they were fast asleep. I switched off the lights and hung up the call with AA after wishing her good night.

Feeling comforted by the soothing sounds of my friends' soft snores, I nodded off.

***

I was jolted awake by the usual nightmares at dawn the next day. I got up and stretched my body, happy to see Winona and Nate still fast asleep on the floor. Ekon was awake, but hadn't gotten up from his position next to Nate. I wondered where Jai was.

When I went to Jai's kitchen to get a glass of water, I spotted him texting someone. Not wanting to startle him, I sent him a text that I was right behind. He turned around and waved. "Why are you up so early?"

I laughed. "I can ask you the same thing."

"Ken's back in town and wanted to come over," Jai said. "I didn't invite him, because he might feel out of place with everyone here."

"We can all leave, Fellow Monster. Spend time with your boyfriend before your parents arrive."

"But it snowed the whole night last night. Nate and Winona live close by, but what about you and Ekon?"

"Don't worry, we'll manage," I assured him.

Winona woke up a few minutes later and said she had to leave to take care of Ribster and Dexter. Nate left soon after because he had forgotten to get his laptop charger and the battery would die out soon. Jai didn't even have to mention Ken to them.

After breakfast of last night's leftover pizza, Ekon offered to drop me home since I was still limping a little, and it was not safe for me to drive in this snowy weather. I protested, because the weather forecast had a storm coming in the next hour, and I wanted Ekon to reach home safely before it started.

"Fine, you can drop me. But if the weather gets worse, you'll come home with me," I finally said.

"Are you sure about inviting me over, Tia? I might be stuck there till tomorrow per the forecast."

"Then let me drive back home. And I will call you when I get there," I argued.

Ekon shook his head. "Absolutely not. You cannot drive with your injured feet."

Stubbornly, I sat in the driver's seat of my car, but soon realized Ekon was right. It hurt to press the brake and gas pedals.

"Okay, you win," I said, shifting to the passenger seat.

Ekon chuckled as he sat behind the wheel in my car. "Let's go in your car. I will take a cab back here to get mine."

On my way home, it started snowing heavily. There was no way Ekon would get a cab in this weather. Somehow, we made it to my place safely. I held Ekon's hand and led him to our apartment. He looked hesitant but followed me.

"Are you absolutely sure about inviting me over?"

I nodded. "Positive. It's not safe to go elsewhere."

Back in my apartment, I took Ekon's jacket and hung it up. "Make yourself at home. Would you like to change into something more comfortable?"

Ekon looked surprised. "I don't think you'd have something that would fit me."

I laughed. "I just might."

I went to my room while Ekon sat on our couch. From my closet, I picked up my baggiest set of pants and a t-shirt. They were fluorescent orange. I had bought them to cheer myself up when I was feeling blue during my period. They were at least two sizes above my standard fit but the most comfortable clothes I owned. I giggled at the thought of Ekon wearing this color.

I changed into the shorts and t-shirt that I wore at home. For a moment, I contemplated wearing pants and wondered if the shorts would make me feel exposed. I decided I looked fine and smiled confidently at my reflection in the mirror.

I handed Ekon a towel and the clothes. "The restroom is over there. Let me know if you need anything."

Ekon examined the set of clothes I gave him. "Er, Tia, you have, um, unique home wear."

I laughed. "No one will see you. I won't take pictures, I promise. If I do, I will get your permission and not show it to anyone. I don't want anyone else looking at my cute boyfriend in fluorescent clothes."

Ekon blushed but laughed with me. "You're crazy. I will be right back."

"Do you want more tea?" I asked.

"Yes, please. Your tea is addictive," Ekon answered.

Ekon changed into my fluorescent orange clothes in the restroom. They fit him well other than the fact that the t-shirt was a little short, and his taut abdomen showed. I tried not to check him out from the corner of my eye, so I wouldn't make him uncomfortable. When he looked at me with a "How do I look?" expression, I whistled at him. "Only you can wear a washrag and still look great."

Ekon blushed. "And you look beautiful. All the time. Whatever you do and wherever you are."

I beamed at him. "Aww. Thanks." I picked up the box I had brought from my room when we sat on the couch. "Do you want to play Monopoly? Or should I say, do you want to lose against me?"

Ekon scoffed. "We shall see."

"R and I play this all the time. And he has never won even once," I gloated.

"That guy is not as smart as I am," Ekon said, making a face.

"Have you met R?" I asked him.

Ekon nodded. "Yes, and he seems to have a problem with me. He asked me not to rub my 'crap' on you the last time he came to Recharge Café."

"And Nate said something similar to me. He said that I should not dare hurt you since he is a hacker," I replied, giggling at the memory.

Ekon laughed. "Our friends are overprotective of us. It feels nice though."

I nodded. "Exactly. We are lucky."

"Hey, aren't you worried about the 'crap' your friend was referring to?"

I shook my head. "I'm sure you'll tell me when you want to."

Ekon scooted closer. "Can I hug you?" He held me in his arms. "I will share everything with you when I'm ready, Tia. I promise."

I smiled and embraced him back. When we pulled away, I smirked at him. "Now, get ready to lose against the best Monopoly player in the world."

I was forced to eat my words when I realized that Ekon was fantastic at the game, and Lady Luck was on his side. He kept getting money from the bank, while I landed in jail more than three times. Ekon was rolling on the floor, laughing. "The jail loves you."

I glared at him. "You jinxed the dice. There was no way I could go there each time, otherwise."

"Alright, alright, let's play something else if you want," Ekon said, still trying to catch his breath from his laughter.

I shoved him playfully. "It's alright. I will let you win today."

Ekon raised his eyebrows and straddled me. "Oh, so you're deliberately letting me win, huh?"

I laughed again, trying to stop Ekon from tickling me. "Of course. The game belongs to me, after all. I told it, 'Eko is here for the first time, so we should let him win.' That's why you're winning."

When we stopped laughing, we realized how close our faces were. I lay on my back on the floor, and Ekon kneeled with his legs on either side of me. He was still holding my hands lightly. I could feel his heart pounding in sync with my own. Ekon tried to release his hands from mine and get up, but I intertwined my fingers with his. He leaned closer, and I noticed how handsome he was. He had long eyelashes and a cute pointy nose. His gaze was intense, and it made me feel warm and fuzzy within. I felt my face getting hot as I thought of how his perfect, kissable lips felt on mine.

Just when I thought we were going to kiss, Ekon lovingly held my face and pecked me on my forehead. He immediately got up and walked to the dining table to drink water. I winced when I realized that my body was trembling from our recent proximity.

Had Ekon noticed my nervousness?

"It's almost lunchtime. What should we make? Can I take a look at your refrigerator to decide?" Ekon asked me.

I walked with him to our refrigerator, feeling like an idiot for showing my boyfriend my fear. "Sure."

He stood in front of our fridge with his hands crossed. "What are you in the mood for? Something simple or elaborate?"

"How about just one dish, which is a one-pot meal," I suggested. "We would just need to wash one pan, two plates, and two spoons."

Ekon chuckled. "Sounds good. I'm going to make jollof, a traditional West African dish. We make it at home all the time." He added shyly, "It's a special delicacy I haven't made for anyone else other than my family before."

"Aww, it's so sweet of you to make it for me. I feel honored."

Ekon took the chicken, six tomatoes, some green chili peppers, and tomato paste from the refrigerator. "Alright, can I see what spices you have? Also, are you good with spice?"

I showed Ekon our spice box. "Here, you'll find all the spices in this. I love spicy food. After all, I'm half Bhutanese, and Madison is from the Caribbean."

Ekon looked pleased. "This is fantastic. It has everything we need—thyme, nutmeg, and bay leaves."

I watched in fascination as Ekon expertly sliced onions, chicken, and chilies. Next, using a mortar and pestle, he crushed the ginger and the garlic. After this, he mixed the protein, the onions, and the spices until they turned golden brown. After that, I lost track of what he was doing, because I was too busy admiring Ekon's expert chef skills and his cute expressions.

"Now, we wait for the rice and the protein to absorb the gravy and the flavors from the spices," Ekon informed me. "Do you want to stream something while we wait?"

Ekon and I put the Monopoly game back into its box. I switched on the television and opened a streaming platform. "What do you want to watch? A murder mystery series? Why don't you choose something?"

Ekon selected a forensic thriller named *Forensix*. "Have you watched this? It looks interesting."

I shook my head. "No, I haven't. Let's watch it together."

Ekon and I were engrossed in the series, but he got up periodically to check on the rice. When the food was ready, I brought the pan and two plates to the dining table. "Do you want to eat while watching the show?"

"I prefer not to, but I'm okay if you want to," Ekon answered me.

I placed the plates on the dining table. "I, too, don't like to eat with distractions. Delicious food and good conversation make the best meal."

Ekon took a seat next to mine and smiled at me. "Great minds think alike. *Itadakimasu. Jal meokkesseumnida. Smaaklike."* Ekon said bon appétit in three languages like the last time.

I put the first bite into my mouth, savoring the burst of flavors. The rice was perfectly cooked, and I noted a variety of tastes—tanginess from the tomatoes, heat from the chilies, and the sweetness from the onions.

"This jollof is amazing. You're awesome, Eko," I gushed.

"It would have tasted better if the tomatoes were riper. Also, I should have sautéed the onions a while longer." Ekon critiqued his own food, as usual.

A sense of déjà vu swept through my mind as I recalled the first time he did that at our picnic in Landfill Hill. I reached out to pinch his cheeks lightly. "Chef cutie."

After lunch and washing the dishes, Ekon and I sat cuddled on our couch, engrossed in the suspense thriller series. Midway, he dozed off. I wanted to stroke his hair, but I didn't, because I was dead against touching anyone in their sleep. I sat next to him and read a book on my phone. I nodded off after a few minutes as well.

Suddenly, I felt a hand graze against my shoulder and my nape. Instinctively, I grabbed it and shoved it away. "Hands off, you sick child abuser demon."

I opened my eyes to see Ekon's aghast expression.

Oh no.

CHAPTER 45

"Eko, that was not directed toward you. Please let me explain," I pleaded with my boyfriend, avoiding his eyes. I couldn't face him and see his hurt expression. It was heartbreaking.

"You were the one who fell asleep on my arm. I was only trying to free it from your body weight. I didn't touch you without consent," Ekon clarified. "I'm sorry for making you feel uncomfortable."

I felt terrible when Ekon apologized for something that wasn't his fault. "Y-You don't make me feel uncomfortable at all."

"Tia, your whole body is still trembling. My staying here today was obviously a bad idea," Ekon said, his tone even but cold. "I'll leave now, before things get worse."

I could feel a sharp pain in my chest, but I was unsure if the sting was from his words or the guilt of my actions. "I swear it was not directed toward you," I repeated my earlier sentence weakly.

Ekon walked toward the bathroom to change back into his damp clothes. "It's fine, Tia. We can talk tomorrow."

I have been through a lot and can't expect my fears to melt away suddenly. There is no need for me to feel ashamed or bash myself. I need to speak up and clear the air.

Listening to my inner voice, I got up from my seat. "Ekon, can you please hear me out first?"

My confident tone worked, and Ekon sat back on the couch. I took a deep breath before speaking. "Look, I'm sorry I shoved you away and called you a child abuser demon. But it was not directed toward you. If I was uncomfortable around you, I wouldn't have been out with you all night or invited you over. As for my nervousness, I-I am afraid of intimacy because of everything that I have gone through. And I'm working on it."

"No, I'm sorry," Ekon said, his voice barely a whisper. "I selfishly thought only about myself. You have nothing to apologize for. I should have been more sensitive, knowing well the trauma you've been through."

"I'm sure you have questions, but—"

Ekon interrupted me gently. "We don't have to speak another word about this. When you're ready to share, I'm here."

I smiled. "Thanks."

"Don't thank me. You've never judged me once, but I did today. I should have realized how deep your wounds were when you called me a *child* abuser demon. I can't even begin to fathom for how long and how much you've been in pain," Ekon said in a low tone, keeping his voice from breaking.

I placed my hand on his and squeezed it reassuringly. "I've overcome most of my trauma. Some of it is still a work in progress, though." I added after a pause, "Do you promise not to treat me differently now that you know? I don't want you to be awkward around me."

Ekon put his arms around me. "I promise. If anything, I feel closer to you."

I melted in my boyfriend's embrace. "Me, too, Eko."

"Now, should we watch more of the series, or did you have something else in mind?" Ekon asked me, stroking my cheeks.

I leaned close to his ears and whispered, "Do you want to make out on my couch?"

He chuckled in response. "I thought you'd never ask."

***

Ekon and I binge-watched the thriller series *Forensix*, huddled together on our couch. The six officers were scientists who used their medical, chemical, and digital knowledge to solve crimes. We paused the show periodically to discuss who we thought the killer was and why. Just when they were about to reveal who the culprit was, the lights went out.

I switched on the flashlight on my phone, relieved that I had charged my battery almost fully. I lit a tea candle and placed it on the coffee table.

It was almost time for supper, and I was beginning to feel hungry. I looked outside and saw that it was still snowing. The visibility was near zero. We hadn't checked our phones or the news in a while because they were switched off, and I wondered how badly the storm affected the city.

"There's a citywide power outage," Ekon informed me, answering my question. "And it's crazy cold outside."

I sighed. "Fantastic, now how do we get dinner ready?" I answered my own question, "Oh, I know."

Ekon got up from the couch. "Let me help."

I gestured for him to remain seated. "I'll fix us something you'll love. I promise."

A few minutes later, I popped out of the kitchen with two steaming bowls of instant noodles topped with an egg and green onions. I had used my battery-operated electric kettle to fix us dinner.

Ekon took his first bite and squealed like a child. "That's my favorite brand of ramen. How did you know?"

I laughed. "I found your secret stash in your car the other day and decided to try the brand. Now, I'm addicted."

Ekon slurped his noodles. "Tell me about it." He looked at me and smirked. "So you know how to use chopsticks. That day was just an excuse for me to feed you."

I hit him playfully. "I genuinely can't pick up rolled ice cream with these."

Ekon laughed. "If you say so."

After dinner, we ate strawberries for dessert and washed the dishes. The temperature in my apartment had dropped, and we were beginning to feel cold. I went into my room to get us blankets. "Hey, let's stay in my room. It's toastier here," I said.

Ekon came inside holding a tea candle lantern. "It *is* cozier. But are you sure you're okay with this? I can take the couch out in the living room."

I grinned at him mischievously. "Oh no, we are not sleeping tonight. It's time for board game wars."

Ekon and I played games for the next few hours. He won all of them, and I was about to throw a tantrum. Ekon laughed evilly after every victory, provoking me further. Though I was usually sporting, my poor luck made me sulk like a kid. And it didn't help that my boyfriend made fun of me.

"Someone boasted earlier that they have *never* lost in any board game," Ekon taunted me.

I threw the dice at him.

He caught it and laughed. "Did that someone lie through their teeth?"

I stuck my tongue out at him. "You're just lucky today."

The lights came back on, and I dragged Ekon and our blankets back to the couch. "I need to know who the murderer is."

We gasped when they revealed the culprit, because neither of us had expected the protagonist's father to be the killer. It was unbelievable, but it made sense. After we finished the thriller mini-series, we midnight-snacked on some chips and fruit, watching a comedy show. Midway through, Ekon and I dozed off blissfully, leaning on each other.

***

I woke up first the next morning and made omelets for both of us.

Ekon hugged me from behind. "Good morning. What's cooking?"

"Non-chef-grade food," I answered, giggling. "No complaining."

Ekon smiled. "I would never complain about food made for me with so much care."

After breakfast, I switched on my phone to check if there were any messages from my parents. I had charged my device last night when the power was back but hadn't turned it on. My heart stopped when I saw a text from Amanda sent more than four hours ago.

Amanda: Affy's missing. Please call me ASAP.

CHAPTER 46

"This is all my fault. I should have checked my messages last night." I paced back and forth in my living room, refusing to listen to any words of consolation from Ekon and my other friends on the AA Squad. After seeing the message, I had first called Amanda and now we were on a conference call with the squad. "I shouldn't even have involved Affy in this in the first place."

"It's not yet twenty-four hours since they've gone missing. We still have a chance to find them," AA said. "Let's not give up hope."

"Has Amanda complained to the police?" Winona asked.

"Yes, but she was told that a person needs to be missing for a longer time to be reported. Two hours is too soon," Ekon replied.

"Can you tell us what exactly happened?" Jai asked.

"Affy was going to stay at Amanda's place this weekend before they moved foster homes next week," Ekon explained. "They had messaged her just before leaving that they would arrive in ten minutes. When there was no sign of Affy, even after two hours, and their phone was switched off, Amanda began to worry and complained to the police."

"We could have done something immediately if I had checked my phone," I complained. "How stupid of me to switch it off!"

"There's no point crying over spilled milk, Tina," AA said in an annoyed tone. I realized that she hadn't morphed her voice. "Let's focus on what we need to do next. Please."

"There is no need to wait to report a missing person," Winona said. "In fact, the earlier it's reported, the better. I wonder why the police said that."

I sighed. "I tried calling the special helpline that got me through to Officer Hussein last Friday. But the line was busy all the time."

"Yes, there must have been an increased report of accidents and other emergencies during these unfavorable weather conditions," Nate said.

"Still, the police should have taken down Amanda's complaint," Winona insisted. "I smell foul play here."

"We had listed Affy as the person with the highest stakes in this case. If they press charges against Nicholas, he is done for. A sexual abuse case against a minor will remove all his chances of getting bail from the court," Jai reasoned.

"We need to find Affy as soon as we can," I said, wearing my jacket and getting my car keys. "I'm going to start searching right away."

AA sighed sounding exasperated. "We cannot go on a wild goose chase. Let's decide a plan of action first."

Ekon took my hand in his and squeezed it reassuringly. I sat down next to him reluctantly.

Nate shared his laptop screen on our conference call. "So, this is the map of Strollfield. Let's mark all the areas that are closed because of the storm." He pointed his cursor at the center. "This is where Affy currently stays with their foster family."

We eliminated the closed routes and were left with only two possible roads where Affy could have been taken.

"Okay, now, we need to find out which of Nicholas's underlings live on these routes," Winona said. "Let's pray that Affy was not taken to some other unknown place."

"That's highly unlikely," AA replied. "Both roads that are still open lead to residential areas. Lady Luck is on our side today."

I crossed my fingers and hoped that AA hadn't spoken too soon.

"Okay, let's mark the addresses of all of Nicholas's underlings," Nate said. "Do we know how many are there?"

"I know the thirteen names. But I have no idea where they live," Jai said.

"Wow, what a fantastic memory," I exclaimed.

Nate cleared his throat. "I could get into the university student database—"

"Wait," Ekon interrupted him. "Tina, do you remember the registration database for the SCF fundraiser last year? All performers and volunteers had to input their addresses. We could find some in that if we still have access."

I hugged Ekon and kissed his cheek. "You're brilliant."

I logged into the spreadsheet on my phone, thankful that I still had access to it. Jai rattled the thirteen names off, one by one, as Ekon and I searched for the addresses. By the time we were done, we had three possible addresses where we suspected Affy could have been taken—Pete Hilton's, Sudesh's, or the home of someone I didn't know named Sam Carson.

"Pete lives with his family. Besides, I think he left Strollfield after getting expelled. Let's eliminate him for now," I said.

"Okay, then let's try the other two. AA and I will see you and Ekon there," Winona suggested.

"And I'll try to get an ambulance and medical help ready," Jai offered. "I'm sure it will be a challenge to get timely healthcare right now with the current situation."

"Can I try to track Nicholas's and Affy's phones?" Nate asked.

"Alright, but nothing extreme," Ekon replied.

"Be careful team. Good luck," AA wished us all.

***

Ekon and I drove to Amanda's place to get something belonging to Affy. We hoped to get Ribster and Dexter's help to find them. Without any questions, Amanda gave us their hoodie. Affy had left a set of clothes at Amanda's house since they stayed over often. Seeing her bloodshot eyes, I hugged her and assured her that we would find Affy soon. Amanda wished that she could help us, but her parents had forbidden her from going out in this weather. I gave her Officer Hussein's card and asked her to keep trying that number until someone answered and to contact me immediately when she was able to get through to the police.

We parked my car at the end of the street and waited for Winona, Ribster, and Dexter. I hugged the two lovely dogs when they arrived and made them sniff Affy's hoodie. Immediately, they ran toward the only non-lit house in the residential area, belonging to Sam Carson.

We stood behind Sam's place not sure what to do next. Ribster and Dexter barked loudly, but thankfully, no one came outside. One part of me wanted to risk everything and break into this house to search for Affy, but the other rational side knew it was a dangerous idea. I kept calling Officer Hussein's number but could not get through.

I stuffed my phone back into my jacket. "This is terrible. What do we do now?"

"AA and I will distract whoever is inside, while you and Ekon search for Affy," Winona replied.

"No way. That's too risky," I exclaimed. "If we get caught, Affy's life could be in danger too. We need to wait for the police."

"But we've been trying to reach them for so long," AA argued. She was shorter than me, leaner, and wore a black mask, sunglasses, and a black cap to cover her face. "We need an alternate plan. Besides, Win and I can fight anyone if they try to attack us."

Winona wore her cap, mask, and sunglasses. "We're going in. I'll signal to you, and then you can come in through the window. We might look suspicious in case there is a security camera at the entrance if too many of us go in. Affy is definitely in the vicinity. Look at the way Ribster and Dexter are going berserk."

"What's your plan?" I asked.

"AA and I will ring the doorbell and request for donations. If no one answers, we'll let you and Ekon know," Winona replied. She pointed toward two people walking toward us. "Look, Nate and Jai are here."

I looked at the two dogs who were barking continuously as Ekon tried to calm them down. When Jai and Nate arrived, they took over Ekon's position.

"We have to call emergency to get an ambulance. I couldn't arrange one," Jai said. "I've got my first-aid kit just in case."

"I tracked Nicholas's phone, and it hasn't moved from his house since yesterday," Nate informed us. "He may have been carrying a disposable phone."

"How do we know he did this himself?" I asked. "He could have made someone else kidnap Affy."

"Affy went missing in the middle of the snowstorm when there was a citywide power outage. I don't think anyone would have risked their life for Nicholas. There's a high chance he did this himself," Jai reasoned.

Nate nodded. "Besides, he probably didn't carry his phone with him was because he was scared of being tracked."

"Okay, what about Affy's phone?"

Nate sighed. "That one's not possible to track without some 'advanced techniques' that you guys have banned me from using."

Jai and I laughed, and Nate stuck his tongue out at us.

"Tina, come quickly. Winona signaled us to go in," Ekon called out to me. "She asked us to go in through the front door since there are no security cameras."

I hurried to Ekon's side. We entered the house and Winona gestured us to go directly to the bedroom as she and AA dealt with the person in the living room. The bedroom was dirty and stank badly. Clothes and opened food packages were strewn on the floor. But there was no furniture. There was a small walk-in closet, and it took every ounce of my willpower to tiptoe in there to look for Affy. Holding my nose, I did a quick search.

Ekon raised his eyebrows asking me if I found Affy, but I shook my head. He had stood near the room door all this time waiting for the next signal from AA or Winona. We saw AA walk toward us.

"We found that the front door was unlocked and let ourselves in when no one answered the doorbell. There's only one person in the house. He's passed out in the living room, and his breath smells of alcohol. Winona is keeping a close watch on him, so hurry and try to find Affy while you can." She turned to Ekon. "You can stay here with Tina, and I'll guard the front door."

I went into the kitchen as quietly as possible and opened all the cabinets, the refrigerator, and the oven. It was filthier than the other room and rats roamed around freely. I tried not to scream as one of the rodents climbed up my shoes. I shook it away and ran to the other bedroom.

This room had a bed and a table, nothing else. Something caught my eyes, and my heart stopped for a moment. I placed my hand on my chest because I could feel a panic attack forming. I started hyperventilating, and my vision became blurry. My stomach started churning, and I felt like I was going to throw up.

I was about to collapse on the ground when I heard my inner voice.

I'm here to rescue Affy. This is not about me or my unpleasant memories. I have a chance to save someone. I need to act fast and do my best.

I took a few deep breaths and calmed myself down. I yanked off the sheet and mattress covering the bed so that I could see the wooden frame and the base of the bed, which were actually two doors with small handles on them. With all my strength, I forced one of the doors open, and it fell on the other side with a loud thud.

I wept silently, relieved that Affy was there. They were unconscious but seemed to be alive.

Ekon called the emergency number and requested an ambulance right away. We set Affy on the floor, gently shaking them, but they did not stir. Jai arrived immediately and performed CPR. We could hear AA and Winona fight the guy who lived here—who must have awoken—and lock him up in the other room. Ekon held my hand tightly as Jai tried to get Affy to breathe again.

"I can feel a pulse, but Affy needs to be rushed to the hospital immediately."

Tears were streaming down my face, but I did not attempt to stop them. My heart went out to Affy, who was battling for their life through no fault of their own. I couldn't control the nausea that doubled me over, and unwanted, unpleasant memories cluttered my mind. I tried to shake off the gory flashes of the abuser demons hiding in my storage bed at night when I was a child. This was the very reason I still slept only on a mattress at night.

Soon, an ambulance arrived, and they rushed Affy to the hospital. Jai broke down, unable to control his emotions any longer. His body shook as he wept uncontrollably. I collapsed next to him and put my arms around him, sobbing. We slowly got up, still not letting go of each other.

Ekon put an arm around both of us and hugged us tightly with his eyes welled up.

When we were about to pull away, I saw AA and Winona holding hands and crying. I gestured for them to join us. Winona threw her arms around us, but AA hesitated. Her face was still fully covered.

"Guys, look what I found." Nate came running into the room but stopped mid-sentence and looked down uncomfortably. "Oh sorry."

"Come on Nate, AA. I think we can all use a group hug," Winona said.

Nate walked toward us and patted each one of us on our backs. Ekon thumped his back and squeezed his shoulder. Nate gave her his rare, child-like smile and a big thumbs up.

AA removed her hat, sunglasses, and mask slowly and finally joined our group embrace. Tears laced her beautiful light brown eyes as she looked down, still trying to hide her face. I tapped on the squad founder's hand and mouthed, "Thank you."

She shook her head, her short wavy hair bouncing, and smiled at me, whispering, "No, thank *you*."

We stayed huddled close together for a long moment, our minds still whirling because of the emotional roller-coaster ride these past few hours. But we were all grateful that we had each other's backs—and I knew we always would.

The police arrived a few minutes later and arrested Sam Carson for keeping Affy hostage.

"You're not allowed to snoop around people's houses like this. That's privacy breach," one of the police officers lectured us. I had never seen her before.

"And it's okay if the police don't register a missing person's complaint, even after multiple calls?" Winona fired back.

"What if it had been too late before we found our friend, Affy Rodriguez? Would you have taken responsibility?" AA retorted. "They are barely alive right now."

The officer walked away without responding. I tapped my feet impatiently as I tried the police helpline number for the umpteenth time. We really needed someone helpful to show up and investigate properly.

"Miss Lauren, you need to leave this place now. It's a police-only investigation area," a female voice called out.

"Officer Hussein, finally, you're here."

She gave me a quick smile. "I'm sorry about your friend, but you all need to leave now. And I apologize for not picking up your calls, and on behalf of the team that did not register the missing person's complaint."

I nodded. "Thanks for coming."

"I'm glad you found your friend. Please call the helpline and report any further details about this case," she said.

I cleared my throat. "I suspect the involvement of Nicholas Parker in this kidnapping incident, Officer."

"We need evidence. Mere suspicion is not enough," she replied.

"I understand, but the only person who would benefit from the disappearance of Affy right now is Nicholas. They are a major witness in his case, and may press charges against him for sexual assault," I reasoned.

"Officer Hussein, I found something in the trash can," Nate added. "Can you please come to the backyard?"

We followed the police outside and saw what Nate was pointing at. It was an old single-use cell phone that had keys. It could only be used for calling or texting.

"These phones are not good evidence in my experience," Officer Lee said, joining us to peer into the garbage can. "They don't have anything useful other than the victim's phone number. Still, we can keep it."

She picked it up carefully with her gloves and placed it in the evidence bag. "Anything else you want to add before leaving?"

"See if you can find any pieces of nails," I said. "Nicholas has the habit of biting them and spitting them out all over."

I knew it was almost impossible to find evidence like that in such a big area. But it had also been almost impossible to find Affy today. We did because our lucky guesses worked.

Who knew? Maybe, Lady Luck would favor us again today.

***

By the time I got back home, the sun was shining bright and smiling on all of us again. I took a relaxing shower and had a cup of Ekon's special hot chocolate to comfort myself after the events of the day. I unlocked my phone and saw a lot of messages on the AA Squad group.

Jai

Affy is out of danger. If all goes well, they'll be discharged tomorrow.

AA

That's great news. Great job, squad. Particularly Tina.

Winona

Yes, that was really quick thinking, Tina.

Nate

I would have thought of looking under the bed, never inside it.

Ekon

Not everyone is Tina Lauren.

Me

Guys, it was a lucky guess. Besides, all of us worked together to save Affy. Three cheers to us!

I smiled as each one of us typed "Hip Hip Hooray!" in the squad group chat. My heart burst with pride and affection for all my comrades-turned-friends.

Just when I was about to set my phone aside, it buzzed again. This time it was a text from Amanda.

Amanda

Soul has been invited to perform at SCF this year. The JustCooking post with our music went viral. So did the one in the plant lovers group. They are saying that our music helps plants grow. Who knew, right? Thanks for working your magic again. You're the best!

I squealed joyfully and called Amanda, congratulating her. She and Yash were in the hospital with Affy. All three of them thanked me profusely a million times for being there for them. They promised to treat me to a pizza party when Affy was discharged from the hospital.

After hanging up with Soul, I wore my jacket, took my car keys, and headed to my car. Now was the right time to do something I had been dreading for the last five years.

Before I changed my mind, I drove to my favorite furniture store in Strollfield. Within minutes, I'd purchased the queen-sized bed I had been longing to get for so long. Later that evening, when it was installed and ready, I sent a selfie of myself with my new bed frame to my parents. They called me immediately, and we chatted about my upcoming trip to Birch Town to meet them. Nobody said anything, but I knew that my parents were ecstatic that I had finally overcome my fears and bought a bed after five long years.

That night, I opened my notebook, striking off more items from my wish list. I was proud of the progress I had made.

I had made progress by uncluttering everything.

I had uncluttered my life—and obtained real friends.

I had uncluttered my fears—and attained peace.

I had uncluttered my mind—and found my inner voice.

If I hit rock bottom again, I shall bounce back ten times higher.

Because I have something priceless with me always—my inner voice.

EPILOGUE

A Few Weeks Later

I rollerbladed to the Strollfield Cultural Festival auditorium, controlling my speed and being careful not to collide with the other students. I knew I was late to Soul's concert, but I couldn't miss Ekon's food truck wars either. When I reached the entrance, I took off my skates and ran into the venue, where Jai and Rory were waiting for me.

"T, you're late," Rory scolded me. "Look, they're closing the doors."

"Tiara was with Ekon on the other side of the venue," Jai told his room-mate, referring to me by my newly changed name. He was one of the few people who remembered to do that. "Cut her some slack."

I was still panting and tried to catch my breath. "I told you I would be present for both the events, and here I am."

I smoothed my yellow dress and adjusted the laces on my matching sneakers, thanking the stars that I didn't decide to wear heels today. I brushed my hair with my fingers, looked at myself in my pocket mirror, and applied my lip balm.

"Is Madison's group performing today?" Rory asked me. "They placed third in the entire country."

I smiled proudly. "Not this time, but their dance group will be touring the country soon."

"And she got her scholarship back," Jai added.

My friends and I waited with bated breath for Soul to arrive on the stage, but due to technical sound issues, there was a delay in the schedule. In the background, their viral instrumental music played. I got up and stretched my arms and legs, exhausted from the day. In the morning, I had been summoned to fix SCF app issues when it crashed. The organizers had paid me three times the usual amount for solving the problem in less than three hours.

In the afternoon, I had stuffed myself at Ekon's food truck and helped promote his culinary creations by wearing the mascot uniform. Now, I was here for the final event of the day: the musical performances. Had Soul not been performing, I would have called it a day.

I sat back in my seat and looked around. The auditorium was packed, with very few empty seats left. The sleek flat-screen TV played a slide show of all the main attractions at the fest this year. The television's main purpose was to help the audience in the back get a closer glimpse of the performances. I noticed the technicians testing the spotlights for the Soul band members on stage and my chest swelled in pride. I couldn't wait to see Amanda, Affy, and Yash glow in front of the audience like they truly deserved.

I yawned and browsed my phone to stay awake. On the squad group chat, Winona had posted photos of Ribster and Dexter, and I reacted with a hundred heart emojis. I smiled when I read the other messages, including AA's and my usual banter and Nate's congratulatory message for fixing the SCF app in record time.

As I was replying a "thank you" to Nate, I felt a tap on my shoulder.

"Tia," Ekon whispered in my ear.

I pocketed my phone and turned to greet him with a hug. He looked dapper in a suit and was beaming.

"We are leading on the first day of the food truck wars."

I whisper-squealed in delight and linked my arms with his. "Congrats, Eko."

"Thanks. So what did I miss?" Ekon asked, intertwining my fingers in his.

I made a face. "Absolutely nothing. They have technical issues. I should have just come with you."

Ekon smirked at me. "See, I told you. We could have been alone in my green room for some more time."

I blushed and shoved my boyfriend playfully. "We would have arrived after Soul's concert then."

Ekon and I laughed at our private joke.

A few minutes later, the introduction speeches started, and I dozed off, leaning on Ekon's shoulder. He nudged me gently when they finally introduced the band on stage. "Good evening, ladies and gentlemen. We apologize for the inconvenience caused by the delay today. Without further ado, we present the first band on stage today, by public demand. Soul!"

The auditorium erupted in thunderous applause as Amanda, Affy, and Yash appeared on stage. I got up from my seat and whistled, cheering for them.

Amanda started the performance with her melodious violin, and Yash accompanied her in rhythm with his dhol, while Affy played the guitar.

Affy announced on the microphone. "This is an ode to our bullies and abusers." Then they started singing,

> "You bullied us because you could
> Because you thought we were weak
> Because you thought we were too crude
> Because you thought we were meek."

Yash sang the next stanza.

> "We put up with your abuse
> And your games of power
> Our silence you continued to misuse
> Putting us through more torture."

Both sang together,

> "You think you can break us
> You think you can make us bleed
> You think you can wreck us
> Oh no, you will not succeed."

Affy continued,

> "You emotionally manipulate
> And threaten to keep us quiet

And should we dare to tattletale
You'll be sure to cause a riot."

Yash sang,

"The world adulates you
And no one will believe us
They will make a cry and hue
And call us pretentious."

Together they sang the chorus.

"Well...
You think you can break us
You think you can make us bleed
You think you can wreck us
Oh no, you will not succeed
No, you will never succeed."

By now, the crowd was in a frenzy, singing the chorus lines. My friends and I were bellowing at the top of our voices, though we couldn't sing. The entire hall raised their hands into the air and waved to the music flashing their phones.

Affy continued,

"We may feel helpless
Because of your influence
But we are not hopeless
We have the power of confluence."

Yash added,

"All of us fellow survivors
And others who stand by us
Will stand united together
And we will be matchless."

They all sang the chorus.

"Everybody,
You think you can break us

You think you can make us bleed
You think you can wreck us
Oh no, you will not succeed
No, you will never succeed."

They ended together.

"You will never never, never, never
Oh no, you will never ever succeed!"

There was thunderous applause from the audience. I was hooting and cheering, my chest bursting with pride.

The crowd chanted, "Once more, once more, once more."

Affy yelled into the microphone. "Before we perform again, can we request that Tiara Lauren come on stage, please? We wouldn't have been here today without her."

I felt my face going hot from embarrassment. I sat rooted to my seat, but Amanda came to summon me, and I blindly followed her.

Hesitantly, I stood next to Affy, feeling awkward about the spotlight being on me, and they started singing again. I just stood there, grinning from ear to ear like an idiot, as the audience applauded.

When the performance was over, the audience gave Soul a standing ovation, and my eyes welled up. This song was a tribute to every abuse survivor in this world—for our strength to bear the pain, our strife to overcome the trauma and move on, and our courage not to let the unfortunate incident define our lives.

I had won the battle against abuse.

Now, I declared war on my abusers—their time is up.

Please consider leaving a review

Thanks for reading. Please leave an honest review on your favorite store. I would love to read your thoughts.

You can contact me on my website https://winnzwordz.com.

ACKNOWLEDGMENTS

Whew! After seven long years, I can't believe I have finally completed *Unclutter: A survivor's story*. I never ever thought that this book would be available to everyone someday when I conceptualized it more than a decade ago when the #meToo and #timesUp movements began. I was inspired by all the people who came out with their shocking stories after suffering alone for so many years. It was heartening to see thousands of survivors worldwide supporting one another. Instead of talking about my personal experiences and those of my friends, I decided to write a book as a tribute to these movements, and thus, *Unclutter* was born.

I have rewritten this story hundreds of times in the last seven years. And finally, it's at a stage where I'm ready to show it to the world. I'm grateful to so many people for helping me come this far. First and foremost, I would like to thank my mother, without whom this book would not have seen the light of day. Thank you, Amma, for not letting me delete this story and encouraging me to keep going whenever I wanted to give up. I dedicate this novel, and all my future works to you. But that's insufficient to compensate for your unconditional love and belief in me. I would not have been a writer without you.

Thank you so much, Shannon Cave, my awesome editor, for helping me shape my manuscript into one I'm proud of. I'm mesmerized by your attention to detail, professionalism, and clarity of thought. I can't thank you enough for your incredibly valuable feedback, which will help me in my future work. If not for you, I would not have had the confidence to publish this story at all. So, thank you for believing in my vision for *Unclutter*.

Thanks a lot, Laura Boyle, my amazing designer, for bringing my book alive. I love the cover and the interior design, and it's exactly how I'd dreamed about it. I can't stop raving about how well the fonts and layout match the theme and mood of my book. They speak to my readers as much as my words do. Thanks for being flexible and rescheduling our collaboration multiple times when I needed more time to work on my manuscript.

Thank you so much, Michele, my brilliant photographer, for making me feel gorgeous. I was a nervous wreck when I entered your studio, but you made me feel at ease within minutes. I felt vulnerable putting my face out there for the world to see, but I'm extremely pleased with the result. You truly are one of the best headshot photographers in the city.

Thank you, Kankana Basu, my first editor, for helping me build a strong foundation for my novel. I'm extremely grateful to you for helping me with the eye-catching summary for *Unclutter*. I simply love it. I would not have come this far as an author without all your help.

Thanks, Reedsy, for having such fantastic professional editors and designers who are excellent at their work. And thank you for being so approachable whenever I needed to contact one of you for any help. You all are simply fabulous.

Before deciding to publish it, an initial version of my book was available on a free writing platform publicly. I'm grateful to all my first readers for their honest feedback. I was encouraged to continue when some of them commented on how well I handled the sensitive topic of abuse. However, some of the comments were also critical, which I appreciate. Particularly, I thank the person who pointed out that all my characters look the same. Thanks to them, my characters are (and will always be) of diverse backgrounds and cultures, just like those around me.

I earned some friends on this platform who've helped me through my journey as an author.

Thank you, Fera, for being my very first reader. If not for you, I would have taken my book off the internet.

Thank you, Naz, for being a wonderful friend, fellow author, and the best beta reader I could ever ask for. Your reviews and feedback will always remain priceless to me. I cherish the memories of our late-night conversations, some of which have made it to this book. Thank you for always cheering me on.

Thank you, Kayla, for your encouragement and helping me spread the word about my book. Your awesome writing and marketing skills always inspire me.

Thank you, Telaya Jackson, for believing in me and reading my book every time I changed the story.

Seven years is a long time to work on a project. And it was impossible to complete it without the most important people in my life: my family and friends. They let me ramble on about my writing, and I'm guilty of sometimes making them bored.

Thank you, my dearest husband, the love of my life, for being so supportive and understanding during this journey. Thank you, my most beloved Annu, for being the best father on earth. You know my lovable male protagonists are inspired by both of you.

Thank you, my darling daughter, for being the best thing that ever happened to me.

Thanks so much to all my other readers and friends: Meghna, Andrea, Pat, Divya, and Anshu, for always being there.

And most importantly, a huge thank you to YOU, my reader, for choosing my book. It means the world to me. I hope you enjoyed reading it as much as I did writing it. I would be extremely grateful if you could write a review on Amazon, Kobo, Barnes & Noble, The StoryGraph, and Goodreads and let me know your thoughts. You can also reach out to me on my website, winnzwordz.com.

ABOUT THE AUTHOR

Winnie D Pagora loves three things the most in her life: her family, her tech profession, and stories. Her fascination with stories started as a mere toddler when her mother read to her, and she began making up her own when she could barely read or write. She was just six when her article first got published in a leading children's newspaper in India. Since then, she has dreamed of writing a book, and *Unclutter: A survivor's story* is her debut novel. Other than reading and writing, Winnie's interests include travel, wildlife, and global cuisines. She currently lives in Canada with her husband and her daughter.